The Third Tablet of the Holy Covenant

To my old friend & colleague
David,

Best wishes

Mike

4/11/13

The Third Tablet of the Holy Covenant

Michael Baum

Matador
9 Priory Business Park,
Wistow Road, Kibworth Beauchamp,
Leicestershire. LE8 0RX
Tel: (+44) 116 279 2299
Fax: (+44) 116 279 2277
Email: books@troubador.co.uk
Web: www.troubador.co.uk/matador

ISBN 9781783061587

British Library Cataloguing in Publication Data.
A catalogue record for this book is available from the British Library.

Typeset by Troubador Publishing Ltd, Leicester, UK

Matador is an imprint of Troubador Publishing Ltd

Printed and bound in the UK by TJ International, Padstow, Cornwall

"Science takes things apart to see how they work. Religion puts things together to see what they mean."
Jonathan Sacks, The Great Partnership:
God, Science and the search for meaning. 2011

Contents

Prologue

August 11th 1960 Jerusalem Post
Earthquake cracks Knesset

August 11, 1960 (9th Av 5720)

An earthquake measuring 5.0 on the Richter scale rocked Israel and surrounding states Wednesday morning, sending frightened people streaming into streets throughout the country, but causing only one indirect injury and little damage.

Israel Radio reported the quake left a crack in the ceiling of the Knesset plenum, Israel's parliament, just 24 hours before lawmakers were scheduled to take their seats for the day's debates. Channel 2 TV reported that Israeli geologists believe a major earthquake could strike Israel without notice, and based on research predict the arrival of "the big one" in the next 50 years. And Channel 1, screening a map highlighting areas of the capital believed to be especially susceptible to damage in the event of a major quake, pointed out that the Al Aqsa Mosque and the Dome of the Rock – both straddling Israel's Temple Mount – were most at risk.

The finger of God?

The earthquake struck shortly after 10 in the morning, shaking buildings in Jerusalem, Tel Aviv, Haifa and Safed. According to Israel Radio, staff in the Israeli Knesset thought a large bomb had gone off, and left their meeting rooms to gather in the building's corridors.

The station reported that an engineering crew discovered a crack in the ceiling of the Knesset plenum, "directly above the table at which cabinet ministers sit." The quake occurred 24 hours before they were scheduled to take their seats. At the top of the Cabinet's agenda right now is the question of unilaterally pulling all Jews out of the occupied territories and handing it over to the Palestinians. Centuries ago, the finger of God was seen writing a message of doom on the wall of Chaldean king Belshazzar's palace, after he desecrated temple objects sacred to the God of Israel. Furthermore the quake occurred on the very day we fast in memory of the destruction of the first and second temples.

Poised for catastrophe

According to a recently released report exposing the shoddy standard of construction in the country, a quake of 6.0 or over on the Richter scale is expected to flatten an untold number of buildings, leaving tens of thousands of Israelis dead – possibly many more. A quake that big could have catastrophic results throughout Israel, where the towns and cities almost all encroach on one another.

Active fault lines run throughout the small Jewish state due to the active tectonic structure of the Dead Sea Rift that runs the full length of Israel.

According to the Risk Management Solutions' (RMS) Israel Earthquake Model, the Jordan Valley Fault in the north of the country "has a high probability of generating a major earthquake."

The RMS believes that a large earthquake there "could create damaging ground motions in every major population centre, all located within 70 km of the rift."

"Research suggests," says the RMS website, "that the Jordan Valley Fault generates magnitude 7 or larger earthquakes every 1000 years. The last major event on this segment occurred in 1033, increasing the current probability of a major earthquake."

Shock report

Continuous quakes

Seismologists say there are earthquakes taking place all the time in the Rift Valley, but most of them are too mild to be felt by man. They do, however, indicate the massive level of instability that exists.

Israel has a long documented record of destructive quakes dating back to 31 BC. On July 11, 1927, a 6.2 magnitude temblor killed more than 300 people and damaged upward of 1000 buildings in Jericho, Nablus, Jerusalem, Nazareth, Tiberias, Lod and Ramla.

Prophesies

The Hebrew prophet Zechariah foretells a final, cataclysmic earthquake when the Messiah comes to Jerusalem, an event that will split the Mount of Olives in two, from east to west, creating an enormous valley. The book of Revelation speaks of a coming earthquake such as "had not occurred since men were on the earth."

Minutes of meeting held under the chairmanship
Of the President of the State of Israel
December 1ˢᵗ 1960

Those present:
The President of the State of Israel: Yitzhak Ben-Zvi
The Prime Minister: David Ben-Gurion
The Speaker of the Knesset: Kadish Luz
The Ashkenazi chief Rabbi: Yitzhak Halevi Herzog
The Sephardic chief Rabbi: Yitzhak Nissim
The Director of Antiquities Authority: Shmuel Yeivin
The Professor of the Institute of Archaeology the Hebrew University: Yigael Yadin
Head of department of ancient Hebrew texts at the Hebrew University: Menachem Stern
Professor of ancient Hebrew linguistics at the Hebrew University: Anthony Zeitman .
The Director of Shin Bet: Amos Manor
(Other experts, including members of the Zinati family were called to give evidence but denied full knowledge of the subject under investigation: See annexe A)

Subject: The Peki'in Papers

Background

Peki'in (Hebrew: פְּקִיעִין) or Buqei'a (Arabic: ﺔﻌﻴﻗﺒﻟا), is a village,in the Northern District of Israel located eight kilometres east of Ma'alot-Tarshiha in the Upper Galilee. The local council in the predominantly Druze village was established in 1958 which has a population of over 5,200 people.

Peki'in is important in Jewish history because it is where Druze and Jews lived peacefully together for hundreds of years. Peki'in is frequently mentioned in historical sources, specifically in reference to its small Jewish community that has existed there almost continuously since the Second Temple period. Near the village, there is a restored Jewish synagogue dating back to the Roman Period. In 1926 and 1930 two old stone tablets dating from the Second Temple period were uncovered at the synagogue. One depicts a menorah, shofar and lulav and the second depicts a gateway with columns on each side, probably symbolising the gateway to the Holy of Holies. The local Zinati family claim to be members of ancient Jewish kindred who have lived in Peki'in, reputedly since the time of the fall of the Second Temple in 70CE.

On August the 11th this year a major earthquake struck central and Northern Israel as a consequence of which the synagogue was seriously damaged and the ancient foundation stones were pushed up to the surface causing one corner of the building to collapse. A young member of the Zinati family, whose task it was to act as custodian to the ancient building, was first on the scene and there she uncovered an ancient wooden box amongst stone work dating back approximately 2,000 years. Realising the archaeological consequences of this find she immediately informed the Antiquities Authority.

SY

As director of the Antiquities Authority I was advised of the potential importance of this find by one of my local fieldworkers and together with YY we made our way to the site and confirmed that the wooden box could only have been found in this context if it had been buried amongst the foundation stones approximately 2,000 years ago. After carefully measuring out the location and photographing the find in situ, I authorised Professor Yadin to take the box to his laboratories at the Hebrew University.

YY

With the help of some lanternslides I will now describe the find in detail. The box measured 50x30x30cms and is made of very well preserved cedar wood. The lid, 1.0cms in thickness, was tightly sealed to the rest of the box with bronze nails that again were surprisingly well preserved. We took scrapings of the wood and the bronze to determine their age. Subjecting the wood to carbon 14 dating and the bronze to chemical assay, we confirmed that the cedar wood was about 2,000 years old and that the chemical composition of the bronze was right for that period as well. We then carefully pried the lid open and noted that the box was lined with lead, which accounted for the perfectly preserved contents. Within were six parchment scrolls with central spindles again made of cedar wood. With no attempt to unfurl them they were transported to the laboratories of the national library at which point they came under the custodianship of my colleague Menachim Stern.

MS

Before attempting to discover the content of these parchment scrolls we again used C14 dating from fragments of the spindle and the scroll itself and confirmed that these were of the same epoch as the box. The parchments were in very good condition, in fact the best it has ever been my pleasure to examine. For classification and for reasons that will shortly describe, we listed them as "the Esther scroll" and the "Jehudit scrolls i, ii, iii, iv, v". The first is much shorter than the other five but analysis of the ink confirms that they are all from the same period. Each scroll was rolled out on a long table and covered with plates of glass. They all have suffered slight damage from the residual water vapour in the sealed container but they were all remarkably supple with few cracks appearing, as they were unrolled. This was probably due to the fortuitous concentration of moisture in the box that made for perfect conditions. There was no evidence of mould. The text was written in the Paleo-Hebrew characters that again date it to the period two millennia ago. The translation of the texts took us nearly three months working day and night to complete, and their content persuaded me to convene this urgent top-level meeting.

The translations into the modern vernacular are attached in annexes B-G. My colleague Professor Zeitman will now describe some remarkable similarities and differences between the first and the other five scrolls.

AZ

As already described the parchments, the inks and the lettering where all of a similar period, furthermore the way the Hebrew characters were formed almost looked as if they were from the same hand. However the remarkable difference was in the style of the language used. The scrolls purport to have been written by twin sisters Esther and Yehudit, daughters of the deputy High Priest at the time of the fall of the second temple in 70CE. The Esther scroll was written with the same poetic rhythm and lyrical language as discovered in the Dead Sea scrolls but the Yehudit scrolls were something else. The latter had such a powerful narrative drive with sparks of humour that have never previously been encountered before the early 19th C. It's almost as if the invention of the novel was anticipated by 1,800 years, beating the Bronte sisters by a long way. From this I have to conclude that these scrolls are forgeries and part of an elaborate hoax but how the deception was carried out is beyond my capacity to speculate. Bearing in mind the awesome content of these texts then even the remote possibility that they are genuine, becomes an issue for the Rabbinate so at this point, through the chair; I'd be interested in the opinions of our two chief Rabbis.

The President
I share Professor Zeitman's concerns and I think we need a two- track approach. I will hear the opinions from our two learned and saintly chief Rabbis but then I wish to hear from our chief of internal security and then I will ask Mr. Ben-Gurion to formulate a plan. Rabbi Halevi-Herzog please give us your verdict.

YHH
Thank you Mr.President. As soon as I knew the content of the scrolls, I convened a small secret meeting of my closest advisors and top Hebraic scholars. We believe that this has to be an elaborate hoax. The suggestion that there might be a codicil to the covenant between Hashem and the Jewish people is outrageous and there is absolutely no hint in the Torah of its existence or an ounce of evidence to support the story contained within the Jehudit Scolls. My concern though, is the malicious intent of those who propagated this hoax. I therefore suggest that the documents are either destroyed or buried deep in the vaults of the Israel museum only to be examined again if any new corroborative evidence emerges in the future.

[YY interrupting – whatever anyone thinks these are valuable artefacts dating back to the late period of the second temple and must not be destroyed!]

The President

I understand your passion Yigael but let's wait to hear Rabbi Nissim's opinion.

YN

I to have also done my share of research on all our biblical sources to search for the slightest hint or fleeting shadow of a secret of such supreme importance to our faith and history of our people. I have to agree with Rabbi Herzog but with one caveat. My own research came up with a hint that there is a long lost tablet of stone prepared at the command of Moses and that can be found in his last words recorded in the "Song of Moses" Deuteronomy 31 verse 26. I also agree with Professor Yadin so I think the compromise suggested by Rabbi Herzog is the best solution, but rather than passively waiting for new evidence to emerge I think we should establish and fund a secret commission to actively follow the clues laid out in Yehudit iv and v, in an attempt to either refute or corroborate the suggestion of a codicil to the holy covenant.

YY

With the greatest respect to our learned and saintly chief Rabbis I think they are wrong in one particular fact. They have searched only Biblical sources for the "fleeting shadow" that might add veracity to the Yehudit narrative but I have already discovered the "footprint in the sands of time" by consulting secular sources. Let me read you this passage from Josephus' "The Jewish War" section VII describing the siege of Masada.

".....but two young women who were related to Eliezer, in intelligence and education superior to most women, escaped along with two infant children and two maid-servants. They had hidden in the conduits that brought drinking-water underground while the rest were intent upon the suicide-pact."

That is almost word for word the description of the escape from Masada in Jehudit v. Of course some might say this merely illustrates the sophistication of this forgery but if is all a hoax it is so elaborate that it's purpose is beyond my imagination. I would therefore support Rabbi Nissim's suggestion but go one step further and start our search where Yehudit v ends, by a complete archaeological excavation of Masada.

KL
That's an enormous undertaking how could we possibly fund and at the same time maintain secrecy of such a project.

The President
As director of Shin-Bet, Amos, how would you respond to that challenge?

AM
That is easy, we would use the bait and switch tactic. The whole exercise must be conducted in the full glare of publicity.

After all Professor Yadin recently completed the excavation of Hazor and the Bar-Kochba caves, this would be a natural progression in the unearthing of our biblical history. The story of King Herod the great and the last stand of the Jews against the might of Rome make for a great news story.

Of course we would need a number of our operatives on site to monitor the finds and leave it to Yigael to keep the secret purpose of the dig within this inner circle.

The President
As there are no further comments I will leave it to you Dovid, as prime minister, to sum up.

DBG
Up until now I have held my peace yet as the debate continued my excitement was hard to contain. The wisdom and scholarship displayed round this table today has made me feel both proud and humble. I totally agree with the decisions you have taken and in my role as your prime minister it is my duty to implement them. The cost will be enormous but I intend to call upon the wealthy of the Diaspora to fund this project with the reward being a place on Yadin's team as amateur archaeologists. This will have the dual effect of opening their pockets and adding to the unskilled workforce of the team. We will also try to sell the rights to the unfolding story to the highest bidder amongst the world's press.

I will personally chair the project team made up of some of those here today and a few trusted additions.

The code name for this covert action will be operation *SHANIT M'TZADA LO TIPOL* (Masada will not fall a second time) **M2** for short.

The President
Thank you Dovid; Yigael, how long will it take you to plan the expedition, recruit your team and start the excavation?

YY
I can start the survey of the area immediately by diverting resources from existing projects. Fortunately it is winter now but we will need to complete the survey before the heat of the spring. So bearing in mind that the site is only workable for say four months in the year, it would be reasonable to suggest the winter of 1962-63.

The President
Would you all now return your copies of the translation of the Peki'in papers for secure storage in the department of antiquities. Professor Yadin is the only one allowed to leave this building with facsimiles of the original scrolls and a copy of the translation as resource material to guide his search for some sort of evidence we might use as corroboration of their provenance.

The President closed the meeting at 11.30 pm

TOP SECRET
Governed by state security act 1949
Section a viii

PART 1

The Piki'in Papers

Israel 70-73 CE

TOP SECRET

Translation by Prof A. Zeitman et al 1960

Chapter 1

The Esther Scroll

.....Yea, though I walk through the valley of the shadow of death, I will fear no evil; for thou art with me: thy rod and thy staff, they comfort me....

This is the last testament of Esther Bat Eliezer, HaCohen daughter of Israel, founder of this temple hakatan[1] consecrated with the word of the Lord out of Jerusalem.

Woe is me who witnessed the fall of the second temple and the fire in the holy of holies on that day. Woe is me who lies on her deathbed as the curse of the crab crushes her chest and her bones. Woe is me who prays for death to relieve her suffering. Why does the Lord curse me? Have I not carried out his last commandment? Have I not been a virtuous daughter and mother? I shall take comfort in the words of Solomon, the son of David, the king of Israel.

..........When the dread cometh as a storm and calamity cometh as a whirlwind then I will call thee and thou shalt answer.............

I raise my countenance to heaven and speak to you oh my daughters of what is pleasant and good in this land. In this the 40th year of my life I embrace you, oh my daughters, and remind you of your holy task. Forget not the testament of my beloved sister Yehudit Bat Eliezer, HaCohen, for I can vouchsafe that it is good and true.

Fulfil the command of the third tablet and protect the walls of the temple hakatan[1] from generation to generation until the time that a third temple will rise again in the holy city of Jerusalem according to the will of the God of Gods for all Eternity and he will shine as a light upon you and he will make known to you His great name. I have taught you in truth of how I came forth out of the fires of Masada and survived the might of the barbarians from the west of how I travelled 40 days and forty nights from that place of death to the hills above the lake Kinneret to a place of peace and beauty how I placed

---

1 Literally means little temple but best to describe it as proto-synagogue.

the word of the Lord within his temple hakatan. May thy father protect you yet even he must not learn of our sacred duty because the future of the children of Israel will come from the loins of the daughters of the Eliezer Ha'Cohen. Be fruitful and multiply but do not trust a man with cunning lips who would wish to learn of your hidden duty. Do not place a slackard in charge of this important task for just as lead melts, so before a fire he will not stand. Bury these words and the words of my sister who turned south to the trade routes of King Solomon to find refuge out of Akaba, yea even onto the southern seas and to bring the lights of the great temple to a temple hakatan and sojourn in a land wherein both she and her kin will find safety and multiply until the time cometh to bring the word of the Lord to the holy city again when the children of Israel will be gathered in once more from the four corners of the earth. Ay! Bury these words and the words of Yehudit in a casket of the finest cedar wood clad in lead and hide them in some place whereby only the wrath of the Lord will bring them once more to the remnant of our people that they might fulfil the last commandment of Hashem. And the tablet of the Lord that was taken forth from the holy of holies lest it fall into the hands of the barbarians, shall speak unto the people at this time but until this come to pass you and your daughters and your daughter's daughters shall keep it hidden and speak not of this to any, nay not even he who lies with you and doth father your children.

If thou carry out my commandments that are the commandments of Hashem then you shall the blessed amongst the daughters of Israel and I shall rest in peace.

Amen, Selah

Chapter 2

Yehudit Scroll I
Jerusalem 9th Av 3791 (70 CE)

The blistering mid summer heat of the late khamsin on the 9th of Av added to our thirst, our wretchedness and above all the intolerable stench. To breath in deeply made us retch and should we vomit our dehydration might be the last straw before our body, the beast of burden for the last flicker of the flame of life, finally collapsed allowing our spirit at last to return to Hashem. Yet the flames around us were real enough as were the deafening roar of hatred and the scream of the dying. The stench was like the breath of hell from the uncapped sewers of all the latrines of all of time. Its components varied from minute to minute according to the direction of the hot winds off the deserts from the south or east. These hot winds carrying the smoke from the conflagration brought blinding tears to our eyes already moist from the tears of our grief and the tears of our fear. We cannot afford this luxury of uncontrolled tears as our store of body fluid is close to empty. From the south it smelt of burning flesh in cruel imitation of a roasted ox teasing our mouths to salivate at the time of mass starvation. From the east was the smell of rotting corpses pilled up, as the strength of the survivors faded away; not enough strength to bury the dead and barely enough to stay alive. The roar of hatred reflected the roar of the uncontrolled flames as they licked at the very portals of the temple of Herod and came from two sources; to the west the Roman legions as they pressed their advantage through the gaping wounds in the protective walls of the last defences on the temple mount. From the south these roars appeared to be reflected as the three factions of the last Jewish defenders of the holy city, desecrated the ground upon which they stood by murdering their brothers in the name of some forgotten feud or arcane detail of temple worship. What Jew did to Jew on this darkest day of our history measured up well in the rank of atrocities with the suffering inflicted by the Roman legionnaires as they took control of what was left of the holy city, our golden city, our Yerushalayim, city of peace. In its dying throes the city's denizens turned mad and turned upon themselves and only a precious few kept their heads, envisioned a future for their cursed people and remained calm enough to plan escape. I am one of those few. My name is Yehudit Bat Eliezer, HaCohen. My father is of the princely tribe of the Cohenim and Segan, second in command to Ananus ben Mordechai, Ha'Cohen Ha'godal, the high priest, murdered by the Idumeans. One of my father's duties was to act as custodian of the sacred vessels and adornments used for the temple ceremonies on the high holy days. As a Jewish princess I had grown up with many privileges yet like my twin sister, Esther, I am not vain and spoilt because of my upbringing. Our mother was of legendary beauty and met my father when she arrived in Jerusalem as part of a delegation of Jews from the Parthian Empire from the country between the two great rivers of the east, a year before our birth. I hardly knew my mother who died when we were three, but my father who brought us up unaided was both strict and kind and when we were the age of 5 or 6, he discovered that we had enquiring minds and a thirst for knowledge. We are now 16 and can read and write in Hebrew, Greek and Latin. We have studied Euclid, Archimedes and Pythagoras and are proficient in mathematics, astronomy and trigonometry. These skills provided practical help during the early days of the siege, when I was called upon to calculate the angle of inclination for our catapults to throw back the Roman missiles from where they were delivered in the midst of the 5th legion. On a more pacific note, I compose verse whilst Esther is a gifted musician. We can both argue with conviction on theology, philosophy and logic, using the Hebrew sources or the philosophers of the Greeks to support our case. With our mastery of rhetoric we can exploit these skills to unfair advantage. My father says that we are loud and opinionated exhibitionists, unseemly characteristics for young women and that we will frighten any suitor away. They say that we are comely and my father has twice denied us offers of marriage in spite of our unseemly demeanour, not that we minded. They say we resemble our mother, but as looking glasses are disallowed by our father's zeal, we assume that our twin is the reflection denied us. My twin is tall and slim with long dark hair that reflects the sun with a russet glow like the sun setting on the golden stones from which Jerushalyim is built. She has startling green eyes. True green, like emeralds, not blue grey that turns green in certain light. My twin is the most beautiful amongst the princesses of our tribe, oh that I should look that way! Yet it matters not as our sacred books and precious secular texts go up in flames and we are unlikely to survive another day. As it is written in the prayer we recite on the holiest day of the year, Yom Kippur, when Ha'Cohen Ha'Godal enters the holy of holies on the Sabbath of all Sabbaths, and calls on God to judge us in the year to come; " Who shall live and who shall die; who shall perish by fire and who by water, who by the sword, who by wild beasts, who by hunger and who by thirst, who by strangling and who by stoning." Well Hashem has at least six out of seven ways to choose from, in determining our premature end. In fact my faith is sorely tested. What kind of merciful and omnipotent God would choose from this menu to end the lives of two faithful and virginal young women? If I meet him in the world to come he will have a lot to answer for. This blasphemy is of course kept to myself. I'm sure if my thoughts became known, even at a time like this when other pressing matters might be considered a priority, the sanctimonious Pharisees would still find time to take me before the Sanhedrin to pass sentence of death by stoning. " God, if you are listening, curse these men and curse these Romans, and if you are not listening to my cry, then you are not my God!"

All these confusing thoughts were rushing round my head as Esther and I awaited our father outside the sanctuary of the holy of holies. This in itself was remarkable as we were the first women ever to have stood so close to the Ark of the Covenant, merely twelve steps and one heavily embroidered silk curtain away. Even more remarkable were the orders from our father hastily written on the parchment carried to us by one of his loyal Nubian slaves, Ishmael. We had been ordered to visit the mikvah, cut our finger and toe nails and crop our hair close to the back of our necks leaving ringlets hanging in front of our ears. We were then commanded to dress in clean white linen garments to cover our nakedness from head to toe and to attend upon him in this sacred place. Under the guidance of Ishmael we were taken from our home in the upper city close to the outer wall in the south west sector, through a labyrinth of streets, past Herod's palace and through the Gennath Gate of the inner wall. From there we climbed the great bridge to the outer court on the temple mount. How we avoided death at the hands of the marauding Idumeans is a mystery. Esther favoured the view that Hashem had made us invisible as a miracle to preserve the daughters of one the last surviving candidates for promotion to the high priesthood. My own view, always the cynic, that money had changed hands and that our unseen protectors were not superhuman beings but heavily armed zealots hidden discreetly along the way and that the screams we heard were not from the innocents of Israel but from the severed throats of the militia lead by John of Gishala. Whatever the explanation we arrived at the outer court exhausted, thirsty beyond measure and our fresh white linen covered in soot. Within the walls of the temple mount were the remnants of the women and children of the fated city. The dead and the dying competed for space with the hysterical living. The wailing and screams were deafening as we fought our way through to the steps of the temple itself. We were ordered up the steps to the magnificent cedar doors without time or breath to recite the psalms of King David. Because of the shame of our appearance we were reluctant to pass through the doors to the temple court. In anticipation of this, Ismael opened his backpack and handed over a goatskin full of precious water and fresh white linen. Having slaked our thirst and changed our linen, whilst Ishmael turned his back and hid his face we passed through the gigantic doors into the temple compound. First we crossed the huge court of the gentiles in order to reach the wall that encircled the Court of Women with its entrance carrying a warning inscription:

Stranger! Do not enter within the walls of the temple
He who is caught will have only himself to blame
For his death that will follow.

From here fifty steps led up to the gate that opened into the Court of Israel, open only to Jewish men. Ishmael urged us on but we were paralysed with fear for no woman had ever crossed that threshold. We were pushed forward roughly and stumbled into the blinding glory of the temple proper. Even I, the great sceptic, expected the fury of Hashem at this desecration to manifest itself as a bolt of lightening. Yet everywhere was silent and golden. The light slanting through the skylights 50 cubits above our head, already gilded by the setting sun reflected off the golden stones of the city, was amplified in colour and brilliance by the silk hangings and gorgeously woven multicoloured wool curtains covering the walls of cedar wood imported from Lebanon by King Herod himself. And then ahead of us we witnessed the ultimate glory of the legendary temple menorah fashioned by a miracle from one solitary ingot of gold, with its seven branches pointing to the heavens standing on a sturdy twelve sided base with each facet decorated with the emblem of one of the tribes of Israel. On one side of this was the golden table, the shulchan, with shelves and pans for holding the 12 loaves of showbread. We were the first women in the history of our people to be afforded this sight and without thought, as one, we prostrated ourselves in worship of the holy icon. We were rewarded by a kick from behind as Ishmael roared at us, " do not bow down to idols of gold or you will suffer the same fate of the children of Israel who worshiped the golden calf, save your prayers and abeyances for when you appear before Hashem within the Sanctuary." From here we were marched eastward to the exclusive court of the priests. At this point our father's loyal slave could go no further, not for fear of death that was inevitable in the last stand of the defenders of the temple mount but out of respect for our faith. "Go onward through these portals oh daughters of Eliezer ben Yakov Ha'Cohen, be strong and of great courage and await your father who will surely be with you soon. I shall return to guard the entrance of the temple against the pagan hordes and will offer up my life to give you time to fulfil your father's wishes". And with that he was gone. Timidly we crossed the threshold and were somewhat disappointed to find that the Court of the Priests was significantly smaller and plainer than the court of Israel. However that disappointment was short lived until we caught sight of the most beautiful object we had ever seen. Straight in front of us, crossing the eastern wall of the court, covering all but a cubit of gilded wood on each side, was a silk and brocade hanging with heavy plaited cords of spun gold fibre arranged to draw back to two halves of the curtain that gave entry to the Cohen Ha'Godal when he crossed into the sanctuary on Yom Kippur. Yet the curtain itself, although by far the most extravagantly woven from threads coloured with the rarest of dyes showing wondrous images of cherubim, lions, eagles and oxen, was not the object that took our breath away. Just above the centre parting of curtain to the holy of holies, suspended from the ceiling was a lamp of divine beauty. It hung from four thick golden chains attached to a gilded rose on the ceiling. These chains were remarkable enough. Each chain had twelve links and each link was cleverly worked to represent the emblems of the tribes of Israel. The chains pointed precisely to the four points of the compass with the one furthest from us pointing due east towards the Mount of Olives. Hanging from these four chains was a crown of gold decorated with precious stones in sequence, amethyst, diamond, emerald, and sapphire. Each sequence was repeated five or six times round the brim of the crown. Hanging down from the brim was a conical woven basket of golden rope and within each space of the weave in descending order of size was a perfect, flawless ruby. From within this cone, the greatest act of craftsmanship in the history of the Jewish people emerged a steady light transmitted ethereally through the gemstones. The ruby coloured light was reflected back from the silk hangings in front of the sanctuary bathed our faces. We turned to look at each other to witness our shared sense of awe and Esther's beauty was amplified as her pale skin turned the colour of sacramental wine. This of course was the everlasting light. It was with some difficulty that we restrained ourselves from lying prostrate on the floor in front of the fabled nair tamid. Directly below the eternal light was the golden altar for the incense offering with each corner crowned by a horn of gold.

As we stood transfixed by this vision there was a sudden commotion to our left as out of nowhere appeared our father supported by two armed warriors from the zealot faction of the rump of Jewish resistance. Our father looked mortally wounded with blood exuding from a rent in his priestly robes high on the right side of his chest. His right arm hung uselessly at his side and his robes with black with soot and signed at the hem. His dignified face was white, his high cheek bones exaggerated by exhaustion and dehydration, his long white beard was unkempt and his right pupil was dilated. In a parched croak he bade his supporters to lower him to the ground and prop him up against the cedar wall to the right of the curtain in front of the holy of holies. He beckoned us forward. "My darling girls please listen to my words carefully without interruption and swear to carry out my commands. I have not long to live and each breath is both painful and precious." He indicated to one of his attendants to moisten his mouth with a rag dampened by a few drops of precious water from his goatskin water carrier. At this point Esther and I dropped to our knees and each clasped one of his hands. I grasped his right hand and wrist noted that they were cold and clammy with a thready rapid pulse. " You are aware that one of my duties in the temple is to guard its treasures and account for the sacred instruments of worship and animal sacrifice. Beyond that I also carried the burden of the temple's secrets and the secret commands that the first Cohen Ha'Godal, Aaron, passed on to our tribe from his brother, Moshe Rabenu as inscribed in the third tablet of stone he gave to the Children of Israel at the end of his sojourn in this world. You are the first of the children of Israel to learn of the third tablet. To this day it has been a closely guarded secret as it contains three commandments handed down from on the last day of Moses' life as he looked towards the Promised

Land. Here our father paused to take breath and moisten his lips whilst holding up a finger as were about to interrupt. He continued thus; "at this time of existential crisis for our people, sacred laws might be broken if it lead to the salvation of the very future of the children of Israel. This point has been reached and you my daughters will have the awesome duty to carry out this duty. Within an hour or so the defences of the temple will be overrun by the Roman legions aided and abetted by our own turncoats and opportunistic traitors. When that happens all those left on the temple mount will be slaughtered and any of our citizens captured alive will be taken into a bondage worse than that we experienced under the Pharaohs.

You now carry the awesome burden of saving our race and our faith in one almighty God from extinction, but to do so I will command you to perform one act of extreme sacrilege. You will enter the holy of holies and stand in front of the ark of the Covenant, before that I shall die but from there thou shalt live, go forth and multiply!" "But why us?" I remonstrated. " Because you and your sister carry the very best of the character and wisdom of our people and through the fruit of your wombs our race and our faith shall survive." He replied. "Now say no more, take these parchments that contain the detail of your mission bow your heads and let me anoint you with the blessings of the matriarchs". With a pause to catch his breath and moisten his mouth, he took a small vial of oil from his tunic and dabbed a drop on the centre of our foreheads, placing his hands on our bowed heads using his last breath he intoned the ancient blessing. " Blessed art thou oh Lord our God; endow my daughters with the spirit of Sarah, Rebecca, Rachel and Leah. May the Lord bless thee, and keep thee: may the Lord make his face to shine upon thee: may the Lord turn his face unto thee, and give thee peace". With that he reached with his left hand and with all the strength left to him pulled down hard on the golden rope that drew the curtains that protected us from force of the divine presence at the epicentre of our faith. The curtains parted and Eliezer Ha'Cohen, blessed of the almighty parted this life with a knowing smile on his lips. On that note his two supporters laid him down, covered his body with a white sheet of linen ripped from the nearest wall of the court, carefully avoiding a glance into the holy of holies, bowed stiffly to us, grunted a muted blessing of their own, unsheathed their swords and rushed out to guard the portals to the gates of the Court of Israel.

Chapter 3

Yehudit Scroll II

As the curtains parted we expected to be blinded with a flash of brilliant white light, the "Shechinah", the divine presence of the almighty. As it was our eyes took a few moments to adjust to the dim light within the sanctuary reflected from the walls of white linen lining the sides and roof from the diffused ruby glow of the everlasting light. As our eyes adjusted and saw what was in front of us we threw ourselves to the floor and lay flat on our faces with arms outstretched in front of us fearful to look at the face of Hashem. Nothing happened and the expected roar of disapproval never materialised, the only sound to leak into this holy space was the muted roar from the battle being fought outside the temple mount. After a minute or two my curiosity took the better of me and I tilted my head and squinted through my right eye. The face I had imagined was a trick of the light reflected back from the central object in this holy of holies; surely this was the Ark of the Covenant, the Aron ha' Kodesh, the light of the world. The Ark was about two and a half cubits in length, a cubit and a half wide and the same in height. It was covered in gold and around each edge of the brim was a crown of great complexity whose details I could not make out, but the most startling aspect of this divine artefact was the pair of cherubim rising from its top surface. The one on my right had the face of a female child and the one on my left the face of a male child. They appeared to be crafted from solid ingots of gold. Each carried the wings of a bird that arched over the ark and touched in the centre as if to protect the tablets within.

We had first met these angels woven into the curtains closing the entrance to the sanctuary and we saw them again worked into the ceiling of the tent. From the side of the Ark facing me I saw two gold rings, the size of my wrist, and through these rings ran two long staves covered in gold. These I had learnt were used for carrying the Ark during the wanderings in the desert over a thousand years ago in our long history. The weight of the acacia wood of the construction and the weight of gold in its ornamentation must have crushed those who attempted to lift it on their shoulders, yet legend had it that the Ark of the covenant carried its bearers rather than the other way round. The staves were permanently left in place, we had been taught, to symbolize that the word of the Lord would always follow his chosen people in their wanderings rather than remain fixed for ever in their resting place upon the rock where Abraham had been ordered to offer Isaac his son in sacrifice. In remembrance of that event the ram's horn is blown from this place at Rosh Ha'Shana, the New Year and Yom Kippur, the Day of Atonement, not only awakening the children of Israel from their slumber but also recalling God's mercy as a ram, trapped in a nearby gorse bush, was accepted as sacrifice in place of Isaac.

We could have lain there in awe and rapt attention were it not for the muted screams getting closer to the perimeter walls of the sanctuary, suggesting that one of the outer walls of the temple complex had been breached. As one we both shot upright and turned to each other with matching eyebrows raised in arcs to express our confusion and uncertainty. What now? At that point I remembered the scrolls clutched in my sweaty fists containing my fathers instructions. Backing in respect a few paces from the Ark, we started to read in unison by the light of the nair tamid. In father's neat Hebrew script, in red ink upon ochre coloured vellum, a numbered sequence of directives appeared as we unrolled the scrolls from their central wooden spindle.

Order number one read; "Scroll this far and no further; fulfil my first command lest you die. Eat of the showbread sprinkled with frankincense to build your bodily and spiritual strength." As we were starving this was a command we hastened to obey. We turned towards the shulchan and each grabbed a fresh loaf of the showbread that would never again be used in the Sabbath ritual, took a pinch of frankincense from the silver spoon on the top shelf, and ate with relish. Whether it was our starvation or not, I'll never know, but this bread was the tastiest I've ever enjoyed with a uniform crust that melted in the mouth and tasted as if it had been baked with honey as on the feast of the New Year. When we had enjoyed our fill I felt restored and strangely at peace with myself, even though in mourning for my beloved father. Nodding to each other we turned the scroll carefully until the number 2 appeared and at its sight the spindle fell from my hands in shock and disbelief. We were commanded to desecrate the Ark of the Covenant! Was our father mad? He had commanded us to break into the Holy Ark and extract the third tablet! *And that was not all–we were commanded to break it in two. Esther and I conferred for a short while and agreed there was no way back. The choice was stark; retreat and end up raped and murdered by the slavering mob or follow the fifth commandment to honour thy father and thy mother but at the same time risk the wrath of God. The choice was made for us as we heard the crash of timber signalling the destruction of the great doors guarding the entry to the first of the temple's courts. Repeating the Shema, "Hear O Israel, the Lord thy God the Lord is one", we approached the Aron and placed our hands on the cherubim, one at each end. Praying that the lid was not fastened to the body of the Ark, we braced ourselves to lift the heavy golden shield comprising the roof, the golden crown and the conjoined cherubim, covering and protecting the access to the tablets brought down by Moses from the mount. To our astonishment the lid and it's superstructure raised effortlessly suggesting either that we had acquired superhuman strength by eating the showbread or that as in legend, the Ark carried its bearers. Either way from that time forth my scepticism was always tempered with doubt in contrast to all my friends and family whose faith was sometimes tempered with doubt.*

We reverentially laid the lid of the Ark on the floor and peered into the dark interior of the box. At once an aroma of old timber and spice wafted past our noses and as one we responded with a hearty sneeze. I could have sworn I heard the traditional response of labriut, bless you, come from above but the sane part of my brain suggested it was an echo. Inside the ancient timbers was another golden box whose elaborate lid crafted in gold with bas relief figures appeared to illustrate the bondage in Egypt. The lid to the inner box also yielded easily to our combined effort and inside that was a third box of ancient cedar wood without decoration that smelt of frankincense and myrrh.

The lid of the third box, made of a sturdy wooden panel the thickness of my thumb, still a perfect rectangle after more than 1,000 years, gave way to our efforts almost as if there were a hand pushing from below as we lifted from above. A cloud of the dust of ages followed the lid as we placed it next to its fellows on the floor of the sanctuary, and we steeled ourselves once more to peer within the ultimate box holding the tablets of stone, inscribed by Moishe Rabenu, Moses our patriarch, brought down from mount Sinai, from the mouth of Hashem, to the tribes of Israel. By now we were trembling in terror and Esther was retching bile. Once again reciting the Shema, we prepared ourselves to look upon the holiest relic in the history of the world. As predicted by our father there were three rough hewn slabs of stone, two were of similar size, rectangular in shape, measuring about one and a half arm's length in size and half that in width. The third laying on top of the other two was a smaller rectangle, measuring about ten hand spans on the long side and six hand's span on the short side.

We paused again, terrified of laying hands on the words of the Almighty as taken down in chisel strokes by the hand of Moses. Egged on my the increasing clamour from without the walls of the Sanctuary, we bent down and with some difficulty this time, lifted out the smaller stone. Its unexpected weight caused us the drop it on the outer edge of the of the Ark, and with a crack that sounded like thunder, the tablet split in two exact halves making two perfect rectangles, as easy as the breaking of the matzah on the first night of Passover. By this time we had run through the full gamut of emotions from terror, to awe, to simple surprise and fell to our knees to inspect the two fragments of the third tablet of stone.

The deeply cut letters appeared in 10 symmetrical lines divided through the centre. They were written in some ancient form of the alphabet that we couldn't decipher but at least from our father's description we had little doubt what they meaning they contained. Without another thought we returned the three lids to their appropriate places and completed the unscrolling of our father's last testament. With an economy of words our directives were made clear.

3. TAKE THIS STONE TABLET AND WRAP IT IN HANGINGS FROM THE WALLS OF THE SANCTUARY.

4. TAKE TWO GOLDEN CANDLESTICKS FROM THE ALTAR AND WRAP THEM THE SAME.

5. FROM THIS POINT ON EACH OF YOU WILL BE CUSTODIANS OF THESE HOLY RELICS ESTHER CARRYING THE TABLET TO A SANCTUARY IN THE NORTH AND YEHUDIT CARRYING THE GOLD CANDLESTICKS TO A SANCTUARY IN THE SOUTH. YET THE BURDEN OF ESTHER'S IS THE MORE PRECIOUS EVEN THOUGH MADE OF STONE.

6. FIND THE PASSAGE OF KING HEROD BENEATH THE FLAG STONE THAT BEARS THE ARK OF THE COVENANT.

THE SCARAB WILL BE YOUR GUIDE.

7. AT THE BOTTOM OF THAT SHAFT YOU WILL FIND MEN'S CLOTHING. REPLACE YOUR LINEN ROBES AND DRESS IN THE MANNER OF A MAN.

8. KING HEROD'S PASSAGE RUNS FROM THE ANTONIA FORTRESS TO THE NORTH DO NOT TURN THAT WAY: FOLLOW THE TUNNEL UNDER THE TEMPLE TO THE SOUTH UNTIL IT REACHES ITS JUNCTION WITH KING HEZEKIAH'S TUNNEL THAT RUNS AT A DEEPER LEVEL. FOLLOW IT 1,200 CUBITS FURTHER SOUTH UNTIL IT EMERGES OUTSIDE THE WALLS OF THE LOWER CITY AT THE GIHON SPRING IN THE VALLEY OF KIDRON.

9. THERE YOU WILL BE MET BY TWO OF MY MOST TRUSTED FRIENDS. DO NOT BE SURPRISED BY THEIR APPEARANCE AND WHEN THEY ASK YOU "ARE YOU THE SONS OF ELIEZER HA'COHEN?" ANSWER YES AND FROM THEN ON CARRY OUT THEIR INSTRUCTIONS AS IF THEY WERE FROM YOUR FATHER WHO NOW SOJOURNS IN GAN EDEN.

10. MAY GOD SHINE HIS FACE UPON YOU AND BE GRACIOUS UNTO YOU.

AMEN

ELIEZER BEN YAKOV HA'COHEN

★ ★ ★

Without pausing for thought we began to carry out our instructions. As an added sacrilege we tore down the curtains covering the front of the sanctuary and tore them into strips. These strips of precious fabric were used to parcel the stone fragments and golden candlesticks bound up with the gold braided ropes that had made up the curtain pulls. We then turned our attention to the Ark. Esther and I grabbed a pair of handles and each of the ends of the staves passing through the loops at the sides of Aron Kodesh, and braced ourselves to lift the heavy object made up of three boxes of cedar and acacia wood, two of which were covered in gold and the outermost one capped with the golden cherubim. In retrospect we estimated that their combined weight must have been at least five talents. We surprised ourselves again at the ease with which we lifted it and placed it to one side. I was reminded by the apparent superhuman strength demonstrated by armed men in mortal combat whilst Esther, the more spiritual of the two of us again recalled the legend of the Ark carrying the bearer. Where the Ark had stood were paving stones of pure white glistening marble in all likelihood seeing the light of day for the first time since King Herod and his priests consecrated the temple. There were four perfectly cut and closely fitting, flagstones and at their central junction one contained a carefully sculptured bas-relief image of a scarab measuring a finger length. The symbolism of this was not lost on us. The scarab, or dung beetle, was worshiped by the Egyptians as the embodiment of the god Khepri, the god of the rising sun who was credited with rolling the sun to the horizon each morning as the scarab rolled is ball of dung to his nest. The crushing of this image under the weight of the Ark surely symbolised the victory of the one God over the pantheon of deities of the pagan faith of the Pharaohs. Gingerly I pressed the palm of my hand on the pagan image but nothing happened. It was only when the scarab felt the full weight of my body balanced on one leg that the flagstone started to tilt on an axis diagonal from corner to corner. Esther grabbed me before I stumbled and we watched in disbelief as the stone turned silently on hidden hinges until it rested in perfect balance vertically, leaving two triangular holes just sufficiently large to allow our entry into the tunnel below. We looked down into the dark space and realised we would need a source of light in order to continue our mission. Our father had left no instructions on this and we were left to our own resources. There was only one source of flame available to us and that was the nair tamid, to rob the everlasting light to show us the way seemed for once strangely appropriate. Once again we tore strips off the wall hangings and fashioned them into two crude torches making a hand grip by binding them around with the remnants of the curtain pull. We carried the showbread table to a point below the light and Esther clambered up whilst I held out the first of the torches which quickly ignited from the flame within the ruby bowl. Her flame ignited mine and both of ours illuminated the tunnel shaft below the tilted scarab stone. Below was a short drop of about three cubits with iron hoops on the wall to act as footholds. At the base of the shaft we saw two bundles wrapped in sheepskin and also two oil lamps with carrying handles. Clearly our father had not left us entirely to our own devices. I threw my legs over the gaping triangular hole and carefully let myself down whilst Esther held the two torches above my *head. Once my feet touched the ground I picked up one of the oil lamps climbed half way back until Esther's flame could ignite the oil lamp. Clearly the wick was new and the oil fully charged. I climbed back down and bent to light the second lamp when I heard Esther scream above my head. As the doors of the Court of Israel came crashing down under the onslaught of the Roman battering rams, she had dropped one of the torches and this had ignited the remnants of the bone dry curtains of the sanctuary and in no time at all the four walls and tented ceiling was ablaze. Quickly Esther dropped through the hole and half way down tilted the stone back in place on its marvellously crafted spindle. The gap above our heads sealed itself with a hiss protecting us from the conflagration we had left behind and the Roman enemy hard on our heels.*

Chapter 4

Yehudit Scroll III

We paused for a moment and took stock. We could hear the pandemonium above but with the fire raging it would be very unlikely that our position would be discovered. Furthermore the booty of the Ark of the Covenant and the Menorah, both in symbolism and the weight of gold, would satisfy the greed of Titus, commander of the Roman legions and distract them from a closer search of the interior of the Sanctuary. We were standing under a secret entrance to King Herod's tunnel stretching northward to his fortress and southward in the direction of the outer courtyards of the temple complex. The ends of the tunnels disappeared in the gloom as our oil lamps showed us merely 20 or 30 paces in each direction. At our feet were two bundles bound together with long lengths of leather thongs.

We unfurled these bundles and found, as promised by our father, two sets of male clothing that we donned immediately. We looked at each other and with our shorn hair; breeches and tabards, resembled handsome adolescent youths. Also within the bundles we discovered goatskins filled with water that we consumed greedily to slake our dreadful thirst. Finally in another leather purse we discovered 100 shekels. Using the sheepskins and the leather thongs we fabricated backpacks to carry our burden of gold and ancient stones of faith; and set off south carefully watching the ground in front of our feet lest we fall down the sinkhole to Hezekiah's tunnel. We found it quickly enough after about 100 paces and fortunately a low wall surmounted by wrought iron winding gear holding an old wooden bucket whose staves were reinforced by rusted iron plates. From here a thick spider's web hung down attaching itself to the foot of the iron winding gear and the edges of the wall.

Clearly this suggested that Hezekiah's tunnel was used to supply water to the city in ancient times of siege. All this presented two new problems to solve. The first problem was the spider, the shape and size of my hand, watching us balefully from high up on the web. The two of us had an irrational fear of spiders yet the venomous species were very rare in the holy land. "Very rare" of course is not the same as "never found" and the identification of species of spider had not played a part in our education beyond the fact that they were not kosher to eat. My concern was whether the spider would reciprocate that feeling. The other fear was rational. If the tunnel from the Gihon spring was full of water above the height of our heads, then we were trapped. In our favour was the fact that in the months of Sivan, Tammuz and Av we expect no rain and Israel had in fact been suffering a drought for longer than that. Peering over the edge of the low parapet we again saw iron foot rests disappearing into a deeper hole than that from the Sanctuary to Herod's tunnel. Using the flames from our oil lamps to frighten off the traif spider, we brushed aside the gossamer threads of its web and descended about 20 cubits down to a dry and sandy floor. This still was no guarantee of our escape as we remembered the stories from the book of Kings how Hezekiah's workmen constructed the tunnel from the two ends each at an inclination of a narrow angle. How they met in the middle was a miracle of engineering but the final result was to provide a reservoir of water in the two limbs of a wide angled V at the point of their junction, even in times of drought. We continued our walk southwards on the sandy floor that gave a hint of its downward inclination. After we had walked about 500 cubits as judged by the length of our strides, we encountered water. At first we noted that the floor of the tunnel was moist enough to show our footprints, then the water covered our ankles and finally through the gloom we could see the level of the water reaching the roof. We sat down holding our heads in despair; to have come this far only to be trapped by the handiwork of Hezekiah's engineers. After a few moments of self-pity I was restored to my normal state of self-reliance. I then remembered my father's favourite aphorism.

"After the fall and the expulsion from the Garden of Eden, The Almighty compensated us with the power of reason and enquiry. From this we were encouraged to continue his acts of creation, with our science defending our faith". How could our meagre knowledge of mathematics and astronomy help us preserve the will of Hashem as inscribed in the third tablet of stone by the hand of Moses? We had only just mastered the teachings of Pythagoras and Archimedes. At the very thought of those names I experienced my own eureka moment and with my finger drew the following diagram in the wet sand:

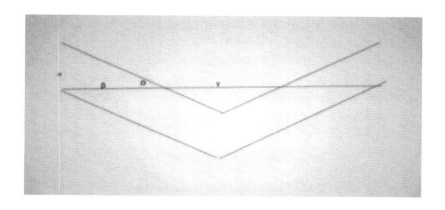

I then explained to Esther, how we might use Euclidian mathematics to work out the distance the tunnel was above head height. Adopting my best didactic teaching voice I intoned as follows. "Let us assume that both branches of the tunnel are of similar height and declining from the surface at similar angles, then following on the teachings of Archimedes, that water will find its own height irrespective of the shape of its container, the problem is easy to solve.

Let alpha describe the height of the tunnel, beta the length of water from its edge by our toes to where it reaches the roof of the tunnel in front of us and finally let theta be the angle between the surface of the water and the roof of the tunnel, the gamma, the distance we would have to travel underwater to reach the far end, would be solved by Euclid's equation for isosceles triangles"

I then started measuring the three parameters within my reach. I estimated alpha as a hand's breadth above my head and then measured beta from the number of strides from where I stood until the surface of the water just covered the dome of my head. Standing back a little so that my mouth was free of the water, I was able to estimate theta using a protractor made from my extended thumb with my index finger lying on the surface of the water.

It took me about ten minutes to make my calculations writing with my finger in the damp sand at the edge of the underground lake. It was also reassuring to remember our father's parchment that gave us 1,200 cubits from the sinkhole of the spider to the mouth of the tunnel. With relief the answer came out as 12 cubits surely not too far to travel on one deep breath.

Having explained all this to Esther I suggested that we practice holding

21

our breath whilst carrying our loads and walking 12 long strides. "That's an awful lot of assumptions" replied Esther, "…and what if we reach the point of no return after 7 strides and your calculations are wrong?" "I will test my calculations by walking 6 strides forward and on my seventh stride judge whether the tunnel has flattened out and begun to turn upwards. I will do this without my burden to ensure that I have breath for my return", I replied with a confidence I didn't really feel. I then strode out with a show of confidence that was somewhat spoilt when I slipped on the wet sand. Further humiliation followed as no sooner had I taken a deep breath and continued walking until my head was completely covered than the buoyancy of my body in the water took my feet from under and floated me upwards until I cracked my skull on the roof of the tunnel. Barely able to control my panic I paddled in a circle and splashed back into the light gasping only to see Esther doubled up in laughter. Two things dawned on me at once. First we would have to attach weights to our legs if we were to stride through the tunnel and secondly, if we resurfaced at the other side we might have to continue our journey in complete darkness. The solution to the first problem was simple, we would simply strap our burden of the fractured tablet, and the gold candlesticks and gold coins so that they hung below our waists or as Archimedes taught, lower our centre of gravity. The second problem demanded that we try and keep the lamps, wicks and flint stone and striker dry whilst somehow holding the lamps in such a way that the oil did not spill. For my second experiment I held the two gold candlesticks below my waist, took a deep breath and once again strode into the water but this time kept my equilibrium whilst counting my strides. To my delight after my fifth stride the angle of the tunnel took a undoubted change of slope and almost immediately turned upwards so that after only ten strides I felt my head break above the surface of the water and after one more step felt secure enough to take a deep breath. My lungs filled with musty air that stank of rotting vegetable matter, a not unpleasant change from rotting flesh. However as anticipated, on opening my eyes it was so black that my eyes ached as they desperately tried adjusting to the dark. I turned around and repeated the exercise emerging triumphantly into the light when Esther fell into my arms with tears of relief blotching her lovely face. Without pausing for words we set about strapping our burdens so that all our treasures both worldly and celestial hung below our waist yet without impediment to our stride. Our last act was to place the flints and strikers in one of the leather *pouches left by our father, pull tight the purse string and tuck them under the necks of our jerkin so that there would be two layers of leather between the flints and the water. Standing waist high in the water we took deep breaths, snuffed out the lamps and strode purposely forward. This time, with the additional burden it took twelve paces and we were desperate for air as we surfaced on the other side of the water trap and the junction of Hezekiah's tunnel. Groping in the dark I found the flints and struck a good spark at my first attempt but sadly the wicks of the lamps were too damp to ignite. I cautioned myself to remember that I wasn't quite as clever as I thought and that for the second time my well thought out plans foundered on the reef of my exaggerated self- esteem. If I remembered the ancient Greeks warned us that Hubris was often followed by nemesis. We had no choice but to stagger on like blind women feeling our way along the walls until after what appeared to be a lifetime, a glimmer of blessed light appeared as an expanding dot at the limit of our vision. With a bit more bounce in our steps but with increasing exhaustion from our heavy burden we approached the source of the light at the mouth of the tunnel. It crossed my mind that after all the excitement of our escape had died down and had effectively been quenched by the cold water of the tunnel, the magical power of the word of the Lord as transcribed onto the third tablet of stone by Moishe rabenu, no longer had the power to carry us forward but relied on us mere mortals, to carry the burden unaided. At last we stumbled through the mouth of the tunnel at the Gihon spring in the Kidron valley. Blinded by the bright summer sun we fell into the arms of two mighty and heavily armed Roman legionnaires. Without hesitation, as if expecting us, they pulled sacks over our heads and bound our arms to our sides. I must have fainted at this point from fear and exhaustion and my last thought as the darkness closed in, was that our father's Nubian servant Ismael had betrayed us.*

Chapter 5

Yehudit Scroll IV

I regained consciousness as I was gently laid down on the sandy floor in a cave somewhere near the foot of the Mount of Olives. Esther was rousing herself at the same time.

As the sacks were pulled off our heads our captors placed their hands on our lips and whispered; "Be not afraid we are here to rescue you. Are you indeed the daughters of Eliezer Ha'Cohen?" We breathed a sigh of relief and nodded our heads in agreement.

They smiled as one and began to introduce themselves and explained their purpose. They were brothers, Ezekiel and Issachar ben Baruch and were proud members of the Sicarii or knife men, who had sided with the Zealot faction in the battle for Jerusalem.

They had killed two Roman centurions, stolen their armour and shaved their beards. Our father had sent messages by pigeon to their leader on the mountain fortress of Masada, that God had commanded that his twin daughters should be rescued and provided sanctuary with the defenders of the main outpost of the Jewish rebellion. Beyond that they knew no more. In their armour and with clean-shaven faces they looked handsome and invulnerable and I'm ashamed to say that I suddenly felt a concern about how we might appear to these two noble warriors. They seemed indifferent to the fact that we were young women disguised as boys and seemed more interested in what was hidden in our sacs than what was hidden under our tabards.

I scolded them and said that the contents of our sacks were holy relics from the Temple and none of their business, we were on a mission for our father, God rest his soul, at the command of the Almighty, whilst their business was to escort us safely to their stronghold. They seemed nice young men who gently teased me for having a scorpion's tongue.

We were told that Masada was three days march southwest but because

24

of the heat of the day and to avoid discovery by Roman centuria out searching for escapees, we would need to walk at night and rest by day. The route was rocky and perilous and our path would plunge 500 metres down to the shores of the Dead Sea. They would use the secret route taken on the Day of Atonement by the priest charged with escorting the "Scape-goat", bearing our sins, to its untimely end. They knew the route well as they had been liaising between the fighting forces defending Masada and the remnant of the Zealots defending Jerusalem for many moons.

Our journey lasting three days was exhausting and despite the heat of the day, the desert nights were cold and we shivered in our thin woollen garments. We had enough food and water for our journey, which was supplemented by wine from leather pouches carried by Ezekiel and Ysacchar. Fortunately our journey was uneventful until we reached Wadi Masada. This was a dry riverbed that flooded every seven years or so. The cunning King Herod the great had erected a wooden aqueduct to collect these infrequent floods and transport the water to huge cisterns excavated in the belly of the mighty free standing rock of Masada. This way Herod knew he could withstand any siege mounted against him by Jewish rebels or Cleopatra's legions out of Egypt. This was the secret route to and from the plateau of Masada from its western flank: It was approached by walking through the winding narrow chasm of wadi Masada. To approach it at night was hazardous enough for any invading force and its defence was easy with guards at each narrow end of the aqueduct and an abundant store of boulders along the rim of the wadi lined up to ambush and crush those foolish enough to attempt a frontal assault.

Our guides expertly manoeuvred their way down the ravine and answered the challenge of the first guard with the password, "Mt'zada lo tipol". We were terrified as we were led along the narrow wooden bridge made by the aqueduct knowing that in the dark, one false step and we would fall 500 metres to our death. We were obviously expected and greeted with great enthusiasm and obvious affection by the Devorah wife of the commander of the zealots, Eleazar ben Yair, and a number of other women. Physically and emotionally exhausted we were shown to our sleeping quarters in a cubicle partitioned off within the twin defensive casemate walls, built by Herod in the south east sector of the plateau. As we still had no idea who we might trust, so the last thing we did before taking to our straw mattresses, was to bury our bag of coins under one of the stones making up the hearth of a little *open oven built into the corner of our cubicle; A simple chimney lead from this soot stained corner out through a gap in the thatched roof above our heads. I fell asleep embracing the golden candlesticks whilst Esther, wrapped the fractured tablet of stone in her coarse blanket and slept the sleep of the virtuous with her head resting on the words of the Lord. We slept for many hours and awoke to blazing sunshine at which point I remembered that I was filthy, stank like a goat, thirsty and hungry for my breakfast. We pushed our way through the rough raw wool hanging that closed off our cubical still in the filthy clothes we had worn since our escape from Jerusalem. Once we had adjusted to the brilliant light it took as a while to orientate ourselves. For a start we had no idea just how big was the plateau on the summit of Masada. It was at least the area of the temple mount in Jerusalem. We thought we might explore our new home but most of all I needed a good bath before meeting any of our new neighbours. Almost anticipating my wishes, the lovely wife of Eleazar ben Yair found us and took us to one side in the shade of the wall blocking the rapidly rising sun as it climbed the sky over the mountains of Moab. She introduced herself as Devorah bat Avraham Ha'Cohen, and that our grandfathers were brothers and thus we were cousins of a kind. "We must get you girls to the mikveh bath house and clothe you like decent women again. After that you are commanded to attend my husband in his quarters and listen very carefully to what he has to say and carry out his orders without question. First you must place in our safe keeping the holy relics you brought from the temple and their secrets can only be shared with my husband and I. If any other learns of your mission they shall surely die", she said imperiously without pausing for breath almost as if her lines had been learnt by heart. She then broke into a radiant smile and hugged and kissed us as if we were long lost daughters. I was shocked and giddy at the significance of what I had just heard and exchanged meaningful glances with Esther. Surely only brides and married women made use of the ritual bath all I required at this time was a good wash in clean water. Maybe we had misunderstood her words. In a daze we allowed ourselves to be lead back to our sleeping quarters. There we gathered up the treasure we had brought forth from the temple, which she guarded as she showed us the way to the mikveh built abutting the casemate walls just north of our cubicle. Whatever the implications of the act we were looking forward to a bath; ritual or otherwise, not only because of our filth and rank smell but we also felt defiled, as we had not yet washed ourselves* since our last lunar flux in the panic and commotion around the time of our escape from the temple compound. The mikveh was a pleasant low standing stone building with a narrow portal through which we had to stoop. We were pleasantly surprised when we saw the sunken bath, clad in cool stone and built strictly according to the command of the Torah, 3 cubits long, 1 cubit wide and 1 cubit deep with seven steps leading down. We subsequently learnt that it was fed from a cistern supplied by a branching channel in the complex network of waterways leading from the aqueduct draining Wadi Masada. Piled next to the bath was a pile of neatly folded fresh white linen clothing. We were happy to get rid of our men's garb and giggled with glee as we immersed and pushed each other under the cool fresh water. Before we were allowed out, Devorah insisted we showed her our hands when she meticulously cut and cleaned our fingernails. We clambered out chattering like monkeys and dried ourselves on waiting towels held up by Devorah. At her instruction we decked ourselves in beautiful white linen and finally modestly wrapped our short wet hair in a turban.

I looked at Esther and my heart skipped a beat as I witnessed her beauty whilst Devorah's smile grew wider and wider as she gave a little clap of delight.

"Come girls", she ordered, "you are now in a fit state to meet my husband, commander of the host that guards this community".

As she led us to the northern tip of the plateau we were amazed to see that the community was not an outpost of savages but a perfectly organised village. The southern and central sections of the plateau, was given over to fruit and vegetable gardens all neatly squared off and free of weeds. Some of the fruit trees were tall enough to provide delightful shady areas beneath which some villagers, if that was what we could call them, were taking a mid morning break. Clearly this had been the work of King Herod's labourers many decades in the past. We passed fishponds and saw a large carp angrily bucking as it was netted out of its refuge. We saw chicken roosts and goat pens with enough livestock to provide an endless supply of milk and eggs for the community. A lean to shed hard against the eastern inner perimeter wall displayed barrels of wine whilst running right across our path as we walked northward were huge storage sheds whose open doors revealed open bags bursting full of corn, nuts and dried fruit. Along the way we also recognised a dairy with cream cheeses drying in muslin tubes hanging from the rafters, *a laundry with bubbling cauldrons of boiling water and well away from this hard against the western wall we could hear the roaring fire of a foundry and could see flames and sparks and hear the crash of iron beaten on an anvil as the armourer went about his business. Everyone was bustling about his or her business with much laughter and shouting. There was even a small market where housewives were bartering or trading with copper and even silver coins. In amongst all this action, screaming young children where running around unchecked, playing the games of village children anywhere in the land of Israel. To add to the sense of normality close to the converted storeroom that housed Eleazar ben Yair and his family, we could hear the chanting of young male voices from a squat freestanding building that must have been a house of study and beyond that a larger building that looked like a house of prayer. The largest and most impressive building stood against the western wall a long way behind us now, raised three storeys high. I thought this was a King's palace and later was to learn that Herod and his family lived there over 60 years ago but today it was derelict and out of bounds. The apparent sense of normality was not to last for long we were brought before the presence of the great leader himself.*

It took a while for our eyes to adjust to the gloom of the unlit interior of the humble living quarters of the ben Yair family. Eleazar was sitting with a young child, maybe 12 months or so, gurgling happily on his lap. He was a tall and imposing man wearing a small circular covering made of brightly patterned wool on the back of his head. Long ringlets and a long beard that appeared as black as pitch against the backlight of the slanting sun reflected off the hangings and kitchenware that adorned the interior of his cave like dwelling, mostly hid his face. He deeply set black eyes were full of foreboding but when he smiled at us his brilliant white teeth lit up his face like shutters opening up on a bright morning sky. Devorah nudged us to kneel at his feet and gave us a bowel of water and a clean rag to wash them as a sign of respect. He waved this ritual aside and begged us to sit on the finely woven carpet at his side. He offered Devorah the child who hungrily rooted for her breast. Holding the baby in the crook of her left arm she busied herself turning up the oil lamps and closing the doors to the ancient Herodian storehouse that was now the modest palace of the leader of the Zealots. With no further ceremony Eleazar ben Simon began to speak and such was the enormity of his message that I can remember it almost word for word. "Welcome oh ye daughters of my dear friend and defender of the faith, Eliezer, the S'gun Cohen Ha'Godal, may God bless his soul and may he sit at God's right hand side amongst the righteous and may his daughters Esther and Yehudit enjoy a long and fruitful life. From afar your father has kept me informed on your development, and your beauty is as he described it to me, but your wisdom that he claimed was second to none, you will have plenty of opportunity to prove to me, but the fact that you have reached this place speaks for your courage. You two young virgins have been given the burden of carrying the most awesome responsibility ever handed down to a daughter of Adam since the time of Avraham Avinu. The children of Israel are facing annihilation as punishment for failing to hearken unto the word of the Lord by hating each other more than we hate the barbarians, those that worship Baal and the graven images of their many little gods. Even now many of our brethren have taken up arms against us favouring the pleasures of the flesh in the name of Epicurus rather than the serene sanctity of the love of mankind as commanded by our Lord through the voices of Avraham and Moishe Avinu. Yet the Lord in his divine mercy has spoken to your father and he has shared the word of the Lord with Eleazar ben Yair before whom you kneel, his humble servant, who addresses you now. It is prophesized in the third tablet of the holy covenant that this day will dawn and he who holds the secret of the third tablet handed to Aaron by his brother Moishe is to fulfil the commandment contained therein, lest the children of Israel are wiped off the face of the earth and Hashem's covenant with the children of Israel is broken like the third tablet inscribed by Moishe Rabenu." By now the excitement was wearing thin and this sermon was boring me. To come all this way to be preached at by a man in a big black beard was almost more than I could bear and I could barely suppress a yawn. Sensing my impatience Eleazar turned to me with eyes like burning coals a spoke the words that turned my bowels to water: " You Yehudit and your sister Esther, have been chosen by the Almighty to continue his work from this day forth. Just as the children of our matriarchs Sarah, Rebecca, Rachel and Leah, multiplied like the stars in the heavens and as the light of these stars flickers and dies, two new matriarchs will rise from the ashes of the temple, to go forth and multiply so that the children of Israel will once again shine like the firmament over the four corners of the earth before being gathered in once more to the holy land, once more to rebuild the temple of the Lord and for the third and last time enjoy the chance of uniting all the children of Adam and Eve in love and worship of the one creator of all things". He managed to say all that without pausing for breath and in those moments I saw with dread how the pattern of my life was now ordained and had the first glimmer of understanding of the burden that Esther and I were expected to carry. We exchanged glances and solemnly nodded to each other; our experiences in the holy of holies offered no other explanation. "Be gone now my children, Devorah bat Avraham will give you your instructions", finished Eleazar and I couldn't suppress the irritating thought that as always it was the women who had to attend to the details.

Devorah ushered us out and led us further northward around more storage rooms and animal pens until we reached the awesome southern wall of King Herod's fabled northern palace and winter retreat. We passed through a narrow gate at the junction with the western fortifications that separated the village area from the palace itself. On our right just beyond the gate Devorah pointed out the public baths that might be used by women between the hours of the sky lightening up in the east and the sun appearing over the edge of the mountains of Moab. We then walked down a narrow staircase hidden from the outside world because of its towering walls on our left. These stairs used to carry the food down from the storehouses and the drinking water up from one of the cisterns hidden in the lowest level of Masada to supply King Herod and his guests during there winter sojourn. We passed three wide terraces on the way down before ending up at a beautiful colonnaded circular garden facing due north. The view was breathtaking and the cooling breeze was very welcome. We were directed to sit on the semi-circular ledge that abutted the high frescoed wall holding up the terrace above our heads. The frescoes had been defaced by the zealots no doubt to hide the scenes of debauchery they once illustrated but enough remained for us to appreciate their grandeur. Having shooed out a young couple that were holding hands whilst enjoying the peace and beauty of the view, Devorah began her instruction.

"We have much to achieve but little time, yet it is the prophesy of Hashem that you will complete your task. First you must understand our position from our enemy's point of view. They will soon learn that our fortress is impregnable. Should the Romans attack from the west the aqueduct will be destroyed, there is then only one route to the summit of Masada and that is on our eastern flank, from the shore of the Dead Sea along the secret snake path. Even if you know the route well only one man at a time can climb it, subtle pitfalls are built into the path and in many places it is like a tightrope. One false step and you plunge to your death. A Roman soldier in full armour could not climb it with his encumbrances, so even if this secret were lost to the enemy the defence of the path would be easy. The Romans will no doubt stage a siege and hope to starve us into submission, that is their usual tactic but what they don't know is that we have enough water in our cisterns to last for seven years, enough food in our stores to last for twelve months but as you've already seen we are self sufficient in bringing forth fruit from the land, fish from our ponds and milk from our goats. The Romans might tire of their siege in a year or two or their legions might be required to fight some more urgent battles elsewhere in their empire. All we have to fear is from within. At present with a common enemy we are at peace with ourselves but I have no idea how long this will last. We are an argumentative people with a strong leader but only God knows how long Eleazer's health and strength will last or how long it will suit the Sicarii to find common purpose with us Zealots. It is an example of my husband's wisdom to choose your husbands from the ranks of these fearsome warriors." "Husbands, matriarchs, siege…. my life is beginning to unravel", I thought to myself whilst seeing my expression mirrored in Esther's face. No, unravel was the wrong word it was the opposite. I felt like a passive shuttle in a loom being whisked side to side dragging my colour to be woven into a complex pattern of someone else's design. Of course if it was the design of Hashem then that at least answered the philosophical question of free will, but if this was the design of the zealots created out of political expediency then I was about to have a fearful tantrum. At that point I remembered my father's dying words and the miracle I experienced in the holy of holies as I lifted the heavy gold crown off the arc of the covenant and in an instant I recognised God's design in all things and meekly bent my back in submission to his will.

"The young men we have chosen for you are the ones who escorted you to this place; the brothers ben Baruch. For you Yehudit, the headstrong, I have chosen Ysaachar who will be a good influence on you because of his devout nature and for Esther, the dreamer, I have chosen Ezekiel for he is a man of action. Please God you find favour in each other's eyes and may your heavenly souls complement each other in their embrace.

This evening you will bathe again and I will dress you both in the finest raiment from our stores and you shall bear the perfume of the roses of Attar. I *will then bring you back to this place and my husband Eleazar shall bring the two young men at sunset and you shall sit and talk whilst my husband and I stand by."*

From that point on Esther and I behaved like puppets barely exchanging a word. Three hours later, bathed, dressed like princesses and smelling of rose petals we stood meekly with our heads bowed under the colonnades with our back to a beautiful sunset that layered the sky in radiant hues of deep red, orange and indigo, running all along the cliff edges towards Wadi Ein Gedi.

The two young men entered the circular garden shortly afterwards in the company of our commander and shuffled around awkwardly obviously feeling like us that events outside their control had overtaken their ambitions. Out of their armour and wearing simple tunics, with bare legs and simple sandals, with a slight shadow of stubble on the chins, they looked young and vulnerable and I liked them more for that.

They sat down on the circular shelf at the back of the terrace, lamps were lit and we were paraded in front of them. They looked up in and in comical unison their jaws dropped as if controlled by the same puppet master. I couldn't suppress a giggle as I compared in my minds eye how we must look to them compared to the bedraggled and soot stained street urchins they had escorted from the mouth of Hezekiah's tunnel to the summit of Masada. These mighty Sicarii looked terrified by our presence and were speechless. Esther and I turned to each other, reflecting our beauty back and forth and our faces broke into radiant smiles that then gave way to good-natured laughter. Clearly we had to take the initiative, as the poor boys couldn't distinguish one of us from the other. I drifted over to Ysaachar, modestly sat at his side and introduced myself. Esther did the same with Ezekial whilst Eleazar and Devorah nodded to each other with approval. The young men were painfully shy but we put them at their ease and we each found favour in the eyes of the other so truly these were to be unions blessed by heaven. The good news was broken to the crowd waiting at the gates to the palace and a cheer went up as we were led up the staircase from below. A formal betrothal was witnessed by a 1,000 souls crushed into the little square framed by the house of prayer, the southern wall of Herod's palace, the storage vaults and an orange grove. Eleazar and Devorah acted in loco parentis for us, whilst the parents of the ben Baruch brothers stood proudly by. Blessings over wine were sung, bread was broken and the ketubah contract was read out. Following this the men joined together in wild dancing in a circle with the two grooms to be sitting in the centre wearing bemused expressions. Some of the older men exhausted by the dance turned their minds to wild drinking whilst the womenfolk looked on with indulgent smiles on their faces. Thus in the space of one day we had completed our courtship and betrothal and could look forward to the chuppah wedding ceremony the next day. By chance or maybe yet again by the design of the almighty, the day we had just lived through was the 15th of Av, the day that traditionally marked the beginning of the grape harvest the day that according to tradition the unmarried girls of Jerusalem would dress in white and go out to dance in the vineyards and "whoever did not have a wife would go there" to find himself a bride.

We spent that night in the home of our adoptive parents but neither of us could sleep because of all the excitement of the previous 24 hours. At day break Devorah roused us from a fitful slumber, listened to us say our morning prayers, watched us as we dressed in plain white linen and whilst still fasting, escorted us to the mikveh. The plateau of Masada glowed gold in the early morning sun slanting across the Dead Sea invisible below our eastern wall. Esther strolled ahead of me and I watched in awe as line of incandescent red and gold against the pale violet colour of the sky formed a corona around her silhouette. After our ritual emersion we returned and enjoyed a frugal breakfast of olives, freshly baked flat bread and goat's milk. Eleazar was shooed outside and stood guard at the door as we put on our wedding finery, a gift of the whole community who seemed better prepared for the occasion than we were, making me feel once again that I was a thread in the design of a beautiful carpet or a puppet in the hands of a master puppeteer. The double doors of our master's home were flung open and Esther and I walked out hand in hand blinded by the sun that shone through our muslin bridle veils. A breathless, ahhh, escaped 1,000 throats as we emerged into the square and we were just able to make out the hazy image of the chupah held aloft on four spears by four of the tallest men from our mountain retreat. There was no prior tradition or minchag for a double wedding involving two brothers marrying twin sisters, so Eleazar in consultation with the elders decided to combine them under a double sized canopy woven in many colours displaying the same iconography we had witnessed in the curtains baring the way to the holy of holies. I took this to be a favourable augury. Eleazar ben Yair stood with his back to the wall of the house of prayer thus allowing the bridal couples to face towards the holy city of Jerusalem. On each side were the two most senior of the elders both from the tribe of the Levites. Behind our master and to one side was a young man I had not yet noticed whose role I was soon to learn. Our two grooms, dressed in long white gowns with their heads, shoulders and backs covered with prayer shawls woven out of the purest white wool, from which hung the fringes died cobalt blue, stood at the edges of the shadow cast by the canopy, upright, tall and rigid like columns of marble.

Devorah gently lead me to the figure on the right, Yssachar the older brother and Esther to the figure of the left, Ezekiel the younger. None of us stole glances as our attention was fixed on the noble face of Eleazar ben Yair, looking like a King in spite of his humble attire. Suddenly as if from nowhere the voice of an angel began to sing the seven blessings. The voice echoed off the vertical cliffs each more than 500 metres in height that surrounded us on three sides. The timing of the echo and its slight change of pitch as it bounced of the sandstone cliffs created an impression of two young men singing in perfect harmony. All this was from the throat of the single young man standing just behind our master. As he was half way through the last blessing the whole congregation joined in and sang these beautiful words as tears of joy blinded my eyes behind the veil:

"Soon O Lord our God, may there be heard in the cities of Judah, and in the streets of Jerusalem, the voice of joy and gladness, the voice of the bridegroom and the voice of the bride, the jubilant voices of bridegrooms from their canopies, and of youths from their feasts of song. Blessed art thou O Lord, who makes the bridegroom to rejoice with the bride"

As the last echo died away our veils were lifted and one Levite from each side offered sips of wine to bride and bridegroom who repeated the blessings. The youth with the voice of an angel burst into joyful song again whilst Esther and I solemnly made seven circuits around our bridegrooms and as they looked at us for the first time they recognised us and they smiled at us in joy, for we had truly found favour in their eyes.

Once we had returned to our places the marriage contracts were read out again, we exchanged vows and rings and then Eleazer began to address the happy throng.

Silence descended like a curtain over the proceedings and his sonorous baritone voice filled the mountain summit. He praised the Lord for allowing us to live to see this day. He praised our beauty and the wisdom and courage of the bridegrooms. He praised the memory of our father and mother, who we never knew. He praised the Lord's creation in all its magnificence and thanked Hashem for bringing us forth from the Egypt to the Promised Land. He quoted at length from King Solomon's Song of Songs. He went on and on and on as the sun rose above our ramparts and began to burn our backs. He most certainly had captured the attention of the multitude but by now he had lost mine. In my father's court I had listened to many such men who seemed to love the sound of their own voices. I thought men like this were dangerous. They certainly revelled in their command of the crowd but this natural gift for leadership might just as easily lead men astray as lead them to a promised land.

Matters were resolved when after an hour during which our master barely drew breath or even repeated himself, there was a commotion as Esther fainted at the side of her bridegroom. She was quickly revived with a glass of water and I spotted Devorah giving the look of daggers to Eleazer whilst gently shaking her head. That little gesture told me who was truly in command and I kept my little smile hidden as I modestly bowed my head. Once Esther was revived and we all took our places again, Eleazer brought forth two long necked glass phials from his pockets. Each contained a little fluid the colour of egg yolk. These looked like the perfume phials wealthy Roman women carried at all times. He gave one each to the bridegrooms and this time spoke briefly. "We are celebrating this time of great joy whilst the fires of the barbarians still consume the holy city of Jerusalem. Nay, this is the first chupah since our golden city was taken by the Titus' Roman hordes, may they forever burn in the flames of God's fury. This day of joy must also be a day of remembrance for our holy city therefore I decree that from this day forth all those who marry beneath the canopy of the Lord shall crush beneath his feet a symbol of our loss. At a nod from Eleazar the two bridegrooms took the perfume phials and crushed them beneath their feet.

After a moment of shocked silence the people of Masada went wild with joy dancing to the music from harp, horn and tambour, followed by singing, feasting and drinking that went on all day. In the midst of this sanctioned period of misrule, Esther and I were lifted high on the shoulders of the two *pairs of the giants who had held the canopy and paraded around the square as we squealed in feigned terror and then we danced decorously with our bridegrooms without touching their flesh, linked only by our bridal veils that were now removed from our brows and held in our extended hands. After we had enjoyed an extravagant breakfast sitting at the head of two long tables with everyone around us competing in the entertainment, that included ribald songs that made us blush, we were urged by Devorah to slip away. She then conducted us to our separate homes a long way from the boisterous celebrations that went on all night. This was the first time that Esther and I were to be separated as we had shared the same sleeping quarters since birth yet as we went our separate ways I felt the threads that held us together, tighten rather than fray.*

Chapter 6

Yehudit Scroll V

Three happy years have past since last I wrote my story. It is strange that happiness and tranquillity does not provoke any enthusiasm to capture my thoughts and feelings for future generations to read, whilst terror and tragedy seem to goad me into action.

I squat here accompanied by a pretty two-year-old child who I've named Naomi, whilst my sister keeps me company with a boisterous little boy named Eliezer after our beloved and saintly father. Yet terror and tragedy have accompanied us for the last four weeks.

I am writing this testament hidden deep within a cave in Wadi Ein-Gedi just one day's walk north of Masada. We hear the Roman soldiers tramping past looking for survivors from Masada but they won't find us because nature, Hashem according to Esther, has closed the entry to our hiding place. This ravine is the happy home and hunting ground of tribes of large spiders that weave elaborate webs across the mouths of caves whereby the disturbed flow of air seems to suck the flying insects into these traps. The entrance to our cave is almost obliterated by cobwebs. Legend has it that King David escaped the clutches of King Saul in just such a way. I give thanks to these spiders and forgive the one that nearly closed our entry into the tunnel when we escaped from the Temple. Esther gives thanks to God.

Our ordeal began two years after our wedding when my husband and I were disturbed from our deep conjugal sleep, by mighty shouts. These were shouts of defiance echoing round the valleys on the three sides of the mighty rock not facing the Dead Sea. These shouts from the throats of 1,000 refugees from the sacked city of Jerusalem, informed us unambiguously that something of cataclysmic importance had happened whilst we had slept.

From where we were standing we could see no sign of life but about 30 steps eastward towards hubbub we could begin to see hundreds of our people screaming abuse and hurling missiles westward over the parapets of the curtain walls guarding the western edge of the great rock. On joining the back of the crowd that stood at least three deep we still could not fathom what had provoked this riotous assembly. I squirmed to the front and caught my breath at the drama being played out before us. The wooden aqueduct that allowed safe crossing to the plateau on our arrival, was now a smouldering charred skeleton. Clearly this had been set fire by the defenders at some time before dawn as scouts signalled the attack of the Roman legions from Wadi Masada. We could also make out the mound of huge rocks that now filled the ravine and no one could guess how many legionnaires had been crushed beneath. Lined up along the edge of the mountainous cliff at the western side of the valley that protected Masada we could see blinding flashes of light as the early morning sun was reflected off the body armour, swords and shields of the VIIth legion commanded by Augustus Silva, their legendary and ruthless commander. Romans and Zealots were screaming abuse at each other and hurling missiles in futile attempts to reach across the chasm that was 500 metres deep and 1,500 metres wide. Even as we started watching, rivulets of armed men started streaming down narrow ravines to the north of Wadi Masada or even abseiling down ropes hanging over sheer cliff faces. I assumed we would soon be overrun but was relieved when the flood of armed men were ordered to a halt around a perimeter just out of range of our catapults, javelin and arrows. The crowd on our side went suddenly silent at this spectacle of military discipline. There was a further commotion starting up from the north end of the plateau that we had not yet seen and as all heads turned in that direction a cry of dismay went up as further centuria of the VIIth legion were seen marching in rigid formation, long rectangular shields guarding their left flank with short swords held pointing to the heavens in their right fist. We later learnt that they had overcome our outpost guarding Wadi Ein-Gedi several kilometres to the north and completed the perilous descent to the shore of the Dead Sea along with a mule train bearing arms and supplies. At the head of this army emerging from the white salt plains whose crystals reflected the low angled sun like diamonds, was a splendidly armoured officer with a bright red brush embellishing the crest of his helmet, accompanied by a legionnaire covered in a lion's skin bearing the golden eagle, the Standard of the legion. For a time my fear was replaced by awe as I watched the dance like manoeuvres of the ranks of soldiers as they gathered into a formation making three sides of a square with the open side facing us.

Rank upon rank came down the cliffs from the west and along the seashore from the north until it appeared that the whole valley was filled with armed men just beyond slingshot range of our defensive position. Then their drum beats filled the air as the officer corps entered the centre of the square and their commander was raised on high, to stand on a wheeled wooden platform that had been manufactured out of our sight, looking like the base of a sling shot catapult that I had glimpsed during the siege of Jerusalem.

The Roman commander resplendent in his armour mounted his podium accompanied by his eagle and a bent old man with a grey beard. The Roman shouted at us in Latin, which I understood perfectly well, whilst the bent old man translated the Latin into Hebrew. In spite of the distance, the crystalline still air and the acoustic properties of the cliffs backing the Roman general, made his words easy to hear. This was very much the experience I once illicitly enjoyed when against the laws of my household I slipped out to hear a Greek tragedy in the amphitheatre built by the Romans outside our city walls in the Hinnom valley. The gist of his words was that we had no hope other than to surrender and throw ourselves at the tender mercy of Rome. Having witnessed this tender mercy of Rome in the sacking of Jerusalem, that included mass crucifixion, I had little doubt what our response should be. Our commander responded as if giving voice to my thoughts, although in language that I blushed on hearing.

The shouting match was nothing other than a ritual and was over in minutes. I then braced myself for a full frontal assault from the VIIth Legion but nothing happened. They were ordered to stand down and set about making their encampment out of our range, building campfires to cook their midday meal and set up an armoury and what only could be described as a brothel although at that distance I couldn't be sure and it might all have been a figment of my fevered imagination. What was not in doubt was the magnificent square tent decorated with coloured fabrics raised on flat land almost due west of the midpoint of Masada, to accommodate the Roman general and his senior staff.

This puzzling anti-climax lasted about a week as the Roman legion settled themselves down at leisure into an encampment and secured their flanks. It then became clear to us what plan that had in mind for us as their slaves and foot soldiers started building a siege wall around the circumference of Masada. Day after day I watched with fascination as the wall, interrupted by watchtowers took shape. It was truly a remarkable feat of engineering as the wall had to follow the contours of the land that included the ravine of Wadi Masada to the south west as well as the flat salt plains to the east by the Dead Sea. It soon became clear that they would be content to starve us into submission by siege rather than by arms. Here they had made a serious error of judgement and clearly their spies had let them down badly. I suspect some of them ended up paying for their errors nailed to a cross. Their mistake was that we were totally self sufficient in food as we farmed the narrow plot of land on our plateau and our storehouses built by King Herod contained dried food that would last for years. Furthermore, unknown to the Romans, Masada was riddled with huge storage tanks for water, enough to last for seven years again thanks to the foresight of "good" King Herod. Fortunately for us the main cistern had recently been filled along the burnt out aqueduct the last time Wadi Masada flooded in a freak storm in the month of Tevet. We therefore entered a strange period where we carried on our life as normal apart from disturbance from our noisy neighbours. It took many months before the besieging army began to appreciate the stalemate during which time by way of rationing, our leaders started minting copper and silver coins distributed to each according to need to be exchanged for food and water. This way hoarding was avoided.

Within a few months of our marriage both Esther and I started to blossom and grow large of breast and belly and felt the first quickening of the first children to be born in the siege. More mouths to fill but our stores were bountiful and we rejoiced. As if in honour of our status the second minting of the coinage of the siege coincided with the almost synchronous onset of our labour pains. All went well and on the next Yom Shabbat in our modest little house of prayer near the western wall, I held my baby girl aloft as our leader announced her name as Naomi bat Yehudit bat Eliezer Ha'Cohen.

Two days later my little nephew Eliezer was circumcised as Esther wept uncontrollably but proudly accepted him back from the mohel with the name of Eliezer ben Esther bat Eliezer Ha'Cohen. It may appear strange that the children's names did not include the father but such was the awe in which we were held as the last living relatives of the S'gun Cohen Ha'Godol, they determined his name lived on through our bloodline. For the next two years as our babies grew chubby on our rich supply of breast milk whilst Esther and I grew complacent in this unreal world. Then suddenly the Roman's came for us and we were shaken out of this state of bovine quietude. After six months of siege it became apparent that the Romans had become bored with this waiting game and had determined on another stratagem of breaking our will. One Shabbat when the day was at its longest and the heat at its highest something changed whilst we were at our devotions on our day of rest. The Romans had cleverly chose that day to prepare for the building of some kind of structure that might carry them up to the level of our walls on the western side. Yom Rishon the day after the Sabbath we awoke to the cries of our lookouts who pointed below. Whilst our minds were on other things the Romans had breached their own siege wall and transported a huge load of timbers and building materials and laid them out in readiness for the building of some kind of siege ramp. Such an undertaking appeared superhuman and was certainly unprecedented in the chronicles of warfare.

As soon as our people understood the Romans plan they reposted with sling shot, arrow and any missile that came to hand. At this distance our efforts were puny and barely slowed the Romans in their work especially as their slaves took the brunt of our best efforts and clearly they were considered as disposable objects with plentiful replacements amongst our poor brethren transported in cages from Judea.

After a few days observing their method with grim fascination I was able to deduce their plan making use of my knowledge of trigonometry. I produced some simple drawings and took them to our council of elders. As judged by the shape and size of the base of their structure built out of massive tree trunks dragged from God knows where, I was able to deduce the size and inclination of a pyramidal dais that would eventually climb to the foot of our fortifications on the western wall aiming a little to the south of our house of prayer. Day by day I witnessed the structure grow and marvelled at the ingenuity of the Roman engineers. They appeared to be building a ziggurat like the ancients of Babylon except at each step they paused to cover the wooden frame with boulders and earth. And so the ramp grew day by day. After a few months the slaves and their masters were within reach of our missiles and started to take heavy loses. This certainly slowed them down but on each Shabbat our foolish leaders insisted that we refrain from work and warfare and these lulls were exploited as the Roman gangs who doubled their efforts and the ramp grew with a slow but relentless tempo.

After a month or two when once again the Romans were given a free reign as we bowed down in prayer to the Almighty at Rosh Ha'Shana the New Year and Yom Kippur the day of Atonement; it became apparent that the Lord had abandoned us to our fate and the new platform on the siege tower allowed the Roman archers a good footing to pour down fire as their flaming arrows arched overhead. Towards the end of Succot it was obvious to all save those who had kept faith with our fickle and petulant God, that we were doomed. About this time Esther and I were summoned to meet with our leader Eleazar ben Yair. What he had to tell made us sink to our knees in despair. Looking gaunt and exhausted he outlined his dreadful plan. Rather than be taken alive all but six of those living on Masada would die. Each father would kill his wife and children and then those left would draw lots to determine the order in which they killed each other. The sight of the 1,000 dead would bring shame on the Romans as they breached our defences. As far as the two of us; we were chosen to live. Following on the precise instructions left by our father in anticipation of this turn of events we must escape not just to continue our bloodline but as custodians of the sacred relics from the temple: the twin golden candlesticks and most precious of all the third tablet of the holy covenant.

The plan was as follows: together with our children and two maidservants, we would hide with adequate supplies in one of the labyrinthine channels of the water cisterns inside the great rock. Entrance and exits to these cisterns where well hidden thanks to the ingenuity of King Herod's architects. We were to stay hidden until the Romans had cleared the site, as they wouldn't stay long once our resistance had been crushed, as the VIIth Legion was urgently needed to put down another rebellion at Jericho.

They would no doubt leave a small garrison to prevent the fortress being occupied so that our final escape would be perilous. We had no time to assimilate all this terrible news and with our husbands summoned and refusing to meet our eyes, we were taken to reconnoitre our hiding place and route of escape whilst our maidservants looked after our weeping children who had somehow sensed that something dreadful was about to happen. The major northern cistern had been built to supply water to King Herod's palace at the northern tip of our fortress. This palace was built with bathhouses on the plateau and three terraces leading down towards the desert below. A water gate was hidden near the bathhouses and slaves could carry jars of water down through a hidden niche in the western rock face to supply those feasting on the lower terraces. From the lowermost terrace was a drop of about 80 metres so escape from this side of Masada would be considered impossible and therefore would not be watched. However unknown to the Romans and unknown to all but the senior council there was indeed an escape route. A flagstone in the courtyard on the lowermost terrace could be lifted by two strong men and beneath that was a near vertical drop with bronze loops set in the rock acting as footrests and ropes to hang on to as one descended. At the foot of this escape tunnel was another rock that would need the strength of two men to shift and from there the coast was clear. At this point the Roman siege wall could easily be mounted. Our husbands were to stay with us to the end to move the heavy stones that blocked our exit but once we were out and they had replaced the rock and the flag stone they were to return to the summit and create a disturbance at the southern end of the plateau in order to distract the remaining guards so we might make good our escape. Their final role would be to lay down their lives for us so that one-day our people and the word of the Lord might go forth from the land of Israel.

With our children and handmaidens we would walk due north keeping close to the edge of the ramparts facing the Dead Sea carrying nothing other than the tablet of stone and the golden candlesticks. They would be bound in protective wool with carrying straps for the four adults to share the load. At day break we would be met by a band of men would be monitoring our escape hidden in the escarpment above. They would provide mules to carry our load as well as being supplied with food and water.

We would then be shown to a cave in Wadi Ein Geddi a day's walk to the north where we were to lay hidden until it was known that the Dead Sea valley was free of Roman legionnaires. On that day the mules would return.

As if all that was not bad enough his last order broke our hearts. Next to our children and even more than we loved our husbands, Esther and I were bound to each other like the twin kernels of a chestnut. Yet once the mules returned we would be parted forever. Esther was to travel northward to the hills of northern Galilee with her child and handmaiden, custodian of the word of the Lord. When she reached a given sanctuary she would sojourn there, build a small temple in which to hide the fragments of the Lord's covenant, if needs be find another husband and choose life for her family and generations to come.

My role was even more hazardous. When the mules returned I was to turn south with the dumb beasts bearing the golden candlesticks and make my way to the southern tip of the Dead Sea and then turn westward to Beersheba. From there I was to join a caravan disguised as one of the spice traders en route to Akaba and then carry on by sea to the spice lands of the Indies. Should I then reach a safe haven amongst the dark skinned ones who traded with us since the times of King Solomon, with my dowry of gold, I was to sojourn there be fruitful and multiply so that the seeds of the tribe of the Levites would take root and flower once more.

With heads downturned and hearts in turmoil we returned to the plateau to prepare ourselves for the ordeal to come. In spite of instructions to the contrary I determined to hide about my person these scrolls that will act as my testament to future generations.

Just as we had completed the tasks of gathering together the essentials for our period in hiding something remarkable happened. Our armed men had built a wooden wall to shore up the breach that the Romans had created above their ramp, but the Romans had thrown firebrands and set the wood alight. Suddenly the direction of the wind changed driving the flames on to the Romans. Then, as if at divine injunction, the wind changed direction again and the flames were driven inwards. The Romans saw this as the work of their gods who had come to their help; I saw it as proof positive that if there was a god he was no friend of mine.

I will say nothing, nay cannot speak of the terrors and torments we suffered in our hiding place nor can I speak of the heartbreak of our separation from our dear husbands save to mention the pledges we made to meet again in the world to come.

That might have comforted Esther but these were empty words as far as I was concerned. Our escape went according to plan and now I find myself at the lowest ebb in my life, damp, hungry and dirty protected from my enemies only by the gossamer threads of a spider's web.

But hush! I think I hear the clip clop of the mules that will finally separate me from my beautiful twin sister. She has promised to bind my written words to her breast and if she survives the perils of here journey to the northern hills of Galilee then one day my nephew will be old enough to learn about his great inheritance as temporary custodian of the blood line of the great temple priest our beloved father. May God rest his soul.

PART 2

The Making of a Man

Chapter 7

Jerusalem, Yamin Moshe (5775) 2015 CE

It is five thousand, seven hundred and seventy five years since the creation of the universe according to the bible or 2015 years since the birth of the Jewish prophet, Jesus of Nazareth. Neither of these calculations is meaningful to me as I'm a secular Jew. All I know for sure is that I've just celebrated my 85th birthday.

> *"I was young and I have grown old, yet I have never seen the righteous forsaken nor his progeny begging for bread."*

So we conclude the grace after meals. When I was young I could sing that verse to a sublime melody that made my parents weep. Now that I am old I have lost my singing voice but I've never been forsaken and remain wrapped in the warm embrace of my beautiful daughter and my grandchildren. But I do so miss the embrace of my wife Sara, of blessed memory. This old man is the child of his former self. When I was young I used the precious commodity of time promiscuously, as if it was limitless and now as my time runs out I value every heartbeat. What little time and energy I had left has been used to record for my child and grandchildren, a story of everlasting love, heartbreak, discovery and redemption. They will never have to beg for bread, not because I am righteous, not because I'm wealthy, but because of their wonderful inheritance. This inheritance is not of worldly goods or sound investments but encoded in their DNA. May they profit from their inheritance of wisdom and beauty.

I'm writing this on the early morning sun lit terrace of my precious golden house in Yamin Moshe. The gold is the reflection of the sun rising in the East and in my face, reflected off these old

Jerusalem stonewalls. On this May morning the birds sing with delight as if intoxicated by the nectar from the blossoms of my bougainvillea, azalea and honeysuckle that cascade in waves over the terraces leading down to the valley of the Sultan's pool. This empty and arid valley still remains brooding in the shadows of the towering Ottoman Empire walls guarding the Old City. Directly in front of me, rising above these ancient walls is the squat form of the Armenian Orthodox Church, whilst a little to the left in my field of vision, the iconic tower of David on Mount Zion, announces a sense of place and a sense of history, although in truth the tower is a minaret from the early Ottoman period close on 2,500 years after the Davidic era. Unseen but ever present, the Western Wall of the Temple mount lies due east, a mere 1,000 metres away. To my extreme right, beyond the church of Domitian, snakes the ugly grey granite wall that separates Israel from the West Bank, announcing that history in all its tragic facets is still being made. If all goes according to plan that wall will soon come down. Walls for defense, walls for prayer, walls for separation; these walls have tears.

I have two houses, two places where I feel completely at home. One is my secular home; a red brick Georgian town house nearly 250 years old in Hampstead Village, North West London, 5,000 miles west of where I sit and meditate. My London home is a flat-faced terrace, with a plaque on the wall recording the sojourn of the landscape painter Constable. The original well with its wrought iron superstructure and bucket, gives off a warm sense of continuity with old London town. This well had to be capped to protect the more adventurous of my grandchildren, but before that I was able to dredge up broken clay pipes, fragments of blue Worcester ceramic and one copper penny bearing the head of Queen Victoria. My spiritual home is here in Yemin Moshe. I claim that I'm a secular Jew, yet here I talk about my spiritual home; surely a contradiction in terms. The answer is simple; I have never rejected the transcendental, searched for it all my life, found it through love and through love found God. Yet I remain a sceptic about religion and choose to define myself as secular. Yemin Moshe was built in 1892 but built on ancient ground. When excavating the little garden in order to plant a shrub, I dug up a terracotta clay oil lamp of uncertain age but in the style common place in ancient Rome, a ceramic tile dating from the crusades and a copper coin bearing the head of King George Vth. This little settlement was the first housing project outside the Old walls of the "City of Peace", Jerusalem. These stone built terraces were decreed and funded by Moses Montefiore who lived in Old London town. Yemin Moshe is Hebrew for "the right hand of Moses". Old Moshe and I not only shared two abodes in close proximity, but also a name. Like most Jews I have two names. My given English name is Martin Tanner (a surname derived after three iterations from the original Tannenbaum) and my Hebrew name Moishe Dovid ben Baruch. I also enjoy a third name by my reputation. I've earned my good name through the spirit of scientific enquiry and through the uncompromising integrity of my research and that is what has brought me to Jerusalem on this occasion. Last night I received the Israel Prize from the hands of the President himself. I have won many prizes for my research including the Kettering prize, the most prestigious and valuable that the USA can offer for cancer research. In fact that $250,000 enabled me to buy this house of gold at the right hand of Moses. However the Israel Medal means more to me than anything before as my spiritual home is so close to where my quest began and so close to where I first found everlasting love. If you fly like a crow over the battlements of the old city, past the gardens of Gethsemane, up and over the Mount of Olives, then down and down to the deepest declivity on this planet you will find that place.

1000 m above the western edge of the Dead Sea is the historic site of Masada. On the western edge of this plateau there is a small synagogue that dates back to just after the fall of Jerusalem to the invading Roman legions in 70 AD. Set in the Western Wall of this ancient synagogue facing directly towards Jerusalem, are two empty niches that once held sacred relics from the destroyed temple. These consisted of two fragments of a granite plaque carved on one side in bas-relief with images of the temple menorah and the great door to the inner court whilst the other was a pair of golden candlesticks that stood either side of the Altar.

The former found their way to Northern Galilee and settled for two millennia in the old synagogue in Piki'in whilst the latter were discovered two or three years ago on the Malabar Coast in Southern India. How these relics made their hazardous journey North and South of Masada was the starting point of my story nearly 2,000 years ago.

I am not long for this world as I sense the knot of cancer invading and extending beyond the confines of my pancreas. The pain is well controlled by the visits of the palliative care staff of the Hadassah hospital nearby. The oral morphine washed down with judicious 15 milliliters of 18-year-old Talisker malt, a luxury I deserve, and makes what's left of my life tolerable. Neither am I afraid of death in spite of having no truck with concept of everlasting life in a heaven filled with saints. That sounds like hell to me. If I were to choose my own heaven creative rascals like Gauguin, Donizetti, Ernest Hemingway and Voltaire would people it. Nor do I live out these precious moments in hope of meeting my Sara again in a world to come, yet my vision is not bleak it is a celebration of the triumph of humanity. I believe that our earth has a fourth stratum in addition to the oceans, the earth and the atmosphere and this I describe as the sea of human consciousness. This remarkable sea covers most of the landmasses of the earth. This sea of consciousness is of course carried somewhere in the cerebral cortex of several billion members of the species *Homo sapiens*. This is a strange sea because on closer examination it is made up of quanta of energy bobbing about inside strange fruit from strange trees. These trees live below the surface of the sea and some have very old roots anchored to the time when man first lost his innocence in the Garden of Eden and recognized that his life was but a passing shadow. These strange fruit are released from the tree at birth but defy Newton's law of gravity and float upwards because of the property of buoyancy within this strange sea. As time goes on this property weakens and eventually all buoyancy is lost and the fruit falls. This fallen fruit is more than compensated by new orbs of living consciousness and as fruit never fall too far from their tree, these newcomers will share and perpetuate the genetic code of their forbears although with ever increasing dilution. In the words of Descartes I am both a *homo sapiens* and a *res cogitans*, something that thinks. As my sapient body dies I know it will be synchronously replaced by one or more innocent children that will in turn become *res cogitans* at an age when they recognize that they exist as individuals with a limited lifespan having made the journey from the age of innocence to the age of knowledge. Legend has it that there is an Angel Lailah who watches over the unborn child. At the point of birth the Angel places it's index finger on the upper lip of the child and quietly whispers "shush", the angel's imprint forms the philtrum that perfects the baby's Cupid's bow. At this point all the memories of past generations of the child's family are wiped out and the newborn starts life as a *tabula rasa*. It is my fondest wish that when I die my beloved granddaughter, would one day bring forth into this sea of my imagination children that will be one-eighth me and one-eighth Sara each successfully completing the journey from innocence to wisdom. It is for these fruits of my genetic tree that I have written these memoirs that will replace those lost in the womb at the touch of the angel's finger.

I have given up on the idea that the tidal ebb and flow of chance explained my life's voyage as there were too many coincidences in my life that brought me to the discovery and de-coding of the Third Tablet of the Holy Covenant. I have now succumbed to the acceptance that I am one of these strange fruit bobbing about like a cork on the ocean carried on a strong current, a veritable Gulf Stream of predeterminism and that like it or not, I have been a pawn in some great eternal chess game in the hands of the greatest grandmaster of the game in all eternity.

Forgive the rambling of a sad old man but I have to stop writing now in order to welcome this lovely young lady that Hadassah Hospital has kindly sent to palliate my passing. Yes I die but my life was fruitful and as we sing at the *Seder* table, *'Dayenu',* it has been sufficient.

Chapter 8

My Humble beginnings

I was born in the east end of London in 1930 at the Whitechapel London Hospital well within the sound of Bow Bells and by that definition I prided myself on being a cockney in spite of my educated accent and an aversion to mussels taken from the Thames estuary. We lived in Sydney Street in Stepney a few doors down from the erstwhile anarchists' house made famous by the siege of Sydney Street in 1911 when Winston Churchill as Home Secretary took charge. Both my parents came from an orthodox Jewish background. My father, Isaac, was born in Odessa in the Ukraine and fled to this country in 1905 following the notorious pogrom on the famous steps when his parents were cut down by the marauding Cossacks, organised by supporters of the Romanov Czar, as a distraction from the threat of a working class uprising. Sergei Eisenstein later rewrote this event for his film "The Battleship Potemkin", as Soviet propaganda, replacing the Jews with heroic Russian workers. How my father escaped from the Imperial Guards and arrived in Stepney as a lad of 16, is an adventure story of it's own, sufficient to say that it involved a perilous journey on foot and by horse and cart across Europe, along a network of Jewish communities until he reached Rotterdam and from there sailed to the port of London. He arrived as a penniless refugee fluent in Yiddish, Russian, Ukrainian and in the dialectical deconstruction of the Talmud. None of these skills were highly valued in working class Stepney but through the charity of the local Hebrew congregation, night classes and self improvement he got by and four years later passed "the knowledge" and got taken on as a licensed London cab driver. The point to note here is that within a few years he was able to master English and master the knowledge of every street, every hotel, every club and every restaurant in London, is a tribute to his intelligence and perseverance. It is claimed with good reason, that to retain all the information of "the knowledge" of the city of London, was equivalent of knowing off by heart every nook and cranny of the human body, every fine tributary of the central nervous system and every word of tractate Sanhedrin of the Babylonian Talmud. The latter was not far from the truth as he was in great demand in the synagogue to help resolve tricky issues of *halachic* law concerning *kashrut*, women's rights and the best bet for the 3.30 at Epsom. He demonstrated these skills of memory much later in life as a finalist in the television contest, Mastermind, with his specialist subject being Palestine at the time of the Roman Empire 100 BCE – 100 CE. He was also a chess grand master and taught the game at the local branch of the Jewish Lads Brigade. Yet it always angered me to hear of him being patronised or insulted by one of his "fares" as he plied his trade in the West-End, carrying chinless toffs from their St James' clubs to the Savoy grill or drunken slobs from the local boozer to a sleazy address in Soho. Yet I'm ashamed to say that when I went up to university in 1948 I was embarrassed to explain how Pater earned his living and reluctant for my friends to meet him because of his comical yiddisher accent.

My mother, Rivka known by everyone as Ruthie, was very different. Her parents made it to the sweat-shops of Whitechapel from Northern Italy and before that on her maternal great grandmother's side from India, before she was born so she spoke perfect English, enjoyed a reasonable education up to the age of 14 and prided herself on her posh accent picked up from the customers she served in the haute couture department at Selfridges in Oxford Street. She won this highly prized position because of her tall stature, natural grace, instinctive style, long slim legs and narrow hipped flat chest figure, that suited the flapper mode of the roaring twenties. However her most striking features were her exotic olive skin and large, lustrous, green eyes. Of course I never knew my paternal grandparents. My maternal grandmother died young in her early forties from what remained a mystery to me until my more mature years. My mother also had an older sister, auntie Millie, whose beauty was legendary, but I only have the sketchiest memory of her before she died in her mid thirties.

Isaac and Ruthie fell in love at a dance organised by the local Zionist organisation and were married in the orthodox synagogue in Stepney in 1925. Sepia photographs of that event show my father upright in his white tie and tails with a startled expression on his face hardly able to suppress his pride in capturing his beautiful bride. My mother is seen standing by his side, towering over him in her high heels, wearing a fashionable short bridal dress with fringes to cover her knees and a beaded band across her forehead carrying a tiny veil.

To start with they lived in one room in my mother's parents' flat, three flights up from the bustling Whitechapel Road, and started saving in order to afford a place of their own. After 4 years they moved to a tiny two up two down terrace house in Sydney Street and about nine months later I entered the world and two years later my baby brother Joseph arrived. Not long after that my uncle and aunt, Hymie and Becky Herschon, moved next door. Becky, my mother's only surviving sister, was plump and plain but was a gifted pianist who played in the pit of the Gaumont cinema on the Mile End Road until the end of the silent movie era and later in the orchestra at the Hackney Empire when she was always able to get a few cheap tickets for us to attend the Christmas pantomime. Uncle Hymie who ran the local deli was also a pretty good klezmer band violinist much in demand for local *simchas.*

My first clear memory, in fact more than just a memory; a seminal event in my life, took place in 1936 just after I'd celebrated my 6th birthday.

My mother had just finished high tea for baby Joe and me, when there were screams and shouts from the street outside our front door that opened straight into our parlour without any kind of lobby or hallway. The door crashed open and my father, with his face covered in blood, staggered in held standing by his best friend Joe Jacobs. Big Joe as we called him to distinguish him from my little brother, was the leader of the local communist party, a burly man who worked as a porter at Smithfield market. Mother fainted and we screamed our heads off. Big Joe and a nurse wearing the uniform of the London Jewish hospital, carried my father into the house, laid him on the sofa, cleaned the blood off his face and bandaged his head. It was much less severe than it appeared and all he was suffering was a gash in his scalp and mild concussion. I was to learn 16 years later, that scalp wounds bleed dramatically but are easily controlled by deep sutures. Later on they took him to the A&E department of the London hospital for stitches but not before the tale of his adventure unfolded. It appeared that the local communist party officials had learnt that Oswald Moseley's black shirted Nazi brigade were being allowed a provocative march through a predominantly Jewish part of the East End of London along the main thoroughfare of Cable Street in Poplar. Well the communists, lead by Joe Joseph weren't going to allow that. They gathered in the party offices in Commercial Street, marched west and turned south down Christian Street where they joined and ever mounting number of anti-fascists. The anti-fascist groups erected roadblocks in an attempt to prevent the march from taking place. The barricades were erected on Cable Street, towards the west end of this long road. An estimated 300,000 anti-fascist demonstrators turned out. Over 10,000 police, including 4,000 on horseback, attempted to clear the road to permit the march to proceed. The demonstrators with Joe and father in the van, fought back with sticks, rocks, chair legs and other improvised weapons and rubbish, rotten vegetables and the contents of chamber pots were thrown at the police by women in houses along the street. After a series of running battles, Mosley agreed to abandon the march to prevent bloodshed and redirected his storm troopers towards Hyde Park. My father had been struck on the head by a baton wielded by a mounted policeman an echo of his father's experience at the hands of mounted Cossacks, but fortunately not a lethal blow. Following this my father became a hero in my eyes and his reputation grew in the eyes of our local community but even though the net outcome was favourable for us all the experience made its indelible mark on my childish brain.

The next occasion I was branded, both figuratively and literally was at the time of the blitz five years later in 1941 when I was aged 11. As the sirens wailed early one Sunday evening we carried homework from the dinning room table and rushed to the improvised Anderson shelter, that we shared with our neighbours the Herschons. Dad and his brother in-law, Hymie Herschon, had dug it themselves after taking down the wooden fence that divided our two meagre back gardens. The pit looked like a grave for twelve people lying in four rows of three. Three wide hoops of corrugated iron laid so that one corrugation at each end overlapped the next in line then covered this pit. Two vertical plates of the same material were erected at each end with one having a rectangle the height of a man to act as a door. The Home Office provided these for a token price. The iron roof was then covered in soil and turf dug out of the pit and the finishing touches included stairs down to the pit bottom made of boxes and primitive wooden shelving to provide bunk beds for the children, the two of us and our two cousins, the Herschon girls.

A simple wooden chest stored a supply of tinned food and fruit juice provided by the Herschon deli and candles, oil lamps, tin plates and mugs supplied by my family. Rushing to the shelter to get ahead of the Nazi incendiary bombs and later on the V1 doodlebugs that devastated the east end in 1944, was a great adventure for Joe and me who felt superior to the terrified Herschon girls. We always claimed the top bunks and nonchalantly continued our homework whilst the little girls whimpered in fear. On the night in question a stick of bombs from a Luftwaffe Heinkel fell in Sydney Street, destroying several houses across the road and wiping out two families who we knew quite well. The nearby explosion made our ears pop, shook the bunk beds so that we crashed to the floor and put an end to our complacency. After the "all clear" siren announced that it was safe to leave our shelter, Joe and I rushed out ahead of the adults to view the damage. It was an awesome sight to see the fronts of the two houses in our terrace ripped open like a doll's house but our main concern was to add to our trophy collection of shrapnel from German bombs. I soon came upon a choice specimen the shape and size of an oak leaf and grabbed it ahead of Joe only to find that it was still white -hot from the burning phosphorous. My screams filled the air and my poor mother had to run to get some cold water from an abandoned stirrup pump left by the air raid warden who had died close by. The instant application of the cold water probably prevented a clawed hand from scarring that would have ended my surgical career even before I'd even contemplated that vocation. I was rushed to the London hospital to add to the burden of casualties that filled the corridors following the raid. My poor hand was dressed by a kind nurse and anointed with a cooling acroflavine emulsion.

I was left with a brand the shape of a dagger across the palm of my right hand but fortunately suffered no lasting deformity or dysfunction. I deserved a thrashing for my stupidity but I think my parents were so relieved that we all survived the raid the matter was dropped.

There was another curious sequel to this event that came back to haunt me, a few years later. About a week after that bombing raid, I found myself unable to sleep and sat at my bedroom window starring at the star lit sky and enjoying the play of the search lights over the docks where another raid must have been expected. Something caught my eye and I glanced across the road and saw that the house opposite had its front window lights on. The bedroom was illuminated like a stage set. A macabre sight met my eyes. A man and woman seemed to be screaming silently at each other. The man started hitting the woman with what looked like a cricket bat and blood seemed to be flying everywhere. The woman fell to the floor and as the man turned away he seemed to catch sight of me and shook his fists with an ugly grimace on his face, before turning off the lights. I screamed out loud and woke the whole household. As my mother was trying to comfort me I told her what I had seen and she told me not to be a silly-billy as I had just had a nightmare brought on by the near miss the previous week and in any case London was engaged in a "black out" to avoid becoming sitting ducks for a Luftwaffe night raid. To confirm this she took me to the window and showed me the two houses opposite us that had virtually been destroyed by the raid had no front windows and in fact, no fronts at all. This satisfied me that it I must have fallen asleep at the window and dreamed the episode. About eight years later, when I was studying medicine at University College, a murder took place in Sydney Street. The bombed out houses had been rebuilt in a hurry to house the work force trying to rebuild Britain's bankrupt economy and one across the road from our old house was the site for a grizzly murder and dismemberment. My interest was kindled as the police were looking for someone trained in anatomy with the skills needed to disarticulate the human body. My year had just completed our course in human anatomy that entailed the dismemberment of a cadaver. However my blood ran cold and the hairs on the nape of my neck stood on end, on learning that the assailant had given himself up because a young boy staring at him from the window of a house opposite had witnessed the murder. There was no such young boy and I took my experience as an adumbration of events still to happen the very reverse of a ghost story. This was the first of a number of life events that threatened my natural scepticism and disdain for irrational belief systems.

This then brings me to the matter of a mass murder: the Katyn massacre, an event in a remote forest near Smolensk in Russia many thousands of miles away, which indirectly launched my career as a heretic. In 1940 at Stalin's order supported by the politburo, 22,000 Polish officers and members of the Polish intelligentsia were murdered. All had been methodically shot in the back the head and truckloads of bodies were taken to mass graves in the Katyn forest. These mass graves were uncovered as the Nazi German forces swept eastward in 1943. There began a propaganda war of words between the two ideological and battle weary adversaries. As far as the British High Command was concerned, it suited them to believe the Russian story of another Nazi atrocity, as the Red Army had opened up the eastern front to take the pressure off the allies. By 1944 however it was impossible to ignore the fact that the Russians were guilty of the mass murder. This then started a war of words between my father and big Joe. Joe insisted that this was all a pack of lies promoted by Wall Street and the Capitalist running dogs of the City of London to discredit communism, whilst my father believed the evidence Roosevelt's emissary George Earle.

They nearly came to blows when my father tore up his membership party card and cancelled his subscription to the red bound volumes of the New Left Book Club. Sadly they never spoke again and big Joe died near the end of the war when a V2 rocket destroyed his home.

To understand the long-term impact this had on me, I have to go back to my bar mitzvah celebrated in June 1943. The service was in the New Road Synagogue, Whitechapel. The Thursday morning before the Sabbath of my induction as an adult into my community I donned my *tefilin,* philacteries, for the first time. I found this ancient ritual, steeped in mystic symbolism an awesome occasion. First I pulled the leather noose carrying the little black box hiding the words of God, up my left arm and twisted it inwards so the box pointed to my heart. I then wrapped the long leather tongue of the *teffilin shel yad,* seven times round my left forearm to represent the days of creation listed in Genesis. Next I bound the *teffilin shel rosh* so that the little black box containing the *Shema* was literally bound to my forehead. *"And they shall be for frontlets between thine eyes".* Finally I wrapped the remaining length on the leather thong from my left arm so that around the palm and middle two fingers of my hand so that the straps approximately spelt out the Three-Letter Name of Hashem, with a "shin," a "daled," and a "yud." *"And thou shalt bind them for a sign upon thy hand".* Then my great day came and wearing a black suit with long trousers acquired on the black market, the whole family walked proudly along the Whitechapel road to the New Road Synagogue. As I sat nervously waiting for my call to read my *maftir and haftorah* from the *bimah,* in front of packed synagogue with my mother, auntie Becky and the two Herschon girls, fondly looking down from the ladies' gallery, I reflected on the plaque that adorned the wall to the right of the great chair occupied by our pious and beloved rabbi, Louis Isaac Rabinowitz who was on leave as chaplain to the Jewish members of the armed forces fighting in Europe.

"On the occasion of the consecration of the above synagogue on May 24th 1892, Her Majesty's birthday; a letter was addressed to the Queen on behalf of the members, expressing their respectful felicitations and acknowledging their loyalty to Her Majesty under whose benign sovereignty they enjoyed the priceless blessings of civil and religious liberties."

I suddenly realised that I how privileged I was to have been born into a country that tolerated the Jews and was sending its young servicemen to defend our liberties with their lives.

I was shaken out of my reverie on hearing my Hebrew name, **Moishe Dovid ben Baruch,** called out by the rabbi, as I was summoned to read *maftir* the last section of the portion of the Torah for that week, *parashas Korach* from the book of Numbers. Reading from the Torah scroll is difficult as the ancient Hebrew is written without vowels with the words recognised by the position of the consonants. Still I mounted the steps to the reading desk full of self -confidence bred of six months tuition from our popular *chazzan* (cantor) Lewi; round of contour with a chubby red smiling face and a beautiful tenor voice trained within the chorus of the Berlin opera. His services were no longer required once the Nazis took over the opera house and he considered himself lucky to get out alive with his adorable little wife.

The story of Korach, Numbers 16 verses 1-30, describes a rebellion of the children of Israel against the leadership of Moses and Aaron. Korach ben Izhar, from the tribe of the Levites, egged on by his ambitious wife, a Lady Macbeth character, assembles 250 men to stand before Moses and Aaron and challenges their authority. *"Why do you exalt yourselves over the congregation of HASHEM?"* Then the mass *kvetching* began. Not enough milk and honey, too little wine, too much hot sun and too much sand between their toes. That though was the least of it. Korach then starts challenging Moses on the illogicality of the laws governing the wearing of fringes and the hanging of God's words from the doorposts, *the mezuzah,* when the whole house is full of sacred books. Korach then goes on to recount a parable of a poor widow who can barely feed herself yet has to leave the corners of her wheat field as a tithe to the priesthood and other hardships brought on by strict adherence to the letter of the Mosaic law. Ultimately she offers her cow as a sacrifice at the temple as an ironic token of her despair before she dies of starvation. This *chutzpah* makes Moses really cross so he calls on the Almighty to punish the 250 upstarts and their families. According to the Torah reading, Hashem causes a large cleft to appear in the earth and Korach and all his followers are swallowed up never to be heard of again.

At the time the content of the portion of the law held no meaning for me and once I'd completed the last verse of Korach, the Torah scrolls were processed around the synagogue and returned to the ark and laid in their velvet lined niches whilst chazzan Lewi belted out the beautiful refrain *aytz chaim he* …('tis a tree of life to those who carry the law). Everyone sat down and you could hear a pin drop as I sung my heart out with my *piece de resistance*, the *Haftorah* from the book of Samuel. There wasn't a dry eye in the house and as I completed the last blessing with a perfectly pitched top C, the house erupted with shouts of *mazeltov* and I was showered with sweets, bought with coupons saved up all year, from my family and friends in the ladies gallery.

As this was a period of wartime austerity, rationing and hardship, my reception in the synagogue hall afterwards, was a modest affair although uncle Hymie had managed to acquire a rare bottle of Johnny Walker for the *kiddush*. Inflamed with that he made a rousing speech to the bar mitzvah boy and once the Sabbath was over we had a party in his next-door house where he presented me with a fountain pen and we all enjoyed a sing-along with auntie Becky at her upright piano and uncle Hymie on his old violin. My most precious present though came from my father and that was a huge second hand copy of the complete works of Leonardo da Vinci, published by the Phaidon press. I treasure it to this day and from that moment on began my love affair with fine art.

Just over a year later when I was 14 and Joe 12, I was expelled from Hebrew school. We went to Hebrew classes on Wednesday evening and Sunday morning that were held in attic classrooms of the old synagogue. Joe was very advanced in his studies and had already completed his pre-bar mitzvah class and had joined me in the post bar mitzvah class. Joe was mature beyond his years, well read with a voracious appetite for books both fiction and non-fiction. He could also read and translate biblical Hebrew better than me. On this occasion we were studying the week's portion from the Torah that was again Korach on its annual cycle. In the absence of our Rabbi who was once again acting as chaplain on active service in the North African theatre of the war, his place was taken by Mr. Finkelstein, a rather sad and grey old man, with an unkempt beard and *payat* dangling in front of his ears. His English was hard to follow because of a thick accent and behind his back we called him a *yeke* (literally jacket in Yiddish) because of his tight buttoned up Germanic ways. After he explained the episode of the rebellion and provided the orthodox way of explaining the lessons to be learnt from the event, I intervened full of righteous indignation. I argued from a counter point of view. I agreed with Korach, I thought he was a democrat whilst Moses and Aaron were despots. I agreed with Korach that the performance of many rituals were nonsense, obeying the letter but not the spirit of the law. Finally I suggested that it was all a myth written by the victors and it was not HASHEM who buried the followers of Korach but the Levites loyal to Moses who blamed HASHEM after the event like the Russians and the Katyn massacre. I was fluent and passionate and felt pretty good about myself. Mr. Finkelstein went white and then blushed beetroot and screamed at me, "Vot you say iz blazfamy!" I quickly responded that by accusing me of blasphemy he was simply finding a way of shutting me up without addressing my arguments. With his last remaining morsel of dignity, Mr. Finkelstein begged me to leave the class and pray for God's forgiveness. The news travelled round our ghetto minded community like a bush fire. Mother was heartbroken and begged me to apologise yet father who whilst appearing to support his wife, took me aside into the parlour as if to beat me, before collapsing with laughter.

"Martin my boy, I'm proud of you," he bleated breathlessly. I then learnt that even as a lapsed communist, he was a bit of a heretic and half agreed with Karl Marx, about religion being the opiate of the masses. He only put on a show of religiosity for appearance sake and would slip away to have a flutter on the dogs on Saturday afternoon with his mates, in lieu of a sanctioned walk in Stepney gardens. Joe's response however was the reverse and lead to our first and only row. He had of course witnessed the whole drama unfold and was ashamed of me. First he said my ideas were not new but discussed in a commentary he had read in the *Talmud*. Secondly it was not clever to try and win an argument with poor old Mr. Finkelstein who was not very bright and so it was an unequal contest. Thirdly had I any idea what he had been through? Finally, just for the record, who knows where we would be if the Korach rebellion succeeded. We are where we are and who we are because of the outcome of every twist and turn in our people's history. I confess that I couldn't follow the last argument but needed to learn what Mr. Finkelstein had been through. It turned out that he was a refugee from Nazi Germany and had lost all his family and all his worldly possessions along the way.

At that I felt like a toad and looked for a stone to crawl under and even welcomed the thought of God's ire once again opening up a crack in the earth to swallow me up. From that time forth though I never changed my views concerning the literal translation of the scriptures and vowed to live by the spirit of the law rather than the letters and rituals of the law. I didn't put on *teffilin* again for about 30 years, although the taboo about eating pork and shell-fish remains with me to this day.

I took an early interest in the study of moral philosophy, reading Kant and Russell, but always turned to Joe as my young mentor in issues concerning the relationship between man and that amorphous concept he called God.

Chapter 9

The awakening of intelligence

I was a clever boy but a long way from becoming a wise man.

At the age of 11, I won a scholarship to Hackney Downs grammar school.

This school had a wonderful reputation and many of the London Jewish East End boys had gone on to brilliant careers from there, with alumni in both houses of parliament, doctors, writers and artists as well. In fact close on half of us were Jewish and our daily prayer assembly nearly matched the Christian service in "big school". It was quite an easy journey for me, five minutes on the rickety old over-ground train from Whitechapel to Hoxton followed by a brisk ten minutes walk. Later on I used to complete the journey by bike. During the war most of the young masters were on active service but the old guard and the newly recruited retirees served us well. They all wore black gowns to cover their shabby clothes and walked within a cloud of blackboard chalk. We were divided into houses for school sports and I found myself as scrum half in my house rugby football 15; I worked hard and played hard. My precocious interest in such writers as Kant, Russell and the Greek philosophers of the age of Pericles, did not go unnoticed and the head of classics assumed I was destined to study philosophy at one of our great Universities, but by then I had set my heart on being a doctor. Why this became my ambition, I'm not sure, but the sight of the runty rickety children from the slums of docklands and the never ending river of amputees and those hideously deformed by facial burns, victims of the blitz and the western front, walking down Whitechapel road to the London Hospital, inflamed my sense of indignation and I decided to work with the kind of philosophy that healed the sick rather than agonized over the meaning of life. From this you might judge I was a bit of a self-righteous prig and you wouldn't be far wrong. I studied the sciences; biology, chemistry and physics but also found time to study mathematics and continue my literary interests in the classics. I was gifted as an artist and spent evenings learning to draw at Toynbee Hall in Commercial Street until my parents learnt that they had introduced life classes. My mother forbade me to ogle the naked ladies. I assured her that the young ladies were nude not naked and I was drawing them not ogling them, but it made no difference. To tell the truth it was a relief to have this excuse as I started to experience difficulty balancing my drawing board on my pubescent lap.

Once in the sixth form I had to consider which medical school to apply for. My headmaster, "Crusty" Crippin MA, DD (Oxon), thought it would be an awfully good thing if I went up to his alma mater, Christ College, Oxford. For a grammar school boy, unlike the fortunate from Westminster or the City of London Schools, the entry process was hermetic and labyrinthine. For my parents the expense, even with a full scholarship, was unthinkable and a place at *Christ's* College was even too much for my father to contemplate.

The London Hospital School of Medicine was an obvious choice and was even within walking distance but the head of 6th Form science, who was aware of my eclectic interests and was a very cultivated old geezer who played the viola in the school orchestra, advised me to apply to University College Hospital School of Medicine. His reasons were cogent. The medical school was part of a great university complex, with all the schools and faculties of the sciences, arts and humanities within a square mile and the Slade School of art in the quadrangle opposite the entrance to University College Hospital. Furthermore as a Jew himself he was aware that there were no "quotas" and that many of the members of the senior common room were Jews as well. That settled it and within no time at all I was summoned for interview where I bamboozled the selection committee with my thoughts on Hippocratic moral philosophy and Kant's categorical imperatives in the practice of medicine. Fortunately I was able to buttress this unforgivable display of half digested and precocious ideas with rather good grades in my higher certificate of education. I was even awarded a state scholarship that paid all my fees and helped pay for my books and travel. Furthermore, with the war ending when I was only 15, and as I was to study medicine, my National Service was deferred until after qualification. I left school after my last exam in May 1948 and looked forward to a long summer break before starting at medical school in the new academic year beginning that September. As if to spoil my plans war broke out in the Middle East. The British Mandate over Palestine was due to expire on 15 May, but Jewish leadership led by Ben-Gurion declared independence on 14 May (because 15 May was a Shabbat). The State of Israel declared itself as an independent nation, and was quickly recognized by the United States, Iran, the Soviet Union, and many other countries. Within hours, Arab forces invaded Palestine. In an official cablegram from the Secretary-General of the League of Arab States to the UN Secretary-General on 15 May 1948, the Arab states publicly proclaimed their aim of creating a "United State of Palestine", in place of the Jewish and Arab, two-state, UN Plan. They claimed that partition was illegitimate, as it was opposed by Palestine's Arab majority, and maintained that the absence of legal authority made it necessary to intervene to protect Arab lives and property. The Israelis maintained that the plan was not illegitimate, since Jews were a majority in areas assigned to the Jewish state. Israel, the United States and the Soviet Union called the Arab states' entry into Israel illegal aggression. The Arab plans called for Syrian and Lebanese forces to invade from north while Jordanian and Iraqi forces were to invade from east. The Syrian, Lebanese, Jordanian and Iraqi forces to link up in Galilee and then turn towards Haifa. In the south, the Egyptians were to advance and take Tel Aviv. I thought that the odds were heavily stacked against Israel and that only my intervention, fantasist that I was, would save the nascent Jewish state.

In those days almost all Jews were fervent Zionists, whether left wing secular or right wing religious. My father an ex communist who still believed in the model cooperatives of the kibbutzim, was a fervent ideologue of the secular left and I shared his zeal. My zeal was fueled by my early memory of the battle of Cable Street and the revelations about the Nazi extermination camps. I was also indoctrinated by Habonim, a Jewish scouting organization that covertly spread the message of the Israeli Labour movement. I rose to become *Rosh Gedud,* or leader of the pack, and wore my blue and white kerchief, stripes and badges with pride and loved strutting up and down the line of timid, whey faced little East End Jew boys, barking out orders in *Ivrit* (modern Hebrew). Much later I learnt of the danger of placing too much influence on the authority displayed by wearing a uniform.

I informed my family that as I was the age when I should have been called for National Service, I would make the journey to Haifa and sign up for the Palmach, a crack infantry brigade of the Israeli Defense Force.

My father screamed, "no you won't", my mother fainted again and it was left to baby Joe, now 16 to talk some sense into me. First off he pointed out that by the time I had got there and learnt which end of a Lee Enfield rifle to point at the enemy, the war would be over for better or worse. Secondly, my school science and cod philosophy were of little value to the young and embattled state and finally in 6 years time, if there was still a State of Israel, they would need all the doctors they could get at which point my *aliyah* would be welcomed. So I heeded his wise advice, backed down without loss of face and listened to the BBC news at every opportunity and followed the progress of the war by pinning little *Magen Dovid* flags on the map of Palestine. The Israelis seemed to be doing pretty well without my intervention although eventually they lost one in ten of their young men of fighting age.

★★★

I entered UCH School of Medicine early in September 1948 and left a few days later to celebrate the Jewish New Year (Rosh Ha'shana) the Day of Atonement (Yom Kippur) and Tabernacles (Succot). I was worried that this might set me back in my studies and set a poor example of my diligence but I needn't have worried as about one in five of the new intake, several senior faculty members and the professor of anatomy, Professor Zuckercandle, missed the bulk of the first two weeks of term as well. In fact within the academic department of anatomy there was a full *minyan* (a quorum of men for daily prayer). As I entered the anatomy dissecting room for the first time at the completion of the high holy days, my eyes wept not for pity for the shriveled grey-green cadavers who demonstrated no remnant of their humanity, but from the fumes of formaldehyde that filled the air. It took longer to adjust to that than the macabre sight of twelve dissecting tables bearing corpses. The professor welcomed us and reminded us to treat these human remains with respect and to remember that like us they were once young and full of hope. The temptation for ribald humor as a natural protective reaction to the grizzly scene was dowsed although later in the year when one of our intake was expelled for stealing an arm and hiding it in the bed of his girl friend in the nurses home next door. The professor continued with his inaugural talk to tell us about the founder of University College London (UCL), Jeremy Bentham. Bentham was an eighteenth century philosopher and atheist, who founded the British school of Utilitarianism. According to his teachings society should be based on the actions that provided the greatest good for the greatest number. He also taught that the human body after death was a pointless husk and therefore for the greater good should be offered up to science and the teaching of anatomy. He practiced what he preached and to this day his reassembled body following its post-mortem dissection, embalmed for preservation, seated on his chair, dressed in his finest attire, is on display in a glass fronted mahogany upright casket under the cupola of the great hall on the east side of the quad leading off Gower Street. No wonder the professors, all doctors of divinity, at Kings College London not far away, described UCL as "the Godless College of Gower Street". Bentham would not have predicted that his foundation, which allowed the professoriate to be appointed outside the requirement for a Doctorate in Divinity, would one day allow the appointment of

Jewish professors and the unimpeded acceptance of Jewish students. Also thanks to Bentham's teachings there was a plentiful supply of cadavers from dying atheists wanting to "leave their bodies to science".

Four students were allocated to each corpse and the dissection of every four corpses was supervised by a "demonstrator" who was an aspiring surgeon studying for the first part of his FRCS. I was in awe of their detailed knowledge but when it came to my turn to study for my FRCS I learnt that the trick was to study the section covering the next day's dissection from Gray's anatomy. We were all required to purchase this huge tome, I loved the detailed illustrations and copied them as an aide memoire but found the text unreadable.

Lasting friendships were forged round the dissecting table. With me there was a real toff, Rupert Bonneville (Bunny for short). He was a good- looking public schoolboy who had attended Harrow, with a floppy blond mop of hair almost covering his right eye. He negated all the hostile stereotypic images of public school boys that I'd built up from my reading. In fact he was charming, warm and friendly. He sported a red MG convertible and introduced us to his gorgeous leggy posh girlfriend. When he casually mentioned over a disarticulated shoulder joint that he had actually experienced sexual intercourse, I nearly fainted. Much later I learnt that he was to inherit a baronetcy on the death of his father.

Next across the table from me from me was Patrick O'Connell. He had grown up in Cork and won a scholarship in the same way as me. Pat was the class joker who introduced me to the rituals of beer drinking and the singing of ribald songs. Until medical school I had drunk nothing other than sacramental wine and it took a while for my liver and frontal cortex to adjust. Physiology is a wonderful thing and within the year Pat and I could be heard singing "The bald Teddy Quill" in perfect harmony whilst propping up the bar at the Students Union. Providing the perfect tenor voice to complete our trio was the fourth at our table, my best friend, Dafyd Williams from the Rhonda Valley in South Wales. His father was a steel worker and like many of his ilk felt no particular pride in his working class status and joked that the best way of avoiding a crushed hand in a steel press was to have a wallet thick enough to throw between the plates and the best way to obtain that was to study hard to join one of the professions. Dafyd studied very hard at the local free school run by the Methodists and was their star pupil who had no difficulty in winning a scholarship like Pat and me. As with all the Welshmen I ever knew, he had learnt to sing like an angel in the chapel choir and could play rugby like a demon. When we were in our fourth year Dafyd played outside me as fly half whilst I played scrum half for the medical school first XV.

The four of us became a clique of inseparable friends, the English toff, the Irish Paddy, the Welsh Taffy and the East End Yid. The only upsetting thing for me was the sudden discovery of my short stature. Growing up in the east end and mixing entirely with Jewish kids I assumed I was of average height at 5 foot 7 inches. It was a shock when on mixing with my new friends to discover that I was in fact a shortie. Bunny was 6 foot one inch, Pat was a burly 5 foot 9 and Dafyd was an athletic 5 foot 11. This did nothing for my self-confidence in the company of young persons of the female persuasion.

My new glamorous life in the company of bright young men and women of many nationalities and faiths, great conversation over foaming pints in the students union, rugby football and Saturday night "hops", soon made me distance myself from my roots. I rarely attended synagogue any longer, using my studies as an excuse, whereas in truth I was enjoying rugby practice.

I even started "dating" gentile girls, although that Americanism had not yet been invented. Things came to a head one Sunday lunchtime, just before Chanukah 1949. The previous Saturday morning I had played in a trial for the second fifteen, studied in the university library all afternoon, had a drink in the union bar with my mates at 6.00 where I picked up a charming young blond student of philosophy from LSE, engaged her by showing off my knowledge of Plato and took her to see "On the Town" with Gene Kelly at the Odeon Leicester Square.

The next day we sat down to our traditional Sunday brunch of schmaltz herrings, cream cheese, pickled cucumbers and bagels. As we started eating Joe started humming the overture to the "Barber of Seville". I looked up with a start only to see him grinning mischievously at me. My bowels turned to water as I realized what he was hinting. "Shut up" I hissed, but he hummed all the louder. I attempted to hit him but he dodged my blow and his grin grew wider.

To understand my fury and embarrassment you needed to know the unsung lyric. I think the parody of words to Rossini's music were written by Berle Goodman a popular Yiddish comedian on the Catskill circuit and all I can remember is the chorus that went something like this:

" *You are lobos, you are a lobos,*
You take shikshers to pictures
On shabbos."

Lobos means naughty boy, *shiksher* is a derogatory name for a gentile girl and *shabbos* is the Sabbath. Clearly someone had spotted me in the cinema queue and the Jewish grapevine had been twitched and to mix metaphors the scandal had spread like wildfire. It didn't take long for my father to understand what the fracas was all about. He went white with fury and I was truly shocked by his anger. The gist of it was that I so much thought of marrying a gentile girl, he would rent his waistcoat, cover himself with ashes and recite *Kaddish* as if I was dead. I couldn't believe what I was witnessing; I hadn't even kissed the girl goodnight. My mother once again collapsed, pale and sweaty with a slow pulse. I now knew that this was a vaso-vagal attack or a faint in laymen's terms. Once the drama died down a few weeks later, I got her to see one of my tutors about her labile cardiovascular system. He diagnosed stenosis of the stays. In other words to try and keep her boyish figure for Selfridges fashion department she had resorted to a whalebone corset that impeded her venous return.

Returning to the melodrama that was unfolding, I have to confess that I was taken completely off guard. I loved my parents and never experienced a cross word or a cuff across the head. That made it all the more shocking for me. I suppose someone could write a treatise about my father's over-reaction but somehow in my bones I had an understanding bred of a group subconscious. You might be surprised that instead of storming out indignantly, I took it meekly, apologized and vowed never to let it happen again. I did my best to keep my vow, I attended charity events in fashionable northwest London in the hope of meeting nice Jewish girls from good homes, but most of them were vacant *becks* only interested in fashion and meeting rich prospects. In those days doctors were not considered a good catch as the early epoch of the NHS offered poor rewards. Gradually and discretely I drifted back to my wayward campus life. Wayward? Hardly. Life on campus was no Sodom and Gomorra. For a start there was a leavening of mature ex servicemen, veterans of the war in Europe and the North Africa campaign. They simply wanted to complete their degree and restart their fractured lives. Furthermore there was no substance abuse except for cigarettes. This was the late 1940s and early 1950s and the association between tobacco and lung cancer had to wait for the RCP report of 1961. Fortunately I never acquired the taste. There was little promiscuity, the pill had yet to be invented and following the licentiousness of the war years, when young men and women had little time or thought for postponing gratification a new-prudishness became part of the zeitgeist. As it might be described in today's argot, "we talked the talk but rarely walked the walk". For female companionship, having given up on the North West London set, I joined the university Jewish society and at their functions and inter functions with provincial universities became acquainted with any number of intense, scholarly, black haired girls with thick ankles. I enjoyed their conversation but again if I may tune in to the modern vernacular, I never really fancied any of them.

Chapter 10

Bonneville Abbey

Just before Christmas 1951 Bunny invited me together with Dafyd and Pat to spend the vacation at his parent's place in Dorset. He had also invited Veronica his latest girl friend from Sloane square and a few of her chums. "Have you got enough room for all of us?" I naively asked. "Not to worry old chap, mater is going to open up the west wing for the hols." he replied. Whilst digesting the significance of a house with wings I respond, "Very decent of you to ask I'd love to but I better check if my folks have anything planned first", thinking that a snow ball in hell would have a better chance.

Before doing so, on a whim, I checked out his family name in the university's copy of Burkes peerage. There I learnt that the Dorset branch of the Bonneville family enjoyed an ancestral home called Bonneville Abbey that boasted 24 guest rooms and a deer park. Armed with this knowledge I approached my father explaining that I had been invited to a country house estate for the winter vac with my student friends to study together for the first part of finals. Surprisingly, my parents who were a little bit snobbish rather liked the idea of me mixing with the gentry as long as I promised not to eat *traif.*

I couldn't wait to tell Bunny that I was free to accept his kind invitation. Pat was free to join us as well but sadly Dafyd was summoned home for Christmas in the Rhonda valley. On a cold late December morning the three of us huddled in the tiny MG roadster with the top down to allow me to squeeze into the gap behind the leather seats. Our suitcases were tied to the pannier frame covering the spare tire. On the road to Dorset that ran across Salisbury plain I nearly froze to death and was revived with hot rum toddy at a roadside tavern. On arrival at Bonneville Abbey I could barely stand up straight. I made for a sorry sight as I walked bow legged and cyanosed towards a welcoming party, of Bunny's parents and younger sister, Annabel. Annabel put her hands to her mouth to stop giggling, whilst my facial color turned from blue to beetroot red on shaking her hand. In that instant I was smitten. She was the most desirable yet the most unattainable specimen of young womanhood I'd ever encountered. In 1945 Evelyn Waugh published "Brideshead Revisited" and I had only got round to reading it the previous year. At once I saw myself cast into the role of Charles Ryder, but he at least was a tall English middle class boy of the Anglican confession, whilst I was a short Jewish boy of humble origins. That aside, unlike the Marchmain family in Brideshead, Rupert's parents couldn't have been more charming and welcoming. I was overcome with awe by both sister and house. Where shall I start, to describe Annabel or her ancestral home? On the principle of age before beauty I will start with Bonneville Abbey.

Why was it called an abbey? According to Bunny, after the dissolution of the monasteries by king Henry the VIIIth, the monarch rewarded some of his favorites with gifts of fine Roman Catholic real-estate, that were then refashioned into stately homes. Little was left of the Tudor structures apart for some outhouses and most of what I first saw was a perfectly symmetrical Palladian mansion. Facing me at the end of a long gravel lane running through the deer park was a three-story block centered on a clock tower rising two stories higher. The octagonal superstructure bearing the clock face was crowned with a cupola bearing a gilt weathervane. At ground level an imposing flight of steps flanked by heraldic beasts, lead up to an arched doorway with intricately carved panels evoking folded linen. Above the arch was a coat of arms almost weathered away by the 250 years of conflict between English climate and Cotswold sandstone. On either side were symmetrical lines of windows obeying the architectural code of the golden ratio. At each flank the east and west wings completed an open rectangle so that the living rooms at the rear enjoyed unimpeded views of the rolling hills and woodland of Dorset. The interior although grand in scale, including a staircase with one flight going up and another coming down, was sadly shabby. Unlike the homes of my well-to-do Jewish friends in North West London, the furniture looked frankly hand-me-down. We were bustled into a drawing room with a roaring wood fire in the grate and offered hot punch that restored my will to live when I started making further observations about these alien living quarters. Drinks were served from a silver tureen with a ladle like chicken soup on Friday night in Jewish homes, except for the silver. Other drinks were displayed in crystal decanters with silver engraved name plates, whisky, brandy, port, sitting on an antique console table at the back of an old leather settee with it's stuffing peeping out of cracks. My wealthy Jewish friends had art deco cocktail cabinets to hold their bottles although hardly any of them drank in a meaningful way. Early 19th century occasional tables scattered round the room, carried back copies of Country Life, Punch and The Tatler, whilst stacked on floor by the battered club armchairs on either side the fire were recent copies of the Daily Telegraph. My mother kept our little house obsessionally tidy and we only displayed the current issues of the Manchester Guardian and the Jewish Chronicle. Next to capture my attention were the paintings, covering so much of the wall that the faded and peeling wallpaper was barely visible. Most of these were old family portraits of little distinction but I could have sworn that the marble floored entrance hall sported two Gainsborough ladies on either side of the grand staircase. I felt intimidated by this evidence of a long historical lineage back to the 16th century even though in theory I could trace my roots back for 3,500 years. Furthermore even amongst the richest of my Jewish friends' homes it was rare to see an original oil painting when the top spot above the fireplace was usually filled with a Baroque framed mirror. In fairness I should point out that most of the world's great collections of the French impressionists, post impressionists and German expressionism, were built up by successful and cultured Jewish families prior to them being looted by the Nazis.

Hot punch in hand I made a tour of the room to study the paintings in greater detail when Annabel materialized at my side and pointed out Joshua Reynolds's portrait of her great, great, great grandfather. I've forgot the precise number of greats in my confusion and ecstasy but refocused with genuine enthusiasm when she drew my attention to a small dark Sickert.

I subsequently learnt that Annabel had recently enrolled at the Courtauld in Bloomsbury, to study the history of art. All of these early impressions called to mind the words of Noel Coward's song "The Stately Homes of England" where he satirized the nouvelle poverty of the upper classes following the end of the Second World War. I remembered the words perfectly having sung them in the end of term medical school variety show. The second verse went something like this:

> *But still we won't be beaten we'll scrimp and scrape and save*
> *The playing fields of Eton have made us frightfully brave*
> *And though if the Van Dykes have to go*
> *And we pawn the Bechstein grand*
> *We'll stand by the stately homes of England.*

That made me feel a little bit smug and superior as I imagined how poor old Joseph Jacobs, the unreformed communist, might have felt under similar circumstances: but not for long as I remembered the third verse:

> *Our homes command extensive views and with assistance from the Jews*
> *We have been able to dispose of*
> *Rows and rows of*
> *Gainsboroughs and Lawrences,* and so on

I hope that gives you a mental image of the abbey and my emotional response that swung between awe and jealousy intermixed with shame of my lowly ranking in the English class system.

Now to describe Annabel: Perhaps the easiest start would be to claim that I thought that I recognized her. It took me 24hours before I remembered where I had met her before; twice in the

Uffizi gallery in Florence and once in London's National Gallery in Trafalgar Square. She was of course Simonetta Vespucci, Botticelli's model for the birth of Venus, Primavera and Mars and Venus. I'd seen the last in real life and the other two in illustrations in my book on the history of art. Long flowing blond hair, exquisite complexion, smiling full lips, blue inviting eyes, slim of waist, boyish hips, long slim legs with tapering ankles and a good two inches taller than me!

Once warm and refreshed we were shown to our rooms.

Mine was on the third floor of the central block close to the clock tower. It had a polished wooden floor with a thread bare mat, the walls were covered with faded blue damask with little pink flowers, the window looked out over the front drive and the furniture was old mahogany. The bed was high with a thin mattress covered with a patchwork quilt and the nightstand carried an antique stoneware washbasin and pitcher with an elaborate black and red floral pattern the like of which I'd never seen outside an illustration for Nicholas Nickleby. This Victorian look was completed with the candle in its carrying holder furnished with a box of matches. Later I was to learn that this was intended to light my way to the nearest lavatory, or *loo* in Bonneville-speak, three floors below. Opposite the bed was a little fire grate with coke and kindling and alongside that was a Shaker style rocking chair carrying a rag doll with a malicious grin. The oddest and somewhat disturbing feature of the room was a long curtain covering a second door to the room on the windowless wall running parallel to my bed. Curious, I tried the handle that turned with difficulty and the door creaked open on rusty hinges suggesting that I was the first to try it in decades. Beyond the door was a dark dusty narrow corridor, barely accommodating my width. There was no source of light and no hint of where the corridor was leading. As there was only half an hour before we were to meet for pre dinner drinks in the library I decide to explore it later. I washed my hands a face in cold water from the pitcher, changed into a fresh shirt, put on my best suit, in fact my only suit and composed myself for the ordeal to follow. I discovered the library by following the sound of laughter, linking up with Pat O'Connell on the way before shyly entering the room where I was to meet the remainder of the family and guests.

The first new face was Bunny's young brother, Anthony, a delightful self-confident young man of 18. He was the only one present dressed informally, sporting a vee-necked cable stitched cricket sweater with his public school colors framing the neckline. Although the cricket season was five months off, he carried it off nonchalantly so that I felt overdressed. Next I was introduced to Annabel's "intended", Nigel, a young history don down from King's College Cambridge. I was determined to hate him from the start but was totally disarmed when he demonstrated a genuine interest in my studies and was quick to agree with me on my ideas concerning Kant and the ethics of medical practice. I congratulated him on his engagement to Rupert's sister and without any hint of false modesty claimed that he was jolly lucky to capture the heart of last year's debutante of the year as featured in a full page photograph in the Tatler. Next I met up with two friends of Annabel, one from her old school at Rodean and the other a fellow student at the Courtauld. The latter was nicknamed Minxy and I never caught her real first name. She was a petite vivacious brunette with dark, long lashed luminous eyes, who hung on my every word.

Finally there was an elderly, war widowed, slightly batty, aunt Jocasta who had lost her husband at the battle of the Somme. She asked me if I was one of the Devonshire Tanners and tempted as I was I denied membership of that clan and by way of a half truth explained that I was one of the Bromley by Bow brigade. That seemed to satisfy her. The party was completed as Lord and Lady Bonneville entered to join us in a glass or two of the finest amontillado. Bunny's mum looked wonderful in a slinky number cut on the bias (this esoteric knowledge learnt from my mother's conversations after work) looked as you might imagine Annabel would look like 25 years later. Lord Bonneville looked dapper in blazer, grey flannels and regimental tie. He walked with a slight limp because of shrapnel in his left thigh a permanent record of his gallantry commanding a battalion of infantry at the fateful battle for the bridge at Arnhem. He spent the last year of the war as a prisoner of war. It was rumored that the King recognized his gallantry but it was considered bad form to enquire further.

Bunny's family had a profound effect on me that influenced in a small way the trajectory of my life. As a collective they had this in common; they were comfortable in their skin, they were comfortable with each other and comfortable in time and place. It was a kind of insouciance yet without the implied sense of irresponsibility. No doubt there were skeletons in their cupboard and I think I was to meet one later that week, but if anything that enhanced their status in my eyes. You might think that all this was the consequence of their privilege and old wealth however threadbare. Yet I saw something of the same when I met Dafyd's family for the first time in south Wales at the time I was acting as best man at his wedding and if anything they were one step lower in the pecking order than my family. It was the sense of belonging to place, history and caste. Amongst such people, however kind, I always felt an outcast: the legendary wandering Jew. Amongst my own people there might have been a greater sense of security but in all our relationships there was subtext of angst, *weltschmerz*, *sturm und drang*. I wanted to be like the Bonneville but was prescient enough to know that I could never enter their charmed circle by marriage, extreme wealth or even success in my profession. The only answer would be to find a land of my own, with a people who shared my history: In other words the land of Israel. In that moment I hardened in my resolve to make *aliyah* once I qualified.

As we were about to sit down I noticed the 12th member of our party who arrived late. He was another very self-possessed young man, a friend of Anthony at Harrow. He quickly went round introducing himself as Bhawani Singh but please call me Bubbles. He spoke English with a cut glass accent and like many upper class Indian gentlemen tended to overdo the compound adjective scattering his conversation with, "awfully good", "frightfully decent" or "jolly good show". I loved the way he called me "old chap" as he held forth on his passion for astronomy. Much, much later I was to discover that he was the oldest son of the Maharaja of

Jaipur whose distant ancestor had built the greatest pre-Galileo observatory in the eastern world. He earned his nickname from the fountains of champagne his father ordered up to celebrate the first son born to this princely family in many generations.

At table I found myself flanked by aunt Jocasta on my left and Minxy on my right. As the old aunt was deaf in her right ear, I spent most of the evening talking and flirting with the young lady on my right. The next cultural clash that I experienced concerned the drinking and appreciation of fine wines. Jews aren't really interested in alcohol in spite of the fact that wine together with it's blessing are central components in our rituals. We are commanded to drink one glass every Friday night, four glasses on the eve of Passover and enough to make one *shikur* (drunk) on the rejoicing of the Torah at the end of the feast of tabernacles and Purim. Perhaps the simple explanation is that kosher wine is virtually undrinkable and we learn avoidance behavior at an early age. Jews don't have cellars except to hide in during the blitz or as a place to store junk.

Yet here the Bonneville cellar was spoken of reverentially as a place where wine had been laid down for generations. Each wine was discussed with unaffected connoisseurship. The fish course was accompanied by an amusing young sauvignon blanc from the Loire valley, the shoulder of lamb heralded in a rather good claret, a pre war chateau Lafite actually, decanted earlier in the evening and the desert wine (I never knew such things existed) was a legendary chateau D'Yquem 1937. It was all absolutely gorgeous and more than made up for the somewhat stodgy and overcooked food. I felt happy and eloquent. I regaled Minxy with my wisdom and started competing with Pat, who was the life and soul of the party, in getting the group to laugh. I had no chance. Pat's accent alone gave him a head start. At 9.00 pm the ladies retired to the drawing room; a discrete touch on my elbow by Bubbles cautioned me to stay put and the men gathered around the master of the house for a goblet of Napoleon brandy and a smoke. I lay back in my chair, stretched out my legs and enjoyed the masculine camaraderie of the moment. At some unspecified time later I was helped to my room, nicely warm and cozy, with the fire having been lit by unseen hands and fell fast asleep with my clothes on.

I awoke a couple of hours later shivering with cold as the fire in my grate had died down. I had a cracking headache and a taste in my mouth like the floor of a parrot's cage. I took a mouthful of water and froze as I sensed I was not alone. The chill in the air was preternatural and I could hear a rhythmic creaking sound coming from the direction of the rocking chair. I quickly turned on the bedside light fully expecting to see that the rag doll in the chair had come alive to haunt me. My relief on seeing that all was as it should be was short lived when I realized that the dreadful creaking noise was coming from behind the curtained door. At that point I remembered the last verse of " The stately homes of England".

The baby in the guest wing who crouches by the grate
Was walled up in the west wing in 1428
If anyone spots the Queen of Scots in a hand embroidered shroud
We're proud of the stately homes of England.

In a panic I wedged the back of the rocking chair under the door knob of the secret door, changed into my pajamas and leaving the bedside light on returned to a fitful sleep. I was woken by the morning sun at about 10.00am feeling dreadful, dressed and staggered down stairs to find the whole assembly wolfing down a healthy breakfast served from a grand credenza by the breakfast room window. I was informed that the bacon and sausages were awfully good but I must try the kedgeree. I had no idea what that was and when Bubbles explained that it was a traditional Anglo/Indian dish made from smoked haddock, boiled rice, eggs and curry powder, I had to excuse myself to rush to the loo and vomit up the previous night's treacle pudding. I returned to the breakfast pale and sweaty and poured myself a cup of coffee. Bunny looked up and exclaimed, "I say old chap you look like you've just seen a ghost".

I responded by saying that I hadn't seen one but might have heard one and went on to make a self-deprecating joke about the events of the night before.

"Do you by any chance have any family ghosts at Bonneville abbey" I enquired. Anthony then broke in with a mischievous grin to remind Bunny of the sightings of Sophie. Sophie apparently was a 17year old girl who burnt to death in the fire that destroyed most of the original Tudor building in the early 19th century and once breakfast was over we were taken to see a charming painting of her by Romney that I hadn't yet spotted in the entrance hall. She was posed sitting on a garden swing with a flowering vine entwined around the ropes. She was dressed in a white chiffon high wasted gown of the Regency style. Her dark brown hair was worn in ringlets and she looked a lot like Minxy. "Come on gang" shouted Anthony, "let's go and find Martin's ghost". Flashlight in hand he lead a group of us up the stairs to my room and we all burst in with squeals of laughter. Pulling the heavy curtain aside young Anthony opened the secret door and gallantly lead us in to the dark dusty narrow corridor.

He pulled up sharp and Minxy second in line bumped into him and let out a scream. In front of us, dimly lit by the torchlight was a cobweb encrusted garden swing hanging from a beam on the ceiling with a cluster of dried flowers wrapped around one of the rope supports, half hidden in the spider's web. A nudge from Anthony's knee produce a squeak from the rusting hooks and eyes from which the ropes hung accompanied by another scream from Minxy. We stood in silent awe with our hair standing up on the nape of our necks. Bunny, who had brought the rear whispered, " Listen carefully". We listened and at once I heard the rhythmic creak that had ruined my night's sleep and it was coming from further down the corridor. "I know what that is, follow me" commanded Bunny. Emboldened, we trooped along behind him and at the end of the corridor found ourselves behind the clock with a clear view of the pendulum swinging in it's casing extending through a slot cut into the floor boards. We had found my ghost at the end of the service passage to the great clock of Bonneville Abbey. We fell into each other's arms helpless with laughter and I knew of the instant that this episode would pass into the folklore of the abbey and that made me feel rather good.

As that day was Christmas eve, the family busied themselves in preparation for their big day whilst I spent most of the day sleeping off my hangover and my haunting and reading old copies of Tatler and Punch in front of the library fire. The plan was to have a late supper and then walk down to the village church for midnight mass. As we assembled at 9.00 pm Bunny, with the best will in the world informed his parents that I should be excused as I was of the Jewish faith. There was a brief silence when I imagined the temperature fall by one degree. This was interrupted when Lord Bonneville bluffly remarked, "By Jove old boy you speak awfully good English for an Israelite!" His wife then added her well meaning reassurance by squeezing my arm and saying, "Darling, I would never have guessed, you don't look the least bit Jewish "

Both these well meant comments hinted to the fact that I was probably the first Jew they had met and the fact that lady Bonneville thought she had paid me a compliment, implied that her knowledge of Jewish physiognomy derived from back copies of *der Sturmer.* Fortunately the ice was broken when Pat chipped in with a screamingly funny joke about an Irishman, a Scotsman, an Englishman and a Jew linked to affectionate stereotypes. I've forgotten the punch line but the story was well judged and well timed. We fell about with laughter partly at Pat's humorous delivery and partly in relief. I mouthed a silent, "thank you" to him across the room. Once the laughter had subsided I spoke up to declare that I would love to join them because as an amateur social anthropologist I felt it my duty to study the religious rites of the natives. This again provoked peels of laughter as we shrugged on our overcoats and scarves and traipsed through a light fall of snow to the pretty little village church about half a mile away. I have to admit that I loved the service in the old stone church with its square tower and Norman arched entrance. It was conducted at the high church end of the Anglican Communion and I joined in with gusto the singing of the hymns although I drew the line at kneeling to pray and sat that out unostentatiously. I could virtually hear the crunch of dry bones as two sets of my grandparents turned in their grave.

The snow had settled whilst we had been at prayer and it seemed quite natural for Minxy to take my arm as we walked back to the warmth of the Abbey.

I went to bed sober that night and enjoyed a hearty breakfast the next morning, avoiding the *chazerei* (food of porcine origin) and excused myself as the rest of the party returned to church. Whilst they were away I busied myself revising from my textbooks and notes in preparation for part one of finals in the new term.

Christmas day dinner was a large and elaborate affair finished in time to catch our new Queen, Elizabeth II, deliver her first Christmas day address to her subjects. After that some fell asleep in their chairs as a physiological response to the heavy meal, plum pudding and vintage port, whilst I returned to my studies in part to complete my reading of Bailey and Love's short practice of surgery, a door step of a book that weighed about 3lbs, and part to salve my conscience that I hadn't really lied to my parents. Again I went to bed sober and slept heavily. The next day, Boxing Day, was fun. The morning was crisp and cold, with a clear eggshell blue sky and two inches of snow crunching underfoot. We enjoyed a long walk through the village and round the deer park with Minxy holding my elbow to help herself over the icy stretches.

The afternoon was spent playing traditional party games and we all had to do our party pieces. Annabel turned out to be a gifted pianist whilst her fiancée Nigel, sang along with a beautiful baritone voice. Bubbles did magic tricks and Anthony had us in fits with his hopeless attempt as a ventriloquist using the rag doll from my room as a dummy. My rendition of "The Stately Homes of England", sung in a tenor voice mimicking Noel Coward, was picked up on the piano by Annabel, went down very well and received tremendous applause. At 6.00pm the serious drinking began. A toast to the Queen following by a toast to our hosts involved getting through a couple of bottles of Dom Perignon and then we took it in turns to fill our glasses from a well stocked bar. Come 9.00pm someone suggested rolling up the carpets in the great entrance hall so that we could jitterbug to gramophone recordings of American big band music and foxtrot to the husky voice of Bing Crosby. I ended the evening dancing a slow waltz cheek to cheek with Minxy and gave her a lingering kiss as we all turned in at midnight.

I think I lost my virginity that night. Now you might expect that such a seminal event, if you'll excuse the expression, as losing one's virginity, would not be open to doubt, so let me explain.

I reached my little room with its two doors feeling a little tipsy and full of good will, washed my face in cold water, changed into my night attire and fell fast asleep. At some time in the small hours I dreamt that a lithe young female body had slipped under the sheets alongside me. Once I was aroused this figment of my dream slipped across my abdomen so as to straddle me. At this point I may or may not have woken up. In the dark I couldn't quite make out her face but her figure and the way she carried her head convinced me that this was none other than Minxy. She put a finger to her lips to shush me and placed her left hand across my eyes to blind me, as she brought our coupling to the inevitable happy ending. As she climbed off my bed and donned her long white nightdress she blew me a kiss and slipped quietly out through the door. I could have sworn it was the *wrong* door.

Full of languor I rapidly fell into a deep sleep and awoke refreshed unsure to this day whether or not I had dreamed the whole episode.

At breakfast I gave Minxy a meaningful look and a sly smile, which was met with a blank expression and raised eyebrows. The party then broke up to go our separate ways and Minxy and I exchanged telephone numbers.

Once again I squeezed into the jump seat of Bunny's MG steeling myself for a freezing drive back to London. As we turned around under the clock tower I glanced up at the window of my guest room and although it was almost certainly a trick of the light magnified by my feverish imagination, I could have sworn there was a smiling pretty dark haired girl waving me goodbye.

Chapter 11

Mother's curse

I returned home from my few days at Bonneville Abbey, late in the evening, frozen to my marrow but walking on air. My elation evaporated like the morning mist as I sensed fear and tension in the household. In spite of my mother's warm embrace and my father's amiable questioning I could tell something was amiss. Worst of all was Joe's inability to look me in the face. Egocentric as always I assumed that word of my "debauchery" at the Abbey must have reached home ahead me, but that anxiety was rapidly replaced by a much more sinister explanation. After dinner my father quietly took me aside and whispered that my mother had discovered a lump in her breast whilst I was away and assuming far too much knowledge on my behalf asked for guidance. Having just completed my three-month attachment to my junior surgical firm, I knew enough to be sufficiently fearful. Although no one spoke openly about the big "C", which carried the same sort of stigma as "a spot on the lung" amongst recent immigrants, a lump in the breast was known to be a harbinger of death. If nothing else I remembered my surgical chief's aphorism that; "a lump in the breast is cancer until proved otherwise". I couldn't face my mother who I heard whimpering in the corner but I promised my father that the next morning I would seek out my surgical tutor, Mr McKenzie, and ask his opinion. "Mac" as we called him, received me kindly and offered to see my mother at once but was honest enough to suggest that if it were his mother he would seek out the opinion of Sir Stanford Cade at the Westminster Hospital, London's top cancer specialist. He then went on to advise that we try to get her seen urgently by our GP who would then write the necessary letter for an appointment with the great man who still generously gave of his time to those patients who couldn't afford to see him in Harley Street. I skipped classes for the next two days and along with my father, dragged mother protesting to the nearest NHS GP surgery. We waited anxiously in a crowded and dirty reception room after giving our particulars to the haughty receptionist who never even made eye contact. The room was full of tobacco smoke and copies of the satirical magazine Punch yellowed by age and nicotine. I watched with alarm as patients were rushed in and out of one or the other consulting rooms at five-minute intervals. When it was mother's turn I thought I might win a few more minutes by announcing that I was a medical student at UCH. The elderly, grey and exhausted GP was unimpressed and didn't even examine my mother but at least agreed to write a letter to Sir Stanford Cade at the Westminster, muttering "you'll be lucky if you see him in person but he holds surgical outpatients on Tuesdays and Thursdays". The letter was scrawled in an instant and a harassed nurse ushered us out. When we got home I opened the letter that in barely legible handwriting read as follows:

Mrs Tanner age 42
C/O LILB
OPA ASAP

I translated that as "Complains of lump in left breast out patient appointment as soon as possible".

The following day being a Thursday, we made our way to the Westminster hospital clutching the letter where the three of us joined the long queue in surgical outpatients. The hospital was situated not far from the Palace of Westminster with views of the river Thames from its upper windows, very close to the Tate Gallery and the Royal Army Medical Corp hospital on Millbank. In those days there was no such thing as an appointment, we registered our arrival with an orderly sitting at a high mahogany desk, who noted mother's name, date of birth and time of our arrival, in a leather bound ledger rather like Ebeneezer Scrooge in "A Christmas

Carol". We then joined the huge crowd at the end of the line on five rows of old wooden benches arranged in parallel, inching along to the side as patient after patient was summoned by a starched nurse to any one of six doors opening off the high vaulted waiting room. During this long wait I tried to read a textbook but kept conjuring up frightening images of Stanford Cade as some kind of booming and pompous Sir Ralph Bloomfield – Bonnington out of the pages of "Doctor's dilemma". After two hours we reached the front of the line and were ushered into a small consulting room with another high desk for the medical notes and a worn out leather examination couch with a unstable free standing screen wobbling on its casters as a token gesture to the patient's modesty. The surgeon who welcomed us was not as I imagined at all being far too young and far too polite to be anyone of importance. When I enquired if by chance he was Sir Stanford, he had the grace to blush and modestly exclaim, "goodness me no, I'm only his senior house officer. My role is to sort the wheat from the chaff in order to save the old man's time. Don't worry if I think your mother's lump is of any importance, I'll call him in": all this without engaging my mother once. He took a brief but efficient medical history then his nurse ushered mother behind the screen whilst I turned my back in order to avoid seeing my mother's nakedness through the wide gaps between in the curtaining. During that pause I mentioned that I was a fourth year student at UCH and he ribbed me about the way we had faired against the Westminster in the semi-finals of the London teaching hospitals rugby cup. We were both smiling as he went behind the screen but neither of us was smiling when about five minutes later he returned. Ignoring my father he looked at me and mumbled, "I'm sorry old chap but I think this maybe wheat rather than chaff". "What do you mean?" I exclaimed. "I think this one's for the old man", he replied and without another word slipped through a communicating door to the next consulting room. My father and I exchanged glances of horror and the next few minutes seemed interminable. At last the communicating door opened and in strode the great man. He was nothing like I expected! He was shorter than me, sported a bristly toothbrush moustache, spoke with a thick Eastern European accent and if it wasn't for his name I could have sworn he was Jewish. A little bit of research in the following week confirmed my suspicions that he was indeed Jewish and had changed his name from Kadinsky to Cade on taking British citizenship after the war.

The great man looked very dapper in his wing collar and morning coat with striped trousers and behaved impeccably like an old fashioned gentleman.

He went behind the screens to re-examine mother and came out looking grave drying his hands on a towel offered by the nurse, and waited for my mother to dress and join us before speaking. Taking my mother's hand he gently patted it and told her not to worry and that she would be safe under his personal care. Surprisingly the rest of the dialogue was conducted with my father. I assumed this was some kind of medical etiquette I would learn later in my career. When my father mentioned that I was a medical student, his eyes lit up and the remainder of the conversation was directed at me. As I recall it went something like this. "Your dear mother has a lump in her left breast that feels neoplastic. I wish to admit her urgently for excision biopsy, frozen section, proceeding to a modified Halsted mastectomy if the biopsy is positive after which I would recommend a course of radiotherapy. As it happens I'm lecturing to my students the day after tomorrow at 11.00am on the topic of the diagnosis and management of breast neoplasia, you are welcome to attend". Turning to his assistant who was looking on with admiration written all over his face, he said, "Turner, please put Mrs. Tanner first on my operating list next week and make sure she gets a nice bed with a view over the river". Turning to my mother with a smile and a courtly bow, he left the room leaving Turner to pick up the pieces.

Once the formalities were completed our sad little family group made its way to my father's taxi cab parked at the back of the Tate Gallery. My mother was white, speechless and sobbing quietly to herself. Even though she could not have understood any of the technical language, the word mastectomy was sufficient to confirm her worst fears. My father did his best to encourage her by saying what a *mensch* (gentleman) Sir Stanford was whilst I lamely added that at least she was in the best of hands. We decided not to alarm my brother Joe at this stage as he was studying for his first year examinations at Jew's College. He had also done well at school but instead of medicine he had opted for a career in the Rabbinate and an MA from London University was the first step along that path.

Over the next 24 hours, with my parent's encouragement, I read everything I could lay my hands on about breast cancer in the university library. Here I experienced my first "library gremlin". For those unused to spending hours in dusty aisles amongst the stacks in old libraries, a "library Gremlin" is the chance discovery of a critically important publication when searching for something entirely different. I was looking for a description of Cade's modification of the classical Halsted radical mastectomy in old bound copies of the British Medical Journal for 1947 when I pulled out the volume for 1937 by mistake that fell open on a paper authored by Sir Geoffrey Keynes of St Bartholomew's hospital. The title of the paper made me catch my breath and I carried the heavy tome to a quiet reading corral in the corner.

The paper was entitled, "Conservative treatment of cancer of the breast" and described a series of 250 patients just having the tumour removed followed by the insertion of radium needles into the remainder of the breast and the armpit that harboured the lymph glands. He went on to describe the results and claimed a near 90% 5 year survival, comparable to the best results reported for radical mastectomy up until that day. Bursting with excitement at my discovery I arrived the next morning at the main lecture theatre at the Westminster hospital school of medicine. The hall was packed and buzzing with excitement in anticipation of the lecture from the most famous cancer surgeon in London. I squeezed myself in unobtrusively in the back row.

Sir Stanford breezed in with a "good morning gentlemen" and without pause launched into his lecture without the benefit of notes or lantern slides.

He was a very gifted lecturer, charismatic, articulate and witty, illustrating anatomical points with rapid sketches on the blackboard.

He repeated Mac's aphorism that all lumps in a woman's breast were cancer until proved otherwise. He went further to describe how the diagnosis and surgery was a matter of urgency as the cancer was capable of leaking cells into the lymphatic drainage of the breast at any time and furthermore warned against too many doctors or students examining the woman as they might inadvertently squeeze cancer cells into the system. He was also reluctant to wait a week for the results of a biopsy as this might disturb the tumour and spread more cells as a result of the delay. For this reason he and his pathologist had perfected the technique of "frozen section" whereby the tumour was removed and deep frozen in liquid nitrogen before going to the pathology department where the solid lump would be finely sliced, stained and looked at down a microscope: The whole process taking only 30 minutes. He made us laugh by describing how he filled the time drinking a coffee and completing the Times crossword leaving his anaesthetist and house officer in charge.

If the result came back benign he would send for the next case but if it came back as a cancer he would rescrub whilst the nurses changed the drapes in case any cancer cells had contaminated the field. He then described his surgical technique in detail having explained the principles of "en bloc" resection. Apparently the cancer cells were capable of spreading centrifugally in all directions along the lymphatic channels like the legs of a crab as described by Hippocrates, hence the name of the disease. Hippocrates counselled nihilism but since the invention of antisepsis by Lord Lister in the late 19thC and the introduction of anaesthesia by Robert Liston into this country around the same time, pioneering surgeons like William Halsted in Baltimore and Samson Handley in London, had perfected the technique of removing the whole breast together with all the lymphatic drainage in one block without cutting across lymphatic channels thus avoiding spillage of cancer cells into the wound. This way also allowed the removal of all the lymph glands in the axilla that were the last bastion of defence against the onward spread of the columns of cancer cells into the body as a whole. He cautioned against excessive radical zeal as we might end up in doubt as to which bit of the woman to return to her bed (hah, hah) and described how he now avoided dissecting the glands from beneath the sternum and above the clavicle, leaving that to the tender mercy of a friendly radiotherapist. He concluded his lecture by saying that in order to avoid any compromise in removing the skin over the tumour, whose subdermal lymphatics might already be carrying the contagion, the very first step in the operation was to take a skin graft from the thigh in anticipation of the closure at the end. Finally he ended on a histrionic note by quoting from Shakespeare's Hamlet, "Diseases desperate grown, by desperate appliances are relieved, or not at all." He then nodded in response to the thunderous applause before asking for questions.

I was the first to raise my hand and about 100 heads turned to look at me as Sir Stanford acknowledged me and said, "You have a question Tanner?"

I flushed with pride that he had remembered my name. I even surprised myself by my own self-possession and gift of speech as I replied, "Please sir I have just come across a paper by Sir Geoffrey Keynes published in the BMJ in 1937 claiming that you might achieve the same results as a radical mastectomy by just removing the tumour and then treating the whole breast and its lymphatic drainage with radium. What do you think of that approach sir?" There was a stunned silence as the great man's face changed colour from pink to white and then to red. Obviously having difficulty in controlling his anger he turned to rest of the class and explained: "Young Tanner is a guest from University College London School of medicine, so he can be excused for asking such a question". This was met with roars of laughter and it was now my turn to perform the chameleon act with the colour of my face. With exaggerated enunciation, as if talking to a native of the colonies he explained as follows. "If you were attending to what I was saying you might recall my warning that cutting round the tumour releases cancer cells into the wound cavity and even if radium was a effective as the knife, by the time it got to work those few thousand cells would have multiplied to several million with open access to the body via the cut ends of the lymphatic tubules draining the cavity. Next question please". At that I crept out with the wind knocked out of my sails and my tail between my legs a very uncomfortable state of being.

I still wasn't satisfied, as what Sir Stanford had described was indeed a plausible hypothesis yet Keynes' results did not support the theory. I decided to keep my mouth shut and as my admiration for figures in authority in the medical world was as yet undimmed I accepted that the flaw in the thinking was my own.

The following week my mother was admitted to the Westminster two days before her operation. The clerk checking her in after we'd waited two hours was surly and offhand but the porter showing us to her bed was friendly and talkative. The ward sister was puffed up like a pigeon and quite intimidating but the staff nurse, who was sweet and rather pretty, went out her way to explain what we might expect. The women's surgical ward was of the Nightingale configuration, with 14 beds down each side, with the night nurses desk in the centre next to the now defunct coke fire encased in green tiles. As promised her bed had a nice view over the Thames with a bronze plaque above acknowledging a donation from its Victorian past and a brass hook carrying the name of Sir Stanford Cade on a shiny card. After she was settled in a young probationer nurse measured her pulse, blood pressure and temperature and dutifully filled these numbers unto a graph hung from the foot of the bed. My mother looked like a prisoner condemned to the gallows and my father could think of nothing to say as he sat wringing his hands. After another hour, Turner the senior house officer we had met in out patients bustled in with a clip board, settled on a chair at the right hand side of the bed and embarked on taking a full case history. I was impressed by his skill and his genuine attempt at empathy with my mother's condition and state of mind. When he was about to examine her behind the drawn screens, he summoned a probationer to chaperone him and politely asked if we wouldn't mind stepping outside. After he had completed his examination he summoned us back and settled down to give a detailed explanation of what was involved in the operation and recovery and for once someone was talking to her directly rather than via her male relatives. Having got her to sign consent for a biopsy of the tumour and to proceed to a mastectomy if it turned out to be anything "nasty", no one had yet used the word "cancer" in her hearing yet, he left with a friendly smile and a pat on the hand with the words, "see you in theatre". We were turfed out of the ward at the end of visiting time leaving my mother looking distraught and alone. On the way down the stairs my father burst into tears and I held him close as we found our way to the cab. The following morning at 8.00am long before visiting time, Sir Stanford made his ward round and marked her up with a large indelible ink X over her tumour whilst teaching his eight students how to carry out a breast examination using my mother as a passive teaching aid. I learnt later from her that he was very polite and asked her permission first but of course she was determined to be a "good patient" and wouldn't have dreamed to say no.

Later on in the day she was sent for chest and skeletal X-rays, to "exclude distant metastases" and blood tests to exclude anaemia. We were with her that evening when a very jolly consultant anaesthetist came to call in order to check her fitness for a general anaesthetic. He promised her a large dose of pre-medication to calm her down and then made us all laugh that he would split it 50:50 with her, as he would also need calming down before gassing for Sir Stanford who was known to be something of a martinet in theatre. Some years later I discovered by chance that this poor man was indeed sharing the pre-medications with the patients and became a hopeless addict to narcotic drugs.

As visiting hour came to its close that evening my mother seemed calm and almost fatalistic, quietly singing to us Doris Day's latest hit, "Que sera, sera, whatever will be will be." At which point my father once again collapsed in tears hugging her tight until gently prised away by the ward sister showing her human side for once. She escorted us out of the ward offering as much reassurance as was possible whilst offering a clean starched white handkerchief to dab dry my father's eyes. Her parting words were, "at least she's first on the list at 8.30am and I'll call you as soon as she's back on the ward."

By this time of course we could no longer protect Joe from the truth and he was far from pleased to have been kept in the dark all this time. None of us slept much that night and found each other drinking tea in the parlour at about 6.30am. We listened to the BBC news, popped out to buy a newspaper and waited. Once the hands on the clock had passed nine thirty I knew that the frozen section had shown a cancer. At 11.30am sister called from the ward and said she was back and fast asleep but we could pop in and visit at two in the afternoon when she would try and get Turner to talk to us.

On our arrival the duty staff nurse smiled sweetly at us and showed us to the bed nearest the daytime nursing station positioned so that the staff might keep a close. There could be no doubting the gravity of her surgery now. She was propped up in bed on a pile of pillows looking almost as pale as the sheets. There was a blood transfusion entering her left arm and two drainage tubes carrying blood from somewhere hidden under the sheets, to bottles hanging down from the bed frame. Another bottle appeared to be draining urine, hung third in line. An oxygen mask hid most of her face much she still managed a bleak wintery smile whilst limply raising her right hand off the bedcover. I deposited a brown paper bag of grapes on the bedside table and took the bunch of flowers we had bought to the staff nurse who handed them to the ward orderly to place in a vase to accompany the grapes. I took the opportunity to enquire after my mother as a dutiful son but I must shamefully confess that I also liked the chance of chatting to this pretty young woman in her fetching uniform with her skirt a little higher than would have been accepted at University College Hospital. Whilst I was away from the bedside, Joe took out his pocket prayer book and quietly recited the prayer for the sick. My father sat holding mother's right hand incapable of words whilst I returned with the news that everyone was happy with mother's progress. We were shooed away when visiting time ended at 7.00pm.

On the third evening after her operation we caught her weeping with pain, the chest pain from the mastectomy was bad enough but the pain from the donor site for the skin graft on her left thigh was intolerable. The donor site of partial thickness skin was equivalent to a third degree burn. I was furious to find her in pain and checked the file hanging from the foot of her bed. She had indeed been prescribed morphine sulphate 20 milligrams four hourly p.r.n. (The latter rubric standing for the Latin version of "on demand".) I saw that the doses had been ticked off every four to six hours for the first 18 hours but nothing since then. I summoned over the pretty young staff nurse to enquire about this and she had the grace to blush and bustled out to call the sister Bentley. Sister strutted towards us with the bib of her white apron pushed out like the prow of a sailing boat with spinnakers hoisted and demanded to know by what right had I the temerity to look at my mother's charts. By this time I was furious and demanded to know by what right she had allowed my mother to suffer pain. As the storm started to gather and the spinnaker filled with wind my mother and father begged me not to make trouble. The storm then broke as sister exclaimed; "Your mother has a very low pain threshold and as a medical student you should know that too much morphine would suppress her respirations and increase her chance of post operative pneumonia!" I couldn't help myself and retorted, "As a ward sister you should know that her chest pains are stopping her taking deep breaths and that could contribute to post operative pneumonia." Sister Bentley took a deep breath and instead of exploding, changed tack and sailed back to her office from where raised voices could be heard. Mr. Turner the SHO emerged looking flustered and did a wonderful job of calming everyone down, reaching a face saving compromise by prescribing pethidine instead of morphine and by the end of visiting time my mother appeared more comfortable. As we left she begged me, "Martin, please for my sake don't make any more trouble".

My mother was in hospital for ten days, her discharge delayed because of a slight wound infection but I never met sister Bentley again.

I took three lessons away from that event that stood me well in my professional development. First in reverse order, I would always be a "trouble maker" in spite of my mother's plea that carried an echo from the ghetto, next I learnt there was more to medicine than science and facts and that I should remember young Doctor

Turner's skills at defusing an ugly situation between patient and staff and finally I would never forget that pain control mattered.

From that day on I could never accept that pain was the inevitable consequence of surgery. I was unable to do anything about this as a student or junior doctor but things changed the moment I took charge of my own ward.

I carried out an audit on the adequacy of postoperative analgesia in my hospital and discovered to my horror that only about a third had adequate pain relief prescribed and only about half of these had it dispensed. Sister Bentley's ill-informed fear of suppressing respiration had been taught to several generations of student nurses since my mother's experience. In fact the opposite was true; too little too late increased the risk of that complication.

From then on, no patient of mine was allowed to experience postoperative pain and my junior staff and nursing staff feared for their lives if I encountered anyone in severe discomfort amongst my patients on my post op ward rounds.

Five days after her discharge from hospital my mother saw Dr. Turner for her first post-operative appointment. He was kind and gentle when removing the stitches from her chest wall but she wept uncontrollably on seeing how mutilated she was. In place of her breast there was her chest wall with all the ribs showing, pressing hard against a saucer shaped skin graft. With the chest wall muscles removed to aid the surgical dissection of her armpit, her left arm appeared attached to her body like a rag doll. Once she had settled down Sir Stanford was called in. He nodded approval at his own handiwork and passed on the good news that the pathology report was favourable. "It has all been taken away my dear. The margins of the breast specimen are clear of disease and only two out of the twenty-four nodes I removed were infected."

Then turning to me he said, "Well Tanner I hope this proves my point. Only radical surgery can achieve this degree of clearance of the disease." "Yes sir" I hastened to agree, partly as a show of respect to a Knight of the realm and partly to encourage my mother. Turning to his SHO Sir Stanford said, "Turner arrange for Mrs Tanner to attend for radiotherapy in two weeks time and get sister to fit her with a bean bag." Nodding politely to mother, Sir Stanford swept out of the room and I never saw him again.

The six weeks of radiotherapy, five times a week were gruelling and exhausting for both my mother and my father. My father drove to the hospital each day, waited two hours for her two-minute exposures to the X rays emitted from the Cobalt 80 unit and then drove her home. To make up for all those lost fares he would work late into the night ferrying the beer-swilling yokels from pub to pub. I would often come home from medical school in the evening seeing mother alone and staring vacantly into an unlit fireplace. She complained of lack of energy, chronic fatigue and most nights I could hear her leaving her bedroom at about 4.00am, padding downstairs, unable to sleep anymore. Her doctors said this was the side effect of the radiotherapy but much later, during my postgraduate studies I recognised, too late, that these were the symptoms of an acute depressive illness. She ceased to care for her appearance and seldom bothered to place the beanbag in her bra, a rather poor substitute for her breast. To add to her sense of mourning she also suffered from phantom breast syndrome where she still sensed the presence of a breast but on raising her hand to her chest all she experienced was loss. The war-wounded amputees at the time, who still attended surgical out patients, also complained of phantom limbs. Once the radiotherapy was finished my father bought her our first TV. It was a 12-inch screen, Bakelite model that produced grainy black and white images that were exquisitely sensitive to the position of a contraption looking like a metal coat hanger, which acted as an aerial.

This novelty cheered her up for a while but I still often caught her out when I came down for breakfast in the morning, finding her asleep in front of the TV test card. She wasn't eating and begun to lose weight then to add to her burden her left arm began to swell because of the accumulation of lymph fluid. Inevitably a letter arrived from Selfridges to explain that they could no longer keep her job open but by then her morale was so low there was no chance of her going back to work. This again threw an enormous financial burden on my father who started working double shifts to make up for the loss of my mother's income. I saw his health deteriorating and the sparkle in his eyes dying like the last ember in the grate of our parlour coal fire. I felt guilty about not contributing to the family income so covertly worked as a hospital porter from 6.00am until lectures began at 9.00am. I handed over my modest pay packet each Friday, lying that I was being paid as an assistant in the anatomy dissecting room. One good thing came out of this as I experienced first hand the patronisation and sheer bloody rudeness the hospital porters had to suffer at the hands of the senior medical and nursing staff. I also witnessed first hand how the work of a great teaching hospital would grind to a halt if it weren't for the poorly rewarded and unappreciated workers at the bottom of the food chain. These poor chaps teased me a lot but treated me well, almost as if they saw me as the young subaltern in a company of privates and NCOs. The senior porter, a fat John Bull like character, had in fact been a sergeant major in the Middlesex Light Infantry and enjoyed regaling me with stories of his daring do.

My mother made a slow recovery but it was a long time before she could face strangers and she derived some comfort from regular attendance at the synagogue. Having lost her elegant figure and along with that her interest in fashion she retrieved some self esteem by joining the ladies' guild and devoting herself to charitable works.

Many evenings I couldn't face returning to my joyless home and spent long hours after ward rounds, lectures and tutorials, and finished bashing away at the textbooks and journals in the university library. I read everything that was to be learnt on breast cancer and noted in passing that all the chapters on the subject in all the surgical textbooks, might as well have been written by the same man. I made a habit of reading the weekly copies of the Lancet and British Medical Journal (BMJ) that demonstrated how out of date on most subjects the textbooks were, although there was little dissent about the management of breast cancer.

All agreed that a family history increased the risk of disease but none commented on a family like ours where every other female member seemed to be struck down. From my meagre knowledge of Mendleian inheritance, it looked to me as if my family carried a dominant gene that no one yet had suggested and I thought that one day I would make that my mission in life.

All that aside, I had developed a visceral hatred about what my mother had suffered; it might or might not have saved her life but it had effectively destroyed it and my father's along the way. I still don't know what triggered the resolve but one dark and freezing night making my way back from Gower Street to Whitechapel, I determined to seek out Sir Geoffrey Keynes.

Tracking down Sir Geoffrey Keynes was not too difficult a task for someone with sufficient *chutzpah* like me. I started off by phoning St Bartholomew's hospital and asked the switchboard operator to be put me through to his secretary. I was firmly but politely informed that Sir Geoffrey had retired from his post as senior surgeon in 1951. When I then asked for his current whereabouts I was told that she wasn't allowed to disclose such details. Not perturbed I visited the library and took down the latest editions of "Who's Who" and "Burke's Peerage". I then began to learn more about this extraordinary man. He was the younger brother of Maynard Keynes the famous economist, climbed with Mallory on Mount Everest and served as a surgeon in the First World War, pausing only to marry Charles Darwin's granddaughter in 1917. He pioneered blood transfusion and set up the first such service in London. In 1939 he joined the RAF as a senior surgeon and returned to civilian life with the rank of Air Vice-Marshal in 1945. In his spare time he worked on a three-volume bibliography of the writings of William Blake the eccentric English 18th century mystic, poet and artist. "Burke's Peerage" was kind enough to provide an address, Lammas House, Brinkley, Cambridgeshire.

I wrote an effusive and very polite letter to this awesome polymath, explaining my interest in his pioneering work on breast cancer and enquiring if he might spare me a half hour or so to discuss this further. To my astonishment and delight, I received a reply ten days later inviting me to tea the following weekend. The following Sunday morning I made the difficult journey to Brinkley. I took the Cambridge train from Liverpool Street Station and then changed onto the branch line to Newmarket. I hung around the station exit for about 30 minutes until I found a taxi to take me to Brinkley. Lammas House was a beautiful rambling early 19th C building with an inviting porch carrying a blue Wedgewood design around its jutting square cornice. Sir Geoffrey and his charming wife Margaret greeted me warmly at the door. It was soon apparent that they were looking forward to this encounter as much as I was. I was shown into a warm and cosy sitting room that in many ways reminded me of my first impressions of Bonneville Abbey with one major difference. In place of the rather gloomy family portraits and the equally crepuscular Sickerts, this room was hung with alarming, flame coloured and frankly insane originals of the work of William Blake. Prior to this I knew virtually nothing of Blake's work but it was love at first sight. Sir Geoffrey who was obviously delighted to register my enthusiasm, sent Margaret off to prepare tea and then conducted me round his collection of watercolours, woodcuts and framed hand written poems of this mystic genius whose greatest claim to fame to my knowledge, were the words to the hymn "Jerusalem" that I had belted out in the village church in Bonneville. Tea arrived and the two of us settled round the fire and scrutinised each other. He clearly could not place me in the taxonomy of the medical profession, whereas I had difficulty imaging this cultivated and kindly gentleman as a senior surgeon at Barts and something of a legend.

Sir Geoffrey was very tall and as a result walked with a slight stoop, either in deference to my short stature or out of habit in coping with the low lintels above the doors of a Georgian house. He was grey haired, with a grey bristling moustache much favoured by ex RAF officers. This moustache balanced his lantern jaw and his pale blue eyes sparkling with intelligent enquiry. Once we settled down with freshly brewed tea, hot scones and butter and some slices of fruit cake, I got round to explaining about my mother's experience and my interest in his publication in the BMJ in 1937. At that point his face flushed as an outward physiological response to the temporary loss of his constitutional *sang froid*, as he launched into his story. He explained to me the logical inconsistencies of the radical operation in a way that I had yet to organize in my own mind, that until this were hovering just out of reach. The greatest inconsistency of them all was that the disease kept stubbornly recurring almost anywhere in the body however perfectly and completely it had been removed. The words "perfectly" and "completely" were uttered with heavy irony. The logical conclusion therefore was that by the time of diagnosis cancer cells had already disseminated round the body via the blood stream planting the seeds that in due course grew into lethal metastases. If true the therapeutic consequence was obvious, nothing could ultimately improve survival so that the best we could offer was to remove the malignant lump and control any residual local disease with radium so if nothing else this offered a better quality of survival than that offered by radical surgery.

He then went on to explain the details of the technique he had pioneered and how he patiently collected a large series of cases treated in this manner and compared them favourably with a similar series treated by radical surgery by Sampson Handley at the Middlesex hospital. He then described how he was invited to talk on the subject by the American Association of Surgeons in New York just before the war. He was so shocked by the hostile reception he received there, that he truncated his lecture tour and returned home. He continued his work in this field in spite of the criticisms from his own colleagues and showed a laudable concern for his students when he warned them off repeating his heresies in front of their examiners in surgical finals. The war intervened and in anticipation of enemy bombing raids he buried his set of radium needles in a lead line box effectively burying the technique for another 40 years.

He clearly enjoyed recounting his story to an attentive audience and the time flew by until Margaret interrupted us saying, "Darling I think we should let Mr Tanner go if I'm to drive him to Newmarket in time for the 17.50 to Cambridge." We exchanged goodbyes and his last words to me were, "Thank you for your interest Tanner but be very careful how you make use of this knowledge". In spite of my protestations Lady Keynes insisted on driving me to the station and along the way told me how much her husband must have enjoyed my visit as almost no one had shown any interest in his work on breast cancer since he was demobbed from the RAF in 1945.

Sir Geoffrey was to die at the grand old age of 95 ironically in the same year that Dr. Bernard Fisher, who was the first to disinter the concept of breast conserving surgery, described his trial of breast conservation, at the world cancer congress in New Delhi in 1982

On the train home I felt elated as pieces in the puzzle fell into place but clearly any useful action on my part would have to await my qualification as a doctor and to pass that hurdle meant listening to the warning not to pass on the Keynesian heresy to my examiners.

The rest of my time as an undergraduate passed quickly in a fog of relentless study that left little time for anything else and I felt well prepared when I entered into the examination halls in Queens Square in May 1954. I found the written papers, clinical exams and the *viva voces* less of a hurdle than I expected and was not really surprised when I was called back for the distinction vivas.

After a four-week marathon I learnt that I had passed with distinction winning the prizes for surgery and morbid anatomy. When I brought this news home my mother beamed with pride, the first natural smile I'd witnessed from her since her operation. My father then addressed me formally saying "Would Dr. Tanner join me in a small glass of Johnny Walker" and then promptly burst into tears. The following day we celebrated the news that Joe had qualified with first class honours in his MA, his course being two years shorter than mine. A few weeks later, on a beautiful day in June, my parents accompanied their two sons to Senate House for the degree ceremony and a photograph of Joe and me in our mortarboards and gowns, flanked by our parents, the four of us smiling broadly, remains with me to this day.

Chapter 12

Walking the wards

One hot and steamy day in August 1954 I stood at the portals of the redbrick cruciform building at the north end of Gower Street. I faced across the road and admired the great cupola of University College London, brilliant white against the cloudless cobalt coloured sky. A few visiting foreign students sat listlessly under the classical Greek colonnade below the dome but the quadrangle was virtually empty as most of our students were enjoying the long vacation. I turned my back on the scene and accepted, with a combination of resignation and excitement, that I wouldn't see the light of day for the next 6 months, other than through the soot grimed windows of University College Hospital. This was my first day as a hospital doctor- the bottom feeder in the food chain–the house officer. I strolled along the tiled corridor to the main staircase, self-conscious of my status that was made apparent by the traditional uniform of the short white jacket with a stethoscope bulging ostentatiously from my right pocket. The Gothic interior echoed to my footsteps whilst the plaques upon the walls venerated charitable donations that built the hospital in the Victorian era or great figures in the history of medicine. I was made to feel humble by all this historical precedent whilst taking the first step in my long career with the ultimate ambition of becoming a consultant surgeon. My first step was indeed on to the granite staircase that encircled the octagonal atrium that was the centre-point of the giant cruciform building. I ran up the stairs two steps at a time until I reached the fourth floor when I turned right through the double mahogany doors leading to the North East Wing of my hospital.

Because I done so well in my final examinations and won the surgical prize, I was effectively given my own choice of where to start my career. As I had got on so well with Mr McKenzie, I elected to join his team. The wards were of the Florence Nightingale design, with 12 bays running down each side and the nurse's station in the middle. In those days the wards were heated with gas fires. The holy of holies, at the far end of NE4, was the office of the sister-in-charge, Miss Mary O'Connell. The entrance lobby on each level held an operating theatre and a side room for the junior medical staff to carry out laboratory tests. The organisation of the team or "firm" as we described it, was hierarchical in the extreme. At the top of the pyramid were the two consultant surgeons, Mr McKenzie and Mr Duffield–Morgan known as "Dudders". Below them in the pecking order were the senior surgical registrar and then the junior registrar. Immediately above me in the hierarchy was the senior house officer. One level below me was a group of third year medical students numbering 7 or 8; that accounted for the medical side of the team. In parallel with the medics there was another hierarchy of the nursing and ancillary staff. At the top, ranking equivalent to a senior NCO or sergeant major was the ward sister. Below her they were the staff nurses, the probationers and the nursing assistants, whilst at the bottom of the heap were the ward orderlies, cleaners and porters. Although we were all terrified of Sister O'Connell I soon learned that her constant presence and her strict discipline, guaranteed the efficient running of the firm and whenever I was in trouble with some minor surgical procedures on the ward, she was always at hand to guide me. Because I treated her with respect and never patronised her, she seemed to like me and would occasionally invite me in for morning coffee and short- bread biscuits.

It's worth describing my two consultant bosses as their very different set of personality traits and skills had a very important impact on the direction of my career and my attitude to the care of patients.

Mac was a gentle Scotsman who trained in Edinburgh. He was soft-spoken and had a beautiful bedside manner, making him very popular with all the patients. He was a handsome man with a ruddy complexion and was never happier than when on holiday fishing for salmon in the Highlands of Scotland. He once even remembered to send the firm a present of fresh salmon that he had caught on his holiday but because of the unreliability of the Great Northern and Eastern Railway, the great fish was past its prime when it finally arrived at the doctor's mess. His attitude to surgery reflected his personality. He was very gentle in handling human tissue though I quickly formed the impression that if anything his surgical approach was too timid. His operations went on too long and the anaesthetists used to joke that they timed him by the calendar not the clock. He often appeared to find excuses to avoid surgery rather than proceed to what might have been a challenging or difficult case. Much to my surprise I discovered that he had adopted the approach suggested by Sir Geoffrey Keynes in treating breast cancer, with a wide excision of the tumour following which he referred the patient to the radiotherapist. How much of this was due to conviction, compassion and concern for the woman or how much of this was his was a reflection of his wish to avoid difficult radical surgery, I could never decide. The most interesting thing about the man was that he was in the battalion of the Royal Army Medical Corps that was present at the liberation of the Belsen concentration camp in 1945. We learnt of this when the firm was invited to drinks party at his house shortly before Christmas. He seemed to have had a lot to drink before we arrived and pulled out an envelope full of photographs he had taken at the time of the liberation of the death camp. We were all shocked and I was overcome with waves of nausea. There were pictures of the pits filled with naked bodies piled one on top of each other looking like rag dolls. There were pyramids of rotting corpses and pictures of horse-drawn carts with corpses spilling over their sides. The survivors in their striped uniforms, were skeletal thin and staring at the camera with sunken vacant eyes. It later became clear to me, that following this experience, that Mr McKenzie became philo-Semitic; he hinted at this in private conversations with me across the operating table and chance remarks when conversation in the Doctors Mess turned to troubles in the Middle East.

Mr Duffield–Morgan was almost the opposite in character and

behaviour to Mac. He was very large in all directions, probably 6 foot 4 and 18 stone, he had a loud booming voice and was "awfully well" married to a woman from the minor aristocracy; and he never let us forget that. As a student he used to play at number 8 in the pack for the Harlequins and of course captained the Medical School 1st team. His self-confidence knew no bounds and a friend of mine described him as having an ego the size of the Isle of Wight. Of course all of this made him a brilliant teacher at the bedside and most of the students loved him as much as they feared him. I reserved my judgement. Unlike Mac, Dudders was a gifted surgeon who loved nothing better than a complex surgical challenge and his catchphrase was, "When in doubt cut it out". In spite of having large hands he operated rapidly and because he seemed to enjoy this the challenge of difficult surgery favoured the radical approach whenever there was any doubt. An anaesthetist colleague told me that Mr Duffield-Morgan recognised three indications for surgery. One; he'd seen it described and fancied having a go. Two; he'd done it before and rather enjoyed it. Finally the third indication was when the patient actually needed it! Unsurprisingly he favoured the Halsted radical mastectomy in the treatment of breast cancer and he even went one step further adopting the "super radical" approach he had learnt whilst spending a year as a senior resident in the Massachusetts General Hospital in Boston. This extension to the radical operation went beyond removing the whole breast all the muscles on the chest wall and all the lymph node contents of the armpit; it also involved manufacturing a "trapdoor" in the sternum in order to dig out any lymph glands lurking behind between the ribs. He preached that without adequate access surgeons would inevitably compromise on the extent of their operations. His two favourite incisions when operating in the upper abdomen were the "Michigan Sabre slash" and the "Rio Branco flap". The former was an oblique incision that crossed the rib cage on the left and extended diagonally southwest across the abdomen ending up in the right flank. There was no question that this provided ease of access for a radical gastrectomy, but the final wound was very ugly. The second was even worse and quite difficult to describe. The incision started at the point where the ribs on the left and right hand side met at the apex of the abdomen and went halfway down to the umbilicus, the wound was then extended in a south-west direction and finally turned to West again to end in the right flank; this allowed lifting up a large flap of the abdominal wall which was held in place by a long-suffering medical student clutching a huge sharp edged retractor. The slightest tremor would earn a rap on the knuckles by the great surgeon wielding a heavy pair of forceps. Indeed this wound provided wonderful access to the right upper quadrant of the abdomen making hepato-biliary surgery extremely easy. However I was deeply worried about this practice and not simply for the fact that I would be left with the almost impossible task of closing the wound neatly but because of certain ethical concerns. Mr Duffield–Morgan, was famous for his surgery and research of the bile duct system. For some reason or other that I never fully understood, he was of the opinion that the hydrostatic pressures within the bile duct system were critical to the formation of gallstones. At each opportunity he would like to insert a cannula into the common bile duct in order to measure pressures before and after injecting drug that was known to relax smooth muscle. This is all was quite unnecessary to the benefit of the individual patient on the table and this research was conducted without the patient's consent. All of this was happening under my gaze with memories of the Nuremburg trials fresh in my mind. To my eternal shame I never had the courage to challenge him on this subject although we effectively came to blows at the end of my attachment.

That aside I loved my time as a house surgeon at UCH. Although officially we had no time off and worked on average 100 hours a week, our social life was wonderful. All the young doctors, mostly men, lived on site in the Doctors Mess. Our little rooms were cleaned, our beds made and our meals provided by a platoon of mostly country wenches from Ireland, who treated us like demi-gods. We had our own bar with fresh barrels of draft beer on tap and the mess officer kept account books for us. The Nurses Home was not far away and as most of the girls had set their hats at capturing a young doctor in order to migrate up a social class with every likelihood of decent housekeeping money in the future, a supply of nubile young women was also on tap. I was able to resist all this temptation not so much because of my moral probity but simply because by the end of the working day, round about 9 or 10 in the evening I was so (.... how shall I put it?) "Knackered", to use the common argot picked up from my grandchildren, sounds about right.

This all changed though during the Christmas/New Year lull in elective surgery that coincided with the doctors and nurses Christmas show.

We had managed to procure the score and libretto of the Broadway show "Guys and Dolls" that was currently showing at the Coliseum and had just opened as the film with Marlon Brando as Sky Masterson and Jean Simmons as Sister Sarah Brown of the Salvation Army. I was chosen to play Sky Masterson and Staff Nurse Katherine Sullivan was given the role of Sister Sarah Brown. I couldn't help noticing staff nurse Sullivan as she conducted the chief's ward rounds when sister was on a break. She had huge brown eyes and long lashes, exquisite slim ankles and looked gorgeous in her blue uniform and frothy white cap. From what I could see she only had eyes for our swashbuckling senior registrar and appeared as much out of reach as my screen goddess Marylyn Monroe.

All that changed at our dress rehearsal on the 23rd December. Nurse Sullivan in her cute Salvation Army uniform looked adorable and I guess I looked rather handsome in my zoot suit and snappy trilby. Whatever the case there seemed to be electricity sparking between us and when we eventually kissed in the last act, her moist lips parted, her little tongue darted swiftly in and out of my mouth and my bowels turned to water. Details of this romance will not be revealed to save the embarrassment, nay mirth of my grandchildren, but the love affair lasted until I was cruelly dragged away by the RAMC.

At the other extreme I experienced visceral hate for the first time a little under a week following the great success of "Guys and Dolls"; on Boxing Day.

The occasion was the New Year's Day firm party hosted by Mr Duffield-Morgan in his magnificent home in Lowndes Square, Knightsbridge. We were invited for drinks and canapés at 6.00pm and I was accompanied by Katherine, looking very fashionable in a wide taffeta skirt with frothy white petticoats and a tight red leather belt that accentuated her wasp waist. We were rather overwhelmed when a liveried footman opened the door and called out our names before passing our heavy coats to another lower ranking footman. Dudder's rather timid and mousy wife, the honourable Daphne Duffield-Morgan, welcomed us in the marble floored colonnaded entrance hall and instructed prim waitresses in black uniforms with white aprons to provide us with sparkling wine. Mr Duffield-Morgan was loud, red faced and clearly drunk on our arrival. He enjoyed being the centre of attention whilst we all guffawed at his jokes and anecdotes. He started to annoy me when in conversation with his senior registrar in a thundering voice he dismissed Mr McKenzie as a lily livered surgeon who couldn't cut his way out of a paper bag. I was further rankled when he turned the conversation to making fun of the Irish, whilst I felt Katherine stiffen on my arm. "Have you heard the one about Paddy and Donal who missed the last bus home after the pub closed? Well they decided to break into the bus station and couldn't find the number 11 so they decided to steal the number 39 and walk home from the stop at Cambridge Circus". Haw, haw, haw. Most of his adoring audience laughed along with him but as he started the next joke the room went silent. "What do you call a bunch of Jewish shyster lawyers at the bottom of the ocean? A bloody good start!" The silence deepened and the atmosphere froze. I was not the only Jew on the firm but I was the only one with the guts to stand up to this bully. Speaking quietly whilst realising that my future was in the balance I stated, " Sir, as a Jew I find that joke deeply offensive". The arrogant and pompous fool blustered for a while and then started shouting at me; "I always guessed you were a slimy Hymie, Tanner, pity Adolf didn't finish the job. Now you can bugger off."

Katherine and I were able to retain our dignity whilst a flustered and embarrassed Lady Daphne showed us out into the freezing air leaving a deeper frost behind us.

The rest of my year as a houseman was blighted by this experience. Even though I was the wronged innocent such was the power and influence of Mr Duffield-Morgan people began to avoid me. The man himself apparently spun the tale to make out that I was an impudent puppy who had insulted him in his own house and apart from those who witnessed the event only Mac believed my version.

My six months as a house surgeon was followed by a rather tame though intellectually stimulating six months as a house physician on the academic medical unit.

At the end of the year I left the cruciform building having been called up for National Service in the RAMC. By this time it had been made clear to me that I would not be welcomed back to UCH to start building my surgical career.

Chapter 13

Royal Army Medical Corps (RAMC) 1955-57

I joined the army in September with the putative rank of second lieutenant and was immediately bussed off to Aldershot for 6 weeks of "square bashing".

This involved ill-disguised systematic bullying by a sadistic sergeant major with a bristling moustache and a peaked cap with the visor cut virtually to cover his eyes. I very quickly learnt that when sah'nmajor Kelly turned his attention to me and with a sneer addressed me as "Sir", then something would transpire that day that would leave me cold, wet and exhausted. Any minor misdemeanor such as a stain on a brass button or the inability of sah'nmajor Kelly to capture his reflection in the toes of your boots would end with the punishment of being sent to the hill. The hill was a sand and grass embankment that rose at an angle of 45 degrees to the height of about 100 feet from a dark corner of the parade ground. Depending on the severity of the misdemeanor, the punishment involved a carefully calibrated number of round trips carrying various weights of kit on your back or dangling from your belt. The maximum punishment, nay torture, was said to be 50 repetitions carrying 70 Kg of kit. The worst I experienced was 10 reps plus 40Kg and that nearly killed me. The parades and combat courses were either boring or exhausting but I enjoyed learning to fire the standard issue Lee Enfield Mk 4 rifle and the Smith & Wesson 0.38 revolver standard issue for officers.

I had a steady hand and was quite a good shot.

After a grueling 6 weeks being kicked out of bed at 05.30 for parade at 06.00 and crawling into bed exhausted at lights out at 2200 hours, I was at last able to swap my itchy khaki battledress for a nicely tailored uniform with a single pip on each epaulette and a shiny Sam Brown belt. My cap and collar dogs proudly announced that I was a member of the Royal Army Medical Corps carrying the rod of Asclepius, surmounted by a crown, enclosed within a laurel wreath, with the regimental motto *In Arduis Fidelis*.

So adorned I felt guilty of the transient self satisfaction I enjoyed by parading in front of the long mirror in the officer's outfitting shop in Aldershot. I couldn't help but remember the strutting officers of Hitler's SS I'd seen on Pathé newsreels, in their glamorous black uniforms and begun to understand why the carapace of a uniform could be so seductive for men who lacked conventional skills and achievements that won admiration from their peers or a natural charm or wit that might attract the attention of young women. Nevertheless I decided for the first and last time to show myself off in my new uniform by surprising my "east end" family on the first Friday evening of my first leave. It was worth it to see my mother's covert smiles of appreciation before and after she covered her eyes to chant the blessing over the Sabbath candles. My father then blessed the wine and the *challah* bread and then to my surprise my brother Joe chanted a *shechionu* the prayer when we thank Hashem for preserving us to enjoy the occasion. We enjoyed an animated meal but I couldn't help but notice how pale and drawn my mother looked and how sad her face was in repose.

My first posting was to the RAMC hospital at Millbank just west along the embankment from Horseferry Road the site of the Westminster Hospital where my mother had begun her ordeal.

Compared with my schedule at UCH my work at Millbank was quite light. In fact apart from the odd case of trauma referred from the assault courses and the occasional case of acute appendicitis, my pattern of work was pretty much like general practice. I had senior officers to call on for guidance but there was little formal teaching. In therefore decided to spend most of my time studying for the primary FRCS using a correspondence course and volunteering as a demonstrator in anatomy at my medical school. During my leisure time I continued my secret romance with staff nurse

Sullivan. The secret of course was with my family not within the officers mess. After about ten months I passed my primary FRCS, a tough exam in anatomy, physiology and biochemistry, and was promoted to a full lieutenant with a second pip on my epaulettes.

Then in October 1956 my world turned upside down. On the night of the 29th we were woken up at 0400 and ordered to present ourselves for an urgent briefing in the officer's mess. I casually assumed that this was an exercise and took my time putting on my uniform and with my fellow officers strolled along the corridors of our sleeping quarters being urged on by our medical orderlies. The tension in the mess was tangible and I sensed that somewhere in the British sphere of influence, the "balloon was about to go up".

We were addressed by the commanding officer RAMC Lieutenant Colonel AJ Llewellyn flanked by our immediate superior Captain JM Elliott, an anesthetist by trade, who would later command us as a unit in 23 Parachute Field Ambulance 2 Parachute Brigade. Our CO told us to prepare for operation MUSKATEER and the only clue he gave us to where or why in the world we were to be deployed, is that we were to be equipped with tropical gear.

Of course it didn't take long before the rumour spread round the brigade that we were heading off to the Canal Zone in response to Nasser's attempt at nationalising the Suez Canal. The army was originally to land at Alexandria, but the location was later switched to Port Said since a landing at Alexandria would have been opposed by most of the Egyptian army, necessitating the deployment of an armoured division. Furthermore, a preliminary bombardment of a densely populated area would have involved tens of thousands of civilian casualties. The final land order of battle involved the Royal Marine Commando Brigade, the 16th Parachute Brigade, and the 3rd Infantry Division with the Mediterranean fleet preparing to support the amphibious operation. On the 29th October Israeli armour, preceded by parachute drops on two key passes, thrust south into the Sinai, routing local Egyptian forces within five days. Affecting to be alarmed by the threat of fighting along the Suez Canal, the UK and France issued a twelve-hour ultimatum on the 30th October to the Israelis and the Egyptians to cease fighting. When, as expected, no response was given, Operation Muskateer was launched.

The 45th Commando and 16th Parachute Brigade landed by sea and air on the 5th November. Although landing forces quickly established control over major canal facilities, the Egyptians were able to sink obstacles in the canal, rendering it unusable. The Anglo-French air offensive damaged Egyptian airfields not already attacked by the Israelis, but failed to destroy oil stocks or cripple the Egyptian army. The 3rd Battalion Parachute group captured El Cap airfield by airborne assault.

On the 5th November, an advance element of the 3rd Battalion of the British Parachute Regiment dropped on El Gamil Airfield, a narrow strip of land, led by Brigadier M.A.H. Butler. Having taken the airfield with a dozen casualties, the remainder of the battalion flew in by helicopter. The Battalion then secured the area around the airfield.

The British forces then moved up towards Port Said with air support before digging in at 13:00 to hold until the beach assault began. With close support from carrier-based Wyverns, the British paratroops took Port Said's sewage works and the cemetery while becoming engaged in a pitched battle for the Coast Guard barracks. The French paratroops stormed and took Port Said's waterworks that morning, an important objective to control in a city in the desert.

At first light on 6 November, personnel from 40 and 42 Commando Royal Marines stormed the beaches, using landing craft of World War II vintage. The battle group standing offshore opened fire, giving covering fire for the landings and causing considerable damage to the Egyptian batteries and gun emplacements. Round about that time I joined the second wave of 23 Parachute Field Ambulance flown in by helicopter mercifully spared the parachute drop enjoyed by the longer serving medics, orderlies and stretcher bearers of the group. The NCOs who had landed 24 hours earlier by parachute drop to a Nissan hut that served as our quarters and housed the operating suite, harried me along the tarmac. I barely had time to drop my kit on my camp bed before being summoned to the operating theatre to start work on a fresh wave of battle casualties. There was no time for the niceties of pre-operative evaluation as that had already been taken care of by a triage supervised by our commanding officer and two dressers in the casualty clearing station. The casualties were deemed beyond help, walking wounded to wait in line at the dressing station or in need of life or limb saving surgery urgently. The latter then had a brief note with description of wounds and instructions on how to proceed from Captain Elliott slipped into a waterproof sleeve and tied round the neck of the wounded soldier. There was no time to change into theatre greens so we worked with rubber aprons tied round our waists over our uniform singlets and shorts whilst resuscitating the patient and then after quickly washing the blood off our hands relied on a sterile gown and rubber gloves to protect the patient from our own bacteria. This was almost tokenism as the greatest risk of infection came from the wounded soldier's blood and fecal stained body together with the foreign bodies in their wounds consisting of fragments of their uniform, shrapnel and debris from nearby explosions.

I'll never forget my third real combat victim and he never forgot me.

He was a short dark haired man in his early 20s rushed into the theatre by two stretcher-bearers from our battalion. The note around his neck read, "Hypovolaemic shock, transfuse-shrapnel wound left groin heavy bleeding-explore and repair wound after debridement."

He was indeed in a state of shock. Even through his dark sun tanned skin I could note the cyanotic tinge and the sweat on his brow. His hands were cold and his pulse barely detectable. Without even bothering to take his blood pressure and with the help of a very experienced RAMC "dresser" we managed to get up an IV line in his right arm in spite of the fact that his peripheral veins were collapsed. I started pouring in saline and yelled out for a unit of group O blood whilst we were waiting for the grouping and cross-matched of a transfusion. Meanwhile an anesthetic orderly gave him oxygen by a mask and 20 mgm of morphine sulphate following which he stopped thrashing around. Having established a pulse and recorded a blood pressure of 90/50 I turned my attention to the damage. The area around the left groin was wrapped with a tight bandage holding a compression dressing beneath which the torn edges of his khakis uniform could be seen. The dressing and the uniform were saturated with blood whilst bright red arterial blood could be seen exuding from beneath the dressing pad. This was enough to alert me to the fact that the wound involved the femoral artery. My dresser and I, using long sharp scissors cut away his uniform in order to expose the lower abdomen and left leg. At the time I noted something odd about his uniform that didn't really register until the next day. Before ordering the dresser to remove the bandages I scrubbed, gloved and gowned up without even bothering about cap and mask whilst the anesthetic orderly put the patient to sleep with gas and air. I draped a wide area around the groin with green sterile cotton squares as I cleaned around the wound with iodophore solution and then asked my aide to remove the dressing. At that point my fears were confirmed as a jet of arterial blood shot upwards and staining the operating light with ruby like droplets. I just had time to note the shard of shrapnel penetrating his groin before the puddle of gore obscured by view.

I then remembered my first formal teaching at Milbank. Don't panic, local pressure will halt arterial bleeding, expose the anatomical areas above and below the arterial bleeding, apply clamps and only then expose the wound.

Exposing the femoral artery below the wound was not too difficult but above the wound I was already at the level of the inguinal ligament. From that point on I made up the operation as I went along with vague memories of illustrations in surgical textbooks floating in front of my eyes. I asked one of the stretcher-bearers to try and find the Commanding Officer to give me advice but I had to keep going.

I opened the inguinal canal and put a sling round the testicular cord and clipped it to the drapes out of the field. My patient would not have been pleased with me if he lost a leg and a testicle at the same time. Following that I was free to cut through the inguinal ligament and dissect out the common femoral artery and vein. I carefully separated the two and slipped a sling of thin rubber tubing round the artery which was held tight by a Spencer Wells clip occluding the blood flow to the leg. Everything then went blissfully calm as the bleeding ceased and the patient's color improved as the blood flowing in exceeded the blood flowing out. But this was the calm before the storm. I yelled at the anesthetist to start the clock as I was now working against time.

I quickly slipped the distal tourniquet around the femoral artery below the wound and removed all the pressure dressings. Cleaned the wound again and inspected the damage in a dry environment. Sure enough the shrapnel had penetrated the common femoral artery just above its bifurcation into the major superficial and deep branches. To tie this off above the wound would mean an amputation so I needed to repair the artery. I removed the metal shard along with some fragments of khakis material and freshened up the arterial wound edges at which point my heart sank as it became obvious that simply to sew up the wound after so much of the anterior arterial wall had been destroyed would have left a channel so narrow that it would become occluded by clots within the hour. By this time I was sweating from the heat and with fear of failure and again with greater urgency called for the CO. My cry sounded pathetic, like a child calling for daddy. As that thought passed through my head I paused I remembered that the one I really needed was my mummy.

I've no idea what a photographic memory is or whether it really exists outside science fiction but I have an excellent visual memory. Sometimes I even lull myself to sleep by wandering round the National Gallery with my visual memory of my frequent visits as my guide. Up until this stage of the operation my visual memory had served me well by dredging up pictures from Bailey and Love's textbook on surgical practice that virtually floated in front of my eyes as I operated but beyond this point I could recall no helpful illustration on how to proceed. My brain then, without effort of will, switched to our sitting room two years earlier. I was studying with my textbooks open on the dining room table whilst my mother sat sewing in an armchair by the fire. She was a gifted seamstress and used to make her own dresses from patterns in Women's Realm. After she lost her job at Selfridges and before her depressive state rendered her inert, she used to take in work carrying out alterations on ladies frocks and blouses to help out with the household budget. On more than one occasion I witnessed her skill at widening the sleeve of a dress at the armhole. She would cut along the seem at the tee junction between the sleeve and the bodice and sew in a diamond shaped piece of fabric of matching color and material from her basket of off cuts from the local sweat shop. That was the answer to my surgical dilemma and appeared self-evident even though I'd not been taught or even heard of the procedure. Again a sense of calm settled over me, as I knew exactly what was required. I cut a diamond shaped postage stamp sized patch of fascia from the abdominal wall just above the inguinal ligament and called for the finest silk sutures. I then closed the defect in the wall of the common femoral artery with this patch working as fast as possible knowing that in theory I only had about 20 minutes for the limb to remain viable as it was hanging on to life by the feeble supply of blood supplied by collateral vessels from the gluteal arteries. The theatre went deathly quiet and others drifted over to witness this surgical first. Once the patch was secured I gingerly removed the clamp from the distal end of the wound and waited a few minutes. The surgical bed remained dry. Even more slowly I released the compression on the proximal tourniquet whilst everyone in the operating room held their breath. Still the field of view remained dry and then to my delight I witnessed the pulse travel across the arterial repair without any ooze of bright red blood between the sutures. I asked one of the orderlies to examine the left foot and he reported that it had turned pink and warm with a pulse palpable at the ankle. At that there was a spontaneous round of applause and as if on cue the CO entered the room. "What the hell's going on here? This is meant to be an operating theatre not a bloody music hall". I called him over and explained the wound and my method of repair." He looked down at the field of surgery with a skeptical expression for a minute or two whilst once again I held my breath.

He then looked me in the eye and sternly advised me to protect the repair by dividing the Sartorius muscle at its origin, swing it over at sew it to the defect in the abdominal wall. I think I detected a twinkle in his eye as he spoke. I left my dresser to clean up and close the wound and administer penicillin and without having a moment to savor my triumph, I was ushered to my next case. This poor chap wasn't as lucky. He had stepped on a mine and his leg below the knee looked like a joke cigar after it had exploded in someone's face. There was no alternative but to carry out a below knee amputation.

I worked non stop for seven or eight hours before being relieved and dead on my feet dropped into my camp bed but just before I fell into a dreamless slumber it suddenly dawned on me what was so odd about that first Tommy's uniform.

All badges of rank and all regimental insignia had been cut off before he landed on my operating table.

The following morning I was woken up by a NCO at 0700 and advised that CO wanted to see me immediately. I splashed water on my face and without bothering to shave put on a short-sleeved khakis shirt and pulled on a ridiculous pare of long khakis shorts. The CO greeted me warmly and suggested that we did a ward round together so that we could plan the amputation of my first casualty's leg. Again I detected that twinkle in his eye.

As we approached my patient I overheard him speaking in an animated way with a young soldier next to him. The animation in his voice was enough to reassure me that he was well and the leg was not gangrenous even without examining him. The odd thing was that he wasn't speaking English and neither was he speaking French. It was some guttural tongue rattling on like machine gun fire. When he saw us he went silent but we were greeted with a wide charming smile in his sun-bronzed face. The CO nodded and asked the dresser to expose the wound. To my relief the wound was dry and clean. Next we inspected the leg and that was pink and warm with a bounding pulse at the ankle. At that point the CO turned to me with a broad smile and said; "Well done old chap you must write this up for the British Journal of Surgery". At that point, the patient speaking with a thick accent yet clearly an educated man interrupted us. "So do I get to keep my leg to fight another day?". "Indeed you do" replied Captain Elliott, "and you've got Mr. Tanner to thank for that."

We completed the ward round with me walking on air thinking that I might specialize as a vascular surgeon once I gained my consultancy.

After he left I had a quiet morning supervising the care of the postoperative cases but was on call for the operating theatre in the afternoon.

Once my tasks were complete I wandered back to the young man whose leg I had saved, settled on his bed and asked his name. "My name is Jamal Atrash" he replied. "Forgive me for asking but what was that language you were speaking and in which unit do you serve?" " The language you overheard was Ivrit but the second question I cannot answer". "Ivrit, do you mean Modern Hebrew?" I asked. He nodded his assent. " But you don't have a Jewish name" I continued. "That's because I'm not Jewish, I'm a Druze" he responded. Because of his accent and my ignorance it took a while to sort out this apparent contradiction but in the end he taught me who the Druze were and how he came to be here in the first place.

The Druze appeared to be an exotic religious sect remotely connected to Islam but secretive about their practices. They numbered only about 40,000 who lived in the Northern region of Galilee, Southern Lebanon and Western Syria. They were loyal citizens of whatever country treated them with respect and for that reason fiercely loyal to Israel. He came from a village in the far north of Israel near to the Lebanese border where the Druze and the Jews had lived together in perfect harmony for centuries. Jamal was obviously very bright, mastered at least three languages and was hoping to go to medical school once he had finished his two and a half year spell as a conscript in the Israeli army. He was a bit vague about how he ended up on my operating table, but claimed to have parachuted from his transport plane west of the Suez Canal because of a navigational error by the pilot. Meanwhile he was proud to learn that the Israel Defense Force (IDF) tank divisions had already conquered Sinai.

At this point in our conversation I was again summoned

urgently to the office of the CO. I stood smartly to attention and saluted in front of his desk.

"No need for those formalities Tanner", he said with a grin whilst shoving a sheet of paper and a pen towards me. "Sign on the dotted line old chap, it's the Official Secrets Act". I gulped looking at him with disbelief, read the paper with the parliamentary portcullis insignia on the letterhead and signed as directed. " Righty-oh" he continued, "now I can let you into a secret. You know that those two Tommy's that we examined this morning, well they're not Tommy's they are Johnny foreigners and by that I don't mean French. They're bleeding Israeli parachutists who were dropping in on us as liaison officers. Apparently we are fighting this war together as secret allies. So Mum's the word, eh?" Suddenly everything made sense and I enjoyed a burst of pride to learn that the IDF and the British army were allies and for once there was no risk of dual loyalties. "Thank you sir, you can rely on me to keep *shtum*- sorry Sir that's Yiddish for Mum's the word. Will there be anything more Sir?" I continued in a bantering tone of friendly and teasing respect. "Well as a matter of fact Tanner this telegram from Blighty just landed on my desk and it seems to be for you", he replied. He handed over the buff envelope and watched with ill-disguised curiosity as I opened it up and read the pasted strips of text.

[Come home at once. Your mother died last night.
I wish you a long life. Dad]

"Everything all right Tanner?" asked Captain Elliot reading the sudden pallor on my face. I showed him the telegram and he looked up at me with an expression of genuine concern and empathy and asked me to sit down.

"Anything I can do to help?" he continued. Trying to control my tears I replied, "Well sir in the Jewish tradition we bury our dead within 24 hours and then have a seven day ritual period of mourning. I don't suppose there is any chance of compassionate leave in the middle of a war?" "As it turns out Tanner we are no longer at war.

I've just heard on the radio that the Americans have succeeded in persuading the United Nations to call for an immediate ceasefire and the UN have voted overwhelmingly in its favor so Anthony Eden had no choice but to give in. So yes as far as I'm concerned you are on the next flight to Nicosia and then see if you cant hitch a lift home from there but there is little chance of you being home in time for the funeral as the best part of 24 hours has already gone by." As he said that my hair bristled on the nape of my neck as I recalled the image of my mother coming to my aid in the operating room at the moment of her death.

Chapter 14

Sitting Shiva

My CO was true to his word, arranged compassionate leave and found me a seat on elderly Dakota transport to Nicosia. From there I hitched a ride on a RAF flight carrying home some of the more seriously injured and those needing reconstructive surgery for hideous face wounds at a specialist unit outside London, where I earned my ride by attending to IV infusions and administering intramuscular morphine to those whimpering in pain from the frightful combat wounds in the short lived battle to control Port Said. I landed at RAF Brize Norton near Oxford and took the train to Liverpool Street. From there it was but a short taxi ride home. I arrived home nearly three days after my mother had died and approached our front door at about 7.00 pm expecting the *Shiva* house to be full of mourners with the door open inviting any passer by to drop in. However something was very wrong as the door was shut tight and as my brother opened the door to my frantic knocks my misgiving was increased by his demeanour. Without a word more than the ritual greeting of wishing me a long life and giving me a brotherly embrace he ushered me into the parlour where I was shocked to see my father alone bent over with his head in his hands. All the mirrors were covered in sheets and the pictures of my mother were turned to the wall. It didn't take me long to deduce that the *shiva* had been postponed pending a coroner's inquest into her death.

Three days beforehand my father had returned home from a late night ferrying fares from the East End to the West End and back and on letting himself in at 1.00am, smelt gas. My mother was found dead in the kitchen with the four gas burners turned on and unlit, having taken the precautions of sealing the cracks round the sash windows and the gap under the door.

Her suicide note was brief but heartbreaking. She judged herself a freak and a burden on the household. She was proud of her son's achievements but ashamed to be in their presence and finally she asked for forgiveness from my father for failing to disclose her family's curse at the time of their betrothal. On reading this I broke down in tears. At the time I learnt of her death I assumed it was related to breast cancer recurrence yet in its way her death was just as much the consequence of the diagnosis and treatment of her disease. At this point I gave up on my idea to become a vascular surgeon and determined that I would devote the rest of my life in avenging my mother's death.

The coroner's court in Horseferry Lane sat three days later and we looked a sorry sight as we listened to the evidence from the police and the pathologist's report on the autopsy. The proceedings were mercifully short and the verdict beyond doubt.

When a Jew commits suicide, she is not permitted a full Jewish burial, and there is even a debate whether *shiva* the seven-day mourning period, is observed or whether the *kaddish* prayer is said. In practice, however, suicide could be treated as a normal death, if there was evidence that the person was not of a normal state of mind at the time. Our kindly GP who had looked after my mother over the last couple of years had no difficulty in convincing our very tolerant Rabbi, that at the time of her death my mother was not of a sound mind, so arrangements were made for her funeral in the orthodox burial ground at Aldernley Road, Mile End the very next day.

The week of ritual mourning was an opportunity for our extended family and wide range of friends from the very different spheres of engagement of the three principle mourners, to say prayers together and offer condolences. My father bracketed by his two sons held court whilst sitting on three low stools, with rent garments and the stubble of unshaved faces. Words of comfort were voiced and practical matters like feeding the three of us were taken care of by my aunt and uncle next door.

This period also allowed me a period of reflection for planning the rest of my life. The first thing was to break off my relationship with staff nurse Sullivan as I could not allow myself to even consider causing more hurt to my father at this time. This was achieved without rancour but in any case I learnt that her side of our religious divide voiced similar concerns. I next applied for a job as a surgical registrar at the nearby London Hospital on Whitechapel Road for when my period of time with the RAMC was up. That would serve the two purposes of studying on the job for my final FRCS whilst living at home when I was off duty to keep an eye on my father. I also started reading around the subject of breast cancer and in particular the subject of familial predisposition to the disease. I further postponed any thought of making *aliyah* to *Eretz Yisrael*.

After the *shiva* was over I returned to Millbank and completed my term of service to RAMC in London, as the Suez crisis had been resolved as far as the British army was concerned. I found myself promoted to the rank of captain for the last few months of my posting.

I secured a good job at the rather unfashionable London hospital having burnt my bridges at UCH and threw myself into my busy clinical work whilst bashing the books until midnight most days in preparation for the final examination to enter as a fellow of the prestigious Royal College of Surgeons of England.

In what little time I had left over I pursued my research on familial breast cancer by the simple expedient of "asking around". I started off with my mother's sole surviving sister and from there sent from Jewish family to Jewish family in the east end of London. Sometimes following up on a lead, I would find myself in the leafy and expensive areas of north west London where the wealthier Jews had moved having made good or bettered themselves within one or two generations since their grandparents had arrived at the turn of the century from eastern Europe, like my father or more recently as refugees from Hitler's Germany. Surprisingly, bearing in mind that cancer was still a taboo subject in polite circles, as a young surgeon I was welcomed warmly into all these households who went to no end of trouble to search out their family records to help me with my research. Furthermore the rabbis of these diverse communities also put themselves out by looking through their burial records to corroborate the age at death of the victims. In a completely amateur way I built up pedigrees of families who claimed that they had more than their share of breast cancer. Sadly of course the more recent wave of immigrants had lost many of their kindred in the Holocaust leaving blanks in the pattern but there was no doubt that a pattern was beginning to emerge. I identified about 30 families where every other female member had died of the disease. The evidence was often hearsay than a death certificate authenticated, but compelling never the less. I also noted two other facts, the age of diagnosis or death was remarkably young, on average 40 compared with 50-55 in most other communities and there was also a surprisingly high incidence of double mastectomies. Although I now had a numerator to work with I had no idea of a denominator: in other words 30 families out of how many? I couldn't claim that my search was systematic in any way as a result of surveying the Jewish population of London or even Whitechapel. It was simply a random collection derived by word of mouth and following up the connections of family and friends. Clearly I needed the help of a professional epidemiologist but who would take me seriously? At the very least I believed that I had identified a set of Jewish families where breast cancer was inherited as if their germ line carried a Mendelian dominant gene that predisposed to the disease. I sat on these observations for the best part of a year before deciding what to do next. In the meantime though I wrote up the case of Jamal Atrash hoping that one-day my new technique of repairing the common femoral artery would become known as the "Tanner manoeuvre". I submitted my paper to the British Journal of Surgery (BJS) and couldn't wait to see my name in print for the first time. Nemesis followed rapidly on the heels of hubris when the very kindly assistant editor of the journal wrote to thank me for my submission whilst drawing my attention to a paper in the Surgical Clinics of North America 1944, when a surgeon from Boston first described the technique invented on the battle fields of Normandy shortly after D day. That taught me the important discipline of carrying out literature searches before committing word to paper and reinforced my determination to pursue one line of enquiry in a topic that appeared to have no mechanistic answers.

My next "breakthrough" followed a chance encounter in my first week as a surgical registrar at the London Hospital. I was changing into my theatre greens in preparation for assisting the professor with an operating list when I got into conversation with another young surgeon using the adjacent locker.

He was a tall handsome man with shiny black wavy hair and dark twinkly eyes. He introduced himself as Jonathan Ashkenazi. After introducing myself in return I asked if his name implied that he was an Ashkenazi Jew like me. He replied that he was often asked that question but paradoxically his family were Sephardic Jews originally from Alexandria in Egypt. This was the first of these exotic and somewhat aristocratic Sephardim I had ever met. Although there was no animosity between the two "tribes", the Ashkenazim mostly from Eastern Europe and the Sephardim mostly from Spain, Portugal, Iran, Iraq and North Africa, our sets seldom mingled. The Sephardic Jews in London were given aristocratic status partly because their community was the oldest with their main synagogue, Bevis Marks, founded in nearly 300 years earlier. Moreover the famous banking families like the Montefiores, Sassoons and Montagues were mostly of Sephardic extraction. He seemed very friendly and not the least aloof as expected and we agreed to meet up for a beer in the doctors mess once our lists were complete. We immediately hit it off and became good friends. When I told him of my family history and my research into a Jewish predisposition to breast cancer he was genuinely interested and promised to help me expand my work searching out other such families linked to his friends and relatives in the Sephardic community. He was true to his word and as a result I made two further discoveries. The first was that these were Jews like I'd never met before. Not only were they mostly very wealthy in a serious way that included second homes and yachts on the Côte D'Azur, they were very glamorous in a Levantine way. Their food was also very different to the stodgy Ashkenazi cuisine and potatoes were replaced by rice and pepper replaced with saffron and cumin.

The other discovery if that's what you choose to call it, is that we could not identify a single family with more than their fair share of the disease. I assumed therefore that my original observations were flawed with some kind of selection bias and once again let the subject drop in order to focus on my studies, as the FRCS finals were now only three months away.

Most evenings when I was off duty I would return home at about 6.00pm having enjoyed the short walk from the hospital in the bustling Whitechapel area to my house on Sydney Street. I would often stop on the way at Blooms kosher restaurant and pick up some salt beef cut fresh and hot at the counter. That together with new green pickles and a potato latke would serve as my evening meal. I would then settle down with Bailey & Love's "Short Practice of Surgery" for intense study. The "short" in the title carried a sense of intentional irony by the publishers, as in truth it was a doorstep of a book. I also brought home from the medical school library volumes of Raven's practice of surgery that described technique rather than pathology and diagnosis. I was a driven man waiting to qualify as a surgeon in order to avenge my mother's death in some ill-defined metaphorical sense. Most evenings father returned from work at about midnight looking more and more unkempt, bearded since the *shiva* and often smelling of alcohol. On other occasions when I'd be operating until late at night and needing a change of clothes for the following morning's out patient clinic I might find him asleep in a drunken stupor on his armchair in the parlour. I was so worried about his behaviour now that I asked my brother to try and help with some pastoral advice.

Eleven months after my mother's death we had the stone setting ceremony at her grave. We had chosen a simple grey granite headstone with her name in Hebrew engraved in black along with her dates and below that the beautiful verse from the Proverbs; *Ayshet Chayil:*

"Who can find a virtuous woman? For her price is far above rubies. The heart of her husband doth safely trust in her, so that he shall have no need of spoil. She will do him good and not evil all the days of her life."

At home with family that evening my father consumed about half a bottle of scotch and staggered up to bed with some support from his two sons and much shaking of heads by the rest of the family and our close friends.

In contrast he was able to celebrate a joyous occasion a couple of months later when I returned from the Royal College of Surgeons at Lincolns Inn Fields clutching my freshly minted FRCS diploma signed and sealed by the great and the good of the English surgical establishment. That night we went out to eat at Blooms to celebrate and as there was no tradition there for alcohol with food we made do with lemon tea yet between the three of us we polished off a bottle of Dimple Haig on returning home.

The next morning on the ward and in theatre I was addressed as **Mr**. Tanner for the first time as a token of the British inverse snobbery after qualifying as a surgeon. This was a nod to Thomas Vickery and the Master Barber Surgeons who first received the royal charter from King Henry VIIIth as illustrated by Holbein in his masterpiece on display in the Great Hall at Lincolns Inn Fields.

We were no longer master surgeons but more simply Mister surgeon.

Again I spent the day floating on air as the word got around that I was a proper Mister. Jonathan Ashkenazi qualified on the same day and we jointly organised a party in the doctor's mess that weekend where we got through a firkin of light ale and danced with the nurses to the music of Buddy Holly until dawn.

I got home on Monday evening with a thick head only to find my father vomiting up blood. I rushed him to hospital and got him seen by the consultant surgeon on call. He diagnosed a bleeding duodenal ulcer and after blood transfusion rushed him to theatre. He invited me to scrub in with his team.

He opened the abdomen through upper mid line incision and palpated the duodenum looking for the tell tale thickening and scarring that would mark out the site of a chronic duodenal ulcer. There was nothing obvious to feel so he opened the gastro-duodenal junction through a long oblique incision. At once we saw that that his stomach was full of blood clots and after those were sucked out and the kidney dishes filled up with this blackcurrant jelly like material there was still no sign of the spurting arterial bleed in the base of an ulcer but instead the dreaded sight of the gastric mucosa oozing blood from all surfaces with multiple tiny gastric erosions. The only way of controlling that blood loss was by an emergency total gastrectomy. The operation was completed with speed and consummate skill but my father had no will to live and died on the ward four days later. We all knew that this was a result of alcoholic gastritis but the death certificate was signed off by the SHO simply as haemorrhage from peptic ulceration.

Chapter 15

Aliyah at last

Joe and I stood at the dockside in Marseilles in the spring of 1959 gazing up in awe at SS Theodore Herzl proudly flying the blue Star of David, the flag of the State of Israel: a Jewish ship with Jewish officers and a Jewish crew. We were wrong about the crew who turned out to be the usual motley crowd of Greeks, Malay and Pakistani drifters. The chef was Jewish though and the food strictly kosher. We stood there with a mix of complex emotions flooding our consciousness. We were orphaned, having buried both parents over the previous 18 months. We were leaving behind all our friends and family and a settled life for new horizons; a mixture of Zionistic commitment and sense of adventure. Neither of us was clean shaven as we had allowed our beards to grow since the death of our father but that was where the similarity ended.

Joe's beard was that of an aspiring rabbi and went with side locks and sober clothing befitting his calling. My beard and moustache were neatly cut with a rather raffish look and more a conceit than a badge of orthodoxy. It matched my open neck shirt, Paisley cravat and loud checked sports jacket. I rather fancied myself as a ladies man.

Each of us carried a money belt wrapped round our chest under our shirts carrying a few hundred pounds left over from the sale of the family home and its contents. We were thus equipped to support ourselves for about 12 months. My plan was to join the *ulpan* "language school" at Bet Brodesky, Ramat Aviv just north of Tel Aviv, whilst looking for employment as a surgeon once the money ran out. I hoped to have learnt to take a medical history and make my orders in the operating theatre understood in Modern Hebrew by then. Joe already had an invitation to join a yeshiva "religious seminary" in Safed up in the hills of the Galil north east of Haifa. He wanted to study Talmud for a year before looking for a religious community to serve.

We walked up the covered gangplank with all our worldly goods packed in one suitcase and one shoulder bag each. We shared a two berthed cabin; not so much a state room but more of an understated room, with bunk beds and portholes just above the water line and riveted bulkheads limiting any frenzied movements. In earlier years this might have been described as steerage but as we had no intention of spending much time below decks it suited us fine. During the crossing we spent most of our time reading in the fine weather whilst passively developing a suntan. Joe attended *shachris, mincha and maariv,* everyday in the ship's little prayer room but I only joined him on the Friday evening and Shabbat at sea. Joe found a group of like-minded and equally hirsute men with whom to argue on the one hand and on the other hand, on some minutiae of Talmudic doctrine. I in the meantime found a group of like-minded young women mostly of Nordic birth, with whom to enjoy a drink at the bar whilst debating the probity and practicalities of continuing or discussions below decks on bunk beds stacked one above the other. Joe and I were happy pioneers each in his own way.

The voyage passed rapidly and we gained our first site of Israel as Mount Carmel and the city of Haifa appeared just after dawn on the fifth day at sea.

As the mist lifted and the sun rose above the high ground, the beauty of Haifa was revealed with the Baha'i temple and the 19 steps of its magnificent gardens cascading down to the German colony at its feet. As the sun rose a little higher, the 19 facets of the temple cupola reflected golden sun on gilded dome.

I was unaware that I was silently weeping until Ingrid Christianson handed me a handkerchief to wipe my eyes just before we parted with exchanges of kisses and poste restante contact details. I suspect that each were fabricated but t'was always thus with shipboard romances as I'd been reliably informed.

Having disembarked Joe and I embraced, pledged to keep in touch whilst exchanging our authentic postal addresses and dragged our cases to the bus station. Joe climbed on the Egged bus to Safed via Nazareth whilst I boarded the bus to Tel Aviv stopping en route at Caesarea. The insanity and crowds at the central bus station in Tel Aviv, the alien smells of street food and the cries of the street vendors left me confused and vulnerable. The pirates at the taxi rank saw me coming and fought for the pleasure and honour of ripping off this self evident English gentleman and I was driven to Bet Brodesky via the "scenic route" that included a running commentary in a mixture of Arabic, Hebrew and American movie English. For this I handed over a fistful of shekels, cheap at half the price. Ramit Aviv was a newly built suburb just north of the Yarkon River that seemed like a pleasant change from the ugliness of what I had so far seen of Tel Aviv. I was expected and warmly welcomed into the hostel and language school for potential immigrants from the English speaking parts of the western world.

I very much enjoyed my few months at Bet Brodesky and made many friends from America, South Africa together with a few Londoners and Mancunians.

We all had similar tales to tell and they formed the kernel of my *chevra,* chums, for years to come. I enjoyed going back to school and very rapidly I was able to ask the way to the central bus station or mention the fact that David was an old man who could be found sitting under a tree, in what I imagined was fluent *Ivrit.* I could count to 1,000, knew the names of the days and the months and learnt the all-important catch phrases of Israeli life; "just one moment", "have a little patience" and "we are closed for the high holy days".

In those early days Tel Aviv was hell on earth. The heat turned from very hot to unbearable within a few weeks of my arrival. Tree shade was minimal at that time although 20 years later those pathetic saplings would grow to give Tel Aviv the character of a garden city. Even worse than the heat was the stultifying bureaucracy of an emergent nation with too many clerical staff to feed. Opening a bank account, drawing money, extending a visitor's visa or getting a drivers licence, required time and patience almost beyond my tolerance. To complete the driving licence process took seven full days traipsing or better described as *schlepping,* backwards and forwards between different agencies at different ends of town. And the queues, the queues! In England we had mastered the art of queuing many generations past but Israel, an emergent country at the junction of the Levant, Arabia and North Africa, had still much to learn. Queuing in Israel in the late 1950s depended on *proctectia* or in other words the clerical officer who owed you a favour, brazen ignorance of the polite British code of conduct and the ability to climb over the heap of bodies stacked up before a booth with a protective grill separating the crowd from the indifferent clerk eating her falafel. In the end I learnt to master this problem by first dressing like an Israeli, which involved open neck short-sleeved shirts and Roman style sandals *without* socks. Next, as I knew I would never succeed with a full frontal attack, I learnt the outflanking manoeuvre of bluffing my way in to the office through the back door and saying that Moishe sent me. I knew no Moishe but it appeared everyone else did and he was owed *protectia* big time.

I had just reached the point of thinking that Israel was a big mistake when my new best friend Ike Vogel from Brooklyn New York, invited me to spend Passover with his uncle's family in Jerusalem. I had hoped to spend the feast with Joe in Safed but he informed me with regret that his presence was demanded by the Rosh Yeshiva, the famous Rebbe Fertleman, whilst at the same time a *shidduch,* marriage proposal, had been suggested between him and Tziporah Fertleman, who he really fancied, and that my presence might in some way jeopardise his chances. I got the message.

Ike rented a car and at midday on the eve of the first night of Passover we drove due east from Tel Aviv towards the Judean hills. The first half hour or so we drove on the fertile plain with olive groves, fruit trees and vines providing an elegant patchwork of different shades of green. Tall stands of palm trees punctuated the fields and groves along with the blindingly white walls of the Arab villages and minarets reflecting the high noon day sun. My excitement began as we started up the incline of the winding road to Jerusalem. Shortly after we drove past the signpost to Latrun and entered the Ayalon valley, site of the famous battle in 1947 between the nascent army of the State of Israel and the Arab Legion, we came across the rusting hulks of armoured vehicles and command cars. These had been bulldozed on to the hard shoulders of the road and can be seen to this day as a memorial to the doctors and nurses killed in the infamous ambush at the time they were trying to break the siege of the Hadassah Hospital on Mount Scopus. The British Mandate forces stood by and witnessed the massacre with apparent indifference.

Twenty minutes later as we made a sharp left hand turn, we enjoyed our first sight of Jerusalem the Golden. The epithet was well earned as the reflected sun from the west provoked the ancient limestone, the traditional building material since biblical times, to appear as if backlit through golden filters.

At two in the afternoon the angle of the sun was just perfect for creating this illusion. A few minutes later once we had climbed another 100 metres the City of David and Solomon shimmered like a diadem in the heat haze. I will never forget my first view of the holy city looking like a mirage floating on top of the hills above our heads.

Jerusalem is a very difficult city to navigate, without any logic to its construction until you remember it was built on seven hills. After another hour having made a number of enquiries from fiercely black bearded and black suited ultra orthodox Jews, scurrying around with a sense of urgency to complete their preparatory tasks for the festival to come, we reached the landmark of the Montefiore Windmill at Yamin Moishe and turned south on Emek Refa'im towards the German Colony.

The German Colony was so called because it was built in the late 18thC by a cult of eccentric Protestants calling themselves the Teutonic Templars. Their houses were therefore built according to Germanic taste rather than ancient Crusader or Ottoman style. Surprisingly the result was charming: heavy stone built villas, entered via balustraded granite steps and porticos with oak double doors. The charm was the incongruity of the cascades of vine and bougainvillea softening the brutalism of the original architecture and the fact that the houses flanked narrow cobblestoned lanes.

We were warmly greeted at the door by an elderly couple who where in fact Ike's great uncle and aunt. At the turn of the century Ike's paternal grandfather and his brother had fled the pogroms in the Pale of Settlement in Russian Lithuania. They became separated along the way, with one ending up in New York and the other in Palestine. Ike's great uncle Izzie was a secular Jew of leftist leaning but still celebrated *Pesach* for the sake of the *kinderlach,* little ones. From the sound within there were clearly many of those in residence for *Seder* night. As the family only spoke Yiddish or Modern Hebrew I was somewhat at a disadvantage but to my surprise Ike was fluent in Yiddish and helped me with the translation. I was introduced to about 30 men, women and children but hadn't a clue as to who belonged to who. This was of passing interest to me as one of the young women with flashing black flirtatious eyes reminded me of Minxy of Bonneville Hall. However there was never the smallest of chances for me to explore that line of enquiry. Ike and I were housed in an attic room with two roll out beds and barely had time to wash before being called to the *seder* table. Izzie Vogelstein lead the service in a beautiful baritone voice and at once I was back in familiar territory. The young children competed to sing the four questions, *Ma nishtana ha'leilah hazer,* the plagues visited upon the ancient Egyptians were chanted whilst spilling a drop of wine each in token of their loss of blood, the *matzah,* unleavened bread, was blessed and we all choked with eyes watering on tasting the *marrah* or bitter herbs in memory of the ancient Hebrew's years of bondage. At the end of a huge delicious *haimeshe* dinner of Eastern European provenance prepared by Rebecca Vogelstein and her daughters and daughter-in-laws, the little children were allowed to run wild searching for the hidden half of the first broken *matzah,* the *afikomen,* for which the finder had the chance of auctioning it back to great uncle Izzie for a few shekels.

Apart from all this familiarity there were four important differences from all my Passovers spent in London. The first was the fluency of the Hebrew that was now the native tongue of the younger generations. The second was the fact that in spite of sitting in Jerusalem we still sang *Le shana habah b'Yerushalyim,* next year may we celebrate this feast in Jerusalem. The third was the fact that they only celebrated the one *seder* night and not the two that we mandated in the Diaspora. Finally the fourth and most important for me was that the wine was actually drinkable. On the first two nights of Passover in England we were compelled to bless and drink the four traditional glasses of kosher wine that punctuated the sections of the service. This was an ordeal, as the only sacramental wine that was on sale was sweet and sickly, giving you the hangover without the transient phase of euphoria. In contrast wine grown in Israeli vineyards and processed my Israeli hands was not bad and might pass as a reasonable amusing little cabernet sauvignon. I regretted that there was only one *seder* night as I staggered merrily up the stairs to my attic bed at midnight.

The next morning rising late with a dry mouth and a mild headache I discovered that the family had left for the synagogue so Ike and I decided to take a look at the old city of Jerusalem. We retraced our steps to the Montefiore Windmill and Yamin Moishe along Emek Refa'im. This is the oldest section of west Jerusalem. Just below the windmill we could see *Mishkenot-Sha'ananim* , Peaceful habitation, the first Jewish neighbourhood built outside the walls of the Old City of Jerusalem, on a hill directly across from Mount Zion. The name of the neighbourhood was taken from Book of Isaiah 32:18: "My people will abide in peaceful habitation, in secure dwellings and in quiet resting places." Sir Moses Montefiore built *Mishkenot Sha'anim* in 1860 as an almshouse. Since it was outside the walls and open to Bedouin raids and pillage, the Jews were reluctant to move in, even though the housing was luxurious compared to the derelict and overcrowded houses in the Old City. As an incentive, people were even paid to live there, and a gate was built around the compound with a heavy door that was locked at night. Much later in my life I enjoyed my *protectia* as a frequent guest of the Jerusalem Foundation staying in one of the luxurious apartments created out of this ancient stone built row of terrace houses overlooking Mount Zion. Down below the steep hillside we could see the Sultan's pool in the valley of Hinnom built at the time of the Ottomans, whilst raising our eyes we took in our first sight of the ancient Ottoman walls built on Crusader foundations, guarding the old city and it's holy sites including the Western "wailing wall", of King Herod's temple, the church of the Holy Sepulchre and the Dome of the Rock, three of the holiest sites of the three Abrahamic religions. Once again the noontime sun was reflected back as golden rain in the heat haze and as I turned my head a few degrees to the north a lump swelled in my gullet taking in the view of the iconic Tower of David on Mount Zion. I wanted to rush across the valley to embrace these old walls until I was reminded by Ike that I wouldn't reach the other side as all that was laid out below our feet was no-man's land and anyone seen running in that direction might attract a bullet from the Jordanian Arab Legion. Instead we turned north and wandered through the cobble stoned alleys and terraced houses of *Yamin Moishe* literally meaning the right hand of Moses, until we found our way to the beautiful art-deco YMCA building and the King David hotel. We nonchalantly wandered into the hotel as if we were guests and made our way onto the terrace that gave us the closest view of the old city and the Jaffa gate. At this point I pledged to myself that one day I would own a property were I could wake up to this view every morning. I am told that this is one of the first symptoms to afflict all those who develop the madness known as the "Jerusalem syndrome".

★★★

I returned to Ramat Aviv after the feast was over but still facing six more days of unleavened bread, known as *matzo* to those of a Jewish persuasion or cardboard to gentiles. Beer was forbidden during this period but for reasons beyond my ken, vodka was allowed if distilled from potatoes. I felt refreshed by the sanctified and rarefied air of Jerusalem with my Zionist fervour rekindled. I also felt that idling my time away learning modern Hebrew in the fleshpots of Tel Aviv when I could be saving lives in the operating theatre or God forbid in the theatre of war, was not the best use of the talents of Mr Martin Tanner, MB, FRCS Captain in the RAMC. Furthermore I was rapidly running out of money. So at first light the next day I packed my diplomas and references and set off for the offices of the Jewish Agency. I waited in various lines ending up at the wrong desk and at the end of a frustrating day was advised to visit the labour exchange. The following day I repeated the exercise this time in the company of a bunch of no hopers, rough artisans and delinquents with my self esteem seeping away by the hour. Having reached the front of the right queue I was offered a job as driver of an Egged bus but they looked frankly disappointed when I showed them my qualifications. They suggested I went to the downtown offices of *Kupot Cholim* the health care system set up by the trade union movement. Here I had more success and was offered a job as second assistant surgeon at their hospital in Afula in the Jezreel valley. The terms included full board and lodgings and a pittance of a stipend. By this time I had learnt that Israel had no shortage of doctors in fact by European standards too many. The same applied to concert violinists I was later to learn. So as beggars can't be choosers I accepted the post and agreed to start work the following week. With what little money I had left I bought a second hand motorbike and packed all my worldly belongings in its pannier bags. My last evening in Tel Aviv was bitter sweet as together with all my newfound friends we celebrated *Lag Ba'Omer* in the traditional way by singing Israeli folk songs to the music of a piano accordion around a campfire on the beach. We finished off with a well-known love song that went something like this:

Put your hand into mine, I am yours and you are mine
Hey Hey Daliaya, Beautiful daughter of the Galilian hills

This turned out to be prophetic.

Chapter 16

The Jezreel Valley

So in the first week of May 1959 I mounted my trusty Ariel 4G Mk II square four 1000 cc motorbike, turned north and headed out on the coast road towards Haifa. Without a care in the world, with all my worldly goods strapped on the back of the bike, with the wind in my hair and aviator goggles protecting my eyes; we didn't use crash helmets in those days, I revved up and hit 90 mph just south of Netanya. Just my luck -that coincided with the first *khamsin* of the season. I hate the *khamsin*. This is the hot, dry and dusty wind that gathers pace over Egypt, dries out and picks up sand over the Sinai and then in turn drives me to distraction. If you haven't experienced a *khamsin* it's difficult to describe. You can't get comfortable. It leaves you full of foreboding and looking for someone to blame. In some Arab countries in this neck of the woods, murder is deemed a lesser crime than normal if committed at the time of a *khamsin* and instead of the death penalty you get a stern ticking off and a caution. That's bad enough, but riding at 90 mph into the teeth of the wind is close to suicide. I slowed down, turned west towards the beach, propped the bike up on its stand, stripped naked and sat down in the sea to cool off. In this way, with the wind from the south taking the wind from my sails I headed northward in fits and starts until turning northeast at Hadera on the road to the Megiddo cross roads, as the wind subsided. The hill outside Megiddo is known as Har Megiddo or Armageddon for short. The Book of Revelation mentions an apocalyptic military amassment at Armageddon to mark the end of the world, so I thought I ought to check it out before it was too late.

The archaeological site was a bit of a disappointment so I kept going on the dead straight road from there to Afula. To say that

Afula was also a bit of a disappointment is something of an understatement. After the hustle and bustle of Tel Aviv, its beach and white cuboid Bauhaus apartment blocks, Afula looked dead and dusty. In fact I was in and out of it before I realised. The downtown area was only vaguely identifiable and the shops and bars looked flyblown and the people on the street looked like they'd just arrived from North Africa. I subsequently learnt that was true and that many were still unfamiliar with the technical sophistication of a flushing toilet cistern.

However *Bet Cholim* Afula outside of town to the east pleasantly surprised me. It was a pretty gated complex with lush gardens and tall palm trees. Here was the hustle and bustle of a busy district general hospital where most of the staff lived in a communal way not unlike a kibbutz but were allowed to keep their meagre salary and care for their own children, although there was a crèche and kindergarten for the children of the nurses and a swimming pool for all.

It took me a while to find the administration block where I was expecting a warm welcome from the chief of surgery and the CEO for Captain Tanner RAMC, FRCS. Instead I was met with cool indifference by some junior clerical officer who received my visa and certificates and who then summoned a little Arab lady to show me to my room. This little lady was called Fatima and knew no English but looked after me as a domestic maid with great kindness for the next two years and for a while was my only friend on the campus. The chief of surgery was to meet me the next day and I never knowingly met the CEO for the three and a half years of my sojourn.

My accommodation was in a wooden hut with a bed/sitting room and a shower cubicle that I shared with a pair of geckos. That made three friends at least and they kept the population of flying insects to an acceptable level but had little impact on the scorpion population who enjoyed the comfort of my slippers. I had no need of a kitchen as there was a communal dining room where I could enjoy carp, egg plant and eggs but little else. The day started at 8.00am and the weekend lasted from sundown on a Friday to sundown on the Saturday. The next morning I paraded before the Chief of surgery, Professor, Doctor, Doctor Goldfarb. He looked about 70 and we could find no language in common. I spoke perfect English and some French and Ivrit with the last two getting mixed up in my anxiety. He spoke German, Yiddish and Ivrit with an impenetrable accent. We loathed each other from the start.

He was a martinet and ran the department according the Germanic hierarchical fashion with one Chief and lots of Indians. He had qualified in Munich in 1925 and got out just in time before the Nazis came for him.

He did long boring ward rounds every morning with a large retinue of doctors and nurses in attendance, at which he determined which surgeon would do which operation on which patient. A couple of Rumanian surgeons in their 40s who were his deputies accepted this meekly but I often tried to discuss the case and suggest alternatives in the British way, only to be met by a steely gaze and ignored, not that he could understand more than a fraction of what I said.

I was appointed as second assistant to the two first assistants who answered to the two Rumanian deputies who only answered to Professor, Doctor, Doctor, Goldfarb. In that role, if I wasn't merely holding a retractor I was directed to dress wounds or remove sutures. All this was deeply humiliating to the man who invented the operation to repair the common femoral artery and to be frank the two Rumanians were ignorant boors and clumsy to boot.

I now understood how refugees must feel, not knowing the language and working way below their level of skill. Not only that, they mocked me in the operating theatre because of my accent and my confusion with vocabulary.

For example to my ear the Hebrew words for scissors, spectacles and a pair of trousers sounded pretty much alike and the nurses thought it was a great joke handing me a pair of green pyjama like scrubs when all I wanted was a pair of scissors to cut a suture.

I made no friends in the first six months because all the young doctors and nurses had married whilst serving time in the armed forces and no one wanted to know this foreigner with his stupid accent. In contrast I loved the patients who were an extraordinary mosaic of nationalities and religious sects. At one extreme there were the left wing secular Jews from nearby kibbutz Merhavia and at the other extreme the Muslim Arab villagers from Na'Ura. There were new immigrants from North Africa and Yemen and the old German and Austrian Jews who had got out in time or survived the camps. How we managed to communicate is beyond recall but having been thrown in at the deep end my Hebrew improved rapidly. Within a month or two in addition to asking my way to the central bus station and reminding everyone that "David was an old man much taken with sitting under trees", I could also ask these old men about the colour and consistency of their stools and young women on the frequency and heaviness of their periods. This was not sufficient for taking out a young nurse on a date and in any case they were all spoken for and there was nowhere to go. Every other week I had 24 hours off when I could make the tiresome journey to Tel Aviv to hang out with my *chevra*. Visiting my brother in Safed would have easier but the strict orthodoxy of his religious community made a visit on the Sabbath virtually impossible although I did get to see him from time to time on my occasional mid week half day. On my other half days I used to like exploring the area on my trusty old 1,000cc Ariel. My favourite spot was up the top of nearby Mount Tabor where I could enjoy the magnificent mosaics of the Church of the Transfiguration of Christ. I would sit eating my sandwiches in the company of basking lizards whilst enjoying the view to Nazareth in the northwest. All in all though I was very unhappy and once again thought of chucking it all in and restarting my career in London. Then something cataclysmic happened and old Doctor Goldfarb had a stroke and, although I hesitate to put it in so many words, my life changed for the better.

After a few weeks with the two Rumanians in control and wreaking havoc-at least old Goldfarb could operate safely even though it might be the wrong operation- the new chief arrived and couldn't have been more different.

His name was Shmuel, known as Sam Mishkon. Sam had just

finished his time as chief resident at the Mass General in Boston. The MGH is one of the greatest surgical centres in the world and Sam was a rough, tough, no nonsense guy who knew when and how to operate. Having become used to the long hours and exacting standards of the MGH he was not going to tolerate anything but the highest standards in his first appointment as chief of service. He had the power to hire and fire. The two Rumanians were the first to pack their bags and then there was a root and branch overhaul leaving me as first assistant with a youngish South African arrival, also an FRCS, as his second in command. So now the top three could speak English, my Hebrew was improving and the South African, Isidor Field fresh from ulpan, was also quick to learn. Izzy soon changed his name to Hebrew equivalent of Yitsak Sadeh, but always remained Izzy to me but I chose to keep mine as Martin Tanner, as the alternative of Moishe Barsochi lost something in translation. We were a formidable team and once Sam had learnt to trust me I was more or less left to carry on unsupervised knowing that I had the expertise of Sam's special interest in vascular and upper GI surgery and Izzy's expertise in trauma and orthopaedics, learnt in the most violent districts of Johannesburg, to come to my aid. Neither expressed much interest in breast cancer as the operations involved posed little challenge, so that field of surgery fell naturally into my lap and I soon set up the first specialist breast cancer centre in the country. In addition to this I did my fair share of GI surgery and acute surgical emergencies. The fast of Ramadan provided some drama for me as the cycle of fasting and feasting lead to a minor epidemic of perforated or bleeding duodenal and gastric ulcers.

The local farmers both from the Arab villages and the kibbutzim had the unfortunate habit of falling off tractors and then to be run over by whatever the tractor happened to be dragging. The wound of the blade of a plough dragged across a leg sadly left me carrying out a number of below knee amputations.

The other trauma we experienced was from the Golan Heights, where Syrian irregulars took pot shots at Israeli farmers tilling the soil at Deganya Alef.

We soon recruited some new graduates from the medical school in Haifa one of whom was from a nearby Bedouin village. His name was Ishmael Khadir and we soon became firm friends. One of seven brothers, he grew up as a shepherd but the local primary school recognised his extraordinary talents, and persuaded the family to let him go on to high school and eventually university in Haifa.

One Saturday afternoon Ishmael proudly invited me for afternoon tea at his village at K'far Misr. Unlike the Bedouin in the Negev who live nomadic lives, those in the Galil are more settled although they still like to live in their black tents whilst their livestock enjoy more fixed accommodation. I enjoyed my usual hearty Shabbat lunch and arrived on the dot of 4.00 pm for afternoon tea with the Khadirs. Here I had badly miscalculated. Afternoon tea in a Bedouin encampment is not quite the same as afternoon tea in Tunbridge Wells. We did indeed enjoy the ritual of sweet black tea in tiny little porcelain cups pored from elaborate long spouted vessels but after these initial pleasantries I was confronted by the feast they had prepared for the English gentleman. They had sacrificed and roasted a goat and the whole beast including its glassy eyes confronted me on a bed of fragrant rice. Sitting nervously in the wings, watching through gaps in hand woven curtains, the womenfolk looked on and waited for my approval. I put on a show of delight and was urged to take the first portion. The sliver of flesh I cut from the flank was a source of much merriment so Ishmael's father pulled off a hind leg and urged me to eat using hand signals. A pint of cold lager might have helped but that was of course out of the question so I put on a good show much to Ishmael's amusement. At least I was spared the eyeballs. On my way home I threw up all the way round Mount Tabor.

Eventually I settled down into the routines of my new life. The work was exciting and fulfilling. Sam and Izzy's families treated me like an exotic cousin and I was never alone on a Friday night. I made friends with the younger generations in kibbutz Merhavia, where contrary to popular myth the womenfolk were far from promiscuous and I enjoyed hiking and even camel riding with my new Bedouin friends. I even learnt a smattering of Arabic.

I was content but lonely as all I could look forward to on returning to my hut at night was the company of George and Gloria my gecko friends.

The highlight of 1961-1962 was when *Kupat Cholim,* at the recommendation of Sam Mishkon, seconded me to the Scottish Mission hospital in Nazareth to make up for the shortfall in surgical staff as their chief of surgery took early retirement. I loved it there. I loved the warm embrace of the cloistered life and the Scottish discipline and training of their nursing sisters. I was treated with respect that might have been appropriate to a consultant surgeon in Edinburgh in stark contrast to the socialist commune I lived at in Afula. The food was wonderful in comparison and included the full Scottish breakfast complete with oatmeal and kippers. I also loved listening in to the plainchant of the sisters at vespers. It mustn't be forgotten that in the 1960s, Nazareth was primarily a Christian Arab town. I even attended midnight mass at the Basilica of the Annunciation on Christmas Eve.

The outpatient clinics were packed with Arab men and women in traditional garb. The husbands gave the medical histories on behalf of their demure and heavily veiled wives whilst the nursing sisters in their starched white wimples and long black habit acted as both chaperones and interpreters. How all these overdressed women kept cool in the summer, was a mystery I never solved.

The Arab women had prodigiously large families and as there was much consanguineous cousin-to-cousin marriage I witnessed my fair share of congenital abnormalities. For example I was woken one night by the duty sister in the maternity ward in order to examine a newly born baby boy with a blue pulsating swelling in the mid line just above the buttocks. Although I'd never seen this before I recognised it immediately from my memory of an illustration in Hamilton Bailey's "physical signs". This was a spina bifida, and what I was looking at was a myelomeningocele. If I didn't act quickly then the baby would either die with meningitis or become paraplegic. I had never witnessed an operation to deal with this problem nor was there a paediatric surgical unit within easy reach. I therefore took myself off to the library and reached for the volume describing surgical techniques for neonates. Although the bony deficit in the spinal column couldn't be prepared, the mobilisation of the membranes and overlying skin in order to achieve some sort of coverage of the delicate neural networks beneath, was not that technically difficult for someone with a steady hand, in a good light and with a decent first assistant. All of that was available and the operation went very well. The baby was christened *Machmoud* in my honour and I was left praying that he would one day learn to walk and not develop the associated congenital abnormality of hydrocephalus.

I also saw a lot of breast cancer in Nazareth. The Arab women out of a sense of false modesty, hid their tumours until they where ulcerated, oozing blood and pus and stinking to high heaven. In addition the affliction was quite common amongst the nuns because of their heavenly vows of chastity meant that they remained childless. This association had been noted in a convent in the early 18thC in France and must be counted as the very first piece in the complicated jigsaw of factors that predisposed to the disease.

I therefore took advantage of this natural experiment and continued to record my findings on the different patterns of disease amongst the different racial and ethnic groups I had the good fortune to observe. Over a period of two to three years I was able to publish a few papers on the subject in peer reviewed journals that could be summarized as follows. Having no children by the age of 40 whether or not you were a nun increased the risk of breast cancer but paradoxically reduced the risk of cancer of the cervix. Arab women developed breast cancer at a younger age than most Jewish women and it appeared to be of a more aggressive type. The exception to this was seen amongst the Ashkenazi and the Mizrachi Jewish women from Iraq and Iran who had the bad family history that reminded me of my mother's family. They also developed it at an early age, say 30 to 40 and it also seemed to run a rapid course.

However my oddest observation was one of negative association in that I hardly ever saw a Sephardic Jewess with breast cancer repeating my experience in my early quest amongst the Sephardim in London.

My first three publications on this topic came to the attention of Professor Gadi Rosenthal, the legendary Professor of Epidemiology at the Haifa Technion and I was very flattered when I received an invitation to visit his department to discuss some collaborative research. My next half day off I made the journey to Mount Carmel and joined with him on the terrace of his department at the University that enjoyed the spectacular view across the Baha'i temple and its cascading gardens that drew my eye vertiginously down to the harbour and then northward around the bay until I could just make out the Crusader city of Acre in the heat haze. We got on famously and he had the grace to compliment me on my work and enthuse me to carry on. I will return to this collaboration and the way it shaped my life later in this story.

After two years living in Israel I elected to take out citizenship having negotiated a deal with the authorities, largely thanks to the intervention of my chief of surgery, that I could avoid conscription for two and a half years National Service in the IDF because of my age and my experience in the RAMC. Instead, like all those under the age of 40 who had already served, I would be called up for one month each year to assist in a military hospital or a combat unit in the case of hostilities. What I would never have predicted was that my first tour of duty would be under the command of General (retired) Yigal Yadin in the winter of 1963.

Chapter 17

From Safed to Masada 1962-63

Chanukah 1962 was bright and sunny with just a hint of a chill from the light winds blowing off Mount Hermon in the far north east of the Galil. This was a delightful alternative to the *khamsin* I faced on my first journey to the north of Israel. From Afula I turned my motorbike due north to Nazareth and then northeast to the hills of the northern Galil in the direction of the mystical city of Safed. The road was tortuous and I lost my way a few times but it was worth the journey because my brother Joe was to be married to Tziporah Ferteleman and I was to be the best man. Safed is the highest city in Israel at an elevation of nearly 3,000 feet. As a result my extremities were turning blue as I eventually entered Safed, one of the holiest cities in the eastern Mediterranean. Now by and large I don't have much time for "holy cities". To me bricks and mortar cannot be 'blessed' and if they are that's usually a cause for bloodshed and mayhem. For every clan who sees their city as holy others will see the city as cursed. Then the two groups will battle it out until the holy streets run with holy blood until there's no longer a bloody holy stone left standing. Safed is different. Safed wears its holiness lightly and is more mystical and "new age" than filled with biblical bombast. My first view of the narrow cobble stoned lanes and tumbledown ancient houses and places of worship wreathed in the mist of a cold evening at 3,000 feet brought me out in goose pimples. Many of the little houses bore *yadaim eyin hora*, elaborate filigree hand shaped artifacts inset with blue stone eyes to ward off the "evil eye". When I came to ask the bustling black gabardine-clad Chasidic Jewish men passing by, directions to my brother's lodgings, they would not meet my eye in case I was the one who bore them an evil grudge. Eventually I found his address one floor above an artist's studio that paradoxically advertised the work of the resident with canvases of scantily clad slant eyed svelte young women of the inviting type.

I climbed up a narrow flight of stone steps that wound their way round the back of the studio until I was confronted with a crooked ancient wooden door painted cobalt blue. Above the door hung a lantern of brilliant stained glass. I banged on the door and at once the lamp was switched on and the multi-colored light was reflected back in the haze of the thickening mist. At once the door was pulled back and Joe and I threw ourselves into each other's arms. His lodgings were humble consisting of only two rooms divided by a narrow passage. One room was for sleeping and the other through a complex system of long curtains looped over poles served all other functions. The passage was virtually impassable because of the mountain of scholarly books. I was to sleep there until the morrow, the day of his marriage and then move to sleep in the yeshiva for the weeklong celebrations of the *sheva brochot,* a party each night of the following week hosted by friends and family of the bride.

First off we had a *l'chaim* toasting each other in fine wine from a nearby boutique winery. After that we settled down to catch up on gossip and plans for the week until it was time for him to join his commune for the afternoon and evening prayers of *minchah/maariv.* I was excused as the heretic of the family. Before that I learnt that we were to celebrate the wedding in the ancient Abuhav synagogue the following afternoon and because they were expecting about 700 guests and only a handful could witness the *chupah* if it was conducted indoors, the ceremony would take place in the courtyard with the doors of the synagogue left wide open. The reception afterwards would be in the home of Reb Fertleman and once the seven days of sanctioned music, dancing, story telling and feasting were over, Joe and Tziporah would start their lives together as the Rabbi and *rebbetzen* of the little synagogue in nearby Rosh Pinah with fine views over the Sea of Galilee.

Whilst Joe went off to pray I thought it wise to prepare for the event by visiting the Abuhav Synagogue. I had my guidebook with

151

me and learnt that this ancient house of prayer was famous for its symbolic paintings on its domed ceiling. The disciples of the Sephardic sage Yitzchak Abuhav who lived in 15thC Spain until the expulsion of all the Jews in 1492, had founded the Synagogue. The *Sefer Torah* Abuhav that had been rescued from the flames of the Spanish inquisition was said to radiate spiritual energy that protected the Synagogue and all those within its walls and allowed the old building to survive the earthquakes of 1837 and 1960 undamaged. In addition, this spiritual energy was also endowed with the capacity of enhancing the fertility of any bridal couple within range.

I found my way to the ancient Synagogue without much difficulty as it held pride of place in the neighboring little lopsided square. The lights were on inside brilliantly illuminating the courtyard where otherwise everything was bible black and seen as if through a muslin veil because of the swirling mist.

I stepped inside the building and was immediately taken by its beauty.

The domed ceiling was raised on four pillars forming a perfectly proportioned square below which was the *bimah* or platform for the celebrants and the reading of the Torah. The *bimah* was made of elaborate fret-worked wood painted in the ubiquitous cobalt blue that I later learnt was also protection from the evil eye. Tilting my head upwards I noted the white dome covered with Hebrew calligraphy, mystical symbols, birds, flowers and ferns. It looked as if it had been painted yesterday. Turning my head towards the eastern wall I noted the elaborately carved and brilliantly colored doors of the ark. Above this was an inverted pyramid of azure blue stained glass inlaid with ruby tinted crystals through which the eternal flame radiated picking up the colors of the glass and projecting them on the white walls beyond. Just to the right of the ark was a man high silver menorah bearing three white Chanukah candles that looked as if they had just been lit. At that point I noticed a young man washing his brushes against the wall opposite the entrance. As I walked towards him he looked up and gave me a wide smile. He was dressed in a long paint stained smock below which he wore baggy white trousers. He had a short wispy beard and matching side locks. A tight fitting crocheted skullcap covered his head and yet he had the face of a young man no more than in his early twenties. His nose was hawk like but beautiful sparkling dark brown eyes redeemed his face. In Hebrew I asked what he was doing there and to my surprise he answered in perfect English. He introduced himself as Yehoshua BenYosef and explained that, because his father came from England he was brought up bilingual and recognized my English accent. He then went on to tell me that he was a scribe and an artist and had just finished work repainting the dome that had been damaged by an earthquake not long ago. So much for the spiritual protection of the *Sefer Abuhav* I thought to myself and so much for the accuracy of my guidebook. I thanked him for completing the work in time for tomorrow's wedding and explained that I was the best man and that he probably knew my brother Reb Joseph Tanner. He gave me a quizzical looked as if I'd said something in bad taste and excused himself before clearing his materials and disappearing into the mist and darkness.

That evening I recounted my story to my brother after he returned to start his prenuptial fast. He expressed surprise as he had heard no mention of damage in the 1960 earthquake but we both had more pressing matters to attend to so never returned to the subject of that brief encounter.

Whilst I ate a light supper and prepared my notes for my speech as best man, Joe spent the evening and most of the night with his head buried in an elaborately leather bound prayer book, one of many presented as a wedding gift from his father-in-law to be.

The wedding day dawned with a crystalline cobalt blue sky, the kind of light that can only be experienced at these altitudes and in unpolluted air. In such a light the evil eye stood little chance. I dressed in my best white shirt open at the neck with my best (only) cream linen suit. Joe looked magnificent with neatly barbered beard and shining eyes that reflecting his joy and spiritual zeal. His head was covered with a wide brimmed black fedora hat and his long black satin coat covered with an embroidered white *kittel*.

As we took the short walk to the Abuhav synagogue we were

soon lost in a sea of jubilant black clad Chassidic Jews. Most fundamentalist religious groups seem to believe that having fun of any kind is a sin. At an extreme the "Shaker" community in upstate New York died out because they couldn't even tolerate the fact that the joy of sex might also be fun! At lesser extremes Islamic fundamentalists abhor music, poetry and the sight of a woman's eyes.

Most ultra-orthodox Jews are a pretty dour lot but encourage the dictum "be fruitful and multiply" but as the old joke says "..as long as it doesn't lead to mixed dancing". They also like to get a little tipsy on *Simchat Torah* at the end of *Succot*.

This lot seemed a happy clappy breed and expressed their joy at the marriage of the daughter of their beloved Rebbe and a brilliant young scholar and ordained rabbi, by dancing in the streets whilst covertly taking sips of schnapps from little flasks hidden in the deep pockets of their black gabardine.

The beautiful hand woven multi-colored canopy of the *chupah* was held aloft on four elaborately turned mahogany poles by four of Joe's closest friends and a deep throated ahhhhh, was heard from the men as the bride emerged on the arm of Reb Fertlemen. Tziporah's white crinoline dress accentuated her wasp waist but I couldn't see her face as she was heavily veiled. In the background the womenfolk ululated like frenetic turkeys and then complete silence fell as the service began.

The chazzan sang in a well-tuned tenor voice with many decorative rococo elaborations on the well-known melodies. As he was half way through the last of the seven blessings the whole congregation joined in and sang these beautiful words, as tears of joy blinded our eyes:

> *"Soon O Lord our God, may there be heard in the cities of Judah,*
> *and in the streets of Jerusalem, the voice of joy and gladness, the*
> *voice of the bridegroom and the voice of the bride, the jubilant voices*
> *of bridegrooms from their canopies, and of youths from their feasts*
> *of song. Blessed art thou O Lord, who makes the bridegroom to*
> *rejoice with the bride"*

As the last echo died away the bride's veil was lifted and sips of wine offered to bride and groom. At this point we all shared the radiant beauty of the bride as she solemnly made seven circuits around the groom. The marriage contract was read out and vows and rings were exchanged.

Joe was then handed a small glass beaker wrapped in velvet that he delicately crushed beneath his right foot. As the glass cracked a mighty cry of "*mazeltov!*" went out from seven hundred throats that that brought the crows out with righteous indignation from their roosts in the nearby treetops and then everything went wild.

A fiddler suddenly appeared on a nearby rooftop. This was not the least bit hazardous as the rooftop was merely four feet above the level of the square because of the steep decline of the crooked streets built into the contours of the mountaintops. Having struck up a chord by way of introduction he was immediately joined by a whole Klezmer band that included clarinets, piano accordion, trumpets and a double basesThe crowd clapped and stamped to the rhythm of the band and the band responded by playing louder. Bride and groom were hoisted shoulder high on chairs and Tziporah's cries of fear harmonized perfectly with the fiddlers tune. Bride and groom made contact with each other by clutching the diagonal corners of a long silk scarf and were soon out of sight in the centre of concentric circles of black clad Chassidim dancing the *hora* arms on neighbors' shoulders one circle clockwise and the next counter-clockwise. The frenzy grew faster and faster until the circles broke and the Klezmer band leapt from the roof and lead the bride and groom still carried shoulder high, down the steep cobbled streets followed by an amorphous black cloud of bearded men looking like bats chasing flying insects.

I looked on in amazement and abandoned any thoughts of the conventional bad taste best man toast to the happy couple. I borrowed a flask of schnapps took a slug or two joined the throng to go with the flow.

The celebrations went on day and night for the best part of a week until the end of Chanukah and beyond and my return to hospital duties was an anticlimax that reminded me of my chronic state of loneliness in my shack with only the two green geckos for company.

★★★

My period of self pity was cut short on the second of January 1963 when I was summoned to the chief of service's office where, with a wry smile, he handed my a buff colored letter with the stamp of the Israel Defense Forces (IDF) prominent on the top left hand corner.

The envelope contained my "call up papers" for my annual month of service in the IDF. In the previous year I had served as medical officer to a tank battalion based in the Negev desert close to the Egyptian border. The work was boring and the heat at times intolerable. Most of the time I was dealing with thrombosed hemorrhoids and in growing toenails or for a bit of excitement the foot of a gun loader traumatized by dropping a shell case on his sandaled foot, boots with reinforced toe caps being too hot and sweaty for the climate. My first reaction was to groan but on further study of my orders my eyes lit up as I was to serve under the command of the legendary General (retired) Professor Yigal Yadin.

Yadin joined the Haganah, the nascent Israeli army at the age of 15, and served there in a variety of different capacities until 1946, when he went to study archaeology at the Hebrew University. In 1947, shortly before the State of Israel declared its independence, he was called back to active service by David Ben-Gurion. He was appointed Head of Operations during Israel's War of Independence, and was responsible for many of the key strategic decisions made during the course of that war. Yadin was appointed Chief of Staff of the IDF on 9 November 1949, and served in that capacity for three years. By the age thirty-five, he had completed his military career and devoted himself to research and began his life's work in archaeology. In 1956 he received Israel Prize for his doctoral thesis on the translation of the Dead Sea Scrolls. As an archaeologist, he excavated some of the most important sites in the region, including the Qumran Caves and Tel Megiddo. Now he was granted permission to achieve his life long ambition of excavating Masada, the mountain stronghold of King Herod the Great and the last bastion of Jewish resistance to the Roman legions after the fall of the second temple in 70 CE. This was a very ambitious project as the archeological site lay 1,000 feet above the level of the Dead Sea, the lowest point on earth in one of the hottest and most inhospitable parts of the world. The project demanded huge manpower but Yadin genius was shown in persuading the Observer newspaper in London to promote this as a great adventure for young men and women all round the world the opportunity to dig where no man had dug for 2,000 years, to help uncover relics, scrolls and precious artifacts dating back to Ancient Rome, with all board and lodgings paid for provided they came at their own cost. In other words he recruited an army of workers who gave their time free. In addition to the volunteers there would be professional archeologists to guide them and a work force of paid Arab labourers to carry out the heavy and dangerous work of lifting huge granite stones from the collapsed defensive walls of the plateau and the remains of King Herod's palace and redoubt.

The free board and lodgings consisted of a tent city and army rations served from a mobile kitchen. Such a throng of people working under dangerous conditions with the intense heat of midday and the intense cold of the winter desert at night demanded a complete military field hospital and I had been seconded to establish and command this facility for the first three months of the operation. For this posting I learnt that I had to thank Sam Mishkon, who had exaggerated my skills and experience along the route of *protectia* via his uncle who was a close political ally of the President who was a close friend of the Professor of Archaeology at the Hebrew University, Yigal Yadin. I could not believe my luck. Although Yadin had no military authority and was acting as director of the archaeological expedition, the IDF commanded by Major Yehudah Ben Tzion, who was in charge of security and my immediate superior. My instructions were to present myself on the 27th January at a military depot in Arad to make our way via a desert track by command car to the camp on the west side of Masada. I knew better of course and couldn't resist the opportunity of taking the scenic route on my Ariel via Beersheba and down the famous winding road to the deepest point on earth at Sodom and then to turn northward towards the eastern side of the great rock. I wrote to my CO asking for permission and surprisingly he replied in Yiddish, " *gai guzenterheit*", literally meaning go in good health but translated into modern English idiom, "best of luck chum".

Once again I packed my pannier bags but this time with the foresight to take clothes for all extremes of weather and set out south west to the coastal road full of excitement at my new adventure. I left at first light expecting an arduous ride that would last until dusk. The road from south from Tel Megiddo to Tel Aviv and the south east to Beersheba was simple to follow and uneventful but my adventure truly began as I entered the barren landscape east of Beersheba making my way to the edge of the great Rift Valley in search of the narrow switch back road leading down to the Dead Sea. The road signs were simple to follow and there was almost no traffic. Along the way I saw many encampments of black tents of the Bedouin and their camels with beautiful long eyelashes belying their temperamental nature.

The first two tight turns on the decline to the Dead Sea were anticlimactic and then suddenly the dramatic landscape opened up in all its savage beauty and I was struck with a sense of déjà vu. I stopped the bike and wiped my forehead, took a swig of water from my canister and pondered. Suddenly it flashed into my consciousness – this was the landscape of the background to William Holman Hunt's painting of the Scapegoat. I remounted feeling rather pleased with myself and continued slowly down the switchback tarmac taking my time to enjoy the remarkable colors of the geological strata exposed by some great cataclysmic event on the third day of creation. Reds and browns I expected but the greens and blues were a bonus. Every so often I'd catch a glimpse of the Dead Sea reflecting diamond chips in a setting of lapis lazuli.

I was so transfixed by this otherworldly beauty that I lost track of time and it was almost dusk when I reached Sodom at 1,300 feet below sea level.

I speeded up as I turned north on the road running along the West Bank of the sea, past the salt pans and desalination plants deserted at this time of day.

An eerie deep purple twilight descended as I wheeled up to the vertical wall of the easily recognizable facade of Masada. Only then did it suddenly dawn on me that the CO's *"gai gezunterheit"* was deeply ironical for I had arrived at the wrong side of Masada and in the gathering darkness there was no possible way for getting to the western side where the camp had been erected, short of risking certain death by trying to climb up and over or risking life, limb and precious motorbike by trying to make it round the wadis at either the northern or southern tip of the ship shaped giant rock. By the time I'd realized my dilemma there was only just enough light to find a shallow cave at the foot of Masada where my bike and my person could snuggle down together with me putting on all the layers of clothes I'd brought and the bike's cooling cylinders holding off the chill of the desert night for an hour or two.

I enjoyed a frugal supper of chocolate bars and cheesy biscuits before settling down for a near sleepless night with the images of mountain lions and snakes haunting my dreams. At first light the next day I lifted my aching body in order to start planning my way to the other side of the mountain. As I stretched and yawned I was greeted by the most beautiful sunrise I had ever experienced as the sun edged its way over the lips of the mountains of Moab on the far eastern shores of the Dead Sea.

I turned to face the wall of the cave in order to empty my bladder when suddenly out of nowhere a voice screamed at me in Hebrew to raise my hands above my head and not to move. I wet my legs in terror but was soon reassured when on turning to see my captor I noted the khaki fatigues of two young soldiers of the IDF making their morning patrol around the perimeter of Masada. They almost wet themselves with laughter on learning of my plight and set out to rescue me. My trusty Ariel was to be hidden in the cave and winched up to safety later in the day whilst I was to be escorted on foot around the perimeter of the east and northern faces of the great rock across the wadis and the remains of the Roman siege wall, to the encampment on the western side close to the remains of General Silva's camp. On arrival at group HQ I was greeted with much mirth by Major Ben Tzion and staff before being kitted out from the quartermaster's store and shown to my tent and a welcome shower.

I was to share my tent with one of the professional archaeologists but before settling down it was agreed that my motorbike should be rescued along with all my worldly belongings. My two captors escorted me up the Roman siege ramp and across the plateau at the summit to the eastern lip of King Herod's desert fortress. Whilst I had been checking in, word had gone out to the labourers at the top to set up a winch on an overhanging wooden boom strong enough to bear the weight of a one-litre British motorbike. The view from there across the saltpans of the Dead Sea to the mountains of Moab was even more spectacular than seen at Dead Sea level. The two young IDF soldiers abseiled down the vertical face of the mountain to the approximate position of my arrest a few hours later. They found my cave as identified by the wrappers of my chocolate bars but they failed to find my bike. I was devastated and heartbroken. It was as if my child had been kidnapped but I was reassured that it would find a good home after it had been sold by the Bedouin bandit boys in the souk of east Jerusalem. Once again nemesis had followed fleet footed after my moment of hubris.

I returned utterly despondent to my tent and sorted out my army issue equipment, from now on I was dependent on the charity of the IDF until the end of my mission. Having changed into fresh oversized army camouflage fatigues I was taken to visit the large marquee that was to house the field hospital and for the first time meet my staff. I was advised in advance that they would include a first assistant third year medical student from Haifa on a monthly rotation and a senior and junior nurse seconded from the Rambam hospital in Haifa who would be with me for the duration of my tour of duty.

As I entered the marquee that was close to the northern end at the foot of Masada I saw three bent figures emptying boxes of equipment and sorting out medical dressings and equipment on long trestle tables. They all looked the same from the rear in shapeless army issue uniforms although I was quick to deduce that one was of the male persuasion whilst the other two backsides were clearly of the female of the species. The male backside was the first to turn and he reacted to my presence with undisguised surprise and delight. He charged over and gave me a manly embrace and shouted over his shoulder to the startled young nurses, "Come meet Captain Martin Tanner the man who saved my leg in Suez!"

I could barely believe my eyes for the man embracing me in this rather un-British way was none other than Jamal Atrash whose common femoral artery I'd repaired 4 years earlier. We gabbled away at each other in delight. He was now fulfilling his ambition to train as a doctor and was in his 3rd year as a medical student at the Haifa Technion, the first of his tribe to go to university. I filled him in on how I came to be there and he fell about laughing at what I thought was the tragic tale of the loss of my one-litre twin stroke Ariel motorbike. During this time the two young women looked on wide-eyed and curious. Jamal apologized and quickly introduced me to the nurses who would be under my command, the senior nurse Sara Zinati and the student nurse Rachel Zidan. All three were from the same village, Piki'in near the Lebanese border and I mistakenly assumed they were all of the Druze faith. Rachel, a petite black-eyed girl was his fiancé. Sara was tall and slender with green eyes. However I paid little attention to them in my delight in meeting up with my grateful patient.

I started helping them unload the crates of equipment but within half an hour I was consumed with fatigue, excused myself, returned to my tent and without even changing crashed out on my camp bed and slept for 12 dreamless hours. I awoke at first light enjoyed a leisurely wet shave in the men's shower cubicles and was first in line at the mess for a surprisingly good breakfast of strong coffee, herrings, olives and cottage cheese. As we only had 48 hours to get everything ready before the first Lorry loads of 300 Northern European volunteers were to arrive, I took myself off to the field hospital to supervise preparations. When I arrived and barged through the tent flap I literally bumped into Nurse Zinati. As I apologized she flashed me a broad smile and invited me to join her with a thimble-sized cup of bitter Turkish coffee. She seemed an amiable young woman so I grabbed a canvas-folding chair and took one for her and indicated that there was time for a chat so that we could get to know each other. Sara was a little taller than me and her outline somewhat hidden by her shapeless army fatigues was slender without being skinny. She held herself very upright and proud and she had an open face. By that I mean she made eye contact that welcomed you into her life without being coquettish in any way. Her eyes carried that spark of intelligence and enquiry that can make the plainest of faces of both men and women very attractive. But she was most certainly not plain and I wondered why I hadn't noticed this the evening before. Maybe it was because at our first meeting her head was covered with some elaborate turban. Today her luxurious strawberry colored hair was uncovered and worn in a curious way with one long plait wound around her head like a coronet. Yet the most remarkable thing about her was her slightly slanted green eyes that gave her an almost oriental appearance. So green were her eyes it was almost as if they were transilluminated. In the presence of such beauty I would normally over-react with bluster and boldness and an irresistible temptation to flirt. Yet I felt different about Sara, she was clearly at ease in my company and I was comfortable and relaxed with her from the start. It was not so much as if I'd known her already for a long time it was more like the comfort I felt in the company of my cousins. We had little time to get to know each other before Jamal and Rachel joined us and we all set to work.

Chapter 18

Sara Zinati

The next few days were frenetic as 300 young men and women decanted from lorries and command cars after a very bumpy ride across the desert from Arad. They were mostly Northern Europeans from Germany, the Nordic countries and the UK. They took a day or two to settle in and many arrived with minor ailments, cuts and bruises and diarrhea picked up on their sometimes exotic journeys to get to Masada. By and large they were an attractive bunch of fit young undergraduates and adventurers travelling the world before settling down to some predictable middle class way of life.

Our clinics in the field hospital were kept busy for 48 hours and then everyone fell into a routine. The volunteers were organized into teams of four and a student from the archaeological department of the Hebrew University supervised groups of five teams. Lecturers and senior lecturers in turn supervised these with professor Yadin ultimately in charge. For their medical support the four of us organized ourselves into shifts taking it in turns to be on call at night time but with arrangements using the military wireless communication to keep in touch most of the time. It seemed natural for Jamal and Rachel to work together and for Sara and I to share the shifts in rotation. During daylight hours when not on duty we helped out the volunteers on the plateau above.

We were directed to complete a group of four if any were short in numbers.

As a result we often ended up working on the eastern lip of the plateau where they were clearing out the debris from between the curtain walls of King Herod's fortress that had been partitioned off as dwelling spaces for the Zealots during the years 70-73 CE. Before joining the expedition Professor Yadin had advised us to read Josephus' account of the "Jewish Wars" that were considered accurate enough to guide us in our search for the details of the life and death of the Jewish fanatics holding out to the last against the Roman legions that conquered the ancient land of Israel. All along the defensive rim of Masada the twin walls had collapsed in on themselves either by the weight of time or the effort of the Xth legion. The hired laborers would winch out the largest building blocks and leave the volunteers to clear and search through the rubble until reaching the ground level of the makeshift living quarters. This was hard work but a lot of fun and excitement. One of each team would fill leather buckets with debris using a primitive trenching shovel. Two of the team would stand upright holding a large flat bed sieve the size of an infant's bed with handles at each corner. The fourth member of the team would tip buckets full of debris on top of the sieve, which would then be shaken vigorously allowing the sand and other small particulate matter to fall through leaving pebbles and "finds" on the tray. The residue would be carefully searched by the bucket carrier for clay potshards, metal objects or pieces of glass. Then the residue was casually tipped over the side of the great rock to a gathering mound 1,000 feet below. Most of our "finds" were shards of terracotta tableware of plain design all too common to create much excitement. Occasionally the sun would catch the brilliant patina of fragments of Roman glass. I even uncovered a near perfect perfume bottle with a long narrow neck glistening like a kaleidoscope. How it survived intact for 2,000 years was a miracle to me. However the really exciting "finds" of both historical and illegal commercial value, were few and far between and these of course were ancient coinage, jewellery and most precious of all, parchment scrolls. Sara and I were at hand in the discovery of coins and parchment in the second month of our tour of duty but I will return to that later.

Night would fall suddenly at about 5.00pm when the penetrating chill of the desert winter darkness would replace the high temperatures that could reach 28 to 30 degrees Celsius, at midday. At 4.30pm we would complete our labors and scramble down the remains of the Roman siege ramp on the western side of Masada and line up for a hot shower followed by a communal and very jovial evening meal in the mess. Following that the group would split up, most to read by the light of a lantern in their tent or take an early night's sleep. Once or twice a week the mess tent was turned into a lecture theatre when one of the professional archaeologists would talk about the famous digs in the holy land illustrated by lanternslides. The highlights I remember best of all were Professor Yadin's talks on the excavations at Qumran and the remarkable artifacts discovered in the Bar Kochbah caves further north along the great Rift Valley.

Most evenings after dinner the four of us making up the medical team retired to the field hospital tent for Turkish coffee and a chat by the light of the operating theatre lamps. These were cozy gatherings where we would swap tales about our adventures in the world of medicine. Towards the end of the second week, Jamal and Rachel took their leave early from our foursome leaving Sara and me alone for the first time. There was not awkwardness in this and Sara offered me a second cup of the thick dark black coffee flavored with herbs, a secret recipe of hers. As we sat chatting in the penumbra of the operating room light I noticed two things about her. Firstly that she had an exceptional beauty that only became apparent with greater familiarity secondly she wore no rings on her fingers. I restarted the conversation by inviting her to tell me about herself. It turned out that she was 24 years old and was indeed Jewish and not Druze as I originally assumed. The Jews and the Druze had lived in happy symbiosis in her village for hundreds of years. The Zinati line claimed a continuous 2,000-year history dating back to the fall of the second temple and that was why she was so keen to join the expedition. In defence of this claim of such an ancient lineage the walls of their little synagogue carried two plaques that had been rescued during the razing of the temple and carried north by founders of her bloodline. She then invited me to visit her family in Piki'in after completion of our tour of duty. Somewhat emboldened by this invitation I went on to ask, "Sara, forgive me if you think this is a *chutzpah* but how is it that someone so beautiful and intelligent as you carries neither wedding or engagement rings on your fingers?" It was difficult in that light to judge whether she blushed or not but at least she answered after flashing one of her incandescent smiles. "I shall take that impertinent question as a compliment Dr. Tanner and I shall answer it truthfully without any mock modesty. Indeed I have had many suitors in the past. Some I seem to frighten off because they find me too clever and unwilling to play the role as the modest young maiden that is expected in these parts and others have been frightened off when they learn of my family's curse". "What curse can that be, surely an intelligent young women like you can't believe in silly superstitions?", I responded with incredulity.

She turned her head away from me and replied choking back tears, "Martin, this is no superstition, my mother, grandmother, one maternal aunt and every other female member of the extended kindred on my mother's side have died of breast cancer before the age of 40". At which point she broke down in tears and I instinctively wrapped my arm around her to give her a hug of comfort. She accepted my embrace and rested her head on my right shoulder and we sat this way in companionable silence for a few minutes after which I gently disengaged and spoke. "Sara my dear, if your family is cursed then my family shares your curse and we have more in common than I had expected".

I then went on to recount my own sad family history of the dreaded disease and to record the fact that we had both lost our mothers within a year or two of each other. She then surprised me by providing a remarkable insight that was to shape the rest of our two lives. Turning to me with her green eyes reflecting back the theatre light she spoke the following and I will always remember her words verbatim. " Martin, when I was at nursing college and we were studying human genetics and we learnt about Mendelian inheritance, I deduced that our family carried a dominant gene that caused breast cancer at a young age. Your family appears to carry a similar gene. Might we have relatives in common?" To which I replied, " I suspect you are right about our family's predisposition and your story reinforces my own beliefs" at which point I recounted my research in London and my recent work with the team in Haifa; " However it is highly unlikely that we have relatives in common as you claim to trace your family back 2,000 years to this part of the world whereas my mother's distant relatives originated somewhere in southern India." "Well all of us Jews claim common descent from a ancient desert tribe lead by Moses out of the land of Egypt 3,500 years ago." she replied with a twinkly smile; at which point I understood two things, firstly why she frightened off young suitors and secondly that I wanted her to live with me for the rest of time. I put these thoughts on one side for the moment as I was enjoying the dialogue so much and responded by saying, "surely you are not suggesting that such a mutation can have been carried on a maternal germ cell line for more than 2,000 years! If these mutations are so deadly as to kill off women in the prime as mothers or caring grandmothers, then the mutation would have died out after a few generations." "Not if there is a compensatory evolutionary advantage amongst those who carry the gene" she replied in a flash. This stopped me in my tracks. After a few minutes silent cogitation I sat up straight and said quietly, "you could well be right and I would like to think more about this and continue our discussion tomorrow, but one more question before we turn in." And what would that be Captain Tanner?" she replied with the first hint of a coquettish smile. "May I kiss you good night?"

"Not until you shave off that silly beard and I can judge what you really look like". With alacrity spurred on by desire, I searched out a shaving set normally used for removing pubic hair before operating on the lower abdomen from the sterile packs in our store room and did the best I could in the inadequate light using the stainless steel cover of the autoclave sterilizing unit as a mirror. I turned to face her unsure how she might react. She gave me one of her smiles that melted my heart and curling the index finger of her right hand beckoned me over.

We kissed warmly and she stroked my cheek as she pushed me away and as I returned to my camp bed in the dark starlit night I considered myself the happiest and luckiest man on earth.

Our courtship was sweet and gentle as we bonded through our

work as doctor and nurse and at other times amateur archaeologists or amateur epidemiologists. Each Saturday was a day of rest and recreation for the encampment and on the last Saturday of our second month together we decided to hike to Ein Geddi 20 kilometres north of Masada. We left at dawn and first climbed up the ramp on the west side of Masada and then crossed the plateau to the secret entry point of the tortuous and dangerous snake path that led down to the shore of the Dead Sea on the east. From there we turned northward and followed the edge of the escarpment until we reached the fissure in the sheer rock face to our west that lead into the delightful cool and shaded oasis of Wadi Ein Gedi. We then followed a winding track through lush foliage past deep caves on each side until we heard the tinkling waters of the cataract feeding the first pool. We climbed up the narrow track alongside the waterfall until we reached the second pool were out of sight of all comers we stripped naked and bathed and splashed under the torrent of the second cataract of Wadi Ein Gedi. The water feeding this hidden oasis emerged from an underground river falling via three further cascades higher up and the water was pleasantly warm heated by the midday sun. Lying in each other's arms I asked Sara to be my wife. She looked at me solemnly with tears in her eyes and replied, " Yes my dearest but with this condition, we can never have children as our marriage carries with it the terrible risk of the union of two cursed families and God alone knows what might become of the mingling of our genetic pools." I nodded in meek acceptance of this condition and we held each other tightly and wept with a mixture of joy and sadness.

Suddenly something at the edge of my field of vision captured my attention and looking upwards I saw the silhouette of a mountain Ibex looking down at us from the lip of the cataract about 20 metres above our heads. At that moment as a cloud passed across the face of the sun that had just past its zenith and was now shining its brilliant light from the west, at that instant the Ibex was suddenly lit up by pure golden light. The beast nodded at us as if he was a witness to our vows and skittered silently away apparently walking along a bare rock face with no visible foothold.

We took this to be a good omen and having dried and dressed ourselves we hurried back to the camp hitching a lift on a passing supply lorry returning to the camp with a band of volunteers who had been exploring caves higher up the Dead Sea valley. We arrived back in the camp just before darkness fell and later shared our news and our secret with Jamal and Rachel over a celebratory cup of Turkish coffee laced with cognac.

★★★

The following Sunday morning heralded the usual busy clinic after the Saturday off that involved most of the young and fit volunteers to set off on hikes exploring the nearby Wadis or climbing the more challenging cliff faces. This inevitably lead to a queue of shamefaced young men and women at the field hospital with minor cuts and bruises that needed dressing or the odd suture. There were also those sprained ankles that needed strapping up and decisions about who needed relocating to some sedentary occupation like cataloguing finds instead of climbing up to the plateau to dig for treasure. Finally there were the less adventurous who spent the day at the "sea side". This often entailed floating on their backs in the Dead Sea, reading paperback books. Many of them were white skinned Northern Europeans who were in no way prepared for the fierce unfiltered sunlight of the region. Their blistered and peeling noses were comical but their pain was genuine and needed salves and analgesics. Once the clinic was over, leaving Jamal and Rachel in charge, Sara and I wandered slowly up the ramp hand in hand looking for a team to join in search of clues to the history of our people. Once again we were directed to the far eastern side of the plateau to join the same team who were now close to completing the work on the Zealot's habitation between the walls. They were standing idle until we arrived as two of their number had sprained their ankles trying to track the mountain Ibex.

Amongst other things we had been taught to look out for where two different kinds of soot staining on the walls on each side of the narrow cavity housing the previous occupants. The first kind was a linear stratum that followed the timber and thatch roof catching fire as a result of the flaming tipped arrows from the Roman archers at the siege or following the vandalism of the conquerors as they laid everything to waste in their frenzied destruction of the last bastion of resistance to the Roman conquest of the land. The second sooty trail was subtler and always ran vertically and usually found in the corners of the chambers. These stigmata hinted at domestic use and if followed to its source might reveal a primitive hearth for cooking or heating the chamber. Sara stumbled across such a soot line almost the moment she knelt down in a corner to scrape away the last remaining layer of debris before reaching the packed earth of the floor of the ancient dwelling place. At this level we were urged to explore more cautiously swapping shovel for trowel or if encountering mosaic, palette knife. Sara following the soot trail down to a segment of floor surrounded by a shallow hearth made out of five brick sized stones. The hearth had clearly been used for cooking and contained burnt organic material and even a few blackened fish bones. This was not unexpected, as it had already been discovered that the defenders of Masada had maintained fishponds. As she was scraping through this residue of a last supper the ferrule on the handle of her trowel knocked against one of the stones guarding the hearth and it tilted backwards. It appeared to be free of the other bricks that were cemented to each other. Driven on by curiosity she lifted the stone and blew away the dust below and immediately gave out a squeal of excitement. We all gathered round and inspected the contents of the cavity beneath the stone. We had been warned that on no account were we to move any major find, so we knelt and inspected the enigmatic knobby object below. Whatever it was it had once been carried in a woven sac as the remaining threads adhered to its contents but beyond that all we could say was it looked metallic and was bluish in color. Just below this strange object we could make out the partial outline of some ceramic object. One of our team was sent to find our supervisor who agreed that the find looked important and he then set out to fetch Mordecai Feldman one of the senior lecturers from the department of antiquities in Jerusalem. He joined us 10 minutes later with a leather satchel of equipment. He set up black and white strips to indicate size and location of the objects and then took a series of measurements in three dimensions before photographing the findings in situ. We then watched with baited breath as he lifted out the bulbous blue object that was the size and shape of a bottle of "Dimple Haig" scotch whiskey. He then laid it gently on a clean white sheet for more photographs then leaned back with a laugh and proclaimed, "Well boys and girls you have indeed found treasure but sadly it's only copper not gold". He explained that it was a bag of copper coins with most of the woven material of the dried out and turned to dust. Over the centuries with what little moisture there was left in the atmosphere the copper had oxidised to the blue of copper sulphate and the coins had congealed into this one lumpen object.

He took out his magnifying glass and inspected the flat surface of a coin on the surface and murmured, " M'mm 73CE I presume". We all were allowed a closer look as he pointed to the crude embossed marking of a pomegranate the symbol used to indicate the third year of the Zealot's occupation of Masada. He invited us to inspect our find in the laboratory at the foot of the mountain the following day when soaking in a dilute solution of acetic acid would separate the cluster of coins. He the turned his attention to the cavity under the hearth again pulled out a torch and illuminated its depth. He then let out a gasp, "Oh my God! Send for Professor Yadin".

He refused to say another word but paced up and down with agitation until the leader of our dig appeared. This was the first time I'd seen Yigael Yadin up close. He was a trim figure of average height, fit looking, tanned and handsome. He sported a bristling military moustache but his most striking feature was a bald shining dome of a head the color and appearance of a chestnut. *Ma nishma chaver?*" He questioned in Hebrew. He and Mordechai continued their conversation in Ivrit unaware that Sara and I could understand. It transpired that Sara had uncovered not only a buried stash of coinage put aside for a rainy day but a tall slim pale terracotta pot used to protect parchment scrolls. What was exceptional in this case was the fact that the container was still intact and sealed with a ceramic lid with its characteristic shape familiar to those who had heard the lecture on the Dead Sea scrolls.

He stood erect and his face broke into a huge wrinkled grin. "Who had the privilege of making this discovery?" He asked, looking round proudly as if a group of his student had scored alpha plus in an exam. "I did sir," replied Sara with quiet modesty. "Well young lady you have discovered an intact parchment scroll container and you will be invited to its examination tomorrow morning", he said and then paused, "haven't we met somewhere before? I could never forget a face like yours." He went on gallantly. "Yes sir, I am Sara Zenati from Piki'in" Sara replied. Yadin looked at her intently with a frown for a moment or two whilst Sara dropped her head as if in shame, then without another word Yadin picked up the precious find put it in his satchel, turned on his heel and strode off with Dr Feldman at his side hurrying to keep up.

"What the hell was all that about?" I asked Sara once he'd gone. She shushed me with a finger to her lips and whispered, "I'll tell you after dinner this evening when we are alone."

Chapter 19

The Eliezer Scroll

After dinner that evening Sara and I drifted back to the field hospital and diplomatically hinted to Jamal and Rachel that we'd rather be alone. With a teasing smile I enquired whether she and the famous professor were guilty of having an affair in the past. She was genuinely shocked by my suggestion even though it was meant as jest and replied, "For God's sake Martin he is old enough to be my father!" I resisted any further attempts at humour and asked her again about the rather awkward behavior of Yigael Yadin earlier in the day. "We'll it's really a secret" she replied to which my rapid rejoinder was, "surely if we are to marry Sara we have to start sharing our secrets." "Sorry Martin" she continued, "when I said secret, I should have said State Secret." My jaw dropped and I replied with a hint of skepticism in my voice, "please enlighten me."

Pledging me to secrecy she then went on to describe an extraordinary sequence of events. Three years earlier there had been a major earthquake in Israel sufficiently serious as to crack the walls of the Knesset in Jerusalem. The earthquake rumbled outwards from its epicenter somewhere in the Great Rift Valley not far north of where we sat. It was sufficiently serious enough as to reach her village close to the Lebanese border and bring down some of the little houses near to where she lived. It also brought down one of the corners of the old synagogue were it abutted the narrow alley leading up to the central square. As her family was custodian of the Piki'in synagogue she was first at the scene. Looking deep into the cavity revealed by the force of the quake she noticed a bronze bound cedar wood casket that looked as ancient as the building itself. She then rallied the elders of the community and they all agreed that nothing should be disturbed until a team from the Israeli

Department of Antiquities was sent for. They duly arrived the next day and took photographs and measurements before lifting the chest from its place of hiding and taking it away with them in their truck.

The next few days she was preoccupied with sorting out the damage and instructing the builders but remained curious about the contents of the box. Three months later she was alarmed to receive a letter bearing the stamp of the President's Office that summoned her to attend a meeting in Jerusalem 48 hours later. Enclosed within the letter was a document describing the Official Secrets Act with a space for her to sign her name, date of birth and home address. Fearing she was guilty of some heinous crime and accompanied by her father, she duly presented herself at the President's official residence where she waited nervously with a number of others until she was summoned into a wood paneled room whilst her father was barred at the door. Facing her, sitting round a large rectangular table she was alarmed to see the President himself, the Prime Minister David Ben Gurion, and some other terrifying old men with long beards but also conspicuous with his trade mark moustache and bald head, Professor Yigael Yadin. They tried to put her at my ease and complimented her on the discovery and the swift way she had alerted the department of antiquities and then cross questioned her for about half an hour on how she came to make the discovery and whether it was in the realms of possibility than someone might have placed the casket in the foundations of the old building after the earthquake. Before she was dismissed she was reminded about the Official Secrets act and sent on her way. "To this day I have heard nothing more about my discovery but will always remain curious about the contents of the box that seemed to have triggered a National Emergency" she concluded. "Well Sara you certainly have a gift for finding hidden treasure but then so am I," I said in response to this remarkable story. "How is that?" "Because my love, I discovered you hidden in the deepest hole on earth and you are more precious than rubies." That was enough to break the spell and earn a kiss before we made our chaste ways to our truckle beds in separate tents.

The following day Just after the noon break as we rested from the early morning treatment of walking wounded, Sara was summoned to attend Professor Yadin in his tented office. About 20 minutes later I was summoned as well. Yadin's tent was erected next to his open-air laboratory and the tented repository for the classification, tagging and cataloguing of the findings from the excavation of Masada. This complex had been erected a little to the northwest of the remains of General Flavius Silva's complex for the direction of an earlier campaign to conquer Masada two millennia in the past. Yadin was sitting at his desk flanked by Mordechai Feldman and another senior staff member whose name was not known to me. Sara was sitting on a campstool in front of the table and looked up saucer eyed at my approach.

Yadin opened the conversation this way, "Doctor Tanner I understand that I must congratulate you on your recent betrothal to nurse Zinati. As this is the first engagement to be announced under my command at Masada I would like to give you both gifts." Then with a twinkly smile he nodded to Dr. Feldman who handed us both little packages. We opened our gifts and both gasped with surprise and delight. In my palm I held a little gilt band set with a glass chip that reflected the patina of two thousand years.

On Sara's palm sat a sturdier gilt signet ring. " You may now exchange rings and I announce you betrothed with the authority invested in me as leader of this expedition" he finished with a guffaw and we all joined in with laughter. I made a formal bow and exchanged rings with a delighted blushing Sara and would you know it, they fitted perfectly, Sara's on her ring finger and mine occluding the blood supply to my little finger; but that was to be easily corrected at a later date. The unnamed third man introduced himself as Professor Anthony Zeitman late of Harvard University but now professor of ancient Hebrew manuscripts at the Hebrew University in Jerusalem and Yadin's deputy. He explained that the two rings had been discovered during the excavation of the synagogue on the western rim of Masada. They were of little monetary value as they were gilded silver but were otherwise of museum quality and almost certainly served as betrothal rings 2,000 years ago. The atmosphere in the tent then turned serious and Yadin took over. "Dr. Tanner I believe that no married couple must hold secrets from each other. We three archeologists in this tent need the help of Miss Zenati but our mission is deadly serious and constitutes a State Secret. Before we can go any further we must ask you to sign the Official Secrets Act." Without demur I signed on the dotted line and sat down on a proffered camp chair. He then went on to recount Sara's tale of the discovery of the cedar wood box after the earthquake three years earlier. I acted as if this was a surprise but my air of surprise became genuine as he continued. "Miss Zinati appears gifted at making archeological finds of the greatest significance and it might surprise you both to learn that yesterday's discovery is connected to her first discovery and might be the missing link we have been looking for and to some extent the covert reason for this entire expedition" Sara and I exchanged glances and raised eyebrows but nothing could have prepared us for all that was to follow. "The ceramic cylinder Sara uncovered did indeed contain a parchment scroll from the time of the fall of the second temple. It is reasonably well preserved and you will be the first to see its content but again remember the price you would pay for any breach of the Official Secret's Act. Please follow me." At that he slipped through the canvas walls separating his office from the repository for the artifacts given up by the dig. The tent next door had been cleared of all its occupants and laid out on a long wooden trestle table we saw fragments of parchment compressed between two plates of glass. The unfurled parchment looked very fractured to my eye and was about one metre long with remnants of wooden spindles at each end.

The parchment was covered in runes that had no meaning to me but we were assured that the words were Paleo Hebrew of the first century CE. Alongside the glass plates was a typed sheet of paper that carried Professor Zeitman's provisional translation and it read like this:

....

....

3. TAKE THIS STONE...... AND WRAP IT IN HANGINGS FROM

THE WALLS ....
4. TAKE TWO GOLDEN CANDLESTICKS .....
5. ....
....FROM THIS POINT ON EACH OF YOU WILL BE
CUSTODIANS OF THESE ..... HOLY RELICS ESTHER
.... TABLET TO A SANCTUARY IN THE NORTH AND
YEHUDIT CARRYING THE ....TO A SANCTUARY
IN............. YET .... BURDEN OF ESTHER'S IS THE MORE
PRECIOUS EVEN THOUGH MADE OF STONE.
7. FIND THE PASSAGE OF KING HEROD ....THE FLAG
STONE THAT...
8. AT THE BOTTOM OF THAT SHAFT YOU WILL FIND.........(?)
CLOTHING. REPLACE YOUR LINEN ROBES AND DRESS
..............KING (?) HEROD ..PASSAGE RUNS FROM THE
ANTONIA (?) FORTRESS TO THE NORTH DO
NOT...
10. THERE YOU WILL BE MET BY TWO OF .... TRUSTED
....FROM YOUR FATHER
WHO NOW SOJOURNS IN...GARDEN.. EDEN.
MAY GOD SHINE HIS FACE UPON YOU AND BE GRACIOUS
UNTO YOU.............

ELIEZER BEN (?) YAKOV HA'COHEN

Sara and I read the translation in awestruck silence. To think these enigmatic words had survived 2,000 years made my hair stand on end and I actually shivered as if the ghost of old Eliezer was passing through the tent. Sara looked up with wonderment shining out of her eyes. "Thank you for allowing us to see this wonderful manuscript before any others, I feel truly blessed and sense the spirit of the author of this text as being among us". I turned to her with a startled expression as her words reflected exactly my own feelings. "Am I allowed to learn how the text is linked to my first discovery three years ago?" she continued will ill concealed excitement in her voice. Yadin then responded "Sara my dear, as we need your help with the next step in our research it is necessary for you and Dr.

Tanner to read the translation of the six scrolls that were hidden in the casket discovered after the damage to your synagogue. They comprise the most important archeological discovery in the history of exploration in the Holy Land yet until this day we were not sure if they were forgeries used for some elaborate hoax or malign political motive. Your discovery yesterday provides conclusive proof of the authenticity of the Piki'in papers as you will learn for yourself shortly." Nodding to a heavy iron safe in the corner of his office he continued, " Apart from the original scrolls that are under heavy guard in the department of antiquities there are a handful of translations into modern Hebrew and English all of which are secured in a secret depository in Jerusalem. I am the only one to have at hand one of these translations to help me in my search of Masada for some evidence to corroborate the authenticity of the scrolls. You and Dr Tanner will be the first citizens outside an inner circle of a Presidential board of enquiry to read these documents." Yadin then strode over to the safe, whirled the numbered spindle wheel through a complex set of movements, and removed a thick file. He placed it on the table and invited the two of us to move our seats forward before continuing, " I want the two of you to carefully read these documents and inwardly digest their contents. This tented compound's security is of a very high level. Amongst the archeologists you see working here are armed members of Shin Bet in addition there is an outer ring of defence provided by the IDF who are unaware of precisely what they are guarding but ostensibly to protect us from marauding bands of Bedouin who have been known to pilfer from our camps as I believe you have already learnt to your cost Dr. Tanner" turning to me with a big smile. "Professor Zeitman will stay with you until you've finished, in case you need clarification of his team's translation but Mordechai and I will go about our business as usual so as not to attract attention by our absence. We will return when Anthony sends a runner but it should only take an hour or two to complete your task but I promise you that it will take a lifetime to recover from the impact of what you are about to read".

With this he left the tent and he would never learn just how precise his prophecy was to be enacted.

PART 3

The Quest Begins

Chapter 20

My first visit to Piki'in

It took the best part of two hours for Sara and I to read and more importantly, inwardly digest, the contents of the extraordinary powerful narrative described within the five Yehudit scrolls. Their authenticity was clearly now beyond dispute as witnessed by the replication of the "Eliezer scroll" in its entirety with the blanks filled in. Sara and I exchanged glances and our expressions of amazement and to some extent alarm were reflected back and forth except that her complexion showed a deathly pallor whilst mine was flushed with excitement. Professor Yadin timed his return almost to the minute that we had completed our reading. Without a word to us he looked across to Professor Zeitman who gave him a solemn nod. He gathered up the papers and returned to the safe before sitting down to face us and speak.

"Perhaps you now understand the importance of these finds. We now face a terrible dilemma. There is no longer any doubt that the scrolls that Sara found three years ago are genuine but if that is the case then it appears there might be a codicil to Moses' two tablets of the law brought down from Mount Sinai. I have to confess that I am by no means a fundamentalist in the interpretation of the Torah but within its covers and together with the results of our biblical archeology lay the very justification for the State of Israel. That is why there is so much political interest in our mission." At this juncture he pulled out his wallet from his back pocket and withdrew a banknote and continued. "Have a close look at the picture on the back of this 100 shekel note, that is an image of the Piki'in synagogue and that is making a political statement. It would therefore be hypocritical for us not to pursue a search for the third tablet but we do so at our peril without knowing its contents. This decision has to be taken at the highest level. Professor Zeitman and I have just convened an emergency meeting with the President, the Prime Minister and representatives of the Chief Rabbinates in Jerusalem. We will be away a couple of days but in the meantime I would like the two of you but especially Sara, to think hard about what you've just read and what it might all mean. Are there any hidden messages and are there any clues beyond the obvious, as to where the third tablet is to be found?"

With that we were dismissed but it was to be another few hours before Sara and I could spend time together in order to talk it through. In the meantime we had to make up story to explain our absence from Jamal and Rachel but we thought it reasonable to show off our new betrothal rings. This at least allowed me to restore the blood supply to my finger and help provide some degree of proof for our elaborate alibi. In spite of that I caught a glance from Jamal that suggested he knew that we were holding something back.

It was after 9.00 pm before Sara and I were alone in the clinic tent with our cups of Turkish coffee when we both started talking at once. Not so much talking as gabbling in our haste to share our excitement, emotions and ideas. We both paused then Sara went on to suggest that I spoke first and she would follow.

I took a deep breath and started by reverting to my native Cockney, " Phew, blimey O' Rielly, would you Adam and Eve it! Well for starters this Yehudit, sounds just like you and from the description of her twin, probably looked just like you. Esther was clearly dying of breast cancer at the time she was writing her last testament and the disease had been described as cancer the crab since the time of Hippocrates 500 years earlier and Yehudit describes how the sisters had studied the Ancient Greek scholars. Furthermore the migration south along King Solomon's trade routes might explain the beginnings of the Jewish colonization of India. So at a stroke we have evidence to support my theory that your family has carried the curse for over 2,000 years and my family might have inherited it from a distant relative of Yehudit always assuming she made it safely to the west coast of India!"

"Oh Martin, why are you so scientific, rational and prosaic?"

Sara responded but immediately saw the hurt look on my face, "I'm sorry *moteck* I didn't mean to hurt you but there's an altogether different perspective by which we can see these wonderful events that have brought us together. It was *beshert,* and whilst you see a linear scientific narrative I see the hand of Hashem. The prophet Zechariah and the book of Revelations foretell of an earthquake the will precede the coming of the Messiah. We have come to think that this would be some cataclysmic event akin to Armageddon and the end of times, but surely that makes no sense if the coming of the Messiah is the prelude to the building of the third temple in Jerusalem. I see myself as the maidservant of Hashem and the last of my line that were surviving witnesses of the destruction of the second temple. I have no brothers; sisters or cousins and we have pledged to remain without children of our own. I see the hand of God striking the foundations of our little synagogue and leading me to discover the scrolls written by my ancestors, I see the hand of The Lord in leading me to unearth the Eliezer scroll and I see the hand of The Lord in leading you to me so that you will be my helpmate in searching for the third tablet of divine instruction from the mouth of Hashem to the hand of Moses *Rabenu*. I believe that when we discover God's hiding place for the third tablet it will be the prelude to a new Messianic era and peace in the world. That I have been chosen for the task fills me with terror and awe, I foresee that I will not live to see my task complete but will be granted the time to start a process by which I will be remembered with honour like one of our beloved Matriarchs."

As she spoke these words of prophecy her eyes glazed over and a thin sheen of sweat appeared on her brow as if she were possessed. She then recovered from whatever had possessed her, shook her head with a self deprecating smile and concluded by saying, " I'm so sorry Martin I don't know what came over me but in our different ways I think we are both right. You tell Professor Yadin your version I'll share my fevered imagination with no one save yourself."

★★★

Two days later we were again summoned to the presence of Professor Yadin who was again flanked by his two senior aides. This time we were aware of two tough looking "archeologists" loitering nearby who were more than likely Shin Bet operatives.

We were invited to sit down and offered coffee when Yadin with a business like manner opened the conversation." It has been decided we will begin the search for the third tablet. The Prime Minister has more or less offered us an open cheque as far as manpower and resources are required but to tell the truth although we know where to start we cannot begin to imagine where this quest will lead and what it will uncover.

For the first step in our search we need a low profile reconnoitre of Miss Zenati's synagogue and after that decide on resources for a new expedition in search for a relic second in importance only to the lost Ark of the Covenant looted from the Temple by the Romans in 70 CE. So tomorrow the five of us will make an unannounced visit to Piki'in." "Can I not let my father know of our coming?" Interrupted Sara. "No my dear, this whole venture has to be kept top secret until we've figured out the extent of the venture and developed some convincing explanations for our activities."

The following morning we packed sufficient for one overnight stay and explained to Jamal and Rachel that we had been granted leave of absence to visit Sara's father so that I might formally receive his blessing on our betrothal. We set off westward on the desert road to Arad in an IDF command car with Yadin in the cab with his driver and Zeitman, Feldman, the two tough looking silent men I'd seen loitering outside Yadin's tent the day before together with Sara and me sitting on the long hard benches either side of the open troop carrying compartment at the rear. The ride to Arad rattled our teeth and jarred our coccygeal bones but from Beersheba to the main coastal highway was easy going. The road from there all the way back to Safed was familiar territory for me but running north from there took us up and down narrow single track roads slowly climbing to the mountainous region of the Lebanese border. It was late afternoon before our truck drew up in a rough parking lot at the foot of the hill where Piki'in had taken root. Further access to the little town's centre was by mule, motor scooter or on foot. We chose the latter leaving one of our "assistant archaeologists" behind to guard our truck along with the driver, whilst the other tough guy took up the rear as we made our way up the steep narrow cobble stoned alleys, lead by Sara, until we reached a pretty little central square built around and ancient well and shaded by a huge and equally ancient cedar tree. Sara asked us to rest there whilst she set off in search of her father, the custodian of the keys to the Zinati synagogue. Across the other side of the square from where we sat in the shade of the tree, sat a group of elders from the Druze community distinguished by their long black robes, handlebar moustaches and cylindrical black head coverings. They sat on a long wooden bench looking at us with a mixture of benevolence and curiosity but in return I was surprised to note that the building that shaded their bench was marked out clearly as the head quarters of the Boy Scouts for this region. For some reason I found the scout hut anachronistic but later on in my sojourn in this pretty little town, I learnt that scouting was a very popular "left over" from the days of the British Mandate and one of these elderly gentlemen, who was the leader of the pack had won the George Cross fighting with the British Armed forces in the North African campaign 20 years earlier.

After about 10 minutes Sara reappeared and beckoned us to join her from the mouth of the narrow alley close to our point of entry to the square. We joined up outside the field of vision of those seated by the scout hut. She suggested that if all of us appeared at once it would be too much of a shock for her father. I should be introduced first and then when my business was complete the others would join us.

We all nodded agreement. Sara grasped me purposefully by the hand a drew me up a narrow flight of stone steps under an arch to a stout wooden door with an elaborate antique looking *mezuzah* fixed high up on the right hand door post. It took a while for my eyes to adjust from the bright sunlight in the square to the subdued light in the long sitting room with narrow windows running down one side. The room had a floor made of ancient granite flagstones that were covered by elaborately woven rugs. The walls also had hangings of a similar weave. There was altogether too much dark wooden furniture and overstuffed settees but the overall impression was of homely comfort that seemed to be provided by inherited furnishing as distinct from new bought. Standing in front of the unlit fireplace was a wizened old berry brown man of about five foot two in height wearing a knitted wool skullcap. He looked old enough to be Sara's grandfather yet I had learnt that he was only 55. He in no way resembled his daughter until he smiled and then the relationship became obvious. After the usual polite introductions were complete I was invited to take a seat and offered a thimble of Turkish coffee that Sara had prepared during her short absence. Formalities complete I then stood up and faced Mr.Zinati and solemnly asked for his blessing on the betrothal of his daughter to an Anglo-Jewish surgeon. With equal solemnity the old man stood up and turned to Sara declaiming," And this is your wish my dearest daughter and can this man bring happiness to your life?" Sara then stood up and replied, "Oh yes my darling *Abba* he will make a good husband and provide for me well". Then smiling mischievously he continued, "It had always been my secret wish that Sara might one day marry a doctor but a British surgical kind of doctor was beyond my wildest dreams." He then gently pulled us to stand side by side and placed one hand on each of our heads and intoned the blessing, " May The Lord bless thee and keep thee. May The Lord make his face shine upon thee. May The Lord turn his face unto thee and give thee peace". He kissed each of us on the forehead and continued, "If you have betrothal rings hand them to me and I will return them in the presence of witnesses before breaking one of your dear mother's (may God rest her soul), second best dinner plates." "Thank you from the bottom of my heart" I responded, "as it happens we came here with three companions who are also anxious to make your acquaintance who will make excellent witnesses." At this Sara's father looked bewildered and wondered why anyone else might be anxious to meet him. Sara pecked him on the cheek and popped out the door returning after a brief interval with the three men who had been waiting patiently outside leaving one behind guarding the alley. As their eyes were adapting to the light Mr. Zinati let out a gasp, stood up ramrod straight and executed a smart salute. "Welcome to my humble house General Yadin and to what do I owe this honour?" "Ah, Staff Sergeant Zinati, delighted to meet you again," then turning to Sara who had a look of astonishment on her face, Yadin continued, " Your father and I are old comrades at arms and you may not be aware that he is a great hero. In 1948 during the battle to control the heights around Safed, your father improvised mortars and led the defence after his commanding officer was killed in action. I personally pinned the Medal of Valor on his chest but he is such a modest man I wager he never told you."

There were smiles of delight all round the room whilst Sara's father puffed his chest out a little before bending over with uncontrollable mirth. "First my daughter returns unannounced, then she introduces me to this young man who claims her hand in marriage and then just as I need a witness or two for a spontaneous betrothal my old commanding officer appears out of the blue; you'll be telling me next that the *Messiah* will be along in time for the wedding!" "As a matter of fact Mr. Zinati if the mission that brings us here is successful you might not be far off the mark", spoke professor Zeitman, at which point Sara's father collapsed backwards onto a waiting armchair and looked up with alarm at the newcomer.

It took all five of us to explain our mission and convince Reuben, for that was the name of Sara's dad, that we were speaking the truth and he was then added to the growing list of those signing the pledge of confidentiality about the Piki'in scrolls.

Once this formality was completed, Reuben collected a set of large iron keys and led us down to the old synagogue just in time to make up a *minyan* for the weekday *mincha/maariv* service. We entered the synagogue via a courtyard surrounded by a low stonewall. The synagogue was small by all comparisons and had a distinctive barrel ceiling. The women sat in the back two rows but that evening Sara sat alone. Facing the ark there were only five rows for the male members of the community and five elderly bearded congregants who welcomed Reuben but ignored the rest of us, occupied the front row. Reuben, as some kind of lay preacher led the service; whilst I was distracted by the two marble tablets set into the wall either side of the ark. Each was rectangular measuring about 20 x 16 inches One depicted the *menorah, shofar* and *lulav* and the other a gateway with columns, perhaps representing the entrance to the temple. The edges of the tablets were a little irregular.

After the service the old men in the front row scuttled off without paying us any attention leaving the rest of us to pace around the inside of the building making mental notes. We eventually gathered in front of the tablet of stone carrying the gateway carved in shallow bas-relief. "If this is truly one half of the third tablet of the covenant then our task is nearly complete but surely it can't be that easy. These stones must in truth be decoys but perhaps in themselves they carry clues," said Yadin and turning to Reuben continued, "*Nu chaver,* can you make any the wiser?" "I know more about our synagogue and its secrets than anyone else but we have always assumed that these were the originals brought forth from the second Temple but you are very welcome to study all our archives which contain the fragments of parchments and old prayer books going back nearly 2,000 years in our *genizah* and if there are any clues to be found that is where you must look."

I stood riveted to the ground because subconsciously I had observed something during the service that now surfaced and confirmed beyond any shadow of doubt that these plaques were two halves of an original stone tablet measuring 20 x 32 inches.

I knew this because if you took the right hand plaque and rotated it 180 degrees and opposed two of the long sides the irregularities fitting perfectly like pieces of a jigsaw puzzle. How I came to make this observation was almost certainly related to my training but later on Sara tried to convince me it was divine intervention.

I then rejoined the conversation, " Reuben you are correct these are the original stones. Alfred Hitchcock's film, 'family plot' featured stolen diamonds hidden in a chandelier. Using the same logic, the best place to hide valuable stones is in a wall. However the clever deception here is that the two inscribed surfaces were turned to face the wall but one was rotated 180 degrees and then the outer surfaces were carved in such a way as to force the observer to see two unrelated objects." "My God I think you're right Martin!" exclaimed Mordechai whipping out a Polaroid camera from his backpack. He then proceeded to take pictures of both stones and printed the instant images. Next he extracted a pair of scissors and carefully cut around the outlines of the two stones and exactly as my eye predicted the two opposing edges were a perfect compliment to each other like two strands of RNA. There was a deathly silence and I sensed that some were resisting the temptation to prostrate themselves before the holy stones but then Reuben pulled at the fringes of his *tsitis* touched each stone and brought the fringes to his lips. Sara then stepped forward and kissed each stone full on without any intermediary. Whilst she was so occupied Yadin turned to us and said, " Gentlemen I think that thanks to Dr. Tanner's remarkable insight we now know where to begin but before doing so we have much to prepare."

That night Sara slept in her own bedroom whilst the four male members of the team were found lodgings in a nearby tourist hostel. I'm not sure where the two Shin Bet operatives and the armed driver spent the night but they awaited us by the command car as we left Piki'in early the following morning on our return to Masada.

Chapter 21

My second visit to Piki'in

Shortly after our return to Masada I was summoned back to Afula hospital to resume my duties and Sara retraced her steps north to return to her duties and to start planning for our wedding. We intended to get married in November a month mercifully free of high holy days and fasts; furthermore we were both due for a vacation period around that time so that there would be time for a proper honeymoon. We warmly embraced Jamal and Rachel goodbye but before that we had recruited them to act as best man and maid of honour at the wedding. The fact that a Druze man and woman could play these roles at a Jewish wedding was testimony of the close friendly relationships between the two faiths in upper Galilee. Sara and I planned to meet on our weekends off in the meantime.

At the same time bureaucracy and internecine strife held up the plans for the formal scientific analysis of the stone tablets. Shortly after our return Yadin and his two senior aids went to Jerusalem to report back on our visit north, to the project team set up by the Prime Minister.

This group contained representatives from the mainstream branches of the Jewish faith, representatives of the government and opposition, representatives from the scientific and archaeological disciplines as well as the security services and the IDF. On the assumption that the Piki'in plaques were indeed the reunited halves of a codicil to the sacred covenant between God and his chosen people, then the political and religious fall out could be of unimaginable importance. I later learnt from Yadin that the infighting and vitriolic debate nearly led to a civil war between the religious and secular groups at the table and this wasn't helped by the resignation of Ben Gurion and his replacement by Levi Eshkol.

Furthermore this change at the top took place shortly after the Presidential election when Zalman Shazar replaced Yitzak Ben Zvi. However the new President was a kinsman of Yadin and his diplomatic intervention saved the day. This was to be the plan.

The security cover was to leak a story to the press that there was credible intelligence of a terrorist attack on the iconic old synagogue as illustrated on the 100-shekel bank note, by a splinter group of the PLO. This would allow for a *cordon sanitaire* to be thrown around the hilltop village and allow a few days freedom from tourists and inquisitive locals.

The plan included erecting a marquee in the courtyard of the old synagogue so that the two wall plaques could be subjected to scientific and scriptural examination in situ before final decisions were made about their long-term disposition. Whatever the outcome the plaques would be placed temporarily in safe custody in the vaults of the Department of Antiquities and would be covertly replaced by facsimiles. Assuming their authenticity was confirmed then their final resting place would be in a neutral ecumenical house of worship linked to the Israel Museum in Jerusalem as the rejoined fragments of the third tablet of Mosaic law would become a holy relic not just for the Jewish faith but also of other faiths that recognized the "Old Testament" as part of their religious canon. Finally by the time all this was agreed the High Holy days of Rosh Ha'shana, Yom Kippur and Succot were upon us, so the expedition was deferred until November to a date that happened to coincide with our wedding! Us against them was an unequal battle so we graciously agreed to defer our wedding by three days on the understanding that we could witness the extravaganza and that the marquee could be left standing to house our wedding breakfast. All parties were satisfied and Sara again saw this as further evidence of some great-preordained heavenly plan, leaving me the tough job of persuading the travel agents who were organizing our honeymoon to a destination that would be a great surprise to my new bride, to postpone the date of departure.

★★★

The "circus left town" on November 2nd coinciding with the breaking news on television, the Jerusalem Post and Ha'Aretz of a leak from Shin Bet of a threatened terrorist attack close to the border with Lebanon. Sara had arrived at her family home a day earlier having been advised by me in advance to pack her passport and some clothes for a tropical climate. I was surprised to learn that she had no passport never having the need or opportunity of leaving the Holy Land. I left her the unenviable task of handling the bureaucracy involved in obtaining a passport. I arrived in Piki'in just before the roadblocks and crime scene tapes had closed off the sensitive areas. I was to be billeted with Jamal's family but again having to dream up some plausible excuse for arriving so early. This excuse based on a half-truth that involved a formal betrothal ceremony, a public exchange of our antique engagement rings in front of witnesses and the breaking of one of Sara's late mother's second best dinner plates a ceremony known as "Vort". The explanation for that act of vandalism escapes me at this time of writing.

Early on the morning chosen for the lifting of the plaques from the wall, Sara and me walked hand in hand towards the old synagogue trembling in anticipation for the two most momentous occasions in our lives, the reunification of the two halves of the third tablet of the Holy Covenant to be followed shortly afterwards by the matrimonial covenant uniting Sara and I as husband and wife. From the square at the centre of the village to the synagogue, there were three security checkpoints that included scrutinizing our passes and checking our person for hidden weapons or explosives. The security staff had no better knowledge of the truth than the general population. The Zinati synagogue was barely recognizable hiding behind a huge white marquee filling its courtyard with cables and wireless lines running to generators and communication nodes. We slipped into the large tent and were greeted by the bizarre sight of about 30 men of rabbinical appearance whose degree of fundamentalism was directly proportional to the length and untidiness of their beards, and the technical staff recognizable by their open necked shirts and clean-shaven chins. However out of respect both groups had some kind of head covering ranging from black wide brimmed fedoras to discrete crocheted saucer shaped skull caps. I quickly slipped on an example of the latter before anyone noticed me.

Long tables ranged alongside the tent walls carrying technical equipment and there was a buzz of excitement in the air. At the far end of the tented area the doors to the synagogue appeared in the gap left in the tenting. Suddenly the double doors were thrown open and a deathly hush fell as Yadin flanked by two ancient looking white bearded men, who must surely have been our two Chief Rabbis, appeared.

"Gentlemen, it has been decided that before we start work we should all put on our *tefillin* and *daven shacharis,* the morning service", bellowed one of the old men.

I was ill equipped for this exercise so I slipped back out of the tent to join Sara who had preceded me after noticing that she was the only woman in the whole assembly. After waiting for about 20 minutes for the morning prayers to finish we unostentatiously rejoined the community just as they were entering the synagogue proper. There was a roped off area in front of the ark and the wall bearing the tablets. A small group of Yadin's most skilled archaeologists then started work on releasing the marble plaques from the wall. It looked as if the plaster around the edges had been softened up overnight by some caustic solution and I took note at the careful way they picked out fragments holding the stones in place leaving the edges that were meant to oppose each other when united until the end. It took two men working on each stone nearly two hours before they could slip a series of long flat rigid metal spatulas under the stones from the sides that had been completely freed up and then very gently lever them away from the walls to be held by another two men wearing white cotton gloves who gingerly carried them to the waiting tables in the tent outside. As the tablets were laid side by side face up and the one bearing the bas relief carving of the temple doorway was rotated 180 degrees and the two long lateral sides were opposed, exactly as predicted the fit was so perfect that the pair of tablets clicked and locked together as if by magnetism. At which point a communal sigh has heard as 30 men and one woman exhaled in unison.

Some of the rabbinical team muttered prayers or wept with joy whilst the secular group of scientists and technicians applauded with unconcealed triumphalism.

Professor Yadin then called forth the Ashkenasi and Sephardi Chief Rabbis who donned white cotton gloves and under his supervision carefully turned the stones over in order that the surfaces hidden for nearly 2,000 years could be viewed and interpreted.

Again a communal sigh was heard but this time the note seemed to my untrained ear, to have slipped into a minor key. There was nothing to be seen! The sense of anticlimax was almost palpable and murmuring was to be heard from lips almost hidden by the extravagant facial hair of the ultra orthodox. Yadin took control and shooed the Chief Rabbis away whilst ordering strong neon lights to be directed on the apparently blank surfaces. He and his two senior colleagues then quietly studied the surfaces carefully blowing or brushing away dust and debris with compressed air and sable tipped paintbrushes. After a while he straightened up, turned to the audience and explained his initial observations. "Gentlemen" and then with a nod at smile at Sara, "and lady, there is evidence of ancient inscriptions just detectable to the naked eye but they have been badly compromised by erosion over the millennia by the acidity of the mortar holding them in place. The next tests we'll carry out will be a simple charcoal rubbing and then some photographs with normal and ultraviolet light. In addition we will take samples of the stone for identification of the type of quarry from which they might have been taken and also send some samples of the mortar that usually contains some organic material for carbon dating using the same techniques that proved successful at the Qumran caves. You may all stay and watch what emerges from the charcoal rubbings as that is literally child's play but then I suggest you all leave us alone to complete our work and then we will reconvene at the same time tomorrow morning. At that a technician rolled out a sheet of tracing paper across the length of the reunited stones and gently rubbed the whole surface will a large chunk of charcoal held in the palm of his hand. With a flourish he whipped of the paper and held it up for all to see.

There was no doubt that there was a ghostly remnant of a human hand at work but it was impossible to make out anything that remotely resembled Hebrew lettering.

The meeting reconvened the following morning but professor Yadin had little to add. Yes the dating and origin of the stone would do for the Sinai region from about 1500 BCE but photography in different wave lengths of light was no more revealing than the charcoal rubbing we had already seen. He had decided to take the stones back to his laboratories in Jerusalem to work on at leisure and to fill up the cavities on the walls with the facsimiles already prepared. He concluded that although many might feel a sense of anticlimax he still felt confident that this was the lost codicil to the Ten Commandments but he needed more archaeological corroborative evidence and to think about other technologies that might yet reveal more of the text lost by the corrosive power of acidity and time.

Everyone then drifted out heads bent over in disappointment but as far as Sara and I were concerned we had nothing better to think of than preparations for our wedding.

★★★

My brother and his heavily pregnant wife arrived the day after "the circus" had decamped totally unaware of what had been going on in the past three days. Joe was to officiate at my wedding and was the bearer of two beautiful gifts. One was an elaborately illuminated *Ketubha* or wedding contract that he had commissioned from a scribe working in the artist colony of Safed and the other was a multicolored *Tallis,* prayer shawl, woven from the finest wool by artisan weavers in the old centre high on the hill above modern Rosh Pinah.

This was to be worn by the groom under the *Chupah.* The gift from Jamal and Rachel was also specially commissioned from a skilled weaver working nearby and this was *the Chupah,* or canopy itself, under which the wedding ceremony would take place. Against a white background the names of the bride and groom together with the date and place of the wedding were woven in gold thread both in Hebrew and English, whilst around the border little blue birds and scarlet flowers were worked into an Arte Nouveau design. For the wedding ceremony itself this was to be held aloft by four stalwart men carrying long mahogany poles to shelter the wedding party but we were told it could then be used as a wall hanging to be used again for the weddings of our children. We were truly delighted with our gifts but couldn't bring ourselves to mention that there were not to be children from this union.

My memories of the event itself remain rather blurred almost as if I'd been intoxicated by love and happiness rather than hard liquor. The ceremony was of course identical to that I described on my brother's wedding day and I don't want to bore my reader by repetition but there are a few impressions left over in my memory. First is that of my bride's ethereal beauty in a gown of some floating gossamer white material that gave the impression of effortless movement such as that of a dandelion clock caught in a light zephyr wind. My next impression can only be described in mystical or Kabbalistic terms. It was almost as if the *Shekinah* of The Lord had been captured by the net made from the canopy of the *Chupah* and for once my restless and ambitious soul was at peace in the right place and the right time and would always be thus as long as Sara was by my side. My final long lasting impression was of a smiling congregation, an admixture of friends and family from both the Jewish and Druze communities, seemingly carrying us on their shoulders on the first steps of our journey as man and wife. To an extent that last impression was both figuratively and factually true as Sara and I were carried shoulder high on gilt chairs from the *Chupah* up to the old square under the ancient cedar tree round the narrow alleys and back down to the marquee for our wedding feast. Joe sang out the reprise of the seven blessings in his beautiful baritone voice ending with the blessing over a silver goblet full to the brim with ruby red wine. Jamal made a dignified and well judged speech explaining how we all came together on a mountain top from where the view was divine and that the bride and groom where now seated on another mountain top from which the view of our future life together was equally sublime. He also saw fit to mention how I had saved his leg in the heat of battle but then had us all doubled over with laughter on stating that he wished I'd done something about his crooked nose at the same time. Then as I recall two unscripted events took place. First Jamal's uncle who turned out to be the chief scout and the most prominent of the Druze elders of the village, stepped forth and placed a chain of cloves around Sara's neck and muttered a silent blessing over her bowed head. I later learnt that this was an exceptional honour to bestow upon a non-Druze bride. Then to cap it all Reuben, Sara's father stepped forward, repeated the priestly blessing and pinned his medal of valour on my chest. "That my dear son is in recognition of your valour in the battle against the captains of the harbingers of death, your courage in taking my daughter off my hands but mostly so that I can be sure that this medal awarded in the defence of our land will be handed down the generations of our blood line for ever and ever, amen" I never had the heart to tell him that Sara was to be the last of his line.

As soon as the festivities were over, very much in the British tradition, Sara changed into a "going away " outfit and we drove off towards Tel Aviv in a white hired car. Joe, for once reverting to his native state, had even remembered to tie tin cans to the rear bumper.

Once we had negotiated the tortuous roads of the northern Galilee and were back on a highway heading towards Haifa I turned to my new bride and said, "Would you like a clue as to where we are going to spend our honeymoon Mrs. Tanner?" "That would be nice Dr.Tanner", she replied.

"Well, tomorrow morning we have appointments to collect our visas from the Indian consulate!" At that that she let out a squeal of delighted surprise.

Chapter 22

In the footsteps of Yehudit

In the months between my two visits to Piki'in I tried my best to research the possible route and final resting place of Yehudit bat Eliezer, Ha'Cohen after she left her sister at Ein Gedi and turned south with the hope of following the trade routes established at the time of King Solomon to a safe refuge. The libraries in Afula provided little prospect for scholarly research so I used my occasional half-day off to travel to Haifa to browse amongst the book stacks at the Haifa Technion. There was no doubt, both from biblical and archaeological evidence that King Solomon's merchants established trade routes to the west coast of India. They sustained a very prosperous market where gold was exchanged for black pepper, ginger, peacock feathers and pearls. The traders left by boat from the port of Aqaba at the northern tip of the Red Sea. To reach that point involved a hazardous crossing of the Sinai desert by camel trains that organized themselves at Beersheba, travelling in the cool of the night whilst resting under black woolen tents in the heat of the day. Survival was totally dependent on those watering holes that were few and far between along the trail, and finding them depended on the guides who navigated across the near featureless landscape by the stars as if they were ships in the night. They were harried by day and by night by marauding desert bandits seeking gold on the southward journey or pepper, also known as black gold, on the return; many of these caravans never made it to the Red Sea. The boats out of Aqaba were little more than the primitive dhows we see today on the Nile yet they were equipped to cross the Indian Ocean. The route southeast along the Red Sea hugged the Arabian coast and put in at Jeddah before turning eastward along the Yemeni

198

coastline at the southern end of the Arabian Peninsula. From here these frail craft struck our blindly due East, using the rising sun as a guide, riding the monsoon winds that took them directly and with little other choice as far as I could see, to the Malabar coast of India, the centre of the spice trade. In the unlikely event that Yehudit and the precious golden candlesticks from the Temple, made it that far, then there should be some evidence of an ancient Israelite Diaspora being established in that area.

That then led to my second and more puzzling line of research. There was indeed an ancient Jewish community living in Cochin, an equally ancient port in Kerala that was likely to have acted as the eastern end of this spice trade, but although they claimed lineage dating back to the time of King Solomon, they had more than likely arrived from Spain or Portugal as refugees from the inquisition in the late 15th C. Indeed many of these Indian Jews from Cochin, who had started to arrive in Israel and settled in the Negev from the foundation of the State of Israel in 1948 practiced their faith according to the Sephardic tradition and word had it that these might be the last of the Indian Jews to have survived in Kerala.

Although I could get no further with my research at least I knew where to start and that would be in the tropical paradise of Kerala on the south west coast of India. November and December were considered the best time of year to visit and what could be better than a honeymoon in the land of the lotus flower, the tamarind tree and the jasmine blossom at a time when the monsoon rains were long gone and balmy winds off the ocean kept the temperature and humidity perfect for the British gentry of the Raj; or so the brochure from Cox and Kings informed me. I had wisely decided to leave my honeymoon plans to this old and trusted travel company who had been transporting the younger sons and their accompanying memsahib, from the English Home Counties to rule the jewel in the crown of the British Empire since the mid 19thC.

We flew out from Lod airport outside Tel Aviv the evening after our wedding in order to spend the first night of our honeymoon in Nicosia Cyprus so that we could catch the following day's BOAC flight to Bombay. We then planned to stay two nights in Bombay before taking the twice-weekly Air India flight to Cochin. The time difference between Israel and India is three and a half hours, a carry over from the days of the Raj, the half hour being added on so that some Victorian grandee in Bombay wanting to know the time in London would simply rotate his pocket watch face 180 degrees. We landed early in the evening and as we disembarked from the ordered, polite and sane atmosphere of the British Overseas Airways Corporation flight, we were immediately plunged into madness. The noise, the confusion, the stink and the constant harassment of self important officials and self denigrating hawkers and beggars added to our disorientation triggered by that three and one half hour time difference. We queued and queued to pass immigration, baggage retrieval and customs, becoming more and more flustered and sweaty in the putrid air stirred lazily by giant fans that had no appreciable cooling effect. Sara desperately wanted to relieve herself but returned ashen faced from the "Ladies" because all the facilities were blocked and overflowing with liquid feces. She determined therefore to tighten her sphincters and grin and bear it. That grin soon transformed itself into a rictus. It was even worse once we made it together with our baggage on to the pavement outside of the arrivals lobby. I had requested a car and driver from the Taj Mahal Palace hotel to meet us but I saw no hope of meeting anyone amongst this noisy hoard many of whom appeared to have set up home and fallen asleep under our feet. I dragged Sara and our wonky reluctant luggage trolley in the direction of a notice saying Taxis and shouted above the din, "anyone here waiting for Dr and Mrs Tanner". Now that was seriously stupid as I quickly appreciated when thirty edentulous and filthy old men in their underwear rushed forward grinning and wrestling each other and our cases like a feeding frenzy of sharks. Then suddenly the scrum backed off as two smartly dressed military gentlemen with bristling moustaches, laid into them with long thin bamboo canes. Once they'd retreated the senior of the two saluted us smartly and enquired of our destination. When I mentioned the hallowed name of the Taj Mahal hotel, he gave a small bow and blew a big whistle. At which point a very handsome, very dapper, very dark and heavily bewhiskered gentleman in smart livery and an elaborately sculptured Sikh turban, stepped forward and in immaculate English enquired if we were Sahib and Memsahib Tanner. The relief in Sara's face was wonderful to behold as he grabbed our bags and ushered us to a large white Austin limousine. This was Vijay Sunil Singh our driver and guide for the next two days. The journey to the hotel that was near the iconic Gateway to India was eye popping. By now it was past midnight yet for most of the drive we seemed to be surrounded by a seething mass of humanity. If they weren't seething then they were sleeping either bundled up on the pavement, in doorways or at the mouths of ramshackle cardboard and corrugated iron shacks making up a twelve-mile long ribbon of a shantytown all the way to the sea. At every traffic light were we stopped, beggar children competing in winning our sympathy by flaunting their hideous deformities or amputation stumps, surrounded us. On other occasions we were stopped by languidly strolling Hindu holy cows chewing the cud yet another opportunity for the tiny fists to beat upon the windows of our car. In spite of this, the noise and the color of passing saris and garlanded biers carrying the dead delighted and excited me. Sara hated every moment but then she grew up in the green hills of Galilee whilst I grew up in the east end of London in the war years. I almost felt at home apart from the cows. I could tell from Sara's distorted expression that she desperately needed to evacuate bladder or bowel or both and explained as much to Vijay Sunil Singh. With extraordinary tact and skilful maneuvering he quickly parked his car beside a large curio shop that he claimed was owned by a cousin and ushered Sara inside. She emerged ten minutes later with a big smile on her face and gave a perfectly executed and gracious Namaste greeting to the shop proprietor and our driver. I've no idea when and how she learnt to do the slight bow forward with the hands held as if in prayer but it looked so natural that I fell in love all over again. We continued on our journey further laden with little teak elephants and pashmina scarves paid for at the asking price to the bewilderment of the salesmen but that was the least we could do in return for the pit stop.

After a ninety minute journey we arrived exhausted at the most famous hotel in India. It looked more like a cross between a Mughal palace and a Victorian railway station, than a hotel, but inside was cool and peaceful. The travel company had tipped off the hotel that we were newly weds so we were shown to the bridal suite with a magnificent view of the brightly lit esplanade around the bay and the square in front of the great Gateway to India. We barely gave it a second look before falling asleep in a huge bejeweled double-posted double bed mounted high above floor level on a gold platform, exhausted from our travails without the strength to unpack or even change into our nightwear.

★★★

We slept well and awoke the following morning refreshed. Breakfast was brought to our room and proved to be a delightful surprise. There were heaps of exotic fruit none of which we recognized. There were thin crisp pancakes filled with I know not what, that melted on our tongues and deep fried onion balls cooked in a mild spice. Best of all there was strong, dark and aromatic Assam tea and a cool sweet yoghurt drink called lassi. Sara became addicted to lassi whilst in due course I became addicted to Kingfisher beer.

We then dressed in light summer clothes in order to explore the hotel. Sara was delighted to find that it was built around an oasis with a beautiful blue tilled swimming pool shaded by tall palms. She there and then decided to move no further for the remainder of our time in Bombay and sent me back to our room to collect her swimming costume. On the way upstairs past the enormous chandeliers and carved mahogany staircases, I smiled to myself thinking that this was the first of my duties as a dutiful husband and a little squirt of pure joy entered my blood stream. I had never before witnessed Sara languidly stretched out on a sun lounger in a swimming costume and couldn't take my eyes off her. That also seemed to be the case with a dozen or so middle aged obese brown men sitting in her proximity at the poolside. Again I felt the little burst of joy.

However beautiful the view, I got restless after an hour and decided to explore the neighborhood. I had dressed myself according to my vision of the white man in the tropics of the British Empire as remembered from the "Boy's Own Paper" I'd read as a child growing up in London. I had adopted the look of the last days of the Raj; desert boots, khaki slacks, bush shirt with breast pockets and epaulettes, silk paisley scarf tucked in open neck and pith helmet replaced by a white straw panama hat, as I strode confidently into Marine Drive. Big mistake! As if guided by pheromones the hawkers and the beggars plying their trades at the Gateway to India homed in on me like bees round a honey pot. I beat a hasty retreat, went back to the bedroom, changed into shorts, took out my guidebook to India and joined Sara at the pool. In the same way I attracted hawkers and beggars it seemed that Sara attracted men of a certain age with morbid obesity. I chuckled to myself and settled down to research India, its customs and its religions from the safety of the pool at the Taj Mahal Palace hotel happy to be a tourist with no pretensions of becoming a traveler. And so, waited on hand and foot, pampered and polished, we spent the first two days of our Indian idyll. Then the madness began again.

We retraced our steps running the gauntlet of beggars and peddlers to the airport and checked in at the domestic Air India desk, waited in the stinking squalor of the departure lounge and boarded the flight to Cochin, removing livestock from our pre booked seats whilst being greeted with big smiles from the other passengers, most of whom showed more gums than teeth.

The contrast between Kerala and Bombay could not have been more extreme.

First of all Cochin airport was peaceful and our driver was waiting with our name on a card. The fact that Air India had lost our luggage seemed of little concern as indicated by our driver with that peculiar Indian lateral shaking of the head with a big smile that seemed to imply "don't worry be happy". He promised us it would turn up on the next flight only two days away. In fact it had been there all along but had fallen off the conveyor belt between the aircraft and the arrival lobby. A spindly-legged old porter rushed out with our cases just in time before we got in the taxi and almost suffered an apoplexy of delight on receiving a 10-rupee note. He scuttled off before giving me time to work out that I'd given him ten times the going rate; equivalent to one dollar instead of ten cents enough to feed his family for a week.

The next thing I noticed was the perfect dentition of the Keralari Indians we saw on our way to the Coconut Lagoon resort ten miles south of Cochin. This we learnt was something to do with the healthy diet and freedom from chewing paan with betel nut paste. The third thing we noticed along the way, were crocodile lines of young children dressed in school uniforms with crisp white blouses and navy skirts or shorts, the girls all looking the same with their shiny black hair arranged in two perfectly symmetrical plaits. I then learnt from the driver that schooling was compulsory up to the age of 14 and paid for by the state of Kerala that could boast a 90% literacy rate. They all carried leather satchels over their shoulders that I hadn't seen since I was a schoolboy in Whitechapel.

The Coconut Lagoon resort was exactly as we imagined. It was arrived at by boat across the backwaters that were carpeted by pink lotus flowers. It sat on a narrow spit of land with the Indian Ocean on the other side. As we arrived we were each given the Namaste greeting by pretty young women in traditional saris who then hung garlands of sweet perfumed flowers round our necks. All the guests were housed in traditional village huts that were far from primitive inside. Our low double bed was also garlanded with hibiscus and jasmine blossom. The shower and toilet facilities were open to the sky but modesty was ensured by a palisade of tropical palms however it did mean we shared our facilities with a pair of bottle green googly eyed tree frogs who served to keep the flying insects at bay. All meals were served in a huge open sided thatched pavilion and the fresh fruit, vegetables and delicate spices, all from local producers, kept us well fed and explained the perfect dentition of the Malabari. This was truly a tropical paradise just as we had imagined. We spent the early mornings strolling along the white sands at the edge of the Indian Ocean watching the local fishermen bring in their long narrow wooden boats lifted on their shoulders against the pull of the high surf. We then watched them unload the nets and pick out the abundant catch of herring like fish whilst in our turn we were watched with undisguised interest by the fishing village children. They were not the least shy but keen to engage us in conversation in order to practice their school English.

In the afternoon we would sit on our veranda and watch the thatch roofed houseboats that doubled up as tea barges, sail up and down the backwaters followed by platoons of tall stately white egrets. Sara would doze off in her hammock whilst I continued my reading of the guidebooks on Cochin and it environs I'd picked up on the way, looking for clues to facilitate our search for any footprints left behind by Yehudit bat Eliezer. In the evening before dinner we would return to the Ocean side and watch the sunset whilst I sipped my cold Kingfisher beer from the well stocked ice box in our hut and Sara sipped sweet lassi up a straw.

After a week of this idyllic life amongst the lotus-eaters we decided to make our expedition in search of the last Jews of Kerala.

★★★

We hired a car, driver and guide. The car was the ubiquitous white Austin Ambassador whilst the driver and guide were local men who both spoke English. Our guide, Ahmed Ali was well educated and had read history at the university in nearby Ernakulam.

On the road to Cochin Ahmed entertained us by explaining the history, demography, flora and fauna of Kerala illustrated with spicy anecdotes about the spice growers and tea planters. He was a gifted storyteller and obviously proud of the achievements of the State of Kerala. There were no beggars on this narrow highway fringed with spice plantations. Tea was grown in the plantations high in the foothills of the Western Ghats the coastal mountain chain. He urged us to book him again for another day to see how the legendary tea planters used to live. In this way we arrived in the pretty little town of Cochin hardly aware of the passage of time. We parked as close as possible to the quaintly named "Jew Town" and were soon walking along the narrow thoroughfare named Synagogue Road.

The road was lined with pastel colored low-rise houses and we could judge those that were Jewish by the Star of David worked into the railings round the small balconies at the first floor windows. Ahmed explained that most of the Jews had left and Muslim or Christian families and the occasional Kashmeri trader now occupied the houses. He seemed to know everyone and nodded left and right to greetings from shopkeepers, spice sellers and antique dealers crying out, "Mr Ali please bring your friends to visit my humble emporium" or words to that effect.

"Later later" he would reply "but first they must see the Mattancheri Synagogue".

At last, close to the end of the road he stopped at a little shop selling Judaica and made an obeisance to a lady who sat embroidering a skullcap in the shade of her doorway.

"Mrs Cohen may I introduce my good friends Dr and Mrs Tanner, newlyweds on vacation from Israel" he announced with orotund diction and great formality. Mrs Cohen was a woman in her mid thirties with a pale complexion that was even whiter than mine, rose with dignity and accepted my outstretched hand in greeting. She went on at length to explain that she and her husband Shalom were also newly married and that he came from the blood line of the high priest of the Temple in Jerusalem and was the last of the priestly tribe amongst the Paradesi Jews of Kerala. There was something of hauteur in her attitude to us as if the name Paradesi should have implied that she was a member of the aristocracy. She invited us into her shop and with no persuasion Sara eagerly purchased a beautifully embroidered cloth to cover the *chalah* bread for the Friday night blessings.

She apologized for the absence of her husband who was away on business but she was sure that the *Shamas* or beadle of the synagogue, Mr. K.J.Joy, would be glad to show us round the Paradesi synagogue. She nodded farewell *en haute au bas,* and we continued our stroll up Synagogue Road. On the way I addressed a question to Ali concerning the naming of the Synagogue. His reply surprised me. "Mattancheri is where we stand and it's a word that is a mixture of Hebrew and Malayalam, the local tongue.

Mattana means gift in Hebrew and *Cheri* means port in Malayalam. This reflects the history of the Jews in Kerala, as the ancient gateway of the spice trade with Israel was gifted by the Raja of Cochin to the Jewish settlers. The white Jews of Cochin prefer to distinguish themselves from the other Jews by describing themselves as the Paradesi." "What do you mean by other Jews?" I responded. "Wait my friend, all will be explained in due course."

We arrived at the gates of the synagogue where we found Mr K.J.Joy waiting for us and bubbling over with his enthusiastic welcome. He was a charming skinny young man wearing little more than a *lungi* and speaking a mixture of English and Gibberish in his hurry to impart his specialist knowledge. We exchanged 4 rupees as entrance tickets but first of all he proudly pointed out how close the Synagogue was to the rather disappointingly modest Raja's Palace. Next he drew our attention to the square clock tower that had a clock with three faces telling the time in Hebrew, Arabic and conventional numbers. The inscription under the clock faces was a quotation from the Psalms that in translation read, "Our days are like passing shadows", obviously lifted from Macbeth's soliloquy written about 2,500 years later, or was it the other way round. We then entered the synagogue precincts and were asked to remove our shoes in the gloomy vestibule as our eyes slowly adapted from the brilliant sunshine outdoors. He explained that this was not a Jewish custom but aimed at protecting the precious tiles on the floor of the main building.

We then crossed the threshold and stood upon the blue and white Chinese willow pattern tiles each one different in design. To our right a narrow wooden staircase led up to the woman's gallery that was hidden behind painted fretwork screens with the idea that the women of the community could be heard but not seen. The interior was brightly lit from tall windows on three sides of the square interior with the far eastern wall claiming the honour of bearing the Ark covered in elaborate velvet curtains. High above the front of the Ark the everlasting flame burnt in a ruby coloured glass oil lamp. This lamp was repeated over and over by a confusing array of coloured glass vessels hanging from the ceiling in no particular pattern, that were only lit on the High Holy days.

At that point Ali whispered in his ear and a few rupees changed hands after which Mr. KJ Joy turned to us with a smile that reflected his name and announced that as we were the only visitors in the Synagogue he would show us the most precious possession held by the Paradesi house of worship. At that, with a flourish he drew back the curtains hiding the Ark to reveal what looked like to my untrained eyes as polished sandalwood doors carved with fantastic designs of the flora and fauna of the land. He threw open the double doors to a breathtaking display of gold crowned *Sifre Torah* enclosed in the cylindrical hinged cases of the Sephardic tradition. We gazed on them in awe but I was secretly disappointed not to be shown a pair of golden candlesticks from the King Herod's Temple. I thought that was it but then KJ Roy bent over and lifted out a teak box the size and shape of that which school children use to carry their pencils and rulers. "This is our most precious possession!" he declaimed. He lifted out the crusty old box and took it up to the *bimah* from which the Torah was read every Shabbat, opened it up and reverentially picked out 6 metal plaques each about 12 by 3 inches in size made of some kind of yellow metal, not gold but perhaps polished bronze, each densely covered in tiny script of a language unknown to me.

He nodded to Ali who took over, "these plates are inscribed in ancient Sanskrit and are the legal deeds by which the Raja of Cochin conferred the land and rights to the first Jewish settlers. They describe how the gift of treasure from the refugees and the respect for the traders who had secured the wealth of his Kingdom, the Jews would be allowed to build their Temple in a foreign land and how their leader Yehoshua Rabeinu would be granted royal status and establish a Kingdom in the empty lands north of Cochin." My pulse quickened at the mention of the gift of treasure. He continued, " This Yehoshua is now referred to as Joseph Rabban and is a kind of semi-mythical individual a bit like Prester John, amongst the Jews of Kerala. Legend has it that his Queen was of a beauty that outshone the Queen of Sheba and that she was as clever as she was beautiful".

KJ Joy then gathered up the metal plates and returned them to the Ark. He indicated that the tour was at an end so I slipped him a few more rupees in appreciation then as we were putting on our shoes, I noticed something that had escaped me when we were entering the building. Along the wall that had been hidden in the gloom beforehand I could make out four large mural paintings. They looked rather amateurish in the execution but intriguing in their content. I asked Mr Roy if he could turn on a light and let me inspect them. He seemed reluctant and almost embarrassed but responded to Ali Ahmed's urging.

As the *Shamas* refused to say any more it was left to Ali to explain that the first painting described King Solomon in Jerusalem greeting traders from the Malabar coast. The second illustrated the destruction of the second temple, the third the landing of the Jewish refugees on the Malabar Coast whilst the fourth showed Joseph Rabban future King of Shingly accepting the Royal charter from the Raja of Cochin in exchange for two golden candlesticks from his future Queen." At that Sara let out a little squeal of excitement and I turned to her with my finger on my lips urging caution. I started out with a flood of question but by this time Mr KJ Roy's tolerance seemed to be exhausted and we were hustled out in manner I thought quite rude as the *Shammas* shut up shop for the day.

As we once more entered the brilliant sunshine of another perfect Malabari afternoon, I turned to Ali and with hurt in my voice asked, "what was all that about, what did we do or say to offend?" "Ah, it's a long and complicated story and there was nothing wrong in your behaviour it's just that the Paradesi Jews have secrets they do not wish to discuss with strangers. Come now let's find somewhere cool to sit where you can drink a light beer and Mrs Tanner might enjoy a refreshing tall glass of chilled sweet lassi. Of course as a Muslim, I can't join you with a beer but you will forgive me if I just have some mango juice."

★★★

We parked ourselves under the shade of a banyan tree overlooking the backwaters where a teahouse had been set up and preceded to order our drinks. Once we had settled down Ali started up again and with his extraordinary talent for narrative, told us the sad story of the last Jews of Kerala. "You were right Dr. Tanner to pick up on something missing in the story recounted by dear Mr Joy. I shall for now describe the Paradesi community as the White Jews of Kerala to distinguish them from the Black Jews. As you surmised the White Jews came here to escape the Spanish and Portuguese inquisition after the expulsions of 1492. As such they are Sephardim. They like to claim that their faith is pure and that they can trace their roots to the ancient Israelites that were sent as slaves to the Iberian Peninsula after the conquest of Judea by the Romans in 70 CE. By this twist of logic they fantasize that they are the true descendants of Joseph Rabban. Yet there is another Jewish community in Kerala who live on the mainland in the city of Ernakulam who we call the Malarabi or Black Jews. They are truly the ones who can trace their line back to those who landed here about 2,000 years ago. Unfortunately for them in the context of this story, in their long history there has been much intermarriage with the native Indian community so they are dark skinned like me, hence their description as the Black Jews. The natives of Kerala are very tolerant people and there has always been freedom of religion in part because the Mughal Empire never reached this far south and in saying that I speak against my own faith.

Therefore the Jews have never suffered any hostility and were allowed to build their houses of worship and grow wealthy on their trading or professional skills. The newcomers from Iberia became very wealthy because of their trading connections whereas the black Jews, as lowly artisans hardly distinguishable from their aboriginal neighbors, could not match their influence. Then the White Jews adopted airs and graces and to their shame began to emulate the Hindu caste system, claiming the equivalent to Brahmin status for themselves and treating the Black Jews as untouchables.

'Intermarriage' was forbidden and a kind of apartheid was established. As a result the population went into decline and once the State of Israel was declared many of the Black Jews went there

210

to try to improve their status and prosperity whilst many the younger White Jews went there to fulfill their mystical belief that transportation to the Iberian peninsula followed by exile in India were merely steps along the way to their final redemption and recognition as the first among equals amongst the Princely caste of the reborn State of Israel. Now the numbers of both Black and White are so small that I fear they will shortly face extinction." "May we meet one of these Black Jews?" I asked interrupting his flow. "With pleasure" he replied, "I intend to take you to meet my friend Babu Joseph and let him complete this story. He lives close to the old Synagogue at Chenamangalam just north of Ernakulom. He is the last *shochet* and kosher butcher in Kerala and of course the White Jews wouldn't soil their hands with such low caste work so they depend heavily on him and when he goes I predict that will be the end of history for the Jews of Kerala".

I paid the bill and we piled back into the Austin Ambassador where the poor driver had been waiting patiently for the best part of three hours.

We drove east across a complex route of bridges crossing the inlets, outlets and islets that made up the intricate geography of the coast and backwaters of this area. One hour later we entered the rundown and ramshackle town of Ernakulom and turned north to Chenamangalam where we tracked down Babu Joseph and his kosher butchery and curio shop. Apart from the skullcap perched on the back of his head he would have passed as native to India. He had a dark olive complexion, with a toothy brilliant smile and wearing a singlet top over a sarong that was covered in a blood stained apron. He greeted us warmly, threw off his apron and invited us in for tea. His nervous little sparrow of a wife served us in silence keeping her eyes downcast in respect. Babu endorsed all that we had heard from Ali but in poor English and additional translation by Ali, he expanded on this sad story. Obviously there was little love lost between the two tribes of Malabari Jews, not only had the Whites treated the Blacks as untouchables they had even stolen their historical heritage. The four murals we had noted at the Paradesi synagogue illustrated the history of the Black Jews not of these upstart newcomers. The metal plates of the covenant with the Cochini Rajas was theirs and taken from them for "safe keeping" when the Chenemangalam synagogue, the last and the oldest of their dying community, fell into disrepair and the Paradesi Jews refused to offer a loan to have it restored.

I then asked him about Joseph Rabban, king of the Jews. He replied that the name was Rabeinu, meaning "our Rabbi", not Rabban and that he was granted kingship of the land of Cranganore also known as Shingly 40 miles to the north. Terrible floods forcing the inhabitants to move southward coincidentally with the arrival of the White Jews from Spain and Portugal destroyed that Kingdom 400 to 500 years ago and that's how their histories were mixed up and exploited by the newcomers in their favour. I stemmed his flow by asking if he knew anything about the first Queen of Cranganore and the golden candlesticks. "Indeed" he replied, "she is central to our oral history and we think we know where the golden candlesticks are to be found". At that Sara and I sat forward in our chairs and held our breath. "The Cochini Rajas grew very wealthy with their trade in spice and hoarded their gold. However 500 years ago their ports silted up and the trade was redirected to the port of Bombay. After that they were also hit badly by the floods that destroyed Shingly and they lost their fine Palaces. To maintain their lifestyle they started to pawn their treasure to the Hindu brokers who in turn left the gold and precious stones with their Temples for safe keeping in deep vaults that were protected by the elephant headed God Ganasha and the curse of Shiva. Eventually when the Raja's money ran out they built a very modest palace, that you probably saw not far from the Paradesi synagogue, losing hope forever of redeeming their treasure."

"So where are the candlesticks now?" I cried out barely able to contain my excitement. "We believe that they are buried amongst the treasure in the vaults of the Sree Padmanabhaswamy Temple in the ancient capital of Kerala, Trivandrum. These vaults are now sealed and no one dare attempt to unseal them because of the curse." Sara and I exhaled in unison and although disappointed, philosophically accepted the fact that we had come to the end of this line of enquiry yet at the same time had discovered Yehudit bat Eliezer's footprint in the sands of time.

We thanked the last kosher butcher of Kerala but his dignity did not allow him to accept the proffered tip instead of which he invited us to put our small change in his JNF money box to help plant trees in Eretz Yisrael. The irony of that gesture seemed lost on him. As we left Cochin in our hired car I looked across at Sara and noted that she bore a dreamy smile that reminded me of my mother as she sat listening to music on the BBC light program. A sudden thought flashed in and out of my mind. My mother's family claimed descent from an ancient Indian Diaspora, could Sara and my mother, by miraculous coincidence, be the last of the lines descending from the twin daughters of Eliezer the priest of the second temple.

Far from disappointing we thought the day out had been exciting and informative and a wonderful break from eating lotuses at the Coconut Lagoon hotel. The rest of our holiday passed uneventfully as we worked at our suntans and prepared ourselves mentally for our life together as husband and wife as well as surgeon and scrub nurse. A marriage made in heaven in more ways than one.

Chapter 23

London 1964-1967 part 1

On returning to Afula, as a newly married couple, we were billeted in a pretty little Arab house, presumably abandoned in the war of 1948, that had thick walls and small windows, designed to keep cool in the summer whilst retaining its heat in the month or two of cold weather in what passed for winter. The one storey house was almost entirely covered in bougainvillea and had three cosy rooms inside: A perfect little love nest that was soon made habitable by Sara who seemed naturally gifted as a homemaker. Yet it was not to be our home for long. Awaiting me on my return was a letter from my old friend Gadi Rosenthal the professor of epidemiology at the Haifa. After wishing me *mazeltov* on my marriage he went on to make an offer that would completely change the path of my career I had assumed was already inscribed in stone. Apparently he was a close friend of his opposite number at the Institute of Cancer Research, ICR, in London, Professor Archie Lambert. Archie had tipped him off that the ICR and its neighbouring clinical facility, the Royal Marsden Hospital on the Fulham road, were establishing a new team to start researching familial and genetically determined breast cancer. The ICR had already put together a group that included epidemiologists, statisticians, pathologists, geneticists and tumor biologists supported by a large MRC grant, what they were missing was an academic surgeon with interest in the topic. They had noticed that one of Gadi's co-authors had an FRCS and might he be interested in applying for the job that had just been advertised in the BMJ. The job description was for a surgeon who would become a full time specialist in breast cancer and set up a dedicated clinic that might attract women with breast cancer from high-risk families and to help collect specimens of serum and malignant tissue to support the work of this new team. The appointment would be at the senior lecturer / consultant level, paid through the University but with honorary status in the NHS. For those in the know that would mean a denial of the right to involve themselves in private practice and that meant there was a dearth of suitable applicants. As I still retained my membership of the BMA I still received the British Medical Journal although I couldn't remember the last time I had looked at the back pages were the small ads appeared for appointments in the NHS.

I rummaged through recent back copies that had accumulated unopened during my adventures over the previous few months and eventually found the advert and thought to myself "why not?" The contract was only for three years in the first instance so I wouldn't be burning my bridges altogether and the salary by Israeli standards was princely. Furthermore having given up on my quest for the "the tablet of the Holy Covenant" I might now join in the more important and more realistic quest for "the holy grail" of the genetic secrets of cancer. I very much doubted that Sara would share my enthusiasm but was pleasantly surprised as she leaped at the possibility of living in the land of murk and money as a change from the boring old land of milk and honey, as long as she could pop back twice a year to see her father. I still thought it was a long shot but applied in any case. Within a month I had a letter informing me that I was short listed and invited to attend an interview on the 1st of April, the fact that this was April Fools' Day did not escape my attention. I thought I had nothing to lose and as I hadn't been back to London for four or five years it would make a good excuse for visiting my aunt and uncle and my two cousins to show off my new wife.

When I suggested this she was overcome with excitement that made me realize that although I took old London Town for granted, for the rest of the world London still remained the Mecca of glamour, theatre, fashion and the latest genre in pop music. I wrote to accept the offer of an interview and also informed uncle Hymie and Aunty Becky, who now lived in a posh area of Northwest London, of my plans.

They replied by return of post that they would be delighted to see us and as April 1st was a Friday they would make a big Friday night dinner for the family that would include my two cousins, their husbands and their first grandchild and we could make use of one of their bedrooms and bathrooms left empty since "the kids left home".

My hospital wasn't too pleased with this but the medical director recognizing that this might be the chance of a lifetime granted me a week's leave of absence.

★★★

We flew to Heathrow and Sara could barely contain her excitement as our flight path took us over the Thames and she recognized Tower Bridge and the Tower of London. Uncle Hymie was waiting for us in Arrivals and greeted me with a warm embrace. He then turned to Sara took both of her hands and examined her at arms length. Turning to me he announced, "Martin, *k'nain hora* she is the double of your darling mother when she was a girl," then turning to face Sara who seemed to tower over his short tubby frame, "booboola you are like an angel and Martin is a very lucky boychick!" Sara blushed crimson but undeterred he took our trolley and bustled us into the short-term car park and from there into his rather handsome Rover limousine. Uncle Hymie appeared to have done well for himself. This impression was reinforced three times over when he eventually turned into his drive in Winnington Road, Hampstead Garden Suburb. He *had* done very well for himself; this house must have cost him at least £20,000!

Auntie Becky as homely and cuddly as ever embraced me like a long lost child and actually burst into tears. When she was introduced to Sara she turned pale, embraced her and again burst into tears without saying a word.

The house was enormous and decorated in the worst possible taste exactly as I used to describe as "Jewish Renaissance". Our guest room and en suite bathroom were done out in turquoise and kitted our like Madam Pompadour's boudoir. It was all so vulgar

216

that it was comical but I wasn't the least bit judgmental. I was really happy for them and knew that his good fortune had come from hard graft. I learnt later on that by working day and night and opening up his shop as soon as Shabbat finished, baking through the night and providing fresh bagels, cream cheese and smoked salmon early on Sunday morning he now owned a chain of kosher delicatessens in Golders Green and Hendon. Over a gargantuan dinner we caught up on family gossip and community affairs and they listened awe struck to tales of our adventures on Masada and in India although we were careful to remember not to disclose any State secrets. Sara listened intently and watched the proceedings as if she were an anthropologist in alien surroundings. Although we all were of Jewish stock she had never previously encountered the rich bourgeois subspecies of our breed.

The following morning I was driven to Golders Green tube station, leaving Sara to get to know the natives. After one change on the line I arrived at a South Kensington and strolled through the early morning sunshine to the Fulham Road and climbed the stairs to the famous Royal Marsden Hospital, the oldest specialist cancer centre in the world. I was directed to an anteroom outside the boardroom and sat down to wait my turn in the company of three heavily pinstriped young men. I no longer owned a suit and I hadn't worn a tie for four years. So sitting there in a casual jacket and what felt like a noose around my neck I felt somewhat out of place. I wasn't the least bit nervous and felt that I really had nothing to lose. The other three seemed to know each other and spoke with that braying accent of the upper middle classes and clearly saw this job as a stepping stone to a good teaching hospital post with private privileges. I also overheard that one of the candidates was Mr. Raven's senior registrar and that Mr. Raven was chairing the committee.

When it was my turn I was ushered in and shown to a red leather seat at the centre of a long table surrounded by similar chairs except for a very high backed throne occupied by the chairman, in the centre facing me. The chairman welcomed me and introduced himself as Mr Ronald Raven and then went round the table

217

introducing me to eight other men whose names I quickly forgot except for professor Archie Lambert, Gadi's friend who gave me a sly wink.

Mr Raven opened the questioning. He was a dapper little man, dressed in Edwardian morning suit with a hawk like face. He had a strange mode of speech more like a Roman Senator declaiming before the Senate and for that reason I had difficulty in judging whether his questions were rhetorical or not. He seemed to wish to learn about my surgical experience. I knew of him of course having used his textbooks on operative surgery to get me out sticky situations in the past and somehow I wove in the story of the newborn with the meningo-myelocele into my answer at one point and noted that he flushed with pride.

The next to speak was some whale of a man with a booming voice who reminded me of Duffield-Morgan from my house surgeon days. I marked him out as an anti-Semite as he insisted on calling me an Israelite as if that was somehow amusing. The others gave me little trouble but I was given the chance to really show by best when Archie Lambert talked to me about the research programme they had in mind. At that I came into my own and it soon became clear that I knew more about the subject than anyone else round the table. It pleased me to see the fat and fatuous man sink lower in his chair and keep checking his fob watch.

After the interviews were complete we were advised to wait, as the appointment would be announced after the committee had deliberated and that we should return in an hour. As it was still bright and sunny outside I decided to stroll around the charming lanes and squares full of white-stuccoed Edwardian villas with impressive porticoed doorways. I was just thinking this meant the Marsden catered for the carriage trade rather than humble artisans when I spotted a blue plaque on the wall of one of these impressive London Town houses that boasted of having been the home of Mr Hansom himself famous for the horse drawn cab that carried his name.

I returned in good time only to hear raised voices coming from the boardroom. After a good two and a half hours the doors were flung open and Mr Fat and Fatuous who I later learnt went by the name of Giles Carpenter-Finch, stormed out and I was ushered in. There were smiles all round as Mr Raven offered me the job and shook my hand and launched into a speech of welcome that would have done Seneca proud. All but Archie Lambert left and he then ambled over a slipped an arm around my neck and with the soft burr of a man raised in Edinburgh said," aye laddie that was a close thing but I'm glad the best man won. You'll ken that four of us from the ICR supported you as the only one who knew anything about our research the other four from the hospital felt threatened by your erudition and just wanted another chinless wonder. In the end the chairman, Ronnie Raven, had the casting vote. We assumed it would go to his senior registrar that brown nosed lad Christopher Humphries, but to our surprise Ronnie gave it to you with yon little speech about seeing something about you that would add lustre to the institution. Make no mistake he's a cannie auld buzzard even though he dresses and talks like a Sassenach toff. When can you start?"

I asked for a gap of one month and watched him walk away leaving me in a daze. I then spent an hour with the admin staff before retracing my steps to northwest London just in time for the start of the Friday night rituals welcoming in Shabbat.

As I crossed the threshold I was met by a phalanx of enquiring faces. I remained deadpan until uncle Hymie asked the question all had on their lips; "Nuh?" I smiled in return and was greeted with whoops and mazeltovs all round and then manhandled into the best room where uncle Hymie brought out his best scotch, a dusty bottle of Dimple Haig unopened since his grandson's *bris* I surmised. After all the men present were served their cut glass tumbler of whiskey I was introduced to Jaqui and Lillian, the Hisrchon Girls' husbands, Sam Goldstone a local GP and Adam Oppenheimer of Oppenheimer and Grant the biggest estate agent in Hampstead. The girls had done well but I also had to admit that the two attractive and stylish young women to whom I had barely given a second look as we were growing up, had flowered and flourished even though they looked somewhat overnourished to my taste. All this time Sara had been standing quietly in the corner with a proud smile on her face. Excusing myself from the enthusiastic throng, I ran over, lifted her off her feet and gave her a big hug and a kiss.

Aunty Becky then shooed us through into a dining room decorated in the style of Louis Kartooz meets Victorian Vaudeville, with a long table covered in a Persil white tablecloth set with the family silver and surrounded by eight high backed chairs and one child's high chair. After Auntie Becky had made the blessing over the two *shabbos* candles, Sara was invited to repeat the blessings over a second set of silver candlesticks that normally only appeared for *Rosh Ha'Shana* the Jewish New Year.

Sara covered her head with a lace shawl and made two passes over the flames before covering her face with her hands and chanting in a sweet voice, *"Blessed art though oh Lord our God who has commanded us to light the Sabbath candles "*

Everyone appeared to be bewitched by her grace and beauty. After a moment's silence Uncle Hymie belted out the prayers for the wine and bread and then barely without a pause the talking and eating began. I couldn't remember when I had last enjoyed a Friday night dinner like this even though I had been living in the land of the Jews for nearly five years. Anyway to summarize the conversation: it was agreed that little Moishele aged two, the son of Jaqui and Sam was a genius and would grow up to be a neurosurgeon, we didn't fancy Arsenal's chances against QPR the next day, Israel needed a tougher more right wing government, Lillian knew this lovely little boutique, Mode de Paris, in Temple Fortune and Sara would look divine in one her creations, Britain was going to the dogs and everyone should make *aliyah* once the Israeli economy allowed it, Sara and I should live in Hampstead and Adam had just the perfect house for us, in perfect condition, and we should look at it tomorrow before he went off to Loftus Road for the local derby with kick off at 3.00 pm. Once the synchronous eating and talking in loud voices came to an end with Auntie's famous *lookshen koogle,* my uncle asked me if I would accept the honour of leading them in grace after meals. I hadn't done this since I was a young man in my parent's house but the words and the melodies were so imprinted in my memory that with only the occasional glance at the prayer book, I could perform the little service perfectly. The difference this time is that words had meaning without the need of covertly checking the translation. I seemed to lose myself in the beautiful melody of the final stanza, *"Nahar hayiti v'gum zakanti v'lo rahiti…"* and as I finished I broke down in tears of happiness.

The following morning we were excused from walking with Hymie and Sam to Norrice Lea synagogue, as I wanted to show Sara Hampstead Heath, my favorite corner of town.

As hoped for, Sara adored the Heath that at this time of year resembled the southern parts of the Galilee yet was within easy reach of public transport and only 20 minutes from the West End. At 11.00 as arranged, Adam and Lillian picked us up and we drove to view a little flat face Georgian terrace house in the centre of Hampstead Village not far from Whitestone Pond, the Heath, Hampstead tube and the little book shops, galleries, pubs and coffee bars for which Hampstead was renowned. It was love at first sight for both of us. The plaque on the front wall recorded the fact that John Constable the great English 18th C landscape painter had lived there and that alone was sufficient to satisfy me. The walls were festooned with clematis and the windows had shutters. The tiny front garden was railed off with wrought iron bars and the red painted front door boasted a lion's head with a brass knocker in its jaws.

Originally it was a "two up two down" workman's cottage but according to the surveyor's report, a basement and back room kitchen had been added in1880. However the most adorable feature was a cobblestone back yard with the original well and wrought iron supra-structure with a bucket on a chain.

A very talented spider had chosen to weave a perfect octagonal web linking the uprights of the arch that supported the winding gear at the top with the chain holding the bucket. The late morning sun catching a few remaining dewdrops on the gossamer threads glistened like crystal glass. I was glad that this passed unnoticed by Sara who suffered from arachnophobia.

This was an official "listed monument" and preserved for the nation. Sara expressed the worry that there were no vertical or horizontal edges to any of the walls or door frames but Adam reassured her that it had stood that way since the Napoleonic wars and should see us out. Sara and I went into a huddle and after a few minutes I disengaged and diffidently asked the price and the required deposit. We went into another huddle and agreed that with her dowry as a deposit and my salary to pay of the mortgage we could afford it, just. And thus it came to pass that we came to own Constable's cottage, Lower Terrace, Hampstead Village.

★★★

We returned briefly to Israel in order to clear out our meagre belongings as fortunately our accommodation on the hospital campus was fully furnished and equipped by *Kupot Cholim*. We also arrived just in time for the *bris* or ritual circumcision of Joe and Tziporah's first born who was named Yehoshua or Josh for short. Sara's father attended for that event as well so she could take a fond farewell. As my work would be part of a collaboration with Gadi's department in Haifa, I would be allowed one visit a year with all costs covered so it was indeed farewell and not goodbye.

On our return to London we set up home in our pretty Georgian cottage and soon worked out a quickest routes for walks on the Heath, shops for groceries and public transport to work; Northern line from Hampstead, change at Leicester Square and Piccadilly line to South Kensington.

A big bonus that went with the job was a grant to employ a research assistant who would collect and collate data on family history. Although the pay was risible it suited Sara perfectly especially as her nursing qualifications weren't recognized in the UK.

I threw myself into my work leaving Sara to buy soft furnishings for the house, appliances for the kitchen and blinds for the windows although they were purely for decoration as the antique shutters still served their original purpose.

We slept on a mattress on the floor at first and gradually accumulated cheap antique furniture from dubious second hand dealers in Camden Town. The first night we slept in Constable's cottage Sara woke me up in alarm as she could swear she had heard ghostly footsteps on the stairs. I checked and course it was nothing other than the ancient timbers shrinking in the cold of the night. I did not alert her to the fact that I sometimes woke in the night to hear the sound of water being drawn from the well. It might have been the antique plumbing together with the clanging of the obsolete boiler but I found it a comforting thought that the ghost of John Constable was keeping a benign eye on us.

To start with I established friendly terms with the nursing staff and the pathology department. The other consultant surgeons, physicians and radiotherapists were a likeable crew but with one exception and that of course was Carpenter-Finch. He saw me as a threat from the start and I rapidly learnt that he was a bigot and a bully. Yet the major difference between us was that he was ideologically committed to the Halsted radical mastectomy whilst I hoped to pioneer a more conservative and humane approach. There would never be a meeting of minds as this was not a scientific dialectic but a clash of ideologies that would never be resolved until he retired and that fortunately was only to be two years after my appointment. I'll say nothing more on this topic as the story of this battle has been told many times over by better men than me but it would take more than 20 years before we heretics were proven right and conservative surgery together with radiotherapy would replace the hideous mutilation my poor mother had to suffer.

I felt very much at home and once again enjoyed the camaraderie of the operating theatre and the doctor's mess. I joined the relevant surgical societies and was delighted to meet old friends who had followed my career choice. After a relatively short time I was put up for membership of the prestigious Athenaeum club in Pall Mall and duly elected. The Athenaeum is a stuffy old gentlemen's club and women were only allowed in the evening provided they are seen but not heard. Sara hated it. On my own initiative I also gained membership of another exclusive club just around the corner from the hospital, the notorious and rather louche Chelsea Arts Club. Women were only let in if they were prepared to take their clothes off and keep still for an hour whilst being sketched and then join the artist in one of the bedrooms to admire his etchings. Sara loved the Chelsea arts and the Chelsea artists loved Sara but never to the best of my knowledge, persuaded her to take off her clothes in spite of frequent entreaties.

But it was through my work that I achieved my fulfillment. I set up the first clinic in London totally dedicated to the diagnosis and treatment of breast cancer and recruited and trained the first cohort of nurses that specialized in their care. Furthermore, I looked upon my patients as both vulnerable individuals coming to terms with a terrifying disease as well as units each of whom might play a central role in the quest for an understanding of the disease. My critics, and I had many in these early years, accused me of treating my patients as guinea pigs, but my patients belied that unkind jibe and looked upon themselves as members of an exclusive club and that was mostly as a result of Sara's kindness, sensitivity and unofficial role as a counsellour.

My involvement in research was two fold. The first was rather passive in the role of collecting blood and tissue for the back room boys in the labs. It was just over ten years since Watson and Crick described the molecular structure of DNA and molecular biology, as it came to be known, was in its infancy and most of my specimens were frozen in liquid nitrogen and stored at -70 degrees Celsius, to await the day that individual genes could be cloned.

My active role was in the epidemiological studies of high-risk families and here I collaborated directly with Archie Telford, Gadi Rosenthal in Haifa and a group based at the Memorial Sloan Kettering Cancer Centre in New York.

Within that remit I had to tighten up on my theories about the Ashkenazi Sephardic nexus and come up with some reasonable theories about an evolutionary advantage of carrying a gene that had the potential of killing off young women before their first child or leaving behind infants without maternal protection.

In these areas Sara came up with some astonishing insights that set our agenda and were taken sufficiently seriously by our collaborators as to incorporate them in their protocols.

This all came out in a leisurely conversation we were enjoying after dinner as a guest of Archie and Caroline Telford in their delightful Chelsea pied a terre in the company of Dr. Bernie Fassbinder from New York. We were discussing our adventures in India when suddenly Sara's face lit up and she did something out of character by interrupting my flow of conversation in public. "Martin, two things have just occurred to me. If the story of the White Jews and Black Jews of Kerala is true and if there is anything in your theories about breast cancer risk amongst the Ashkenazim and the Sephardim then we have two perfect populations to study who were forbidden to intermarry. Most of these have now migrated to Israel and they would be an ideal starting point for Professor Rosenthal. If that is confirmed then I know with great precision the date of the breast cancer germ line mutation", she claimed. You could have heard a pin drop. "Please go on my dear" coached Archie. Without giving any secrets away she described her family history and the legend of the Zinati clan. "After the fall of the second temple Jewish slaves were transported to the Iberian Peninsula and went on to establish the Sephardic branch of our faith but families like ours stayed on in the Levant to this day. I can only assume that the matriarch of us unfortunates who carry the curse was the mother or grandmother of the first of our line born early in the first century BCE" she concluded. After a few more moments of silent cogitation round the table Bernie Fassbinder burst out with, "That's some smart cookie you've got there Dr. Tanner, it's a long shot but worth the punt. Let's go for it". I turned to Sara and tried to compose a smile that expressed love, pride and astonishment.

Later on the evening as we became more and more mellow under the influence of the first single malt I've ever tasted, a 12 year old Talisker if my memory serves me right, Sara again took us by surprise. I was grinding on with my half baked ideas that the evolutionary advantage was something to do with the co-expression of genes that coded for brains and beauty based on a sample size of two, Sara and my mother; although on reflection I had no idea whether my mother was clever or not as women of that generation seldom had the chance of exploiting their brain power, when again Sara intervened. "Martin please forgive me but although I can accept that cleverness has intrinsic survival advantages, beauty in the eye of any beholder, has no intrinsic value. If a man has learnt to judge women with certain physical characteristics as ideal breeding partners then, this thing we call beauty must in itself be indirect evidence of fertility or the pelvic capacity to carry a baby full term." Archie choked on his Talisker and we all fell about laughing. Sara blushed not sure if she'd made a fool of herself until Archie intervened. "Aye yon lassie's smarter than the rest of us. Martin I want you to promote Sara to senior research fellow but on the same salary and then write an opinion piece for Nature based on Sara's fresh insights and although the authorship will be Tanner and Tanner the Mrs will be first." At that the party ended and we made our way home on the tube I held Sara's hand and exalted in my luck at being one half of Tanner and Tanner.

....

Chapter 24

London 1964-67 Part 2

Following that extraordinary meeting at Archie Telford's home, Sara and I had to settle down to implement our plans and protocols. First off Tanner and Tanner decided to write their paper. Nothing so concentrates the mind than transcribing fireside chat into a fully referenced and coherent form suitable for publication. Nature turned down our first version but with some very helpful suggestions from one of their referees. After a bit of fine-tuning it was eventually accepted by the Lancet as an opinion piece with the provocative title; "What is the evolutionary advantage of beauty?" In parallel we wrote a second paper authored by Tanner and Tanner where we reversed the authorship wherein we formalized the hypothesis that a germ line mutation predisposing to breast cancer appeared shortly before the fall of the second Temple leading to differing risk profiles between Ashkenazi and Sephardic Jews and recommending that the populations of the White and Black Jews of Kerala would be an ideal testing bed for the theory. The British Journal of Epidemiology and Public Health accepted this but not before it had been seen and endorsed by Gadi who had already sent out his fieldworkers to track down these communities. I then made contact again with my old friend Jonathan Ashkenazi who had recently been appointed as a consultant cardiologist at the Brompton hospital just the other side of the Fulham Road to the Marsden and he expressed delight at the opportunity of working with me again. Jonathan had recently married a dark eyed beauty from a family of Jews who had been kicked out of Iraq in 1948. Her name was Sonia and the two of them made up a friendly foursome with the Tanners and we often went to the National Theatre at the Old Vic together as well as joining the proms at the Royal Albert

Hall. They both came from wealthy families and lived not far from my aunt and uncle in a pretty cul-de-sac that by coincidence was named Constable Close. One evening in the interval of "The Merchant of Venice" at the old Vic starring Sir Laurence Olivier, I made the gaff of describing Sonia as having the classical beauty I'd come to associate with the Sephardim. This was meant as a compliment but Sonia seemed put out and insisted that she was Mizrahi not Sephardic, I was not aware of that distinction and quickly apologized. At the time that exchange meant nothing but about a year later the memory of that moment reignited my research that seemed to have hit the buffers. For the time being both Jonathan and Sonia agreed to help us with our search for high-risk families amongst their communities.

The next part of our research proved problematical from the start. Along with collecting kindred with a predisposition to breast cancer that suggested a Mendelian inheritance of a dominant gene, we wanted to try to identify any feature that might suggest an evolutionary advantage and therefore imply that it was co expressed along with the cancer gene. In laymen's terms this meant that it sat on a chromosome close by the mutant gene. I was often asked to speak to lay audiences in the London Jewish community in order to promote my research and I hit on a good analogy. Jews love to play bridge and many became world class. It is always a pleasure to play a hand with a new pack of cards freshly delivered from its cellophane wrapping and freshly divested of the jokers in the pack that play no part in the game. However the more you play with that pack and the more sweaty palms handle the cards, the more the pack starts to get sticky. You deal out 13 cards to each player and then one complains they only have 12. We all count our cards and one will announce they have 14 with the pesky two of clubs stuck to the ace of spades. Now the human genome is very ancient and each time an ovum is fertilized the genes from the male and female are shuffled and the genes dealt out to the embryo, but the shuffling often fails to produce a completely random distribution of the genetic code. The equivalent of the two of clubs, the lowest ranking card in the pack might be associated with the equivalent of the ace of spades, the highest ranking in the pack. In other words a gene that coded for favorable characteristics might compensate for a mutant bad gene in the hand dealt to the newborn if it sat close by on the same chromosome. This way if we could find a characteristic in these families with evolutionary advantages and if one day we might learn which chromosome carried the gene that coded for that characteristic, we might be able to home in on the malevolent mutant.

The simplest thing to test for was intelligence using simple IQ questionnaires although that was very time consuming and two other simple parameters, hair and eye colour were self-evident. We then designed a pro forma to collect these data on "morphometrics"; for example height and girth. Pelvic capacity was an obvious choice and we got ethical approval for a single X-ray frontal view of the pelvis. We also had ethical approval for one blood specimen to measure blood count of red and white cells and for the examination of the shape of the red cells in case of unsuspected thalasaemia or sickle cell disease. Finally we calculated the ratio of weight to height because of the recent discovery that fat deposits could produce small quantities of estrogen although the majority was from the ovaries up until the menopause. We decided not to attempt to codify beauty on a scale 1-10 because firstly it could only be a surrogate for something else and secondly Sara wasn't going to let me risk my life if our records fell into the wrong hands! Instead we agreed to collect frontal views of the face taken on our Polaroid camera of our "controls", those developing breast cancers without a family history, and the "study" group, of those developing the disease with a family history suggesting a genetic predisposition. Some day in the future we might analyze these pictures once we'd thought up a plausible hypothesis linking "beauty " to sexual attraction as a result of the male linking these physical attributes to the capacity to breed.

All that sounds scientific and dispassionate but I wondered if Sara noted the cruel irony in the fact that I loved her passionately for her beauty, wit, intelligence and kindness with absolutely no intention of us breeding. That was in the terms of our pre-nuptial contract.

Once set in motion the work took off at a frightening speed and we were swamped with data in the days when computerization and analysis of data sets was in its infancy. Within a year we were confidently able to assert that apart from a slight trend for height and IQ we had drawn a blank and I was particularly disappointed that greenness of eyes failed to show any correlation. However on redoing all the stats I found that I'd placed the decimal point in the wrong position and in fact the coefficient of correlation was less than 0.001 and not 0.1 but that only accounted for about 20% of the variance and we knew nothing about green eyes because the text books only wrote about brown and blue eyes and apart from bile, that takes its colour from the metabolic end products of dead red blood cells, there were no other known green pigments in human physiology. So it had to be a trick of the light. All of this was published in scholarly journals and slowly Tanner and Tanner achieved a degree of notoriety on a rather small island located in the great sea of clinical science. Those who shared our esoteric interests even made a joke with our names. In those days a "tanner" was cockney slang for six pence and two times sixpence was a shilling in old money before decimalization. Cockney slang for a shilling was a "Bob". So we often heard comment in the corridors of conferences centers to the effect, "I see Bob's published something interesting in the Journal of Irreproducible Results". Of course part of this interest in us as a couple was that Sara had blossomed into a stunning young woman with all the glamour and polish of a catwalk model yet with virtually no artifice and with no comprehension of the damage she was doing to the cervical spines of young men who turned the heads as she walked past. I swear that on one such occasion, I think it might have been the day after the night before on January the second in Glasgow at the Surgical Research Society, one young man knocked himself out walking into a lamppost.

Early in 1966 word came from Haifa that Gad's research on the immigrant Jews from Kerala that it looked as if our hunch had been confirmed but because the sample size was small the confidence intervals on their findings were wide. We needed to look elsewhere for confirmation. It was at this point I was visited by one of Popper's proverbial "black swans": a single observation, an ugly fact that tainted the complexion of my beautiful hypothesis.

A Sephardic family pitched up in my clinic with the stigma of early onset breast cancer in every other female member of a large and tightly knit kindred. As chance would have it they had come to my attention thanks to Sonia Ashkenazi putting the word around at the Spanish and Portuguese synagogue in St John's Wood, the seat of our Sephardic Chief Rabbi.

If I had one quality to pride myself on, I would like to claim scientific integrity. Here I'm not being sanctimonious or self congratulatory, it is simply that from a young age I read philosophy and whilst a medical student had become highly influenced by Karl Popper even to the point of skipping lectures in pharmacology to hear him lecture at the London School of Economics where he held the chair of the history and philosophy of science. His philosophy, unlike that of Wittgenstein, was easy to understand and practical, it simply distilled down to one word, falsificationism: Although in truth it took 1,000 pages of dense turgid prose in his magnum opus "The Logic of Scientific Discovery" to say so. In practice we set up our hypotheses in order to knock them down and from the rubble of ugly facts and false leads, build new and better hypotheses with greater explanatory power. In other words in proving that I was wrong- I was right. It took me until the early summer of 1967 before the memory of that exchange with Sonia Ashkenazi at the Old Vic came to mind at a time I had just encountered my second "Black Swan". Sonia was Mizrahi which was Hebrew for eastern which implied that her forbears came from the east, Mesopotamia to be precise, but their religious traditions were those the Maaravi, the west, meaning the Iberian peninsula. It took one hour in the library to work this out and learn that the Mizrahi could trace their roots back to the fall of the first Temple and the Babylonian exile.

When I got home for dinner that night I explained it all to Sara and she immediately worked it out. There had to be two separate mutations and from this observation alone we might deduce that there was a genetic genealogy that paralleled the biblical genealogy of the Jewish race, the Sephardim did not carry the mutation that appeared shortly before their expulsion from the Holy Land, the Ashkenazim carried mutation alpha that dated back to the fall of King Herod's temple whilst the Mizrahi carried mutation beta that appeared in Mesopotamia sometime between the fall of King Solomon's Temple between 700 and 500 BCE and the fall of King Herod's Temple in 70BCE. This was a bold conjecture, to adopt the words of Professor Popper, but it would take nearly 30 years before the new molecular biology and global research consortia finally corroborated Sara's sudden insight. Sadly we never formally recorded that conversation and in any case our work was interrupted the following day, the 3rd of June when Sara and I both got telegrams to say our grandmothers had died and their funerals would be in 24 hours. These of course were the coded messages summoning us back urgently as we were both reserve officers in the medical corps of the IDF and a war was imminent. This event closely coincided with the end of my three-year contract.

Chapter 25

Israel/London 1967-1973

On receiving our call to arms we made a few hasty phone calls to colleagues, friends and family who offered condolences yet remained bewildered by our haste. Fortunately as breast disease is rarely an emergency, medical cover was readily available for the period of the "funeral and the *Shiva"* and as it turned out that was all the time needed for the IDF to defeat the combined might of the Egyptian, Jordanian and Syrian forces. We grabbed our ready packed kitbags and took a taxi to Heathrow. We boarded the El Al night flight to Lod airport with seats made available at the last minute by the simple expedient of bouncing a couple of outraged American tourists off the flight. As we landed squadrons of the IAF Mirage IIIs had already taken out most of the Egyptian Air Force on the ground with a pre-emptive strike. With our military kitbags as our only luggage we were taken in a waiting bus and driven at breakneck speed to our posts at a field hospital close by kibbutz Kfar Ha'Nassi virtually on the front line at the foot of the Golan Heights and about 6 miles due east of Safed and 6 miles due north of the shores of the *Kineret*, the Sea of Galilee.

I had the rank as a major in the reserves and as such was responsible for triage and advice on complex procedures. Sara was a reservist sergeant acting as scrub nurse and first assistant in the OR. We were both delighted when Jamal, our best man, popped up as young lieutenant and junior surgeon. So the old team who used to dig up shards of pottery at Masada were now together again but this time digging out shards of shrapnel from the combatants of both the Israeli and Syrian armies. In addition to this reunion I discovered that my young brother Joe was posted a couple of miles west of us and the frontline, at Machanayim, a temporary base for the Military Rabbinate Corps, where they had a landing strip that could fly out those with very serious injuries that we had patched up, to the major hospitals in Tel Aviv, or the bodies of those where we had failed. Joe had the macabre task of gathering up and burying body parts that could not be reunited with their owner. He also presided over the burial ceremonies of the intact corpses. When the dead were local boys or combatants from the Syrian army, they were buried nearby, later to be exhumed and repatriated if required.

We worked day and night only snatching the odd hour of sleep when there was a lull in the fighting and we were so focused on the job we had no idea which way the war was going and it was only by the fifth day and when the flood of casualties became a trickle and we had enough time to listen to the news broadcasts, did we realize that the IDF was at the point on winning a famous victory. Having amputated so many limbs, patched up so many ravaged faces and constructed so many colostomies following bowel damage from abdominal wounds, we felt only relief with no sense of triumphalism and as much sympathy for the poor bloody Syrians who had been dragged into this war as for our own boys and girls. An armistice was declared on the 10th of June and the next day we were given 24 hours' leave. Together with Sara and Jamal, we joined Joe in a commandeered Jeep and drove the short distance to Rosh Pinah. Tziporah welcomed us with open arms and bowls of chicken soup. Then after we all had showered and the men had shaved we slept for close on 14 hours. We were stood down shortly after we returned to base and allowed to return home so we caught an El Al flight back to London on the 14th of June allowing us time to visit Sara's father.

On the flight back we discussed what I should do next as my contract at the Marsden would soon be up. That decision it seemed had been pre-empted whilst we'd been away. I opened a letter amongst the pile of junk mail that carried the emblem of the ICR. It appeared that my employers were so pleased with my scientific output that not only did they want to extend my contract they wanted to offer me a personal chair with tenure. We were overjoyed yet all I could think of was how proud my parents would have to lived to see this day.

Of course I accepted and when Sara and I showed our faces again in the clinic, operating theatre and the laboratories of the ICR we were welcomed like conquering heroes as if we had somehow contributed to the extraordinary successes of the Israeli armed forces. Those of you who have no recall of that time in the days before Israel had been demonized by the western leftist liberal press, might be surprised to learn that Israel was lionized like David after slaying Goliath.

Uncle Hymie and Auntie Becky made a grand celebratory feast for the family and us and although I was happy to discuss my future as the new Professor Tanner, I had no stomach to talk about the victory of the Golani Brigade.

★★★

Our research output now slowed down, effectively awaiting the developments of new methodology in clinical genetics and molecular biology but I had numerous other interests that allowed me to publish on surgical topics and the pathology of breast cancer. I also began to take note of some intriguing new research coming out of the laboratory of the Fisher brothers in Pittsburgh that would one day contribute to the paradigm shift in our thinking about the very nature of the disease. My interest in their work eventually led to an invitation to visit their department and deliver some lectures and talk about setting up a new collaboration. Sara and I loved our first of many visits to the USA. We found the Americans warm and hospitable but most of all fun to be with. Sara developed a taste for "whiskey sours" which I thought an abomination whilst in my turn I developed a taste for corn fed, doorstep sized, T bone steaks broiled, that's American for grilled, medium rare over a barbecue flavored with hickory. I was by all accounts, a talented lecturer and one famous American surgeon described me as having the perfect combination of talking British but thinking Yiddish. This was not the least bit racist as the author of that quip was Jewish and in any case, Jews, because of their number and prominence in American medical circles, were no longer as hypersensitive to perceived insult as their co religionists in the UK.

Each successful lecture at an international cancer research meeting seemed to be followed by two invitations to other foreign venues and I began to join the ranks collectively known as "The absence of professors"

Following one of my tub-thumping plenary lectures at the UICC World Cancer Congress in Florence in the summer of 1971, I was cornered by a charming bunch of tall blond Swedish delegates whilst enjoying a nicely chilled Campari orange in the Piazza della Signoria. They flattered me on my talk and endorsed everything I had to say about the Halsted radical and would I kindly introduce them to the Bella Donna by my side. We all got along famously and the happy hour was extended by a further four hours of fine wine, women and song. The upshot of all this was that Sara and I were to be invited to a "ski slope conference" in a famous winter sports holiday resort somewhere close to the Arctic circle in March the following year.

★★★

We had never been skiing before and were very excited at the prospect but first we needed to equip ourselves with all the right insulated clothing and thermal underwear. So off we went to John Lewis on Oxford Street. When fully kitted out I looked like the fabled Michelin Man whilst Sara looked like err.., even more divine than usual. A day before the conference was to start we flew to Trondheim in Norway and hired a car with winter tires. That day was crowned with a crystalline blue sky and the snow crunched like meringue underfoot as we loaded up. Our route took us over the spine of mountains that divided Norway from Sweden, straight along the E14 to our destination, Äre. The scenery looked wonderful in the snow and all this was new to us as London or Northern Israel had nothing similar to offer. We checked into the conference centre at the Sunwing Hotel where a wonderful welcome awaited us and we were advised to unpack and dress ourselves for a group sauna before drinks and dinner. When we asked what the dress code for a sauna was they said we were only allowed one item. Sara assumed that this meant a towel so she changed at the spa and wrapped a towel around her torso whilst I wrapped mine around my waist. We the entered a large wooden cabin on the roof of the hotel to see a mixed group of Swedish and Norwegian academics with both men and women wearing nothing but a necktie, bursting into uproarious laughter at our obvious confusion. Sara quick to catch on dropped her towel to much applause whilst I decorously crossed my legs and let my towel part. Schnapps was past round to celebrate that we had passed some kind of initiation test. The friends I made that night have supported me through thick and thin to this day.

We rapidly settled into a daily ritual. Up at 0700 lectures from 0800 to 1100 then skiing from 1130 until 1530. Shower and sauna on return then lectures 1630 until pre dinner drinks at 1900. They worked hard and played hard and we loved it. Sara seemed strangely reluctant to learn downhill skiing and I didn't blame her. After taking a tumble or two on the button drag lift of the nursery slopes I thought wiser if we learnt cross country skiing or *langlauf* as they called it, together. It looked simple and elegant but we had bought the wrong sportswear, so we had to hire knee breeches, long thick socks and special shoes to clip to the long thin skis. I have to say we both looked slimmer in this garb. And off we set to try our luck on the nearby oval track for beginners. We soon got into the rhythm; right stick forward left ski back, left stick forward right ski back. Piece of cake: easy peasy. Having convinced the instructor that we were ready to go out on a cross country trek, we set off guided by him along a narrow path between the forest of tall evergreens already clearly marked by the neat parallel tracks of those who'd gone before. We were all right on the flat but on the first slight downward incline I realized I had no idea how to slow down let alone stop. "Sit down, sit down" shouted the instructor; I thought he was mad, but just before panic set in a short incline appeared in front of me and the force of gravity slowed me down until I very nearly got to the top of the slope-but not quite. I then started sliding backwards directly into the path of Sara who had neatly completed her descent. We impacted and collapsed in a heap of sticks and skis and arms and legs and powdery snow, in fits of laughter. Unfortunately Sara hurt her back in the fall and after a while took off her skis and with her arm round the shoulder of the tanned husky skiing instructor limped back to the hotel. She decided that was enough for one day and decided to soak up the sun in a deck chair on the terrace of the hotel watching the little kids learn to ski. How I envied those little ones learning to ski at the same age they learnt to walk and zipping fearlessly down the near vertical faces of the black slopes before they were seven.

Sara must have twisted a muscle as the pain lasted a couple of days but after a couple of hot saunas had worked their wonders she was ready for a second attempt and this was much more successful and we reached the point of completing the 5km blue track by the end of the week. Like all good things that memorable eight days came to and end, we made our fond goodbyes, agreed to rejoin them the following year somewhere in Lapland, packed up our Volvo and set off towards Trondheim just as the first cloud of the week crossed the sun as it rose over the fir trees to the east.

★★★

As we started to climb up the mountain pass towards the Norwegian border the sky darkened until the sun was completely eclipsed by thick clouds gravid with snow. And then the clouds burst open and we experienced a blizzard like nothing we could ever have imagined. The windscreen wipers could barely keep up with the torrent of plump fluffy flakes and beyond the windscreen my field of vision was limited to about 20 metres. The road was soon covered with a thick blanket and to my alarm, the edges of the road became indistinguishable but at least they were marked by tall reflective polls at regular intervals. The snow became so thick that my tires had problems seeking purchase with the tarmac and my exhaust pipe was sinking into drifts so as to choke the engine. I was at the point of seriously thinking of abandoning the car when we saw the roadside sign pointing to a ski lodge at Störlien, we had noticed on the way down eight days earlier. We turned into the forecourt and found ourselves in the good company of many Volvos and Saabs and much relieved, crunched our way into the packed and steaming lobby and determined to sit out the storm whilst warming ourselves with tall glasses of hot gluwein. The blizzard lasted two hours and once it had cleared the skies were all cobalt blue again. I made enquiries at the registration desk and was reassured that the road to Trondheim was open as the snow-ploughs had already been at work but to beware the black ice. I wasn't sure what black ice was but I was sure I'd recognize it when I saw it. Full of reborn optimism we set off again singing along to the car radio. As we crossed the border and started our descent into Norway en route to the airport I took a tight corner too fast and hit black ice which I did not see because it was hidden under the freshly ploughed thin layer of snow and the car refused to respond to my frantic efforts at the steering wheel and majestically continued on its straight path seemingly in slow motion, over the edge of the road, turning two somersaults before landing upside down on a ledge about 20 feet below the mountain pass. The seat belts held us suspended without which I suspect we would have been killed, and the glass in the door panels had shattered. I felt surprisingly calm and my first concern was whether broken shards of glass had disfigured Sara's beautiful face. We released the seat belts and dropped the short distance onto the roof of the car. Sara turned her face to me and was white with shock but fortunately without any bleeding cuts apart from slight lacerations on one ear. I had some notion from memories of car chase scenes at the movies, that cars blow up under these circumstances and urged her to knock out the remaining glass in the side windows with gloved hands and crawl through the gap. I contrived to do this without much difficulty but Sara seemed stuck and when I crawled through the thick snow to the passenger side of the Volvo to help she cried out, "Martin, I can't move my legs!" She had just managed to get her head and shoulders through the empty side window so I grabbed her under the armpits and dragged her through and laid her flat on her back in the drift. I held out my arm to help her stand but in horror I soon had to accept the fact that she was paralyzed from the waist down.

For once I was so overcome with despair that I couldn't for the life of me think what to do to get us out of this nightmare mess. Fortunately for us, that was left to others to do so. A car following a short distance behind us had witnessed the accident and had stopped to offer help. They seemed well equipped to deal with this emergency. The young man in the driving seat collected climbing ropes and blankets from the trunk of his car, tied one end of a rope to a tree near the edge of the rope and let himself down to our level in order to assess the situation. He quickly understood our plight and shouted up to his young lady companion, in what I took to be Norwegian, a string of instructions. She did a U turn and drove back to Störlein whilst he wrapped up Sara in a blanket offering words of comfort in perfect English whilst I stood by helpless and hopeless. Within a remarkably short time the emergency services were with us. An ambulance crew well practiced at mountain rescue slipped down a sledge like stretcher at the end of a rope attached to a winch, strapped a neck brace round Sara's neck, and then strapped her securely to the stretcher before winching the sledge back up to the ambulance. Two policemen then joined the ambulance crew leaving the blue and red lights on their patrol car flashing. They helped me up to the road with my white face reflecting back the alternate red and blue lights of the car. Sara was driven off at high speed to the hospital in Trondheim with me in the patrol car in hot pursuit. I never even had time nor thought to thank that young Norwegian couple for saving our lives but they were just the first two of many Norwegians we had to thank for their kindness and efficiency with at no time money changing hands. I later learnt that the car was a write off but the insurers and the police dealt with all that without bothering us and they had also phoned ahead to the hospital emergency staff who where waiting for us as we were rushed to through the A and E department to be seen promptly by a senior trauma consultant. Again all this was taken care of by the hospital staff and police working through an efficient insurance system. I can imagine how it might of turned out in some parts of Southern Europe or some ghastly banana republic in South America, I probably would have been thrown in prison and it would have cost my last penny to get out on bail let alone pay for Sara's emergency treatment.

I sat trembling with shock in a cubicle to be checked out for injury by a young doctor who again spoke perfect English; having been passed as fit, a nurse served me a mug of hot coffee whilst a policeman took my statement and seemed satisfied that no crime had been committed and I was not to worry and that he would take care of all the formalities and hoped that Mrs Tanner would make a quick recovery. I could have kissed him but instead the moment I was alone I broke down in tears.

About half an hour went by when the curtains were drawn and two tall and serious looking doctors in white coats came in. The first was the trauma consultant who introduced himself as Dr Stieg Larson he then introduced me to the second doctor, Thorstein Harbitz who explained that he was a neurosurgeon.

They both sat down and Larson nodded to Dr Harbitz to start. "Professor Tanner, I'm sorry to inform you that your wife has crush fractures of thoracic vertebrae five and six. The displacement is compressing the spinal cord and I must ask your permission to allow me to operate immediately to decompress the cord and stabilize the spine. Without that, I'm afraid she will be confined to a wheel chair for life. Mrs Tanner would now like you to join her whilst she signs consent" I nodded assent but need helping up as I was literally weak at the knees, and on the arm of Dr. Harbitz made my way to another cubicle housing Sara who was now garlanded with IV tubes, catheters and a face mask delivering oxygen. She was deathly pale and heavily sedated but offered me a wintry little smile and a shrug of her shoulders. There was something about Dr Harbitz that instilled absolute confidence. He bore himself with a modest self-assurance and established eye contact when answering my questions with the kind of detail that told me he was a man at the top of his game. I urged Sara to sign consent once I was confident she understood what was going on. The doctors then left us and I snatched a quick kiss by lifting the oxygen mask of her nose and mouth and two minutes later the theatre staff came in with a trolley to wheel her into the operating room. I was then left alone

241

blaming myself for this accident and wishing I could call upon a God to intercede on Sara's behalf. I sat like that for four hours.

★★★

I awoke with a start to find Dr. Harbitz by my side shaking me gently. I must have fallen asleep in the chair. He was still wearing his theatre scrubs with his facemask hanging limply round his neck.

"I'm sorry the operation took longer than expected but we had difficulty stabilizing the fractures because the screws would not hold in the damaged vertebrae because the cortex of the bone was softer than normal, in fact I took some biopsies in case there was a pathological as well as a traumatic explanation for the injury. Anyway the good news is that we got there in time and although bruised the spinal cord and the nerve roots were intact. I predict that she will be walking again within two weeks." I breathed a sigh of relief but the first part of the message seemed to have been censored out by some primitive protective function of the brain. He went on to explain that Sara would have to stay in hospital for another week and that I would need to find lodgings nearby. He even went so far as to suggest I stayed in his house as a distinguished colleague but I turned down that generous offer so as not to impose but in all honesty I couldn't face playing the role as a house guest for a week; so instead he recommended a little bed and breakfast chalet one block away. Finally he advised me to wait about an hour before seeing Sara by which time she should have been transferred to the ward from the recovery room.

I was waiting by her bed as she was wheeled back from the operating suite and sat holding her hand until dawn when she was sufficiently awake to recognize me and take sips of water. The nursing sister on the ward urged me to freshen up and catch up on my sleep until two that afternoon when Dr. Harbitz would be making his ward round. I dragged myself off to the " Alpine view" guest house which was a warm and cozy little place furnished in the traditional Nordic fashion; washed, shaved and slept for a couple of hours before returning to the hospital. Sara was still dozy but became a little more alert when Dr Harbitz and his entourage of students arrived. He was very charming to Sara and asked permission for the students to join him. She mustered up a smile and nodded assent. He then performed an efficient neurological examination and expressed delight to note the return of sensory and motor activity to her lower limbs and promised to call back at about 5.00pm the following day. I returned to "Alpine View" that evening to enjoy my first meal in 48 hours followed by a full night's sleep. The following morning I received a note from the hospital asking me if I would be so kind as to pop into Dr Harbitz's office before his ward round at about 4.30pm that afternoon.

Thinking little of it I spent most of the day with Sara who was now sitting up and wiggling her toes. She also acknowledged that I had tickled the sole of her right foot with a little giggle, two good signs. I excused myself just before my appointment with the surgeon and was ushered into his Spartan office by a pretty blond secretary. Harbitz looked worried, indicated a chair and then avoiding my eyes started nervously shuffling some notes and X-rays on his desk. As if suddenly coming to a decision, he lifted his head and spoke.

"Professor Tanner, there is no kind way of saying this, but the biopsies we took from her spine show deposits of secondary adenocarcinoma most likely to have arisen from a breast primary." I felt the blood drain from my face and I broke out into a cold sweat. "That can't be" I blustered, "I would have noticed"

"Professor Tanner we share your surprise, my junior staff have examined her carefully both before and after admission and no lump was detected. Is there any family history of the disease?" Choking back tears I told him about the Zinati curse whilst he nodded sagely. "That more or less confirms my suspicions she must have an occult primary as you more than anyone would have deduced by now. Would you mind if we requested a mammogram?"

I nodded and looked down at the floor.

"I have something else to tell you. Are you aware that Sara is about three months pregnant?"

"What did you say? That can't be. We had an agreement. What am I to do?"

I was now utterly consumed by despair and confusion.

The good doctor then summoned a senior nurse to comfort me whilst we planned how to break the news to Sara.

I then tried to take control of myself first and then also the medical dilemma, which was clearly within my area of expertise.

"OK, this is what we are going to do. First Sara must have a termination and then she will need radiotherapy to the spinal metastases. At the same time the radiotherapist might include the ovaries in the field of treatment as there is about a 30% chance that would slow the disease. Then I must get her back to the Royal Marsden Hospital for some chemotherapy and then..."

At this point Harbitz interrupted me in full flight on my high horse with these words of wisdom. "Martin, if I may, I think we need to have Sara's opinion on this before we go any further." I stopped truly chastened and apologised.

The three of us then made our way to Sara's bedside as she watched our approach with happy expectancy on her face that was quickly replaced by an expression of alarm as she interpreted the set of my expression.

I sat by the bedside held her hand dropped my head and listened to Dr Harbitz breaking bad news in the exemplary manner of a man of compassion gifted with communication skills. He then went on to explain the therapeutic dilemma we faced.

I looked up to witness an extraordinary change come over Sara and witnessed an expression on her face I had never seen before. Her complexion was as pale as the sheets that covered her but there was a look of steely determination in her eyes that now appeared as if they were backlit by fire.

"I will not abort this pregnancy. I know my expectation of life is short but I will allow nothing that might damage the development of my child. My life so far has been a wonder, full of love and adventure, more than most will experience who live out their allotted span of three score years and ten. I will not deny my child the right of such a life that was gifted to me." Then turning to me she continued, "Martin I want you to cherish and bring up our child and I want her to be loved for herself as well as for any memories she might carry for you in the future. On that I stand firm however much suffering I might have to endure."

There was a moment's silence after that and I raised my head and smiled agreement with tears misting up my vision.

Harbitz then took control. "May I then suggest the following? We will send you home with an adequate supply of painkillers and fashion a plaster of Paris corset to protect your spine during your flight home. I advise you make contact with an obstetrician shortly after your return so you have someone to monitor the pregnancy. Perhaps they will advise a Caesarian section at about 37 weeks following which the experts at the Marsden will take over control of the other problem. Before you go I wish to arrange a mammogram to confirm my suspicions. If that is all agreed then you can be on your way in about 4 or 5 days". There was a last a consensus and before leaving Thorstein Harbitz did something strange. He took Sara's right hand and with a formal bow raised it to his lips and said, "Madam, you are very courageous and I consider it to have been a rare privilege to care for you during this difficult time." With that he made a turn with military precision and marched to the door, a wonderful humane physician who was in a hurry to avoid others seeing his tears.

Chapter 26

Tisha B'Av 1973

As predicted the mammograms demonstrated an impalpable cancer about 0.7 centimetres in diameter deep in the left breast. That in itself posed no immediate problem as, to put it crudely, the horse had already bolted.

We made it home safely by air ambulance care of our travel insurance although the transfers caused Sara considerable pain. The family then rallied round to offer help and advice.

Sam Goldstone recommended an obstetrician he always made use of, a brilliant and charming young consultant at the nearby Royal Free Hospital in South Hampstead five minutes away from Constable's cottage. He had inherited a Baronetcy and was officially known as Sir Rupert Bonneville. I could not believe my luck, my old classmate! We had lost touch after I joined the RAMC and somehow the fact that he had ended up in O & G did not surprise me. I made an appointment to see him as soon as possible after Sara had seen my colleagues at the Marsden.

We made our way to the Fulham Road a week after we had arrived back, by which time Sara had regained most of her feeling and movements in her legs and she was now able to sit up in the car seat.

Whilst she was having her back re X-rayed and her mammograms reviewed I took her slides to be checked by my friends in the pathology department.

They confirmed the diagnosis and at the same time the radiologists satisfied themselves with the results of the spinal surgery. Finally I took her to see my good friend and partner in the crime of breast conservation, Diana Brinkley.

She fully endorsed our plans but suggested that to speed healing of the spine and control the pain a short judicious course of radiotherapy to the dorsal spine, protecting the foetus with lead sheeting, would be a good idea once the obstetrician was satisfied that organogenesis was complete. Sara shook her head at that but I suggested we wait to see what Bunny Bonneville had to say.

The following week we made the short journey down the hill to Pond Street and then to the obstetric department where I took Bunny by surprise and we gave each other manly bear hugs. He had already read Dr Goldstone's referral letter but hadn't picked up that Mrs Tanner was the wife of his best friend at medical school. He was of course primed about the complexity of this pregnancy and left old friends tales for later and immediately switched his attention to Sara turning on his famous megawatts of charm. For a moment or two I felt a pang of jealousy when this tall handsome blond haired aristocrat succeeded in getting Sara to laugh for the first time in weeks by describing my disastrous drive to his little stately pile one Christmas many years ago. He then quickly changed roles to show his professional side and the gravitas of the specialist. He asked about her dates and I was alarmed to learn that she must have known she was pregnant without alerting me. In return she asked him about the safety of radiotherapy to her spine at this stage of foetal development. He postponed giving an answer until he had examined her.

He closed the curtains around the examination couch then drew back the curtains after about five minutes to report his findings, "We'll Sara, either your wrong about your dates or you're expecting twins" he said with a chuckle. Sara and I exchanged glances of alarm. He then continued, "Before I go any further I'll do one of those fancy new ultrasound scans to check on the contents of your womb, it won't take long" True to his word they were back in about 15 minutes with Bunny wearing a puzzled frown on his face. "Martin, old chum I was right about twins but it looks a bit odd in that one twin seems to be much further developed than the other. If we consider the larger one alone, then Sara is about four months pregnant in which case all the organs are fully developed and if we protect the little mite from scatter radiation that might damage the thyroid gland, then I see no problem. Whatever the case I still think Sara should have a Caesarean section at 36 weeks." He then suggested she came back in another month after the radiotherapy in order to repeat the scan and invited us round for a drink at his town house in Harley Street that weekend. We declined the offer claiming we were not really in the mood for socializing but looked forward to meeting him again next month.

Once we were back home I gently raised the subject of this concealed pregnancy and Sara replied, "Darling, I was terrified you would ask me to abort the baby and I wanted to wait until that option would be too late." I did my best to disabuse her of this thought and reiterated my delight that the pregnancy was going forward. Later that evening when she was asleep in bed and I was nursing my tumbler of scotch, I was plagued with dark thoughts of Sara's premature death leaving behind twin motherless babies for me to care for.

The following week Sara kept her appointment with Dr. Brinkley for radiotherapy to the dorsal spine with everything below the field of treatment draped in lead lined aprons. The effect was astonishing, within one week she was pain free and our mood lifted.

A month later we met Bunny Bonneville. He expressed satisfaction with progress and remarked how much she had blossomed since he last saw her. Together we all witnessed the ultrasound scan being performed and I had to swallow a lump in my throat as I saw the moving shadow of one of the twins. Its companion though was clearly not thriving and we were warned that in all likelihood only one would survive.

Sara's girth expanded at an alarming rate and she was booked in for an elective section on the 2nd of August. Bunny invited me in to witness the procedure. Once she was wheeled in fully anaesthetized and covered in sterile drapes, I could momentarily forget that this was my wife and adopt the manner of dispassionate observer, although not for long. Bunny's experience and skill with the scalpel were those of a man who had conducted hundreds of such procedures. In a flash the transverse supra pubic incision of the abdomen was complete and the gravid uterus bulged obscenely through the defect. Another quick movement of the knife and the membranes of the foetal sac were exposed. Almost at the blink of an eyelid a healthy pink baby was delivered and the cord cut and clamped. The baby was then handed to a waiting nurse who held, what at a quick glance appeared to be a baby girl, upside down by her feet and gave her a pat on the back at which this new quantum of human life gave a loud cry of outrage. I turned back to look at the ongoing procedure as Bunny winkled out a tiny cyanosed stillborn baby boy.

I witnessed the placentas being delivered and noted that the little girl's placenta had greedily occupied most of the available wall space inside the uterus leaving the male foetus to whither on the vine. The little runt of the stillborn child was discretely wrapped in a baby shroud and the bundle left to be disposed of according to whatever tradition our faith determined.

A quick check by the paediatric nurse confirmed that the baby girl was perfect in all departments and weighed in at a healthy 7lbs or 3 kilograms for those who had gone metric. Closure of the wound was quick, slick and neat and once surgeon and proud father were satisfied that the newborn was safe, Bunny tipped me the wink and indicated the way to the men's changing room.

He threw his bloodstained gown on the floor and opened his locker pulling out an ice bucket and a bottle of Bollinger 1962. "Brought this baby in from the cellar at Bonneville Abbey on the off chance we might have something to celebrate, 'fraid we'll have to make do with coffee cups but I think you'll be amused by its musky bouquet and long après gout. Here's to baby Tanner, chin chin."

That night as Sara surfaced and was given the baby girl to suckle, her joy was so complete that I was lost for words but fixed that picture in my mind as if I was a camera.

★★★

Mother and child returned home within a week and Sara was so besotted with her baby girl she seemed to have forgotten about the stillborn twin so I arranged with the hospital mortuary to dispose of the tiny corpse without ceremony. We hired a private nurse to help Sara through the early weeks of nursery care. She was a lovely bubbly West Indian girl named Mercy MacDonald who became so popular with the three of us that I begged her to stay on as a nanny when Sara's health began to fail. The baby girl was bottle fed from the start as Sara never established lactation and in any case her medical treatment would have negated that. Once she had her strength back I took her back to see Dr Brinkley who delivered a short course of radiotherapy to ablate the ovaries. She then enjoyed six months of remission during which time mother and father watched with delight as their adorable baby girl, clearly the most beautiful child on the planet, began to develop. She had Sara's olive skin colour and once she reached the point when she spent more time awake than asleep, I had to acknowledge with mixed feelings, that she had also inherited her mother's beautiful emerald eyes. In the early weeks our little house was bursting at the seams with flowers from well-wishers and my cousins were particularly attentive.

The late summer and early Autumn weather was particularly clement that year and our greatest joy was when we wheeled the pram down the hill to Hampstead village on shopping errands only to be interrupted on stroll by the "Oos" and "Ahs" from complete strangers admiring our baby girl.

Early in the New Year the pains returned and X-rays suggested that the disease in the skeleton had progressed so her analgesic regimen had to be stepped up. Diana Brinkley the suggested that Sara started on chemotherapy and we reluctantly agreed: The favoured combination of drugs in those days was known by their initials as CMF. Another short remission was achieved but at the cost of nausea, vomiting and alopecia. One morning in April I noticed that the whites of her eyes had a tinge of yellow, what doctors describe as *icterus,* and I knew all was lost because this was the first evidence of involvement of the liver, concurrently I also noted that she was beginning to lose weight. On the pretext that it would be nice to spend the Passover with her father who had yet to meet his granddaughter, we flew off to Israel with Mercy in tow. At that time I was the only one to know that Sara would not be returning. Passover in Piki'in was a joyous occasion and Sara's dad was delighted with his first and sadly last grandchild. There were also short lived but happy reunions with Joe and his family, Jamal and his family and old friends from the hospital. Mercy, as an evangelical Christian, could not believe her luck to be able to visit Jesus' birthplace at nearby Nazareth as well as Tiberius on the Sea of Galilee where Paul trawled for fish and "Da Ribba Jordan where John da'Babtish did his babpterizations" Her enthusiasm was infectious and her good humour was sorely needed at this difficult time.

Although the heat of an Israeli summer is almost intolerable, here in the uplands close to the Lebanese border the temperatures were less extreme and our little family of three was content to sit under the shade of the cedar tree near the communal well in the central square of the village of her birth, as if holding court. As the days went by Sara's cheekbones became more prominent and she realized that she had become jaundiced as well as losing weight and she understood precisely what that meant. At the same time her pain became more and more difficult to control until I insisted that she must have 20 milligrams of morphine sulphate IM every 6 hours. She became virtually bed ridden by the beginning of July and she had to be forced to eat a little or at least drink cups of Tziporah's delicious chicken soup. As she wasted away she assumed an extraordinary ethereal beauty. Her eyes appeared to grow is size and luminosity and together with the golden yellow tint of their sclera, she took on a feline appearance. By the 5th of August her pain was constant and every movement made her cry out and I could no longer bear it. I suggested that I should double her dose of opiates and true to her character; she chose to debate the issue on *Halachic* grounds of Jewish medical ethics.

"Martin my love, the Talmud states that life is of infinite value and as you know you cannot split infinity so every moment of life is of infinite value. Correct? *Ergo* if my life is shortened by the dose of morphine that is adequate to control my pain, then that is against our *Halachic* teaching and would be judged as unethical; equivalent to assisted suicide" To which I responded, " Sara my darling if the intention of my injection of morphine is to relieve your suffering then I have the moral duty to treat your pain with adequate doses and clearly in that respect I have failed you. If the unintended consequences of that act are to shorten your life by a few hours I can't be held culpable even by the standards of the toughest court of *Dayanim,* so please allow me to carry out my duty as a doctor." She allowed me to win the debate and smiled with relief as the opiate flooded her system but when I laid her down to sleep she resisted and demanded to be propped up on pillows.

I sat with her like that for the next 36 hours topping up the morphine as required until she died in my arms just after midnight on August the 2nd, that happened to be the 9th of Av in the Jewish calendar.

She was buried the next day in a plot next to her mother in the pretty little graveyard beside the ancient synagogue, with my brother Joe conducting the service. I sat *shiva* for the ritual seven days but I couldn't bring myself to leave the proximity of her remains even though my rational half kept telling me that her physical remains would soon turn to dust, whereas her spiritual legacy would be in my heart forever irrespective of my footfall on this earth, so as a compromise to my internal struggle, I decide to stay on until the closing prayers of Yom Kippur on October the 6th that year. As it happened the Egyptian army crossed into the Sinai and the Syrian army invaded the Golan Heights on that day but by then I was beyond caring.

PART 4

Breaking the Code

1998–2018

Chapter 27

Kibbutz Hagoshrim

Hula Valley November 1998

"It's a Bulbul"

"No, it's a red backed Shrike"

"Forgive me but that is definitely a Bee Eater"

"With the authority as a guide on the Hula valley nature reserve I can assure you that it is a Sunbird", laughed a fourth voice. He was indeed an expert on the ornithology of the great bird migration between Europe and Asia via the bottleneck of the Hula valley. Everyone clapped whilst I observed something quite extraordinary. The little bird of iridescent blue and green seemed to have been attracted to the lifelike blue birds embroidered in the canopy of the *Chupah* that was enjoying its first outing since my own wedding 35 years ago to the day. Furthermore the disturbance caused by the little blue green bird trapped under the canopy made me realise that my sense of joy was experiencing its first outing since Sara departed this world.

The four men holding the poles supporting the canopy gave a shake and the little bird escaped, but instead of flying away, decided to perch on the tip of one of the poles to observe this strange human ritual conducted as a prelude to building a nest.

I allowed myself the little indulgence of imagining that the brilliant feathered sunbird was in some way the embodiment of Sara's spirit, come to witness her daughter's wedding. This rare detachment from my usual scientifically rational world view, was heightened when I noticed that the colours of the bird perfectly reflected the patina of the Roman glass chip embedded in the betrothal ring worn by the bride; a little sentimental gift from her father and a keepsake from her late mother.

Kibbutz Hagoshrim is set in the centre of the narrow tongue of land that marks the north east extreme of Israel. From where I was standing I could see the Golan Heights and the Syrian border to the east and the Lebanese borders due north and due east. In spite of being surrounded on three sides by hostile neighbours it is a place blessed with much natural beauty. Like most kibbutzim in Israel it was founded as an agricultural commune but lately had exploited its natural resources for capitalistic purposes. Its founding fathers would be turning in their grave. The new kibbutz elders had decreed a pleasure dome or to be more precise, a resort hotel with luxurious facilities that catered for weddings, bar mitzvahs and the annual migration of foreign tourists to witness the annual migration of exotic birds and water fowl in the period late October to mid November. The gardens of the hotel are exquisite and populated with abstract modern sculptures but the centre piece in the grounds is the waterfall flowing through the garden, a branch of the river Ayun itself a tributary of the river Jordan that flows through the Hula valley to the wetlands and then onwards to the Sea of Galilee. At this time of year the wetlands are host to hundreds of thousands of waterfowl whilst the uplands on both sides of the valley witness the arrival and departure of uncountable little songbirds and their sinister companions, the raptor species.

To the south side of the cataract in the garden of Hagoshrim, half way up the rock face is a natural plateau. Steps had been carved in the rock to allow easy access for wedding parties and that was how I came to be standing under canopy at this time and in this place. As the bride circled the groom seven times and the cantor sang, "blessed be she who has come": the bird song and the tinkle of the waterfall made a perfect accompaniment.

The bride, my daughter Judy-Esther, known as Jess for short, wore her mother's wedding dress that fitted her perfectly. She held herself like Sara and her eyes also reflected the coloring of the sunbird that continued to enjoy the spectacle from his perch.

The bridegroom was Daniel Cohen, whose family claimed descent from Aaron the first High Priest. He was tall and tanned and his glasses gave him a scholarly appearance. They had met whilst serving together in the IDF intelligence service based close to Mount Meron that carried on its summit antennae that could monitor the chatter over the airwaves from the neighboring Syrian and Lebanese armies in addition to the irregular forces of Hezbollah. He was her commanding officer at the time although only a year older. They had discovered Kibbutz Hagoshrim whilst on leave from army service about three years earlier when Daniel proposed to Jess at this very spot.

I have recently turned 68 and although retired from my chair in London I was granted the title of Professor Emeritus and I also carry the title of visiting professor at the Hebrew University and Hadassah Hospital in Jerusalem. Much has happened in the last 25 years but my own life is of no account. After Sara died my life was over but I continued living for the sake of my daughter and for the sake of womankind.

Chapter 28

Judy Esther Tanner

After Sara died and I eventually got back to London with baby daughter and her nanny Mercy MacDonald, I took stock of my life and whether or not it was worth extending. I considered myself worthless yet with an undeniable duty to bring up my child. After my ritual period of mourning, as on two previous occasions, I did not bother to shave off my beard. This time this was not out of vanity and not even as some permanent expression of my loss. It was simply that I no longer cared about my appearance and that it wasn't worth the effort to shave each day. As they say, "I let myself go". I wore the same dirty old jacket and old corduroy trousers each day because it was too much effort to think up another ensemble. I couldn't be bothered to prepare an evening meal and picked up junk food on my way up Heath Street from Hampstead tube at the end of the working day. I put on weight and drank too much. The only proper meals I had been on the Friday nights when I was invited round to my uncle Hymie and Becky's place or my cousin's houses. They tutted about my self neglect but I wasn't suffering from self-pity I was simply beyond caring. I viewed the years ahead without the companionship of my wife as something to be endured whilst I completed my duties as a father and as a research scientist. Everything beyond the call of those duties was of no consequence and I spent most evenings reading and writing scientific papers.

Without Mercy I've no idea how I might have coped. She seemed content to devote her life caring for my little girl and in contrast to my total lack of affect she was constantly cheerful, livening up our gloomy little household by singing hymns in her beautiful contralto voice. I gave her every Sunday off and on each Sunday morning she would go to the little Baptist church in

Central Square where she sang in the choir and often acted as a soloist. She was simply a good person and the finest example of practicing Christianity I've ever known. She clearly adored my little girl and called her Jessie and Jessie adored her in return.

She was a well-behaved baby, pink and tubby with curly golden hair and eye colouring that seemed to vary from day to day, but to be honest most babies up to the age up 18 months looked pretty much the same to me. In fact there is nothing more boring that to be expected to applaud and express delight at the performance of some friend's baby doing nothing more remarkable than rolling over, smiling in an unfocused way and giving a burp.

Come to that I didn't really have any friends. Bunny Bonneville gave up on me after one too many refusals of hospitality and I gave up on Jonathan and Sonia after one too many attempts at being patterned up with some dumb unmarried friend of theirs. To my eternal shame, it ended in a row with an idiotic young woman who understood all the secrets of the universe, preached vegetarianism at me and lauded the benefits of homeopathy and astrology.

When I tried to set her right on all of this she smiled at me in that patronizing and sanctimonious way favoured by vegetarians and described me as typical of those members of the conspiracy of the medical establishment to deny their patients the remedies of the elders of the lost city of Atlantis or some such bullshit. In return I accused her of being a half educated, credulous idiot typical of those conspiring to return us to the dark ages and stormed out.

Forgetting all my bad behaviour let me return to my baby daughter. Once she reached 18 months I could no longer deny that had inherited her mother's eyes. By this time her skin tone had darkened from ubiquitous pink to a subtler olive colour. She was a pretty child and her blond baby hair had developed a russet tinge. She was comfortably within the upper quartile in passing her milestones but conversationally she had little to say, although Mercy assured me that she could say Mercy. By the time of her second birthday there was now doubt that she was both adorable and exceptional. She chattered non stop in a language that resembled Munchkin, could scale the heights of my bookcases if I wasn't looking and took pleasure in teasing me with a Puckish sort of fun that involved hiding my car keys in the laundry basket. By the time she was three she would engage me in earnest conversations that involved many questions about the nature of the universe. The first time it snowed on Hampstead Heath she was not only enchanted by the beauty of the landscape but also puzzled about the nature of snow, its origins and why it was slippery. The older she grew the more she looked like and sounded like her late mother but with one exception that she had obviously inherited from me. As well as the spirit of enquiry and the capacity to formulate naïve hypotheses, she also had a pragmatic approach to life as a problem solver. There was one remarkable occasion when she was five when all these talents came together and I recognized that I had conceived a budding scientist.

If I remember correctly the story went like this. As I've already mentioned I really had no friends apart from Mercy yet I still felt the need for companionship so acquired a shiny black cat with emerald eyes and a slinky walk. Jessie was enchanted by the pussycat and named it Lucky. Lucky was a very self-sufficient cat whose demeanor suggested tolerance of the lodgers in her household rather than affection. That suited me because she was very low maintenance – a bowl of milk, a tin of Whiskas, a scratch pole and a cat flap was all she needed. In return she would occasionally elect to curl up on my knee and purr whilst I was trying to work at my computer. One night Lucky was not so lucky and was crushed by a car speeding up Frognal. Jessie was devastated and I tried to assuage her grief by fabricating and conducting a burial service that involved wrapping the cat in a shroud, placing the corpse in the bucket of the well in our courtyard and lowering the bucket slowly to the mournful tune of "Ding dong bell pussy in the well". The cat was buried out of sight by tipping a bag of garden compost down the shaft.

That evening as we were sitting in front of the television I asked Jessie if she wanted a replacement pussycat. She paused before answering and adopted the pose of Rodin's thinking man and then turned to look at me all solemn saucer eyed and with a piping voice uttered these words, "Daddy, I think I would like another cat but this time I want a white cat that will show up in the dark and not be run over like Lucky but I don't want to call him Lucky, 'cause that may bring bad luck. I want to call him Blossom like the cherry blossom is white on our tree." Finding a white cat is not easy as they are quite rare but eventually Winston, the young man from the Baptist church Mercy was walking out with, found me one. Winston worked as a theatre attendant at the Royal Free Hospital and he occasionally took me for a beer at Jack Straws Castle nearby. He was streetwise and always knew a man who knew a man.

Jessie was delighted with Blossom who differed from Lucky in three ways: white fur, pink eyes and a friendlier disposition.

A few weeks later I heard a timid knock on the door of my study on a Sunday morning when I was left alone to look after Jessie who liked to play at housewife. Jessie entered in her demure ladylike way and said, "Daddy I'm worried about Blossom. He is fast asleep on the rug by the fire and doesn't wake up when I Hoover around him. I tried shouting but I think he is deaf and if he is deaf he wont hear the cars coming" So much thought, so much reasoning and so much deduction from a five year old was quite exceptional. So we took Blossom to the vet on the High Street the following week who listened carefully to Jessie's tale. The vet winked at me a did a mock examination that include inspection of the ears before explaining that Blossom was a pure Albino cat and these animals are very rare and precious and are congenitally deaf and that Jessie was a clever girl to notice this and yes to try and keep him away from the roads at night. That seemed to please my little girl and she smiled to herself as the cat was put back in the carrying basket. On the way home walking up Heath Street, Jessie turned to me and asked, "Daddy what is genital deaf?"

I tried not to laugh but suddenly realized that this cat posed a similar problem about co-expression of genes and evolutionary advantage to the one that occupied my working day. All I could think of saying was that she was a very clever girl and that I would buy her a book on her sixth birthday that might explain all these things.

At the age of 11, I elected to send Jessie to the Jewish Free School in nearby Camden Town. She excelled academically and on her 12th birthday we celebrated her Bat Mitzvah at Norris Lea synagogue where her exegesis on that week's portion of the Torah was spell-binding and demonstrated true scholarship and wisdom quite unheard of for a girl of that age. By the age of 16 when she took her "O" level exams she had already developed into a young lady I could be proud of. She was tall and coltish and exceptionally beautiful and wore her long auburn hair in a ponytail. Yet she was totally unaware of the impact her appearance had on the young men in her group. She avoided the social butterflies known as "Becks" in north west London and preferred the company of other earnest young ladies as well as the adult conversation around the table on our occasional Friday night dinners with my cousins, leaving her male second cousins gawping and blushing in her presence. As predicted by her teachers she scored alpha star in all the subjects she had been entered for. Her most outstanding attribute was an instinctive understanding and love of mathematics. She was even accelerated to sit A level mathematics two years ahead of her peer group along with her O levels where again she scored alpha star.

In the sixth form she was encouraged to add to her successes in mathematics by studying philosophy and theology. She was of course by this time fluent in Modern Hebrew because I had insisted that we communicated that way at home because with two parents of Israeli citizenship she enjoyed dual nationality.

When it came time to think about a choice of university and subjects to read, she had no doubts. She would major in mathematics and also study archaeology at the Hebrew University in Jerusalem but that would of course entail completing her statutory two years of National Service first of all.

By the time she was 18 and having collected stellar grades at A level I knew it was time to let go and accept that from this time forth she was her own person. I consoled myself with the fact that I was close to retirement but also fortunate to have been granted a visiting professorship in Jerusalem so it would be easy to keep in touch whilst not getting in her way.

The IDF rapidly recognized her mathematical skills and also her natural gift for breaking codes. It was therefore inevitable for them to appoint her to HAMAN the intelligence corps of the IDF. That was how she came to work in a cabin half way up Mount Meron close to the Lebanese border under the command of Major Daniel Cohen, her future husband.

In spite of having a daughter with all the attributes a father might hope for, I could never forget that she had one attribute that filled me with dread. She carried the morphometric stigmata of the Ashkenazi curse and that set a deadline for me to unravel that code and find someway to pre-empt the inevitable outcome. From the day of her wedding I gave myself 10 to 15 years to solve the problem, yet officially I had retired.

Chapter 29

The double helix unravels

Between Sara's death in 1973 and my daughter's 21st birthday in 1994 it is true to say that molecular biology, the study of human genetics in health and disease, also came of age. In that year the BRCA I mutation was cloned and the risk of cancer in the carriers of that mutation was confirmed by International Breast Cancer Linkage Consortium. It took some pride in being one of the many players in that collaboration. But along the way there were many milestones of note. To even begin to understand the enormity of the task and the genius of the scientists involved it is necessary to turn back the pages to the beginning of the story.

Watson and Crick discovered the structure of DNA in 1953 and subsequent biological scientists have come up with mind-boggling statistics as awe inspiring as those related to the discovery of far away galaxies and the expanding universe. My old friend Richard Dawkins put it this way. There are 3×10^{12} cells in the body and 46 chromosomes per cell. 2 meters of DNA are packed into the nucleus of each cell tightly wound on these chromosomes. That is 6×10^{12} metres of DNA in each body, which is equivalent to the distance to the moon and back 8000 times! Each time the cell divides there is the hazard of a somatic mutation as a random event. Some cells divide every 48 hours. Richard Dawkins in his most readable and mischievous book "The Blind Watchmaker" describes the fidelity of the transcription process beautifully and I wish to quote one of his passages: *"DNA's performance as an archival medium is spectacular. In its capacity to preserve a message it far outdoes tablets of stone. Letters carved on gravestones become unreadable in mere hundreds of years. The DNA document is even more impressive, because unlike tablets of stone it is not the same physical structure that lasts and preserves the text.*

It is repeatedly being copied and recopied as the generations go by, like the Hebrew Scriptures, which were ritually copied by scribes every eighty years to forestall their wearing out. It is hard to estimate how many times the DNA document has been recopied in our lineage; probably as many as twenty billion times. It is hard to find a yardstick with which to compare the preservation of more than 99% of the information in twenty billion successive copying."

Yet in spite of this exquisite fidelity of transcription it is a result of the very rare failures in the system that progress in my subject of interest was made. Having deduced that familial breast cancer was a result of a "germ line" mutation that persisted down the generations, there was a race on to track these faults in the fidelity of transcription, to their address within the nucleus and then work out what function within the healthy cell had been perturbed.

The first break through occurred on the 17th October 1990 at a meeting where I happened to be delivering a plenary lecture in the USA. This was reported in an unscheduled paper at the evening session of the American Society of Human Genetics in Cincinnati, Ohio and turned out to be the highlight of the whole conference. At 10.30 that evening Mary-Claire King took the podium and announced to a hushed audience that her group had traced a gene that predicted a very high risk of developing breast cancer to chromosome 17 thus at a stroke narrowing down the search from about 70,000 genes to a region that housed less than one thousand genes. On the 21st of December she published the milestone paper in Science, entitled "Linkage of early onset familial breast cancer to chromosome 17q21". This gene was named BRCA 1 and was cloned 4 years later. "Game on" as sport's commentators like to say. Overnight the subject became glamorous and fertile as research funding flowed in from the MRC in the UK and NCI in the USA. Mike Stratton's group at my own Institute of Cancer Research in London localized BRCA 2 to chromosome 13q in 1994. This work then took off in many directions including the critical observations that both these mutations impaired DNA repair or in other words contributed to the failure of the fidelity of transcription exalted by Richard Dawkins. However the area of greatest interest to me was the subject I discussed with Sara at our second meeting in a tent at the foot of Masada. Is it possible that the mutations in the genes newly described as BRCA I and 2 might also bear the imprint of the 4 or 5,000-year history of the Jewish people? And indeed they did!

★★★

My son-in-law is a "Cohen" and I am proud of this fact that my daughter has married into this princely and scholarly lineage. My son-in-law's father is a Cohen and through the oral tradition they can trace their routes back to the High Priests of the Temple in Jerusalem. We now know that this oral tradition has been scientifically confirmed by studying the Y chromosome of Cohenim. The Y chromosome is associated with the male sex and handed down through the generations from father to son. The Y chromosome of the Cohenim has certain characteristics that are common to all the Cohenim in the world known as the "Cohen modal haplotype", confirming the veracity of the oral tradition.

Perhaps more remarkable and certainly more relevant to this book is the tradition that our Jewish ethnicity is handed down through the maternal line. Every cell in the human body has two sources of DNA. The major source is within the nucleus and this can be described as the blueprint that codifies our personhood, in other words the way we look, our height, the colour of our eyes and to a large extent our attitudes and intelligence.

Hidden in the cytoplasm between the nucleus and the cell membrane and only clearly seen on electron microscopy are the *mitochondria*. These tiny structures are vitally important in burning food in order to provide the energy for cellular activity. In other words they are operating as power stations at the molecular level. The mitochondria are peculiar. Way back in the very early days in evolution of living organisms, there was once a tribe of primitive "bacteria", that appeared to have made a pact of mutual self interest whereby the primitive cell would provide the primitive "bacteria" succor and protection in return for them to take over the task of providing green energy. This remarkable symbiosis can be judged by the fact that eons later these saprophytes still retain some of their own original DNA that codes for a few proteins that are essential for the organization of these powerhouses. This mitochondrial DNA is now known to be entirely maternal in origin, handed down through the generations via the female line. The reason for this is simple. The ovum has many mitochondria, whereas the sperm is essentially a motorized packet of nuclear DNA. So the mitochondrial DNA in the fertilized egg is all maternal. As is the case for the Y chromosome, mitochondrial DNA also differs in subtle detail, between individuals and through this it is possible to trace the origins and migration of peoples of different ethnicity from the first hominids who evolved from the apes in Central Africa in the dark distant past. Subtle differences in this coding also allow us to follow the migration of the Jewish people over time and even suggest that our origins might indeed be traced back to four different matriarchal lines. Here I am not describing the biblical matriarchs but the genetic matriarchs surviving the major genocides that scarred the history of my people. Each attempted genocide lead to a molecular bottleneck through which only the fittest to survive might crawl.

Sadly, along the way the Jewish people have collected a number of deleterious mutations within the nuclear DNA of the germ line that has also been passed on through the generations. These include the mutations that are associated with Tay Sachs disease as well the BRCA mutations that increase the risk of developing breast cancer. As intuited by Sara and me at our meeting in 1963, the origin of these mutations in time can be traced by considering the migration and dispersion of the Jewish people in ancient history. The story appears to start about 3000 years ago.

In 586 BCE following the Babylonian conquest and the fall of the first Temple, the major Jewish dispersion was to Mesopotamia; "By the rivers of Babylon, there we set down yea we wept when we remembered Zion" says Psalm 137. Some Jews migrated to Egypt and others North into Syria. After the passage of years many Jews drifted back to the land of Israel but after the revolt against Persia, 359-338BCE many Jews migrated North towards the Caspian Sea with gradual migrations through trading further North into Europe. The Jews whom migrated to Mesopotamia enjoyed a long history emerging ultimately as Iraqi Jews, all of who were expelled after the 2nd World War.

The next cataclysmic event in Jewish history was the sacking of the second Temple by the Romans in 70CE. At this point 80,000 Jewish slaves were shipped across to the Roman province of Hispania and settled in the region just south of Cordova. This colony ultimately gave rise to the Sephardic population. Some Jews remained behind in Cities such as Jerusalem, Hebron and Safed not forgetting the village of Piki'in, with descendents to this very day, whereas others continued their migration through Asia Minor into Eastern Europe. Until the expulsion of the Jews from Portugal and Spain at the end of the 15th Century, there was very little inter-marriage between the Sephardim and the Jews in Mesopotamia, Asia Minor and Europe. With these historical facts in mind it is then all the more interesting to look at the distribution of the BRCA 1 and BRCA 2 mutations amongst women from the different Jewish communities.

My Israeli colleagues at the Haifa Technion, the Hebrew University and Hadassah hospital not forgetting the *Sharre Tzedek* Medical Centre in Jerusalem, did a phenomenal job of tracing these genetic mutations amongst affected and unaffected Jewish women in Israel.

To put it into perspective, mutation within these genes in the majority of populations occur with a frequency of between 1 in 300 and 1 in 800. The second highest frequency is seen in Iceland where about 1 in 170 (0.6%) of women are affected. However amongst Jewish women within Israel 1 in 40 women (2.5%) are affected and then when you look at the individual genes you see how the history of the Jewish people have been reflected, once again at the molecular level. First of all as originally noted by Sara and me, Sephardic women do not carry any of these mutations. Therefore the mutations that have been identified must have occurred after the fall of the 2nd Temple or amongst those families who remained in Mesopotamia or migrated North after the fall of the first Temple. There are three "Jewish" mutations. These can be roughly dated by analysis of mitochondrial DNA. The oldest mutation (let's call it alpha for short) on the BRCA 1 gene occurs in 1% of both Ashkenazi and Iraqi Jews and is estimated to be between two and a half and three thousand years old. This therefore must have occurred by a founder germ line mutation in Mesopotamia shortly after the fall of the first Temple and also have been carried North amongst those Jews who ultimately contributed to the foundation of the Ashkenazi tribes.

The second mutation (beta) is on the BRCA 2 gene and is found in 1.4% of Ashkenazi Jews only and is estimated to be about 700 years old. Clearly long after the fall of the 2nd Temple and almost certainly the founder germ line mutation must have arisen from the Jews that had settled in Eastern Europe. The third mutation (gamma) is on the BRCA 1 gene and occurs in 0.1% of the Jewish population. This mutation is also seen amongst high-risk non-Jewish women of Eastern European origin and is now thought to reflect intermarriage with members of the population of Khazars from Central Asia who converted en masse to Judaism in the 11thC. These three BRCA mutations are distributed amongst Jewish people in an identical way in New York and Manchester. Both the Israeli and the British experience confirm that women carrying one of the BRCA 1 mutations have a close on 80% chance of developing breast cancer by the time they are 80, whereas those carrying the BRCA 2 mutations have about a 35% chance of developing breast cancer by the age of 80. The experience of all the workers in this field has confirmed that what marks these cancers out as uniquely difficult problems is the early age of onset which is on average ten to fifteen years younger than what you might expect with sporadic breast cancer.

So to place all this in the context of my story, Sara's matriarchal lineage must have carried the BRCA mutation alpha, from a time between the fall of the first and second temples and my earliest assumptions were wrong. Interesting support for this conjecture comes from the first Yehudit scroll that suggests the mother of the twins was born in ancient Persia in the epoch of the Parthian

Empire. Secondly her line probably included one of the four "molecular" matriarchs whose fitness for survival through the Roman attempt at genocide meant that her mitochondrial DNA is similar to that of close on 25% of Ashkenazi women in the world today. Finally the early age of onset of her disease and her short survival were typical of the Ashkenazi curse.

All this is very complex but suffice it to say that the biblical genealogy of the Jewish people is confirmed by their genetic anthropology.

★★★

One late spring morning in the year 2000, close to my 70th birthday, I took myself off to meet with my old friend and colleague Neil Bradman who directed the centre for Genetic Anthropology at University College London.

Neil alongside his son Robert, had described the Cohen modal haplotype in 1997 and I was seeking their help with my search for the evolutionary advantage of the Ashkenazi mutations that not only allowed them to survive for nearly 3,000 years but might even have allowed a minority of women of Jewish decent to squeeze past the bottle-neck of one of our history's cataclysmic events. Neil is an extraordinary character, larger than life with the same stocky build as me. The first time a met him I called him professor but he laughed that off. In fact his whole department is funded through the profits of his many business interests and he is effectively a self-taught geneticists picking up the subject from the textbooks of his three children all of whom had postgraduate degrees in human geneticis. As far as I know he runs his department by grace and favour, with the University of the opinion that it has nothing to lose and much to gain.

We took our morning coffee in the open air in order to enjoy late spring sunshine, in one of the quadrangles hidden from sight behind the amorphous white facades of UCL buildings lining Gower Street. We were both wearing the uniform of elderly academics at UCL that consisted of white trainers, blue jeans with an abdominal bulge overhanging a wide belt and T-shirts with agitprop logos, although on this occasion as an acknowledgement to the ambient temperature we also wore almost identical bomber Jackets.

We sipped our cappuccinos at leisure and gossiped about friends and acquaintances and how we might build peace in the Middle East before lunchtime.

He then returned to the topic of earlier discussions. "Well Martin I've been giving the matter some thought over the last few weeks. As you've not found any morphometric clues so far except for the rather obvious fact that your daughter, who you say resembles your late wife, is very beautiful, then I have good news and bad news. Which do you want to hear first?" "Bad news first as always please, Neil" I replied. "OK then, the bad news is that we are simply witnessing genetic drift with Darwin being vindicated yet again. As for the good news, the one critical genetic mutation that might not show up in your morphometric studies might be in the placenta that is so often overlooked in the studies of human development." "Well who knows, maybe beauty is an outward expression of the capacity to make healthy placentas?" I replied with a laugh. Neil looked at me with the expression of the Sphinx as if in deep thought before responding softly, "You just might be right on both accounts."

After that I was in such a hurry to head back home to think this through, that I rather abruptly thanked him, paid for the coffees and jogged up Gower Street, turning left down University Street towards the Warren Street Tube station at the top of Tottenham Court Road, in my hurry to head home.

Chapter 30

The evolutionary advantage of beauty

That afternoon as I arrived back home from my meeting with Neil Bradman, I was full of excitement at the challenge ahead of me to link the health of the placenta in some way, direct or indirect with the BRCA 1 and 2 mutations. It was a beautiful late spring afternoon as I approached Constable's cottage in Lower Terrace with the setting sun casting a pink appliqué of colour on the white flowers of the clematis that climbed over the north face of my pretty little terrace house that Sara loved so much. How gorgeous they looked. The clematis flowers seemed to blush in unison as if they could read my thoughts.

I stopped for a moment and for the first time noticed something rather puzzling. My cottage was the mirror image of the neighbouring cottage that shared a party wall. My neighbour's cottage looked equally pretty in the late afternoon sunshine yet its walls were free of the ornamentation by any climbing plant. Why therefore do I always describe my flat fronted Georgian cottage pretty when it has nothing to do with its decoration or even the colour of the painted door? I stepped back to look again at the twin cottages from a longer perspective nearly being mowed down by an angry woman driving a huge Mercedes SUV who shook her fist with rage whilst her tiny little passenger wearing his private school uniform looked on safely, cocooned in the tank like vehicle. Having got to the other side of Lower Terrace I took my time in trying to understand the prettiness of my home. Suddenly the penny dropped it was nothing to do with decoration but something integral in the proportions. The proportions of the height and width of the house were replicated by the proportions of the door and the windows and again at a smaller scale in the panels on the door and the size of the individual windowpanes. I then remembered something I had read many years ago in a book I bought shortly after moving to Lower Terrace, called "The Georgian House". I was witnessing the beauty of Palladio's golden ratio of 1:6. For reasons that were obscure at the time I recognised that the ratio of height to width of 1:6 was intrinsically beautiful both in art and in nature. I then remembered how struck I was by the architecture of Bonneville Abbey in my youth. It was the same but multiplied up a hundred fold.

I entered my pretty house, poured myself a double measure of my favourite 18-year-old Talisker, settled in my favourite comfy chair by the front window and went into a reverie. Is it possible that there is an evolutionary advantage of beauty or is the ratio of 1:6 the common currency of health in the animal and plant kingdoms that has found expression in architecture and design since ancient times. I gazed out of my window to look at the willow tree planted in the little village green that bifurcates Lower Terrace and it found favour in my eyes. Against the early evening sky its branches and feathery hanging leaf complexes where seen in perfect silhouette. I picked up a pencil and just as I was taught in evening art classes when I was a boy, I measured the branches by extending my arm and squinting with one eye whilst marking with my thumb nail the proportions between each bifurcation. And so it was that the ratio of the length of the trunk to the length of the first branches was 1.6 and that ratio remained self similar with second, third and fourth order branches. Even the terminal leaf complexes repeated this beautiful symmetry. I knew there was a word for this and "Googled" for it on my laptop. What I had just rediscovered was known as fractal geometry. I then turned my attention to a pencil portrait I had made of Sara shortly after we had moved into this house and discovered many ratios of 1:6 in the distribution of her features around her beautiful face the most extraordinary of which was the ratio of the length to the thickness of her pouting lips that was again repeated in the almond shape of her eyes. I then picked up an almond from the little dish of nuts I always keep alongside my tray of scotch whisky and cut glass tumblers and popped outside to the back yard to collect my tool box from the shed, found my callipers and measured the length and breadth of the nut and, hey presto!-a ratio of 1:6 again.

It then occurred to me to consider the internal anatomy of the human body so I reached for my well-thumbed rather ancient copy of "Gray's Anatomy".

The obvious place to start with was the aptly named bronchial tree and once again I saw perfect fractal geometry and golden ratios. A sprig of broccoli almost perfectly reflects the structure of the bronchial tree. The same applied to the vascular trees supplying most of the organs and the collecting system of tubes making up the calyx of the kidneys. I then turned my attention to the milk collecting system of the breast. This proved more difficult to analyse but I did come across a picture of an 18th C attempt at producing a wax cast of the breast's internal anatomy that again hinted at a fractal geometry. At this point I suddenly realised that all along I had known the answer to the question that I hadn't quite yet framed in my mind but to expand on this I turned back to my days as a surgeon at the Royal Marsden Hospital.

It is hard to convey the enthusiasm we surgeons display in the study of pathology in our chosen discipline. Certainly for me and I'm sure for others, there is an aesthetic as much as a scientific interest in the subject. The aesthetics of the subject can be appreciated by the exquisite microscopic anatomy and molecular biology of the normal breast before trying to explain the malignant transformation that literally turns this transcendental beauty into life threatening ugliness. Broccoli, as well as resembling the bronchial tree is an almost perfect representation of the mammary ducts and glands at the time of lactation. The main difference of course is that the branches of the mammary gland are tubular. Imagine a tree like tubular structure and then imagine taking transverse or random oblique cut sections and magnify them up. If the structure is perfectly symmetrical and the cuts are perfectly horizontal you will see a symmetrical plain scattered with circular structures. Of course in real life the organs are not perfectly symmetrical and the pathologist's cut is not perfectly horizontal to

274

the central tubes of the system. In fact when you examine the breast carefully you will find up to about 12 ducts opening at the nipple. Each of these is the mouth of a tree like system for gathering milk at lactation from the glandular elements at the terminal ends of the system that look a little like the florets on the surface of broccoli. You can now picture what normal breast tissue looks like under the microscope. It will appear as a collection of circles of varying diameter or as ellipses where the tubule has been cut obliquely. You will also see clusters of tightly packed cells representing the glandular elements that secrete milk. Sometimes you will even spot a tiny terminal tubule emerging from the lobule itself. If you then increase the power of the magnification you can look at the detail of the individual tubular structures. In health they are quite banal; one layer of simple cuboidal duct epithelial cells surrounded by a single layer of spindle shaped myo-epithelial cells that are involved in expressing the milk by squeezing it along the tubules. Next let's up the power of the simple light microscope to its highest magnification and then we start seeing something of the extraordinary internal organization of these simple looking cells. In the same way most folk on trying to contemplate the magnitude of outer space and the expanding universe feel giddy with the effort, I feel giddy whenever I try to contemplate the miraculous miniaturization of at the other extreme of the microcosm. The most prominent structure is the nucleus that in health is nice and round and pretty central like a fried egg. This floats in a gooey sea of cytoplasm that also suspends the mitochondria that stoke up the energy to keep this micro-system going. The cell is enclosed by a membrane that looks simplicity itself until you have to start envisaging the comings and goings of molecules and the recognitions of chemical signals by specific receptors on the cell surface that alerts the interior mechanisms to either speed up or slow down. Beyond all that and even beyond the highest magnification of the electron microscope we have to try and imagine what's going on at the molecular level. The fact that such a complex and beautiful system retains its integrity is a miracle; the fact that some trivial molecular mismanagement can cause the whole system to crash leading to the death of its host, should not be a surprise.

Returning to the aesthetics of the subject, surgeons and pathologists often describe breast cancers under the microscope as "ugly looking lesions". Along with all this ugliness, the duct and lobular epithelium lose their fractal geometry. The prognosis of the cancer is literally in direct proportion to the ugliness of what we see. Could it possibly be that one of the first steps in malignant transformation is a mutation in the genes that control fractal geometry and a universal law that controls our appreciation of beauty?

For advice on that, like all serious scholars, I turned to *Wikipedia* and apparently it's all down to symmetry and ideal ratios. For example this page seemed to sum it up nicely and supported my intuitive beliefs.

"Evolution taught us to lust after symmetry, a nicely balanced body and face, because asymmetry signals past illness or injury. We therefore define beauty quite elegantly, right down to the most ideal ratio of hips to breasts and upper lip to lower lip."

So in other words external symmetry might act as a surrogate marker of internal symmetry and that is determined no doubt by sequences on the human genome that control fractal geometry. Loss of fractal geometry is associated with malignant transformation but what is the direction of causality? Was the ugliness the cause or consequence of the malignant change or was one or the other a necessary but insufficient trigger? Yet how did the ration 1.6 enter this equation and what if anything has this got to do with placental growth? The more I thought about it the more complex it became with more questions than answers until by 1.00 am that night my head began to spin. What that a consequence of too much thinking or too much drinking? Almost subconsciously since arriving home that afternoon I had polished off half a bottle of my rare 18 year old Talisker. Clearly I had now reached the point where I needed extra-specialised help and I had no doubt where that would come from. Jessie my darling daughter had recently completed her PhD wherein she combined her two undergraduate interests of higher mathematics and archaeology into a thesis that received one of the highest rankings in the history of the Hebrew University in Jerusalem. The title of her thesis says it all; "A non-linear mathematical model with great explanatory power to map population drifts through the study of mutations in DNA retrieved from ancient burial sites: 3,000 years of evidence that evolution of homo-sapiens is still an active process."

I then set down my thought processes in a Word document and sent it to Jessie as an attachment on this e-mail.

To: Jessie.sixpence@huji.ac.il

Dear Jessie,
I hope that you, Daniel and the twins remain in good health. I have been up half the night trying to understand the meaning of and evolutionary advantage of beauty and how this might impact on placental development. Please don't think I'm losing it in old age but read the attachment below and see if you can help me find the missing link i.e. between fractal geometry and placental health.
At the same time why do I keep getting the 1:6 ratios?
Love,
Dad

It was 3.00 am before I got to bed and because of the two hour time difference I expected a reply by the time I resurfaced from my sleep.

At 10.00am the next day I awoke with a sore head and blurred eyesight but felt somewhat restored after two large mugs of strong coffee made from freshly ground beans. I turned on my desktop computer and as expected Jessie's response way the first message to download in my in box.

To: Martin.sixpence@ucl.ac.uk

Dear Dad,
Lovely to hear from you and delighted to learn that your brain is still ticking over in top gear. I don't think you are losing it, in fact I think your ideas are fascinating. The answer to your last question is "easy". You have rediscovered Phi although the precise number is 1.61803399! This is

linked to the Fibonacci sequence $F_n = F_{n-1} + F_{n-2}$ but don't worry about the maths. It remains a puzzle why our concepts of beauty and the organisation of plant and human anatomy seems to be controlled by Phi but no doubt it relates to an evolutionary advantage linked to the economy in energy v. protein synthesis balance.

Your principle question will take longer to answer, as I will have to search the human genome dictionary both for functions and loci. I'll come back to you this evening after work and domestic duties are complete.

Daniel and the boys are thriving whilst I am four months pregnant and the ultra sound scan suggests you are expecting your first grand-daughter!!

Love

Jessie

I was so overcome with emotion on reading her letter that I burst into tears of joy. I could barely contain myself waiting for her next response so I decided I'd pass the time by visiting the National Gallery in Trafalgar Square followed by lunch with amiable company at my club nearby. I returned home that afternoon at 4.00pm, 6.00pm in Jerusalem, to find Jessie's second e-mail waiting in my in box.

To: Martin.sixpence@ucl.ac.uk

Dear Dad,

OMG! I think you are on to something of enormous importance linked to the H19 gene locus. This seems to be involved in maintaining symmetrical development of the foetus and only the maternal allele of H19 is expressed in the placenta, by way of genomic imprinting. In other words any germline mutations carried by the mother will always appear in the placenta. Furthermore variants of this gene can be over-expressed, knocked out or even translocated to be co-expressed with other genes on other chromosomes. I think between us we could come up with a mathematical model based on chaos theory that might explain why beauty might be an outward expression of the mother's capacity to develop a healthy placenta and thus provide an evolutionary advantage. In addition factoring in your other thoughts on the matter it is possible for the model to explain the degree of penetrance of the BRCA I/II that might be controlled by co-expression of translocated H19. Please send me all you know about the possible clinical and biological factors that are associated with the Ashkenazi breast cancers, including growth factors and other gene products. The more the merrier as my mathematical models thrive on

278

complexity and can be reiterated thousands of times a second when I have access time to the university's Big Bertha computer.
Love,
Jess

To translate all that into English it would appear that my daughter had discovered the missing link to complete the circle between our ideas of beauty, symmetry and evolutionary advantage that allowed the survival of the matriarchal line of Ashkenazi women carrying a curse that in most cases would lead to a premature death in their early 30s. There was now a race on to complete the mathematical model that might faithfully reproduce this sequence of events and lead to the development of therapeutic interventions for prevention and treatment of early age onset familial breast cancer. This race was fuelled by scientific hubris but more importantly to reach the finishing line before Jessie's mutation took its toll and for the sake of my unborn granddaughter.

It took almost a year for us to complete a mathematical model that perfectly described our predictions and several more years for others carrying out basic and clinical research to confirm that our predictions were almost entirely correct.

Without any need to understand the mathematics, the model that was generated appeared in a virtual three-dimensional space on our computer screens. Recreating the model of the breast in health was relatively simple, as we knew what we were looking for and as predicted it looked like 12 stems of broccoli with common origins just deep to the nipple. We then played around by knocking out, over-expressing and translocating the putative genes that controlled fractal geometry and judged how that impacted on the morphology of the cells lining the ducts. We then reversed the process and witnessed the destruction of the perfect internal geometry that followed impairment of the function of genes that controlled the repair of DNA that included the Ashkenazi mutations on BRCA I/II. The first breakthrough came about when we detected a synergy between the two sets of genetic functions when the destruction of our beautiful virtual reality breast within a few hours, two to three years in real time, came about when the

H19 locus was over-expressed and translocted to the long arm of the 17th chromosome close to the locus of the BRCA I gene. It appeared that H19 was like the two faced god Janus, in its normal location it acted as a tumour suppressor gene yet when looking the other way, depending on its location on the genome, it lost that beneficial function whilst at the same time enhancing its role for placental health. Other factors that remained to be discovered might have explained something similar going on to explain the persistence of the BRCA 2 mutations over the millennia.

The mathematical model, its predictions and therapeutic consequences were published by Tanner and Tanner in Nature in 2002 entitled, "Mammary morphogenesis and the evolutionary advantage of the BRCA I mutation: a mathematical model". This effectively redirected the global research endeavour in our field. Dear old "Bob" riding to the rescue 30 years after the death of Sara. Within a few years a group of scientists from the Hebrew University that included authors with the names of Mizrachi and Levy, had described gene therapy for these cancers using a diphtheria toxin A chain-H19 vector.

As a footnote to all this work Tanner M and Tanner JE also uncovered the significance of the beautiful green eyes shared by mother and daughter. The gene OCA2 is located on the 17th chromosome and has two common variants A and G. A promotes brown eyes and G, a recessive variant, promotes blue eyes. Only if you inherit the G variant from both parents do you have a chance of blue eyes but even amongst this minority only about 25% will develop eyes the colour of emeralds. Therefore the GG variant of OCA2, can continue to spread even if they are associated with deleterious effects given the Western ideal of beauty. This genetic complex is expressed just one post code away from the locus of BRCA 1.

Our research work lead to fame within our narrow community of scientists and also lead to my nomination for the Kettering prize in America. With that money I was able to buy a pretty little cottage with perfect geometry in Yemin Moshe overlooking the ancient walls of the old city of Jerusalem but I would have given everything back to have Sara with her emerald eyes sitting by my side again.

Chapter 31

Vishnu's Vaults 2012

The Athenaeum club is housed in one of the finest mansions in St James'; with an address on Pall Mall although in fact its grand entrance faces an elegant square, Waterloo Place, whilst its back gardens overlook Carlton House Terrace and The Royal Society.

At any one time the Club and the Royal Society will be playing host to the great and the good of the literati and the scientific aristocracy of the United Kingdom. The Club was built in the early 19th C but in the style favored by the Greeks of the golden age of Pericles. The entrance is just behind the mounting block used by the Duke of Wellington, victor at the battle of Waterloo. The whole facade is glittering white like a wedding cake reflecting the low winter sun just rising over the Institute of Directors on the eastern side of Waterloo Place. The portico consists of a row of Corinthian columns surmounted by a long triangular architrave surmounted by a golden statue of Athena in full armor, the Goddess of knowledge. The date is February the 23rd 2012 and I still have the cutting from the Times to prove that my memory of that date is precise. I mount the wide granite steps under the ostentatious portico and enter my club. I nod to Arnold the hall porter and check the pin boards for messages, not really expecting anything but giving me a pretext to catch my breath before climbing the "North face of the Eiger" as it is referred to by us octogenarians, but is in fact the famous grand staircase that has in the past echoed to the steps of Michael Faraday, Thomas Huxley, Charles Darwin, Charles Dickens and every Archbishop and Ambassador to the Court of St James in the last 150 years.

I was on my way to the great north library to join the ghosts of the pantheon of great British authors who had elected to write their works of genius in the peace and quiet of an exclusive London gentleman's club. At the age of 82 whilst still *compos mentis* and still capable of climbing the great staircase, I was settling in to my daily routine of writing my memoirs hoping to be inspired by the lingering miasma of the great Victorian authors, men of science and men of literature, who had completed their greatest works at these very same antique writing desks. At the age of 82 I also reasonably assumed that I was already living in my final chapter but the events of that day proved me wrong.

My ritual when I was in London was to walk down Heath street at about 9.00 am each morning, catch the Northern line tube from Hampstead to Charring Cross, then walk across Trafalgar Square past the National Gallery to Waterloo Place. The background muffled sound of the traffic that came through the tall windows of the club I imagined to be the echoes of past victories of the British Army at Waterloo and the British Navy at Trafalgar.

I would then write for an hour before taking my coffee on the dot of 11.00 whilst reading the Times, then write for another hour and a half before joining other club members for lunch and gossip downstairs. On that particular day the Times carried a short piece on page 38 that caught my eye with the caption "Strict dress code as officials defy curse to seek temple's treasure."

I had to read it twice before I could believe my eyes. My mind was instantly thrown back to my honeymoon in Kerala. Apparently the treasure vaults of the temple Trivandrum where being opened after 150 years at the order of India's Supreme Court and a treasure with an estimated value of £12 billion was about to be uncovered. At that point once I'd recovered from my shock I did something shameful that might have had me suspended from the Athenaeum, a crime worse than letting your mobile phone ring, I covertly used one of the club's paper knifes to cut out that news item and with a guilty glance over my shoulder, fold it and slip it in my wallet.

I couldn't concentrate after that, thinking back to the day in Cochin when Sara and I learnt the history of the Black Jews of Kerala and the probable hiding place of the golden candlesticks of the Temple. By 12.30 I'd given up and walked back down the grand staircase just as the dinning room was opened.

I made my way to the member's table that occupied the full length of the eastern wall of the room and sat with my back to the windows that looked across to the Institute of Directors. As a lonely old man I chose the one table where other members who were on the own could sit and strike up conversation confident in the knowledge that he (and often enough, she, these days) would be someone of interest, scholarship, high rank in the Church of England or even a long haired poet or playwright. I was first at the table and ordered a glass of club claret, soup de jour and a Dover Sole. The first person to join me was a very handsome elderly Indian gentleman with a grey military moustache. We greeted each other politely and in the way of English gentlemen commented on the unseasonal fine weather. I then thought I recognized him but for the life of me couldn't think when or where we had met before. So in order to search for clues I asked, "what are you doing these days?" "Oh you know, still Maharaja of Jaipur" he replied with a laugh. The penny dropped, "not Bubbles?" I exclaimed. "The very same, but these days they call me Bahawani Singh; how do you know my nickname old boy?"

I then reminded him of one Christmas 65 years earlier and before long we both fell about laughing on remembering that week and the "ghost of Bonneville Abbey".

He seemed in no hurry so we went to the coffee lounge and spent to next hour catching up on our back-stories. He seemed impressed by my high achievements in medical science and I was even more impressed to learn that he was *chargé d'affaires* at the Indian High Commission. He seemed in no hurry to leave so I recounted the story of my honeymoon, the search for the Temple candlesticks and then surreptitiously showed him the cutting from the Times.

"I say old boy that's jolly interesting and such an amazing coincidence that we met today. I have a cousin who is a judge at the Indian Supreme Court and if you like and think you're up to the rigours of another trip to Kerala I might be able to fix up for you to inspect these treasures and see if you can't find those jolly old golden candlesticks. Come to think of it I've got some family business to complete in Jaipur next month and the weather in Kerala's pretty good at the moment, things are quiet at work, in fact my job is something of a sinecure, those embassy wallahs like to impress visitors with my title, I might join you for the ride. A treasure hunt and some hot summer sunshine might reignite my will to live. Lost the lovely old Maharani last year and half the time I'm damned if I know what to do with meself." His cut glass English accent and his use of compound adjectives hadn't change after all these years. After a few rather lame excuses and a little hesitation I thought to myself, "Why the hell not. I'm not dead yet." I then remembered that I was expected in Safed for the Bar Mitzvah of one of my brother Joe's grandsons in late March and that would fit in well: London, Mumbai, Cochin, Mumbai, Tel Aviv, London; on second thoughts too much for an old man. Bhawani Singh wouldn't take no for an answer, "Leave it to me old boy, I'll get my office to fix your visa and arrange your flights and this time I'll make sure you do it in comfort, first class all the way!" "That's very kind but I don't think I could afford that" I replied. "My dear chap you won't be paying, this will be counted as a diplomatic and cultural visit and I'll see if I can run it through my department accounts. Plan B I'll pay for you out of the totally unspendable interest on the interest of the fortune I was left by dear old Pater. Plan C I'll sell one of my empty palaces to the Oberoi hotel chain but I'll not take no for an answer."

And so it came to pass that on March 3rd, The Maharaja and I boarded the first class cabin of the Air India en route to Mumbai where his private jet would pick us up for the short hop to Cochin. Unlike my first visit 50 years earlier this was like a magic carpet all the way lubricated with lashings of Dom Perignon encouraged by Bubbles who had of course the duty to live up to his birthright and nickname.

★★★

We stayed at the Jockey Club in Cochin that seemed to enjoy

reciprocal membership with the Athenaeum and at every turn we were greeted with Namaste and somewhat cloying respect. Through his cousin in the Supreme Court and helped along the way by a modicum of corruption that involved sums of money changing hands that were sufficient to encourage the most devout and unworldly devotees of the supreme God Shiva, Bubbles had arranged a private inspection of the legendary hidden treasures of the old rulers of the State of Kerala in the underground vaults of the Sree Padmanabhaswamy Temple two days after our arrival.

We were greeted by a phalanx of Hindu priests, security guards, journalists and press photographers as the story of our secret visit was no longer a secret because of the systemic corruption in the system and even Hindu priests weren't deterred from accepting the occasional backhander from the Times of India for a good story. Even so security was very tight as we were conducted through a labyrinth of tunnels via a number of airport like security checks until we reached the heavily padlocked gates of the first of the huge vaults. Looking through the iron struts I was reminded of the reaction of Lord Carnarvon on first catching sight of Tutankhamen's burial chamber; "Gold everywhere the glint of Gold". To be more precise the vault looked like Aladdin's cave in the Disney cartoon I'd seen as a child. Jewel encrusted golden jars and lanterns, crowns and coronets bearing rubies and pearls. Golden coins and chains in elaborately decorated caskets competed for shelf space with beautifully bound and bejeweled Holy Scriptures. Even the scattered furniture was inlaid and overlaid and under laid with gold. All that glittered was in this case genuine gold and my chance of finding the golden candlesticks of King Herod's Temple looked remote as this was only one of three vaults and furthermore all this treasure that we could see was standing or lying on tea chest sized brass bound mahogany boxes containing I knew not what.

The gates were unlocked and thrown open. So far no attempt had been made to start an inventory and I had no idea where to begin. The second vault along the subterranean corridor was much the same and the third was still sealed off with a plastered wall. Yet it seemed unconscionable to come this far and abandon the hunt. The Maharaja then turned to me and murmured to me, "Martin dear fellow, we Indians believes in the principle of Kismet. There has been a long chain of events that has brought you to this point and that can only be described as Kismet. Put your trust in Shiva, who amongst many attributes determines our fate, don't try to find the golden candlesticks of the Temple, let them find you." There is a Yiddish word more or less with the same meaning as Kismet and that is *beshert* bearing in mind the limited time available and the monumental task involved, I saw no alternative. So I wandered without looking too hard through the two open vaults each the size of an aircraft hanger and each brightly illuminated by arc lights. The first day yielded nothing but was only the most superficial of inspections. On the second day after a couple of hours I began to think the task was impossible and as I entered the second vault the arc lights suddenly fused and everything was pitched into complete darkness. There were screams and shouts whilst I, completely blind in the dark, tripped and fell heavily dislodging some of the golden Baroque decanters I'd been inspecting, from their shelves. As the lights went on I knew immediately that the Temple candlesticks had found me. I was lying on my side facing the deep shadows of the shelving thrown on the floor by the arc lights and there they were in a penumbra half hidden in the shadows. I then realized my mistake. I had been blinded by all this overblown grandiose treasure while what I was looking for and seemed to have found was modest in comparison. These candlesticks were only a little larger than those my mother used on a Friday night and were very simple in design. How I knew beyond any shadow of doubt that these were the ones was the fact that the circular base was subdivided into twelve facets and each facet carried the emblem of the tribes of Israel. I saw Dan, Judah, Zebulon, and Naphtali and had little doubt that the others were hidden in the shadows or at the other side from my angle of vision.

I lifted them out and confirmed my suspicions and then carried them out without too much difficulty and announced with some theatricality, "Behold, the golden candlesticks of the holy Temple of the ancient Israelites".

All the Indian press picked up the story and the story became more and more elaborate and fantastic with every retelling. One version in a British tabloid portrayed me as a rabbi with mystical powers and suggested that the return of the candlesticks to the temple would presage the second coming. The evangelicals in the "Flyover States" in the USA seized on this and their press somehow got hold of pictures of me and then, with the touch of computer generated halo, hailed me as the Messiah. This foolishness was soon exposed when the British broadsheets provided a true biography and reported on interviews with me during my stop over in Israel for the Bar mitzvah. Eventually after the fuss had died down and scientists from India and Israel confirmed the likely age and provenance of the holy artifacts, some behind the scenes wheeling and dealing initiated by Bubbles and his Israeli counterpart at the Embassy in Delhi clinched a deal whereby the candlesticks would be returned to Jerusalem in exchange for a precious golden statue of Garnesh of great antiquity that was no doubt looted from Rajasthan at the time of the collapse of the British Empire and spirited away to mandated Palestine in about 1947, that ultimately found its way to the Israel museum in Jerusalem. I will return to this matter later but before doing so wish to recount a strange occurrence during my stop over in Safed on my way home to London.

★★★

I traveled business class to Ben Gurion airport just outside Tel Aviv from Mumbai where Joe's oldest son Joshua now earning a modest living as an artist in Safed, was waiting in a car for me at the airport met me. He had studied at the Betzalel School of Art in Jerusalem and then did his MA at the Slade School of Art at University College London. During that time he stayed with me and I acted in *loco parentis*. We became close friends and enjoyed debating our differences. Joshua is deeply religious and something of a mystic. His work reflected this by conjuring up incandescent but disturbing images built out of Hebrew letters using the letters both for their shape and their hidden meaning. For example the second letter of the Hebrew alphabet is *Beit*. The letter in his hands takes on serifs that look like flames but the letter has the numerical value of two, is the first letter of the word for house of prayer and has other meanings of a Cabalistic nature beyond my understanding. He is clearly at home in Safed where his youngest son Samuel was to celebrate his Bar Mitzvah in the same synagogue where his parents were married.

On the long drive north he kept me talking as he wanted to learn every detail of my adventures in India. For once he won the argument with me when I confessed there certainly was a metaphysical spin to my experience. As we turned northeast off the coastal road he said, "Talking of metaphysical experiences uncle, I experienced something weird last week. You may have heard that the Abuhav Synagogue was severely damaged by an earthquake last year, well the dome collapsed and after it had been rebuilt I was commissioned to repaint the interior according to its original design. I was just putting the finishing touches to the work on the eve of Mum and Dad's Golden Wedding as the light began to fade when this guy strolls in. He was maybe in his late twenties but he had a beard so I couldn't accurately judge. He wore rather old-fashioned clothing and spoke dreadful Hebrew with an English accent. He was quite relieved to find that I spoke English and explained why he was there. He asked me if I knew Rav Joseph Tanner and claimed that he was going to be best man at his wedding the following day. I was at a loss and thought he might be taking the piss so I packed up and left without saying another word. Weren't you best man at Mum and Dad's wedding Uncle Martin?"

Once again the hair pricked on the back of my neck as I counted this as the third "time slip" of my life and wondered if this all had some hidden meaning. I replied simply that indeed I had performed that service and agreed that he must have seen my ghost as a young man. He chewed that over all the way to Safed giving me sidelong glances from time to time before responding. "Uncle Martin on the eve of Dad's wedding did you somehow look into the future and see me? If so you and I share a rare gift in experiencing time slips and this is not my first but I have never spoken of it before lest they think I'm mad." I nodded and he smiled triumphantly knowing that there were more things in the heavens and the earth than are dreamed of in my philosophy.

Chapter 32

The Golden Ibex of Santorini

There were of course more important reasons why the Indian government and their Israeli counterparts were anxious to make that exchange. Since the murderous attack on Mumbai by Islamic terrorists in 2011 where they massacred guests at the Taj Mahal Palace Hotel whilst a few of their number made a minor detour to take the lives of a young rabbi and his wife in a nearby Jewish community centre, the Indian government found common cause to share intelligence with Israel. Furthermore the history of the Temple candlesticks provided proof positive of Israel's 2,000-year attachment to the land that could dismiss the Palestinian and their fellow travelers' revisionist narrative. All this diplomatic activity was conducted under a smokescreen of cultural exchanges that involved a golden statue of Ganesh that for all I knew never existed.

The Israeli Department of Antiquities in collusion with their foreign office decided that the original two stone fragments from the second Temple should be reunited and displayed together in the same glass cabinet in the section of the Israel Museum devoted to the Roman period that spanned the two eras by which we count our years. There was then another twist of fortune in my life. My son in law, Professor Daniel Cohen, at the very same time I was in Cochin, had received the letter confirming his appointment as curator of the department of the Ancient Roman period of the Levant in the Israel Museum in Jerusalem.

The President of Israel in the company of the Prime Minister organized a high profile event for the unveiling this special exhibit, on Independence Day May 2013 in front of the world's media. Coincidentally that happened to be my 83rd birthday, three score years and ten, plus thirteen, traditionally the time to celebrate one's

290

second Bar Mitzvah. A glass cube was created that was impenetrable to high velocity ordinance and this was to be supported on a matching black cube full of sensors and alarms their combined dimensions obeying the laws of golden ratios. The museum itself was built up of a chain of glass cubes linked in a knight's move pattern. The whole complex had been reopened in 2011 after extensive refurbishment and was in pristine condition reflecting the late spring sun of the Judean hills off every surface. To reach the sloping underground entrance to the museum one had to pass through beautifully landscaped gardens with spectacular views over the seven hills of Jerusalem and each viewpoint is occupied with a piece of contemporary sculpture from the world's most famous sculptors.

Daniel and I planned the display together, where he could make use of his esoteric knowledge of the era and I could make use of my first hand experience. All he knew was that the original twin tablets were in his protective custody whilst their facsimiles were in their original nests in the wall of the Zinati synagogue. He has no idea of the real reason they had been transferred to the museum vaults and it then occurred to me that I was probably the last living witness involved in the abortive search for the deciphering of "Third tablet of The Holy Covenant". The search and discovery of the Temple Candlesticks could easily be explained away by my follow up of the legends of the Black Jews of Kerala and my chance friendship with the Maharaja of Jaipur.

The glass cube that housed these holy artifacts was artistically lit with a pale mauve tint to bring out the deep gold patina of the candlesticks and reflect the brilliant light of the "marble" plaques. The fractured stone was in fact granite but the sides on show, as I later discovered, achieved the appearance of carved marble by the application of several layers of thick plaster that was then incised, glazed and fired. The catalogue and the audio-guide merely retold the two legends and how modern scientific analysis confirmed the legends to be factual and this alone provided sufficient historical provenance to support Israel's claim to the land ahead of the Palestinians.

The unveiling ceremony was pompous and tedious. I was introduced as the "warm up act" to describe my recent adventures in Kerala. Daniel followed describing the science that dated and placed the three items on display. Then the heavy guns went into action as the Indian Ambassador, the Israeli Prime Minister and finally that wily old bird, the President of Israel, delivered well-scripted rhetorical speeches. As the party broke up and canapés and wine was served, I drifted away to explore the neighboring room containing archaeological treasures from Ancient Egypt.

I was strolling round the tastefully arranged exhibits lost in contemplation when a little golden object surfaced into my realm of observation and I came to a juddering halt as my heart went into a run of sinus tachycardia.

I was reminded of the days when my twin grandsons would play video games with little black boxes held in their hands as their fingers and thumbs frenetically flew over a key boards. Without looking up they would greet me with, "*Shalom Sabba*" and carry on regardless. Once they tried to explain the arcane wisdom required to rise through the ranks of proficiency in order to end up as the grand wizard of some order of chivalry in a game called "Dungeons and Dragons; the search for the Holy Grail". I was allocated an "avatar" of my choosing. That was the first time I heard that word. I entered the fray with certain given attributes of wisdom and or strength. As my thumbs manipulated my journey through a fantastical labyrinth, using my avatar's native skills, I might acquire additional gifts of treasure or valour destroying or being destroyed by fiendish monsters along the route of my quest. Suddenly in front of my eyes was the key to unlock the secret of the stones and I now had no choice but to accept my humble role as God's Avatar in the divine cyber world we inhabit known as human life. The key to this mystery was hidden in an ancient Egyptian household god fashioned out of matt textured gold, a golden Ibex the size of my hand. It stood there along with other burial items from 1,500 BCE but seemed to be illuminated by a spotlight that wasn't there. This was the third of its kind to enter my life. The first I saw in the pool at Ein Gedi on the day I asked Sara to be my wife but the second golden ibex I knew with absolute certainty, would help me recover the lost wording of the Third Tablet of the Holy Covenant. Let me explain.

★★★

3,600 years ago the Island of Santorini (Thera) blew its top. In the most cataclysmic volcanic eruption in the recorded history of our planet, 30 cubic kilometres of magna in the form of pumice and volcanic ash buried the Island and its civilization. These dramatic events have given rise to a number of legends and myths. Firstly the destroyed civilization of the Island of Stronghili, as the Island was known before the eruption, gave rise to the legend of the lost City of Atlantis. The apparent sudden destruction of the Minoan civilization on the Island of Crete has been ascribed by some, to this catastrophic event and the tsunami that followed in its wake. Finally the timing of the volcanic eruption was undoubtedly close to the timing of the exodus of the Jews from ancient Egypt and a rational explanation for the ten plagues described in the Old Testament. Some of the predicted events with a volcanic eruption of this magnitude might account for the plagues. For example the column of ash above the volcano could produce a shadow long enough for the sun to be obliterated at noon over ancient Egypt. Furthermore the inflow of the Mediterranean Sea into the volcanic cavity followed by the mighty tidal wave or tsunami, might have accounted for the dry crossing of the *Red* Sea by Moses and the children of Israel, followed by the destruction of Pharaoh and his legions, shortly thereafter. Bible stories and legends of lost civilizations are romantic but the reality might exceed the expectations of many sceptics.

In 1995 a shaft was being dug to provide foundations for a permanent protective cover over the archaeological excavations at Akrotiri, a site at the southern tip of the crescent shaped island. Amongst the rubble, a workman discovered a perfectly preserved wooden box that was thought to serve some late bronze-age domestic role. On opening the box, the archaeologists were

293

astonished to discover a most beautifully crafted and perfectly preserved Golden Ibex about the size of a newborn kitten. Closer inspection revealed that it was hollow with all four limbs welded at the junction with the trunk. The local experts assumed it was fabricated by using the lost wax technique but the technique for welding the limbs onto the trunk was a mystery, as was its role within this lost Civilization.

As an object this sublimely proportioned artefact could be looked upon in three ways. Firstly as an object venerated for its beauty and for all we know, venerated in its time as a household God, a pocket size adumbration of the Golden Calf worshipped by the children of Israel in the same year as the exodus from Egypt. Secondly it could be looked upon as an archaeological curiosity capable of throwing light on the bronze-age civilizations of the Cycladic Islands and their trading links with ancient Egypt to the South and the biblical Kingdoms to the East. Finally it was a technological challenge to assay the gold and interpret the technique for joining the limbs to the trunk without damaging the find that in its own way would shed light on its archaeological provenance.

In the last week of August 1997, a group of us assembled on the Island of Santorini as guests of Mr. Peter M. Nomikos, the founder of Photoelectron Corporation for a scientific advisory Board meeting. I had been working with Photoelectron Corporation for about three years developing a technique for intra-operative radiotherapy in the treatment of early breast cancer using a miniature X-ray generating source developed by the Company. This device about the size and the shape of a shoebox accelerates electrons down a metallic capillary tube which then hit a gold target generating soft X-rays from a point source at its tip. Introduced within the cavity following wide local excision of an early breast cancer it can deliver a full booster dose of radiation to the excision margins. The *Thera Foundation, Petros M. Nomikos* supports the archaeological studies of Akrotiri and for that reason I was privileged to witness an historic first in the history of archaeology.

On Sunday the 31st August, a group consisting of archaeologists, technologists and oncologists gathered in the subterranean laboratories of the archaeological Museum in Thera. The Golden Ibex was placed upon a laboratory table and the miniature X-ray source was directed precisely at the weld at the junction between a hind limb and the trunk of this enigmatic beast. The device was switched on, electrons were accelerated down the capillary tube and X-rays from the gold target at the tip of the device excited the molecules within the Bronze Age weld of the ancient gold of the Ibex. The signal from the excitation of these molecules was then picked up by another extraordinary technological invention developed for the NASA Mars exploration project. This detection probe then provided us with a waveform printout describing the precise content of the solder. Thus with the benefits of modern technology the artisan of an ancient Cycladic culture was able to speak to us over the centuries. It is difficult to describe the sense of wonder we all experienced at this unique amalgam of art, archaeology and technology. The results from this experiment were quite remarkable and confirmed that the artisan was a visitor from the time of the 18th dynasty of Ancient Egypt and the golden Ibex was buried at the time of the biblical exodus from Egypt. To think that I handled a household god manufactured by a similar technique and within a few years of the golden calf at the foot of Mount Sinai, still makes my hair prickle on the back of my neck. Shortly after that experiment we all retired to the Nomikos castle for a celebratory drink only to learn of the tragic death of Princess Diana in an underpass in Paris.

★★★

I have grown old and indeed wear the bottom of my trousers rolled – as a result of an osteoporotic kyphosis. My increasing age is also acknowledged by the little rows of plastic boxes marked and colour coded for the days of the week with each having sub compartments labeled am and pm. This way I don't forget to take my statins, beta-blockers, diuretics, H2 receptor antagonist and something else whose name I forget, that is meant to shrink my prostate. Clicking my little boxes is effectively an organ recital but there is one organ left that is fit and muscular from a lifetime of exercise 8 hours a day, and that is my cerebral cortex. At four in the morning I curse it as it kicks into action following the second prostatic awakening of the night. My brain says to itself "OK frontal lobes get thinking-the old man's awake. Today's agenda is to unravel the meaning of life and other easy questions". After 30 minutes pleading with my brain that I really do want to go back to sleep, I give up, make my way to the kitchen, make a hot drink and shuffle to my computer to figure out the meaning of life. However at most other times I'm proud of the fleetness of foot exhibited by my grey matter.

This was such an occasion. The physicists at the Nomikos Foundation had analyzed the solder holding the legs to the trunk of Santorini's golden Ibex and I was reminded of this at the sight of the Golden Ibex in the Israel museum. This time round we could reverse the process and tune the X ray detectors to recognize the signal of ancient bronze particles left behind by the tools of the scribe taking down Moses' dictation. I could even visualize a rectilinear scanner that would traverse the stone backwards and forwards moving forward an millimeter at a time whilst each quantum of X-ray energy carrying the wave form signature of bronze from the time of Exodus, would be transformed as a bright dot on a plasma screen. All that was needed was to share my secret with my daughter and son in law, convince them I was not mad and dragoon the physics department at the Haifa Technion to build the machine and talk the radiotherapy department at Hadassah hospital into lending us their 50KV electron generator to attach to the assembly. Fat chance but then as *Hashem* would never leave anything to chance it was predetermined that all concerned would jump at this opportunity for offering a helping hand to the will of God. It would be a *mitzvah!*

Of course not everyone shared my vision yet I got off to a good start.

I wandered back to find Jessie and Daniel just as the party broke up and in time to shake hands with the visiting dignitaries. I then cornered my daughter and son in law and put an arm on each of there shoulders and in a wheedling old man's voice started with, "*kinderlach........*", the diminutive term of affection for young children. God knows why I use Yiddish words whenever I'm in Israel. I've never spoken Yiddish but have picked up a few common words from elderly Viennese friends I've linked up with in Israel. I seemed to have adopted the role and the manner of the little old Jewish guys you meet playing dominoes at corner coffee shops on Ben Yehudah Street in Tel Aviv. In London at the Athenaeum I talk posh. Whatever. "*Kinderlach,* I have a very important secret to share with you. Daniel please may we retire to your office?" Daniel nodded assent as in any case that was going to be his next port of call so that he could file away his notes and lock up the department's laptop and data projector that he had used for his presentation. His office was nearby and having tidied things away he and Jessie looked at me with expectancy. "Please sit down because what I want to say will take time and will challenge your belief in my sanity." They sat down but by now Jessie was looking alarmed. "What I'm going to tell you is not just a regular secret but a State secret! In telling you this story I am in fact breaking the law so please I beg you keep it to yourselves. It is likely that I am the only living person who knows this story but I can't be too careful. Daniel please remind Judith-Esther of the date the two original tablets were taken from Piki'in into the safe custody of your department" Daniel reopened his file and confirmed the date as November the 6th 1963. "Jessie, does that date have any particular meaning for you?" She shook her head. "Well the 6th November 1963 was the day before your mother and I were married and we were both witnesses to their removal from the synagogue walls and replaced by facsimiles. Daniel what was the reason for this exchange?" "My records describe and earthquake a week earlier that damaged the walls of the synagogue and threatened to dislodge the stones so the originals were carefully removed and stored in the vaults of the Department of Antiquities and once the walls were repaired the niches were filled with the facsimiles in case the same might happen again in the future"

"OK Daniel now turn on your computer and Google the dates of earthquakes in Northern Israel" Looking puzzled Daniel did as

I requested and tapped a few keys and looked even more puzzled. "Well according to both Wikipedia and the Israel geological website the last major tremor was felt in Safed in February this year damaging the Abuav synagogue and the one before that was in 1960 causing damage in Piki'in, funnily enough I can't find one for 1963" he eventually replied. "Nu Daniel? Who's wrong-the World Wide Web or your departmental records? Now would you please search for a description of the Eliezer scroll amongst Yadin's inventory of findings from the Masada dig in 1963 in the records of your own department that I'm sure are by now fully digitized." Daniel turned back to face the screen of his desktop PC and tapped away until suddenly he jumped back as if he had caught an electric shock. Speechless with shock he turned the screen so that Jessie and I could see for ourselves. In bold letters the last window he had opened read, "ACCESS DENIED. FOR FURTHER INFORMATION ON THIS FILE PLEASE CONTACT THE OFFICE OF THE DIRECTOR OF THE DEPARTMENT OF ANTIQUITIES OF THE STATE OF ISRAEL DIRECTLY AFTER GETTING CLEARANCE FROM THE OFFICE OF THE DIRECTOR OF SHIN BEIT".

"OK Martin, what's all this about? You have my attention and I swear on my mother's grave that I'll take your secrets and the State's secrets to my own grave if necessary."

Jessie remained pale and speechless and merely nodded an agreement whilst clutching Daniel's hand tightly.

I then asked Daniel to hand me his photocopy of the twin stones from the old synagogue, borrowed some scissors and repeated my trick of lining up the two complementary facets of the images to reproduce the outline of what I assured them was the third tablet of the Holy Covenant. By this time I had really captured their full attention and I then launched into the whole story of the discovery of the Piki'in papers and the Eliezer scroll by Sara and the abortive attempt to uncover the text on the hidden side of the single tablet.

It took close on an hour to complete my story frequently interrupted by intense questioning from my audience of two. In the end they had to accept my story and Daniel asked me how I intended to continue my quest to decode the stone. He nodded sagely as I explained my sudden flash of inspiration and agreed it just might work. Jessie expressed concern about the security issues and the inevitable bureaucracy that would be involved but after another hour we had hatched a plan.

First I would approach Hadassah Hospital for a loan of their electron generator and then Daniel would exploit his contacts at the Department of Antiquities to set up a meeting for us with the Minister of State. In parallel with this Daniel and I would call in favours from friends in the relevant departments at the Haifa Technion and the Hebrew university to help construct a scanner to meet our needs and then recruit experts in paleo Hebrew to help us to translate anything we uncovered as a result of the scanning for fragments of bronze from an era 3,500 years in the past. All this time of course it would be essential to keep the real reason for our project a complete secret so we would have to concoct a convincing cover story. We intended to stick as close to the truth as possible but instead of claiming to have discovered a codicil to the Ten Commandments we would tell everyone that in moving the Piki'in tablets to a new setting in a new light we had caught sight of some faint shallow inscriptions on the obverse side of the stones.

That night I couldn't sleep for my excitement and the following day the three of us, my daughter, my son in law and I launched the operation code named "Zinati".

We then hit the buffers. No one we approached looked upon it as a *mitzvah* to help us. Hadassah Hospital's response could be summarized as, "You must be joking!" I secured one half promise of help from the manufacturers of the electron generator, Carl Zeiss, who offered me the use of the next decommissioned unit that had outlasted its warranty.

After a few months wheeling and dealing, Daniel achieved a breakthrough.

His coup over the Temple candlesticks and the twin tablets placed him in a favourable light with the director of the Israel Museum, Moishe Ginsburg, and he was able to arrange an appointment with the Minister of State for the department of Antiquities, Professor Aaron Ben Tzadick. Like Yadin in the past he had served as a general in the IDF and then developed a second career as an archaeologist and ultimately ended up as a MK for the Likud party. When Professor Ben Tzadick learnt that I had worked with Yigal Yadin at Masada he was quick to offer us an audience whilst at the same time being briefed with our cover story.

His office was in the Rockefeller Museum in Jerusalem. Through his windows we could see the Knesset and along side his windows were bookshelves packed with archaeological finds. He was a tall, bronzed and freckled elderly gentleman with a broad welcoming smile. He was clearly an ex lady's man as well as ex general and was obviously bewitched by my daughter's beauty. He offered us coffee and wanted to learn first hand about my experiences with his hero Yadin. Once we had completed all these pleasantries and got down to business he wound up our discussions with a promise to do his best for us but thought that our chances were slim. At this point I interrupted him with the words," Professor Ben Tzadick, have ever heard of the Eliezer scroll unearthed at Masada?" He shook his head. "Please forgive my *chutzpah* but would you check your computer files of Yadin's inventory of his findings at the dig in the winter of 1963." He smiled across at Jessie with a wink as if indicting he was indulging the whim of her poor old father, then turning to his computer screen started click clacking away. On reaching the named file his reaction was like Daniel's, he looked like he was stung by a bee but clearly a man of action he pressed a buzzer and we heard automatic locks click and a security guard with an Uzi sub machine gun levelled at his hip entered from a side room. Ben Tzadick turned to the guard as said, "Dovid, lower you gun these fine folk are not dangerous but they won't be going far for a while," then turning to us he continued," My dear lady and gentlemen, my Ministry is in lock down and I'm afraid you need to be detained for a while whilst I arrange a meeting for you with my dear friend Avi Jabotinsky Director General of Shin Beit".

Chapter 33

The third tablet of the Holy Covenant

Shin Bet, the nick name for *Sheirut Ha'bitachon* , is the organisation for internal security in Israel equivalent to MI5 in the UK or Homeland security in the USA. It is loved and feared in equal measure. Loved for its efficiency by those loyal to the State and hated in equal measure for the same reasons by terrorists and other who were less than loyal to the State. The role of its director is considered so important that he or she reports directly to the Prime Minister bypassing all ministries. Avi Jabotinsky its current director is a shadowy figure related to one of the founding fathers of the State and he carried ultimate responsibility for our fate. We were kept in Ben Tzadick's office until the arrival of two Shin Bet operatives. They looked tough. They were tall, tanned and shaven headed. Their ill fitting suits did little to hide their overdeveloped biceps and the bulge below the belt was not because they were happy to see us. They sported little white coils of wire behind their ears and from time to time interrupted our cross examination to speak to their chunky cuff links. They interviewed us separately in a neighbouring office and seemed to be angry and confused at the same time. They even forgot from time to time who was playing good cop and who was playing bad cop.

I had to keep choking back my laugher as it became more and more like "Keystone Kops" than "The Manchurian Candidate". Our stories crossed checked and none of us had criminal records or posed any kind of security threat, although in fairness, Daniel had collected 3 penalty points for crossing on red at the Latrun junction on his way down from Jerusalem one day. The problem for Mutt and Jeff as I named them, is they hadn't a clue what we had done or what breach of security we were guilty of. All they knew for sure was that I had signed the State Secret act many years before they were born and then shared that secret, whatever it was, with my daughter and son-in-law. All along they kept trying to reassure us that it was just routine whilst threatening us with grievous bodily language.

They kept rolling their eyes in disbelief at our explanations involving buried treasure and long lost tablets of Mosaic Law but at the same time they hadn't a clue of the nature of our criminal offence. It was a bit like Kafka's "The Trial" but in reverse. Eventually I took pity on their plight and suggested they should contact their boss Avi Jabotinsky himself explaining that Avi and I were bridge partners in the Jerusalem team playing once a fortnight during the months I spend in Israel. Mutt and Jeff blanched at the mention of Jabotinsky's name and both then engaged their cuff links in intimate machine gun rapid conversations. When finished they both turned to me with big smiles that involved the mouth only whilst their eyes burnt with fury. "You should have mentioned that earlier Professor Tanner, the chief is on his way now" said Mutt, as the two of them backed out towards the door as if leaving the presence of minor royalty. At that the four of us, including Ben Tzadick fell about with laughter. Once Jessie had caught her breath she asked, "Is that true daddy, do you really play bridge with the director of Shin Bet?" I nodded assent and we all fell about laughing again.

Half an hour later the bear like figure of Avi Jabotinsky barged through the door and gave me a bear like hug. "Nu, Moishe Dovid, vat kindda trouble you in now?" Avi always used my Hebrew name as a mild rebuke for my decision to make no attempt to change my English name, Tanner to its Hebrew equivalent. Once greetings and introductions were complete and coffee and pastries served the mood changed as the five of us settled round Ben Tzadick's desk and I started to explain why the "Eliezer" scroll dug up at Masada over 40 years ago was considered a threat to National Security and thus ranked as a State secret. Avi was a good listener and let me complete my story with only the minimum of interruptions for clarification. He made no notes but I knew that his memory and powers of deduction were prodigious and that was why he sometimes played in Israel's National bridge team under a *nom de guerre*. Once I had finished my story, the director of Shin Bet and the director of Antiquities, both old friends, embarked on an intense debate on how to proceed. At this point it is worth pointing out that Jabotinsky was completely secular in his beliefs whereas Ben Tzadick was *Dattei,* or modern orthodox as might have been deduced from the neat crocheted skull cap he wore on the back of the bald dome of his head. They argued for an hour back and forth on the wisdom or otherwise of decoding the "Third Tablet" in case the last words of Moses delegitimized Israel's claim to the land. In the end Jabotinsky asked the killer question, " OK Aaron my dear friend, say the wording on the tablet is interpreted in such a way as to lead the expulsion of the Jews from this narrow strip of land and return to the land of their forefathers, would you accept that and where would that place you?" To which Ben Tzadick replied. "If that was the wish of Hashem I would accept it without question and that would land me in Hebron where my family lived since records began!"

At this we all once again laughed out loud with a mixture of relief and a touch of hysteria. And so it was decided that the director of the Ministry of Antiquities and the director of Shin Bet would approach the Prime Minister to argue the case for the permission and the resources for one last attempt to decode the Third Tablet of the Holy Covenant.

★★★

After this things moved very quickly. The Prime Minister was quick to seize the political advantage of the Third Tablet being discovered on his watch and that was the same sentiment of the President. The Israeli Foreign Secretary approached her German counterpart who in turn encouraged Carl Zeiss to lend the Israelis a miniature electron generator and the company agreed to deliver one to us fresh off the production line. The Minister of State for Higher education contacted the Vice Chancellor of the Haifa Technion for a chat about the rather large increase requested in their triennial grant and off the cuff suggested that it might help his argument with the Treasury if the university might see their way to help a pet project of the President that one way or another involved building a rectilinear scanner that might identify various wave patterns in the spectrum of X-rays. The Vice Chancellor said he would have a quiet word with the chairmen of the divisions of physics and engineering. The relevant departments in the control of the Minister for Antiquities and the Israel Museum were already onside and Shin Bet would of course be responsible for security. The only hold up encountered was within the ranks of the extreme wings of the religious groups. The Ashkenazi and Sephardic Chief Rabbis had no trouble in agreeing to attend the event along with their closest advisors but the extreme right wing orthodox sects of *Charedi* refused to sit down in the same room as the "centre left" representatives of the modern orthodox. The leading Rabbi representing the Liberal Jews refused in any case as she was expecting and couldn't face the stress of sitting in the same room amongst a bunch of bearded old men. In the end the controversies were settled from an unlikely source, the right hand man and close confidant of the Ashkenazi Chief Rabbi, my brother Joe.

My brother Joe has appeared only a few times in my story very much in the background and very much in a passive role yet Joe had enjoyed a spectacular career of his own in a very self effacing manner. We left him after he had taken up his post in the little synagogue at the top of the hill in Rosh Pinah. He and his wife Zipporah rapidly gained the love and respect of the community through their pastoral work and through the wit and wisdom of Joe's Sabbath sermons. These sermons started drawing in members of other communities who wanted a change from the dry wrath of the Almighty rants of the majority of the local rabbis. He was eventually persuaded to publish his sermons in book form, "Sermons from the Mount", and these sold about 2,000 copies. Emboldened by this Joe, with the encouragement of his publisher, wrote another book after many e-mail exchanges with me entitled, "On the other Hand", where he beautifully illustrated and reconciled the differences between faith and science explaining that science asked the "how" questions leaving faith and philosophy to address the "why" questions. Because of his light touch and wry sense of humour this book sold 8,000 copies and he soon became a minor celebrity on demand for chat shows where the sweetness and sincerity of his character shone through as he disarmed the proponents of religious fundamentalism on the right and evangelical atheists on the left.

His next book was an even greater success because it addressed a very controversial issue that was in danger of tearing Israel apart. That book was entitled, "Why fundamentalism keeps the flame yet tolerance teaches us to live in its light". In this very provocative book he made the argument that all religious groups needed to keep the flame of their founding fathers alight by tending it with daily rituals, whilst modern orthodoxy taught us how to live by the code whilst not being burnt by flying too close to the flame. This book soon became a runaway best seller both in Israel and the USA. With these two books and his chat show appearances Joe had managed to reconcile secular Jews with the modern orthodoxy and modern orthodoxy with fundamentalism. As a result of these activities he was invited to a pulpit in Jerusalem but refused because he and his family loved their community and the surrounding mysticism and beauty of the northern Galil. Never the less he happily accepted the low profile role of advisor and envoy to the Ashkenazi Chief Rabbi. The leading Charedi Rabbis who were flattered by the way they were portrayed in the book on keeping the flame were yet to learn that they had made themselves hostage to fortune.

★★★

A year later the equipment and personnel were assembled in the underground bunkers of the Israel Museum laboratory. Security was tight around and within the museum that was closed temporally for "stock taking". Two rooms were in use, the laboratory where the stone tablets were to be scanned and a nearby lecture theatre where the decoded X-ray spectra were to be projected.

In the laboratory, a shallow rectangular tungsten impregnated metal box stood on supports that raised it to waist height. The lateral edges of the box carried a line of finely tooled cog teeth. Sitting on top of this was a carriage running on matching finely tooled cogwheels. The carriage bore the assembly that would run lateral courses slowly as the carriage moved down the longitudinal tracks at a controlled pace. The assembly carried the Zeiss electron gun that focussed on the target that sat in the space between the carriage and its lateral tracks. Alongside the electron gun was the sensor for a low energy electron induced X-ray emission spectroscopy (LEXES). The X-ray spectra were then run through a computerised analytical detection devise and every time the complex spectrum of "bronze age" bronze circa 1,500 BCE, was detected a bright red dot would be displayed on a screen that represented the tracking plane across the target. The targets, of course, were the two halves of the Tablet that lay accurately aligned along their fractured edges, fixed in place by clamps in a shallow tray on a soft bed of tungsten impregnated rubber. Before the main study began the surface of the target had been examined under high power fibre optic microscopy. This confirmed that very shallow marks existed together with tiny flecks of bright yellow bronze like particles but in addition the whole surface was adulterated with a patchy very fine layer of what looked like ancient plastering material. After heated and highly technical discussions amongst the experts in the technologies of studying ancient biblical artefacts, it was decided to try and get rid of the remnants of the plaster with a dilute solution of acetic acid. This seemed to do the trick.

Next the spectrometer was tuned to recognise and signal ancient bronze spectra making use of a variety of objects spanning the era of interest held in the museum's collection. And within a few hours the technicians stood back satisfied that they were ready to start the motor that would drive the detector in its search for the imprint of the chisel of Moses or his lithographic scribe.

As soft X-rays would be generated it was thought that the technicians might stay in the laboratory as long as they wore lead aprons but radiation safety protocols had been conducted and the laboratory, was found to be well within a safe dosage range.

Meanwhile in the adjoining lecture theatre a more complex process was going on in deciding on the correct hierarchy amongst the politicians and clergy as they argued over the best seats. Joe once again showed his diplomacy by stating that it was the man who honoured the seat rather than the seat that honoured the man and then taking his place at the back on the extreme right hand side. This was followed by an unseemly scramble to find seats equally humble in position. Jessie and I found the jostling for position hilarious and could barely control our giggles. Meanwhile Daniel was occupied in a huddle with his colleagues who were overseeing the project that included two experts in the reading and translation of paleo or proto Hebraic script. A non-Jewish Englishman, Peter Fleming, who was a professor of ancient languages at the Hebrew University was then given the honour or as he described it, poisoned chalice, of reading and translating as the runes appeared on the screen.

Once Daniel was satisfied that everything was ready to go he nodded to Aaron Ben Tzadick who then nodded to the President of the State of Israel who had modestly taken up position in the centre of the front row.

The President then stood up and made a short well-judged speech pointing out the solemnity and grandeur of the event we were to witness and how we should prepare ourselves for failure or success. Success might change the course of history but even failure would at least leave us with the knowledge that we had in our safe keeping a tablet of stone that indeed was a holy relic of the Temple of King Herod. As he sat down and the lights were turned off Daniel signalled over his telephone link that the motor driving the scanner should be turned on.

The tension was high as the audience of the great and the good of Israeli society held their communal breath and as the first scatter of red dots appeared on the top right corner of the screen there followed a communal exhalation that sounded like a deep sigh.

***

After about 5-10 minutes two straight lines of red squiggles appeared on the screen and the audience started to become restive whilst Professor Fleming frowned in deep concentration before doubling over with laughter that I thought was a bit staged or exaggerated. When he finally caught his breath and caught sight of the horrified expressions on the faces of his audience he apologized and went on to say, "How stupid I am, how stupid have we all been. We have been brain washed in assuming the tablets of the law were written in Hebrew letters. From the time of Michelangelo's horned statue of Moses in Florence to Cecil B. De Mille's "Ten Commandments" starring Charlton Heston, we have always portrayed them in Hebrew lettering. Yet what I am seeing coming up before my very eyes is hieratic script from around the time of the 18th Dynasty and that would just about do for the best estimates of the dates for the exodus from Egypt. I'm pretty sure I'm right but I'm no expert in this area and for a translation I will have to call in Professor Uri Ginsburg head of our Department of Egyptology whose PhD thesis was based on the decoding of the medical papyri of this period. I'm really sorry for my foolish assumption but I'm going to have to adjourn this session until I can track down Uri." The sense of anticlimax was tangible and only Jessie and I saw the funny side. Daniel then took control. "Ladies and Gentlemen, may I suggest the following? It has taken us so long to set up and fine-tune the decoding of the stone that I think we should let our technical staff finish the job. We can then send the complete image of the text to Professor Ginsburg who I have just learnt is attending a conference in LA. I can alert him to the urgency and sensitivity of this matter and see if he can complete the translation overnight, which should work out well for him because of the 11-hour time difference. I will then arrange for the translation to appear line by line below the ancient Egyptian script in Hebrew and in English, to show you on the screen tomorrow morning." There were mutterings amongst the audience and some of the politicians present raised their hands to explain that they already had a full diary the next day and would have to leave to the rest of us to decide how to take the matter further. I then caught sight of my brother in deep conversation with his Chief Rabbi, he caught Daniel's eye and raised a finger as if to say wait a minute. Joe then walked down the bank of benches to the front of the lecture theatre, had a quiet word with Daniel who then raised a hand and begged for silence. Joe then stood tall and proud on the floor below the platform of the lectern and spoke, "Gentlemen, whatever the language of the inscription and whatever the content of the tablet of stone, Chief Rabbi Horrowitz and I are convinced that we are in the presence of the words of the Lord handed down from Heaven to Moses our father. We therefore suggest that when we reconvene tomorrow morning we fast and bring our *tallaitim and tefillin* so that we can say the *Shacharit* service together and when standing during the *sh'monā esrei* we should face the words of the law inscribed on the tablet of stone next door rather than to the east as is conventional". There were loud murmurs of agreement and shouts of Amen as the congregation dispersed and I remembered that I didn't own a set of phylacteries and wouldn't know what to do with them even if I had.

★★★

That night, as always when Joe and I were both in Jerusalem, he stayed with me in my residence in Yemin Moishe. On arrival we kicked off our shoes, reclined on two easy chairs and helped ourselves to generous measures of Ardbeg's smoky single malt. I was quick to compliment him on his diplomatic interventions in the day's dramatic events. I then went on to express my concern that although I had a *tallit* somewhere in the house that I had taken to the Bar Mitzvah of his youngest son, I was completely out of phylacteries. He smiled and with the manner of a magician extracting a rabbit from a top hat, a small velvet sac suddenly appeared from his overnight bag.

"I guessed as much" he said, " and I also guess that the last time you completed the ritual was on your own Bar Mitzvah or at the very latest during the time of sitting *shivah* after Sara died in 1973". He was of course right and I there and then urged him to remind me how it was done. As he bound the little prayer boxes to my head and pointing from my left arm, to my heart, a beautiful thought occurred to me. To reach this point, the night before the decoding of the codicil to the Mosaic Law, had taken the best that head and heart could offer. Furthermore I flattered myself that us two brothers embodied the head and the heart working in happy harmony as lucidly explained in Joe's book, "On the Other Hand" that had explored the dialectic between science and religion reaching a synthesis of mutual dependency.

I was then suddenly plagued by doubts that tomorrow might yet turn out to be my nemesis and asked, "Joe, what suddenly made you so confident today that we had really discovered the Third Tablet of the Holy Covenant?"

As we sat down and I unwound my *tefillin* Joe replied. " Martin my dear brother forgive me for playing the scientist for once but I learnt something new today that confirmed my suspicions that you were right and I now know with certainty the nature of your discovery. You remember that when Yadin carbon dated the organic material left in the plaster on the hidden side of the plaques, it suggested that we were dealing with something of great antiquity. Well yesterday I was chatting with one of the technicians in the Museum laboratory to try and find out the reason for the delay at the beginning, he then explained that the high magnification fibre optic microscopy scan had demonstrated remnants of a film of plaster that they thought would adulterate the spectroscopy as it seemed intimately encrusted within the shallow crevices carrying the bronze particles, and this layer had to be cleaned off with acetic acid before we started. That's when I knew for certain what we were dealing with!" "Quite the detective Joe. So where can I learn about this subject of your deductive powers?" At this Joe reached up into my book shelves and drew down a volume of the Art Scroll *Chumash* he had given me on the occasion of my 70th birthday and asked me to turn to page 1073 and read the passage from Deuteronomy 27 verses 1-12.

Moses and the elders of Israel commanded the people, saying,

310

"Observe the entire commandment that I command you this day. It shall be on the day that you cross the Jordan to the land that Hashem, your God, gives you, you shall set up a stone and you shall coat it with plaster. There you should build an altar for Hashem, your God, an altar of stones; you shall not raise iron upon them. You shall inscribe on it all the words of this Torah, when you cross over. You shall erect this stone on Mount Ebal, and you shall coat it in plaster. You shall inscribe on the stone all the words of this Torah, well clarified."

Having read the passage my heart started beating rapidly and looked up at Joe and was about to say something when he held up his hand and said in a commanding voice, "Now read from the Song of Moses, his last words. Deuteronomy 31 verse 26".

Take this tablet of the Torah and place it at the side of the Ark of the Covenant of Hashem, and it shall be there for you as a witness.

At that I was convinced and fell asleep that night confident in the knowledge that whatever the wording on this tablet of stone it was truly from the hand of Moses but dictated by the highest authority.

★★★

At 7.00am the following morning we all reconvened for *Shacharit*, the morning prayers. My daughter together with two other women, one a scientist in Daniel's department and another who might have been a Shin Bet operative, sat in the back row out of decorum. The service was conducted in turn between the two Chief Rabbis with occasional contributions from the fearsome looking, huge bearded figure of the leader of the *Charedi Lubavitcher* movement Reb Mordechai Ben-Tovim. As it was a Thursday morning it was traditional to read from that week's *Parasha,* section of the Torah, which happened to be *"Ki Savo"*. Someone, probably my brother, had the foresight to bring along a small *Sefer Torah,* scroll. Joe had a beautiful tenor voice and was invited to chant the verses. Before he started he gave me a rather ostentatious wink. I looked over the shoulder of another Charedi patriarch who had his own copy of the book of the text and went weak at the knees when noting that the portion of the Pentateuch, Ki Savo, included the verses 1-12 of Deuteronomy 27.

Once the service was completed about an hour later, coffee and doughnuts were served to break the fast during which time the secular members of the privileged group drifted in and I was amused to note that this included some of the government bigwigs who the day before claimed that their diaries were too full.

By 9.00am the preliminaries were complete and Daniel rose to take the podium looking unshaven and exhausted. He explained that they were able to complete the scans the day before by about midnight, 13.00 West Coast time, and they had tracked down Professor Ginsburg on his mobile phone. He was deeply sceptical at first, but after speaking to Professor Fleming he agreed to take on the task. At about 03.00am Israel time, Daniel was woken when Uri called from LA with the simple question, "Danny, is this for real?"

Apparently it took another hour of cross-examination to persuade him to continue. The work had been completed 7.00am that morning and they had just completed the task of lining up the translation from the Egyptian hieratic script to both modern Hebrew and English and this would now appear line by line on the screen. The lights were dimmed and the audience breathed in as one, before the first line of text appeared.

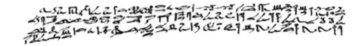

Blessed art thou O Lord our God, King of the Universe, the God of Abraham, the God of Isaac and the God of Ishmael.

At that the hall erupted with shouts from almost all of the clerical throats in the audience in unison, "NO, it's can't be Ishmael, it's Jacob."

Daniel had to shout above the din to get himself heard. "Wait, wait a moment, the next line of the translation will confirm that Professor Ginsburg's translation is correct". The audience eventually settled down again and a stunned silence reigned until the complete text was revealed.

Remember the angel of God who called to Hagar from Heaven. Fear not for God has heeded the cry of the youth and will make a Great nation of him and the daughters of Sarah shall be cursed for Her cruelty.

△△△△△△△

The land you see to the west of Mount Ebal, yea unto the sea, that shall be the promised land of the Children of Israel and the land you see to the east, yea unto the Mountains of Moab, that shall be the promised land of the Children of Ishmael.

△△△△△△△

And you shall build an altar for the Lord, your God, an altar of stones; yet you shall not raise iron upon them so that it becomes an altar of peace for all to share set in a holy city of universal peace. Only then will Sarah's curse be lifted.

△△△△△△

Thou shalt love thy neighbour as thyself

Once I'd finished reading the text I looked around the audience to judge their reaction. The silence was deafening in ways more profound than that overused cliché could ever express. The silence was accompanied by an extraordinary loud "volume" of facial and body language with many of the clergy impersonating fish feeding off the surface of a pond. Some also got up to speak but quickly sat down as they failed to find the right words. Eventually it was left for my brother Joe to intervene and fill that silent space with words of wisdom. He strode to the front and mounted the podium, uninvited but unopposed.

His face glowed with an inner light and he spoke as if in a trance. "Gentlemen allow me to provide you an exegesis on the verses you have just read and please forgive my impertinence to take a lead in the presence of the greatest thinkers amongst the Israeli clergy of this age. I have one advantage over you all in that I am the brother of Martin, Moishe Dovid, Tanner, the one whose persistence and ingenuity lead us to the discovery and decoding of this sacred stone tablet. Last night Martin and I, the scientist and the spiritual leader, explored the events leading up to this momentous occasion and agreed that our lives had served a sacred purpose and that our combined knowledge and complementary ways of thinking helped us determine what this tablet of stone truly represents and what is the true message sent by *Hashem min ha'Shamayim*, to our people from the hand of *Moishe Rabbeinu*.

First of all I now know with certainty, that this is the tablet of stone referred to in the Song of Moses Deuteronomy 31 verse 26." At this every one of the clergy in the audience started to riffle through their personal copies of the book of the Pentateuch. "Next the reference to the Angel of the Lord speaking to Hagar after she and her baby son, Ishmael were expelled from Abraham's tents to die in the wilderness, will be found in Genesis 21. References to building the Altar from stones that have not been cut by iron can also be found in Deuteronomy 27 verses 1-12 and again in Exodus 20 verse 22 alongside the details of the 10 commandments. Maimonides interpreted this to mean that iron is the material for making a sword and the Hebrew word for sword is *cherev* and that derives from the word meaning destruction. From this I think we can agree that the Altar can only be built in peace and that the City of Peace, *Yr Shalom* is indeed Jerusalem. The tablet then goes on to insist that this applies to the whole world therefore Jerusalem must be the epicenter for spreading the message of peace and therefore belongs to all. Mount Ebal was the point where Moses stood as he delivered his last testament so we now know with clarity the will of Hashem as passed down to Moses and it is clear to me that the western ridge of the great rift valley is a natural border between two nations with Jerusalem, the city of peace, a shared spiritual capital and that a simple cairn of uncut boulders is all that is needed to make this claim and not elaborate Temples and that was the mistake made by King Solomon and King Herod. These Temples appealed to the vanity of Kings and twice ended in destruction and dispersion of our people, whereas we should be humble in the presence of Hashem. Finally it is stated in Deuteronomy 27, that the words of the law should be "clarified" on the stone. I think that was a mistranslation and the word should be "summarised" and what better summary do we have for the Torah than, *"Thou shalt Love thy Neighbour as Thyself"*. This is the summary the great Talmudic sage Hillel used when asked by a would be convert to teach him the Torah whilst standing on one leg. This is a universal truism of all faiths and our Muslim brethren quote: *None of you truly believes until he wishes for his brother what he wishes for himself*; (Hadith in al-Bukhari).

I now appeal to my brothers amongst the *Charedi* and the *Chassidic* communities, you are the ones tasked with bearing *Aish Ha'Torah,* the flame of the law to carry the divine word of the Lord to the Children of Israel, now is your chance. You are amongst the elect who are privileged to be present on this day, go forth and carry the flame of peace to all your followers in the four corners of the earth and kiss the third Tablet of the Holy Covenant with the four corners of your prayer shawls to pledge your allegiance to Moses our father.

The hall erupted with cheers and cries of Amen or Umain according to preferred pronunciation. Reb Mordechai Ben-Tovim gave the Ashkenazi Chief Rabbi a bear hug that made him wince. The Chassidim hugged the modern orthodox and the clergy hugged the politicians. The technicians did "high fives" to each other whilst Joe slipped down quietly and whispered in my ear, "I will leave you and your science to rescind the curse on the daughters of Sarah our Matriarch."

I later learnt that when the rabbinical leader of Israel's Liberal Jewish community heard the news she went into premature labour and opportunistically named her son Ishmael.

Epilogue

The last time I saw my father was shortly before his death and he seemed to have fallen asleep with his laptop computer precariously balanced on an old collapsible table on the veranda in front of his house in Yamin Moishe. As I approached a beautiful tall young woman was taking her leave with a peck on his cheek. I heard her wish him goodbye but promised she would see him again soon. As she turned it looked as if she recognized me and I was rewarded with a brilliant smile that lit up her face. I thanked her for her visit and the kind support that the nurses from Hadassah provided. She nodded, smiled again and disappeared in the direction of the windmill without a word.

He died peacefully in his sleep that night.

Needless to say he was buried alongside his wife, the mother I never knew, in the consecrated grounds near to the ancient synagogue in Piki'in.

The days of the *shiva* were attended by so many friends, well wishers, and the President himself, that they could only be accommodated along the terraces that made up the little lanes traversing the slope that led down to the Sultan's pool. Once my period of mourning was over I started the process of clearing out the house and fulfilling his last wishes spelt out in his will. It was during this activity that I discovered the text of this book both in hard copy files and with the last chapter open on the screen of his laptop. I thereupon accepted the task of editing the text and getting it published.

I had so many other duties and so many letters of condolence to cope with that it took a couple of weeks before I completed all my thank you letters.

Eventually I got round to writing to the palliative care department at Hadassah to thank them for the wonderful care of the nurses in their outreach program with special mention of the young woman who attended him on the day before he died. They sent a nice letter back saying what an honour it had been to look after this great man but expressed puzzlement about the nurse visiting on that last occasion. In fact they had been at the point of apologizing that the visit in question never took place because of a traffic accident on the perilous winding road down from Ein Kerem.

When I read that the fine hairs at the nape of my neck stood on end and I realized whom I had met that day. It seems I have inherited something else from my father and that is a capacity, on rare occasions to experience cracks in the space/time continuum or what those who believe in the paranormal call "Time slips".

August 2nd 2016
Professor Judy Cohen
(Yehudit Esther bat Moishe Dovid)

Acknowledgements and author's notes

The idea for this book has been gestating for well over 7 years from the day I became interested in the links between biblical anthropology and molecular genealogy.

This came about indirectly as a result of my involvement in research into the diagnosis and management of breast cancer that occupied the second half of my career as a surgeon and clinical scientist. The fact that the "Ashkenazi mutations" that lead to an early onset type of breast cancer was itself some kind of proof of the biblical history of the Jewish people, is too good a story to keep within the scientific community. Furthermore the fact that the first BRCA mutation is over 3,000 years old and yet survives has always puzzled me and I chose to try an explore this question by way of a novel. Along the way I got to read most of the writings of Richard Dawkins, the celebrated geneticist, and inevitably found myself wrapped up in the debate between science and religion. I then started to find myself drifting away and denying my roots as an orthodox Jew but this drift was arrested after reading the book by Jonathan Sacks, the Chief Rabbi, entitled "The great partnership; God, Science and the search for meaning" (Hodder and Stoughton 2011). This book then acted as the catalyst I needed to settle down and write. Of course as a clinical scientist I have written and edited many books but I really enjoyed the freedom and release offered by writing fiction for a change (although some of my scientist friends tease me in saying that much of my science was fiction as well!).

Although Martin Tanner is a fictional character born 7 years before my time he has acted as a mouthpiece for my views on science and religion fed by my two literary heroes, Dawkins and Sacks. In this book, as well as writing what some might think is a good yarn, I truly wanted to inspire my readers about the beauty and honesty of the scientific method and what it reveals, whilst reminding scientists that all this awe inspiring detail on how the biosphere is organised must be teach us something of the transcendental. It might of course be "signifying nothing" as in Macbeth's soliloquy, but that is a rather nihilist and barren set of beliefs and it pleases me to think otherwise. Even if in the end there is no meaning, the search for a "meaning" by the greatest philosophers and thinkers since the authors of the Bible to the modern era, has been a laudable activity in my opinion. We live in an era where liberal democracy, justice and freedom are the preferred options by which rational beings organize their lives and I think that the moral philosophers of the past, whether secular or religious, have to be thanked for this.

I could be wrong and that this state of affairs is all a question of evolutionary advantage, yet the four words, "*I could be wrong*" is the central tenet of the scientific method, just as "*love they neighbour as thyself*" is really all you need to know about religious teaching.

Critics might think that this narrative relies on too many coincidences. Yet when one considers that there are billions of men and women on this planet and each has millions of "events" in their lifetimes, then there maybe an almost infinite number of permutations of life events. Monkeys typing the works of Shakespeare is a crude analogy but I prefer the words of Archbishop John Tillotson (1603-1694) discovered by *chance* as I was looking through my dictionary of scientific quotations:

"How often might a man, after he had jumbled a set of letters in a bag, fling them out upon the ground before they would fall into an exact poem, yea, or so much as make a good discourse in prose! And may not a little book be as easily made by chance as this great volume of the world?"

To which I would reply, "given an infinite number of throws, at least once".

Or to put it in the context of this book all of man's greatest achievements have occurred as a result of a very fortunate and random sequence of events seized upon those rare great men whose minds were truly prepared.

Prologue
The newspaper cutting is genuine but the TOP SCRET minutes of the meeting in Jerusalem December 1st 1960 are of course fictional.

Chapter 4
The experiences suffered by Martin's mother are precisely what I had the misfortune to witness at the start of my career. Sir Stanford Cade was the doyen of cancer surgery in that era although I was too young to meet him but I built up a clear picture of the man from anecdotes provided from

my senior colleagues and reading many of his classical papers. Early in my career as a professor of surgery at Kings College London I was called upon to deliver the annual Cade memorial lecture at the Royal College of Surgeons in Lincolns Inn Fields. I expounded at length why I completely disagreed with his radical surgical approaches and was embarrassed to learn that his daughter was in the audience. Afterwards she very graciously came up to congratulate me on my talk and said, that speaking as a radiation oncologist, she completely agreed with me. I never got to meet Sir Geoffrey Keynes but I did start some correspondence with him when he was in his 90s. Much of what I've written about the fictional meeting between Martin and Sir Geoffrey was imagined after reading his autobiography, "The Gates of Memory" (Clarendon Press Oxford 1981).

Chapter 5
All the surgeons mentioned in this chapter are completely fictional although their characters have been cobbled together piecemeal from the best and the worst features of individuals I worked under or learnt about from friends.

Chapter 6
I missed conscription by a year but my oldest brother did serve in the RAMC in the Canal Zone and some of Martin's better characteristics are modelled on him. For details on the experience of surgeons during the Suez crisis I relied on the excellent account by Parker and Kirby, "Operation Musketeer-The Suez Crisis", in the Journal of the Royal Army Medical Corps volume 154 (4).

Chapters 9 and 10
Much of the content of chapter 9 is based on my personal experience as a young surgeon working in those parts in 1963/64 but apart from professor Yigael Yadin, all other characters are fictional. My description of working at Masada is based on my experience as assistant medical officer there in 1963 together with the help of Yadin's book, "Masada, Herod's fortress and the Zealot's last stand" (Weidenfield and Nicolson London 1966). This was augmented by G A Williamson's wonderful translation of Josephus' "The Jewish War" (Penguin Books 1959).

Chapter 13 and 14
The details concerning the structure and contents of the Tabernacle are

taken from the English translation from the Hebrew and the Rabbinical commentaries in the Art Scroll Chumash (Mesorah publications Ltd. New York 1995) Exodus 35-38

Chapters 19 and 20

I made two visits to Piki'in to research this book once I had learnt of the legend of the tablets rescued from the second temple. On the second occasion I met the last surviving member of the Zinati clan. Their story can be read in, "The People of Piki'in" by Rivke Alper (Am Oved, Tel Aviv 2004).

Chapter 21

I also made two visits to Kerala and Cochin to enjoy wonderful holidays with my wife whilst researching this book. However I must acknowledge the excellent, readable and scholarly book by Edna Fernandes, "The Last Jews of Kerala" (Portobello Books, London 2008).

Chapter 22-25

All the characters in these chapters are fictional but the diagnosis in pregnancy and the terminal illness of Sara is based on tragic cases of young women with breast cancer that I have had to look after in the past. In part I dedicate this book to their courage and to their memory.

The first of a number of uncanny coincidences happened when I'd just finished writing chapter 24. The car crash on the way back from Äre was based on a true event when I was driving back from a ski slope conference in Sweden in 1988 in the company of my oldest daughter Katie then aged 17. Fortunately we both escaped unscathed apart from scratches and delayed shock. On the day I completed this chapter I was invited back to speak to a Swedish group of oncologists in Äre. I accepted the invitation as long as I could fly into Stockholm and not Trondheim.

Chapter 26

I visited Kibbutz Ha'Goshrim as a guest of Jamal Zidan, professor of oncology at Ziv Hospital in Safed, where he had organized a conference on molecular biology and cancer. Jamal as you might guess is a Druze and any resemblance between the character Jamal Atrash and professor Zidan is entirely intentional.

Chapter 28

For the history of the discovery and cloning of the BRCA mutations I made use of, "Breakthrough" by Kevin Davies and Michael White (Macmillan London 1995). Neil Bradman allowed me to make use of him in a vignette on the understanding that it was all a work of fiction and that I point out that the initials for 'The Centre for Genetic Anthropology', TCGA can stand for the four nucleotides Thymine Cytosine Guanine Adenine, building blocks of DNA. This sequence can be read backwards as with Hebrew, right to left, AGCT. These two strands of letters would make complimentary bonds e.g. Thymine=Adenine et seq. I thought this was too much of an esoteric joke for my lay readers but I hope that any of my biologist readers can see something of the supernatural in this coincidence.

I also wish to thank professor Ros Eeles of the Royal Marsden Hospital for instructing me on morphometrics in the search for evolutionary advantage and professor Stephan Beck from UCL for instructing me on the co-expression of genes.

For those interested in the complex story of the molecular anthropology of the Jewish people I commend "DNA and Tradition; The Genetic Link to the Ancient Hebrews" by Rabbi Yaakov Kleiman (Devora pub. New York 2004) and "Abrahams Children's; Race, Identity, and the DNA of the Chosen People" by Jon Entine (Grand Central publishing New York 2007)

Most of what I have written is an accurate account of the latest findings but with a degree of simplification and artistic licence so as not to inhibit the narrative drive.

Chapter 29
In contrast to chapter 28, most of this is pure speculation although everything about fractal geometry and both internal and external beauty amongst plants and people is true.

Chapter 30
Whilst I was struggling with the problem on how to finish the book the Times news report on Vishnu's vaults appeared exactly as I describe. Those in doubt can search the back copy of the Times. This was the second extraordinary coincidence linked to writing my book.

There is of course a Maharaja of Jaipur but I had no way of contacting him for permission to employ him in my story but as he appears as a guardian angel to our hero I'm sure he wouldn't mind. An earlier holder of that title did carry the nickname "bubbles" for the reason explained in the book.

I do indeed have a nephew (Joshua Baum) who is an artist and had the honour of re-painting the dome of the Abuhav synagogue.

Chapter 31

The story of the golden ibex of Santorini is true and the device described is now in use in the treatment of breast cancer. This episode illustrates another facet of the scientific method by way of making connections between apparently unrelated observations as a way of building hypotheses.

This is where a leap of imagination or "artistic creation" is required. There is an Art of Science.

Chapter 32

Not long before I was about to embark on this chapter I had run out of ideas about the nature and content of the lost codicil to the Mosaic Law when the third and most remarkable "coincidence" in writing this book, occurred.

I was in the synagogue attending the Bar Mitzvah of the grandson of one of our close friends and started to follow the reading of the Torah in English together with the rabbinical commentaries and, lo, there it was, a lost third tablet of the Holy Covenant. The biblical quotations I've used in the text are exactly those I found by chance in the Torah that day but in fairness I should quote Pasteur's aphorism that "chance favours the prepared mind". Rabbi Dr Jeffrey Cohen, the father of one of my sons-in-law, has double-checked my findings and supports my exegesis.

However the inscription on the "rediscovered tablet" is totally fictitious so I hope it won't start another war. Yet the final commandment, " Love thy neighbour as thyself " might have been what Moses had in mind and could easily be true.

★★★

I wish to thank my good friends Jackie Gerrard, Maurice Summerfield, Geoffrey Feld and last but not least Alan Fox, for reading my early drafts, editing and correcting my English and searching out typographical errors.

Finally I wish to acknowledge my wife Judy (*Yehudit bat Reuven*), the very embodiment of Sara Zenati (apart from being only five foot four inches) who accompanied me on all my adventures whilst researching this book as well as tolerating my "absences" when lost in my bubble of creativity. She is the spine that holds the chapters of my life together.

Glossary of Hebrew and Yiddish (y) words

Abba; Father

Aliyah; Literally, to go up, but used to mean immigrate to Israel.

Avraham Avinu; Abraham our father.

Ayshet Chayil; From The Proverbs, "A Woman of Worth".

Bar Mitzvah; The coming of age of a Jewish boy at 13: a rite of passage.

Besheft (y); Preordained

Bris; Circumcision.

Chanukah; A festival of lights usually celebrated in December, close to Christmas, lasting 8 days and on each of those days a child can expect a gift. Celebrating the miracle of the everlasting light in the Temple that burnt for 8 nights without fuel during the Hasmonean period of war with the Greeks.

Charedi; Ultraorthodox or fundamentalist Jews.

Chupah; Literally canopy but used to describe Jewish wedding ceremony.

Chutzpah (y); Nearest English equivalent might be "bloody cheek", as in the convicted murderer of two parents throwing himself at the mercy of the courts because he is a poor orphan.

Dayanim; Judges of the Jewish religious court.

Eretz Yisrael; The State of Israel.

Gan Aden: Garden of Eden.

Haftorah; Reading from the Prophets chanted after the Torah scrolls are closed on the Sabbath.

Haimeshe (y); Homely, used to describe traditional eastern European kosher cuisine.

Hashem; Literally "The Name" but used as a respectful way of talking of God outside the synagogue or home based rituals.

Ivrit; Modern Hebrew.

Ketubha; Marriage contract.

Kiddish; The ritual blessing over wine.

Kinderlach (y); Little children.

Knesset; Israeli houses of parliament

Labriuth; "bless you" after someone sneezes.

Lag Ba'Omer; A jolly festival of song and bonfires to mark the mid point in the solemn season between Passover and Pentecost.

Lulav; Bunch of palm leaves and myrtle carried in ritual procession on the festival of Succot (Tabernacles)

Ma nishma, chaver?; What's going on brother?

Ma nishtana ha'leilah hazer; "Why is this night different from all other nights?". The four questions chanted by the youngest child present at a Seder service.

Maariv; The evening prayers.

Maftir; The last portion (*parachas*) of the Torah read out on the Sabbath.

Magen David; Star emblem on shield of King David

Mazeltov; Literally "good luck" but used to mean congratulations.

Menorah; Candelabra

Mezuzah; A slim casket holding the *Shema* prayer that is nailed to the right hand doorpost of every room and including the front door, in a Jewish household.

Midrash; Local tradition of Jewish religious practice.

Mikveh; Ritual bath.

Min Ha' Shamayim; A command direct from heaven.

Mincha; The afternoon prayers.

Minyan; 10 male Jews over the age of 13 to make up a quorum for prayer.

Mitzvah; A good deed.

Moshiach: Messiah

Motech; Sweetheart

Mt'zada lo tipol; Masada shall not fall.

Nair Tamid; Everlasting light above the Sanctuary of the Ark in the biblical Temple still be seen above the ark for the Torah in all synagogues around the world.

Parachas; Portion of the Torah.

Pesach; The Passover.

Protectia; A system of mutual support and favours returned systematized in Israel.

Schlepping (y); No English equivalent but suggestive of building up a sweat whilst dragging a heavy burden from one place to another.

Seder; The service in the home on the first two nights of the Passover.

Sefer Torah; Book of the law.

Sh'mona Esrei; The 18 verse prayer read standing at the centre of each service of prayer.

Shabbat; Sabbath

Shachris; The morning prayers.

Shammas; Beadle in the synagogue.

Sharre Tzedek; Gates of heaven.

Shechina; The divine presence of Hashem or the aura of the presence of the almighty.

Shema; Prayer that starts off with "Hear O Israel.."

Shidduch (y); An arranged marriage.

Shiva Brochot; Seven blessings at a Jewish wedding.

Shiva; 7 days of ritual mourning.

Shofar; Rams horn used as trumpet on high holy days.

Simchat Torah; Festival of the rejoicing of the law.

Succot; Festival of tabernacles.

Tallis; Prayer shawl

Talmud; Rabbinical commentaries on the Torah.

Teffilin; Phylacteries worn on the left arm and forehead during morning prayers.

Tisha B'Av; The 9th of Av a day of fasting in remembrance of the fall of the Temple.

Torah: The Pentateuch or five books of Moses.

Traif (y); Non-kosher food.

Tsitis; Fringes at the four corners of a prayer shawl.

Ulpan; Israeli language school.